THE
AGE
of
MEN

Book Six
of
THE NIGHTFALL WARS

by

JACOB PEPPERS

This book is a work of fiction. Names, characters, places and incidents are either the product of the author's imagination or are used fictitiously. Any resemblance to actual persons, living or dead, or to actual events or locales is entirely coincidental.

The Age of Men: Book Six of The Nightfall Wars
This book is licensed for your personal enjoyment only. This book may not be re-sold or given away to other people. If you would like to share this book with another person, please purchase an additional copy for each person you share it with. If you're reading this book and did not purchase it, or it was not purchased for your use only, then you should return to the retailer and purchase your own copy. Thank you for respecting the hard work of the author.

Copyright © 2021 Jacob Nathaniel Peppers. All rights reserved, including the right to reproduce this book, or portions thereof, in any form. No part of this text may be reproduced, transmitted, downloaded, decompiled, reverse engineered, or stored in or introduced into any information storage and retrieval system, in any form or by any means, whether electronic or mechanical without the express written permission of the author. The scanning, uploading, and distribution of this book via the Internet or via any other means without the permission of the publisher is illegal and punishable by law. Please purchase only authorized electronic editions, and do not participate in or encourage electronic piracy of copyrighted materials.

The publisher does not have any control over and does not assume any responsibility for author or third-party websites or their content.

Visit the author website:
www.JacobPeppersAuthor.com

*This book is dedicated to my newborn daughter
Norah Alaina Peppers
Okay, sure, fine, so your initials are N.A.P
But don't hold it against your mother and me, alright?
What can I say? We live in hope*

Sign up for my new releases mailing list to hear about promotions, launches, and, for a limited time, get a FREE copy of *The Silent Blade,* the prequel book to the bestselling epic fantasy series, The Seven Virtues.

Go to JacobPeppersAuthor.com to claim your free book!

Chapter One

They came with the darkness.

The enemy soldiers swarmed against the castle walls like thousands of rats scurrying toward a fresh kill, eager to feast on its flesh. They swept against the battlements, *over* the battlements by way of their siege ladders like some great ocean tide, one which seemed impossible to stop, one which only a fool would think to stand against.

But Alesh and those defenders on the castle wall *did* stand, doing their best to ignore their exhaustion and fatigue, to ignore also the aches of the wounds they'd already received, some minor and some bad enough that those brave defenders who had received them would not see tomorrow's sunrise.

Yet wounded or not, doomed or not, Alesh and those who stood with him fought with everything they had against the enemy's greater numbers. After several tense minutes in which it appeared that this might be the end, that the city might now fall, they managed to cut down those who had gained the walls and rushed toward the siege ladders, working together to heave them away. The men and women who were climbing them were left with nowhere to go as the ladders—and they along with them—were cast away from the walls, and they rode them to their deaths where they smashed into the ground far below.

Perhaps they screamed. Perhaps they begged or prayed to the gods for forgiveness, for salvation, but if so, then their prayers were left unanswered. And if they did pray, then Alesh could not hear them just as he could not hear the sounds of them striking the ground over the cacophony surrounding him. All the screams and shouts, the roars of anger and pain, the chiming of steel on steel as the defenders came to grips with their attackers melded into one great and terrible sound that did not quiet and did not abate.

It was a maddening, terrifying sound. It was, Alesh thought in those few brief moments he found between cutting down one of his opponents and moving to the next, the sound of the world breaking. He hated that sound, hated it as much as he had ever hated anything, but that did not stop him from adding his own shouts, his own cries of fury to that wild chaos. For faced with such destruction, such pointless loss of life, how could a man not scream? Alesh's own voice had gone hoarse hours ago, just as his sword arm had grown numb with exhaustion, but there was no end in sight, so left with no other choice, he fought, he screamed, and he listened to the sound of the world dying.

It was late afternoon now. They had been at it since the early morning, and he was tired. In truth, he had left tired behind hours ago, somewhere in the early morning when the sun had only just risen from its slumber. Now, the only thing that kept his feet beneath him, the only thing which gave his arm strength enough to swing the blade it held again and again was his will. A will which, after hours of bloodshed, was beginning to fail him.

A woman old enough to be Alesh's grandmother gained the wall with a dexterity he would not have credited her and charged at him, her eyes wild, her mouth twisted into a snarl as she brandished a knife. Alesh pulled his blade from the opponent he'd just slain and turned so that his left side was to the woman. Just as she was beginning to bring the blade down in a blow, just as her mouth was slowly turning to a grin, one which showed she was convinced he could not—or, at least, *would not*—move in time, he did.

He stepped backward, avoiding the blow, and his own sword came up, propelled by muscles numb with fatigue. There was the slightest resistance as the blade entered her unarmored chest, barely more than a man might feel sticking his finger through a spider's web. Then the woman came to an abrupt halt, impaled on his sword. Her eyes went wide, her mouth opened into a surprised "o" as if she had never considered, not until this moment, that in battle men and women, young and old, all died alike. Then the light left her eyes and whatever her final thought had been died with her as she slumped off his blade and onto the blood-slicked stones of the castle walls.

Alesh stared at the dead woman, lying there crumpled and old and dead when she should be sitting beside a hearth with her grandchild on her knee, and he felt another weight added to the despair which set heavy on his shoulders. Yet he turned away a moment later. After all, there had been other grandmothers in the last hours, and those who might have been their grandsons and granddaughters too, for it seemed that the promises the Darkness made tempted the young and old, the healthy and infirm alike.

He said nothing, for there was nothing to be said; he felt no regret, for the fog which had settled over his thoughts did not allow anything so considered as that. There was only the lifting of the sword and the swinging of it, only the placing of one foot in front of the other and trying not to lose his balance on the slick cobbles.

A witness might have thought him callous and cold knowing that he felt nothing, might have thought all those defenders along the wall callous and cold—and perhaps he would have been right. But if he looked closely enough, that unknown witness might have seen the hardness in the eyes of those defenders, might have seen lines there, etched into their faces by grief and pain and despair which they had not greeted the morning with. Or...perhaps not.

Perhaps, Alesh thought, those lines were only visible to those who had them themselves, scars only able to be understood by those who shared them and who had shared the wounding which left them. There was a brief moment of respite, then, as the few remaining siege ladders were heaved away and the walls were clear save for the dead and those weary defenders standing among them, their uniforms and armor stained in blood that might have been their enemies' or their own. The difference had stopped mattering hours before. If a man could stand, he stood, and if he could fight, he fought. There was nothing else.

Alesh looked about him at those brave, unenviable souls as they stood with lost expressions on their faces, as if now that the killing was done, at least for the moment, they did not know what else they were meant to do. What use were eyes that had seen so much pain and blood in such a short time? What use the hands which had wielded the blade except to lift it once more?

The men and women of Valeria's defenders turned and glanced at him with weary expressions, and he thought that he should have said something to them. Some words that might acknowledge their sacrifice. A leader would have. Certainly, Chosen Olliman would have. But Olliman was dead, Abigail, and Chorin, too, and there was only Alesh now. And whatever else he was, he was no leader, so he said nothing, choosing only to slump to his knees instead. He did not sit, did not dare to for fear that if he did, he would not be able to rise once more, and the next grandmother would find him sitting still as her blade entered him.

Perhaps a Chosen of the Gods would have used his or her great power to embolden the defenders, to give them strength and courage and determination where now there was only an emptiness, one Alesh knew well for he felt it himself. But the flames and the light obeyed his commands no longer. He was *Chosen* no longer, and so he did nothing but slump and breath ragged breaths which plumed in the cold air, a promise, if any was needed, of winter's approach, the time in which those things the year had birthed would die.

"Chosen."

He turned to see Captain Nordin standing beside him. "Captain. It is good to see you well."

The men they had been the day before might have laughed at such folly, for whatever else he looked, the captain did not look well. But no one laughed. Nordin, like the other defenders, was covered in blood practically from head to toe, and there was a ragged cut across his left forearm which gently oozed crimson. Alesh wondered idly how much of that blood belonged to old men and old women or young men and young women, and then decided it did not matter. The tragedy of such deaths as he had witnessed, as he had *caused* was not in that it sometimes struck the old and young, but that it struck *anyone.*

"It seems, sir, that they are retreating. We have beaten back the assault," the captain said.

He said the last loud enough for his voice to carry across the sudden relative stillness of the walls, to carry over the moans of the dying and wounded as others helped them down the battlements to where healers waited. Some men sent up a ragged cheer but most did not. The day's events, it seemed, had left little joy in them.

Alesh understood that well enough. After all, they had not won any victory or defeated any foe. They had only survived a little longer, managed, like some parasite feasting on its host's flesh, to hang on. Sometimes, most times, in truth, it seemed to him that that was all he ever managed to do—hang on. They had beaten back the first assault, yes, but it was only the first, and any child or fool knew that if anything could be said of darkness, it was that it always returned. "That's...good then," he managed, because the captain seemed to be waiting for him to say something.

Nordin gave a single, weary nod, then eyed him closer, a troubled expression of concern on his face that might have been more at home on a mother examining a child who had taken a fall. "Forgive me, Chosen, but you do not look so well yourself. You should see a healer or—"

"Later," Alesh said, rising to his feet and nearly falling as a wave of dizziness brought on by exhaustion threatened to make his knees buckle. "For now, we need to see to the wounded, to make sure that the archers have arrows, and that every man still has a weapon."

He started away and was surprised when Nordin reached out, grabbing his arm. "Sir."

Alesh's first urge was to pull away from the man, to say something scathing that would bite for the captain thinking to stop him. In the end, however, he did not, not so much because he did not want to but because he found that, just then, he had little bite left in him. "What is it, Captain?"

"I-it isn't right, sir," Nordin said, fidgeting now, obviously uncomfortable with whatever he would say but also just as obviously not prepared to let it go.

Alesh held back a weary sigh. "No, Captain," he agreed, "it isn't right, not any of it. But when were we ever promised that it would be?"

Nordin winced. "I...I don't mean that, sir. I mean you, being here, on the walls. There are others who can fight. We have hundreds of soldiers, sir, but we only have one leader. Lady

Katherine has come by at least a half a dozen times to check on you. One of my men just told me she is here even now."

Alesh felt anger roil through him. Perhaps he had a little bite left after all. "You let her up?" he demanded, his eyes trailing meaningfully along the walls where the dead were being dragged away by men and women who looked little better off than the corpses they carried. "I told you—"

"I did not let her up, sir," Nordin said. "I told the men to keep her and the other citizens off the battlements, just as you requested. But, sir...she's right. You should not be here. Forgive me, Chosen, but—"

"No, Nordin," Alesh snapped. "I do not *forgive* you. You are the captain of Valeria's soldiers and so you remain, but it seems that you have *forgotten* that, that somehow you have begun to believe yourself my caretaker. Or is it my nurse?"

Nordin recoiled at Alesh's furious tone as if he had been struck. "Chosen, I didn't mean...only that, forgive me, sir, but without you...without you to lead us, we are lost."

We're lost anyway, Alesh thought. *How have you not yet seen it?* But to say as much, to state the truth that he already knew for those other men, Nordin included, who had sacrificed so much in the last hours to hear it, would have been a terrible crime, one to stack among those others of which he was guilty. He was not a leader, no. He was not a Chosen, not any longer if he ever truly had been, but he would not be needlessly cruel. *I am not evil,* he told himself, but then he thought of Tom, Lord Gustan's servant, the man who he had first abandoned and then killed, and his anger gave way before his shame. "Forget it, Nordin," he breathed wearily.

"At least," Nordin pressed, a tone in his voice that one might use trying to calm a panicked horse, "at least, you might rest with the others? They've all been fighting in shifts, sir, and all of them have had a rest, all but you."

Alesh turned away from the quiet desperation in the man's eyes, for he could not bear to look upon it, not anymore. How much worse, that look, once Nordin realized the truth? Once he learned—and in time, he *would* learn of it, that Alesh did not doubt—that the man he followed was not worth following, that each step he had taken in his path had been a wasted one, and not just wasted, but one which had led him and all those he cared about to their doom?

"Go and have a healer look at that arm, Nordin," Alesh said. "It would not do for the rot to set in. We need you, up here. The men need you."

"They need you, too, Chosen," Nordin said. His voice was barely more than a whisper, but the words brought the anger back, and Alesh spun to glare at the man, his chest heaving not just with exhaustion but with an anger that demanded to be given its way.

Nordin must have seen something of that rage, that fury in Alesh's face. He took an involuntary step back, his already pale face paling further. Then he gave a quick bow and departed, moving off down the battlements.

Alesh watched him go, hating himself in that moment as he did in all moments. It was not Nordin at which he was angry, not really. It was himself. He was angry that he could not be the man they needed him to be, hated himself because he had stopped even wanting to. He did not hope for victory, not now, for such a thing was beyond hope, beyond even his wildest dreams. All he hoped for then, was an end.

He shuffled to the edge of the wall and looked out at the enemy army. Nordin was right. They were not coming forward, not anymore, and the mass of Kale's forces lurked just inside the tree line. He wondered, for a moment, how many there were, but not for long. The answer was clear enough a blind man might see it. How many were there? Too many.

A brief spark of anger lit in him as he thought of Kale. The man was out there, somewhere, had orchestrated the day's tragedy and pain while refusing to take part in it. Alesh wanted to kill him. And the worst of it, he knew, was that he did not want to kill the man to save Valeria or the men on the walls, not even to save Katherine and Rion and his other friends. He wanted to kill Kale simply because he hated him, would have happily sacrificed himself, in that moment, if it meant that he would be able to do so.

But would such a sacrifice, even if it were possible—and it was not—stop the tide of darkness from sweeping over Valeria and its people? No. Of course not. Only a fool would think as much. A man might be killed, but evil remained and would always remain, was in the very air they breathed and passed from the breath of one man to another. A man might slay another, but no man could slay the Darkness.

Alesh gazed once more at the battlements, at the bodies moving and unmoving alike, and in the end there was little difference. "I'm sorry," he rasped, and had someone asked him then, who he spoke to, he would not have known. No one, perhaps.

Or everyone.

Chapter Two

Marta treaded her way carefully among the bodies, doing her best to keep her rising gorge in check. She had thought she had seen evil before, had run from it, hidden from it in the streets. But the day had taught her that evil had many forms and many shapes. And degrees. That it had in abundance.

The men who had lurked in the corners of the alleyways, in the shadows, watching like lions in the tall grass for one of the herd to fall behind, to show weakness, *had* been evil. Those men, when they had found such an opportunity, had pounced much like the lions would, but unlike those beasts which sought only to eat that they might live, those shadow-lurkers had done what they did not out of necessity but simply because they enjoyed it. They *were* evil men, yet their evil seemed a small, sad little thing compared to the evil the day had wrought, the proof of which could be seen in the hundreds of corpses scattered outside Valeria's walls, dotting the field between the forest in which Kale's army lurked and the city in which Alesh and everyone Marta cared about sheltered. A field of blood and the dead and the moaning of some who wished they were, who likely would be, soon enough. The last place in the world Marta would ever have wanted to be.

And yet, here she was, walking among those broken bodies, some filled with arrows, others shattered from their fall from the castle. She was here because she had been told to be here. It was amazing the sorts of things a person could do if she knew her life depended on it, a fact that the guards who'd come for her and the other slaves had made all too clear. Amazing what a person could do…and terrifying.

She and the other slaves had been tasked to work in shifts, searching the dead for those who might yet live so that the army's healers—pitifully few as it turned out, for an army bent on conquest and wanton destruction shockingly didn't tend to attract the sort of people who had dedicated their lives to healing—could see to them. Not out of any concern for their well-being, that much had been obvious, but because every man or woman that could be made well enough to fight was expected to rejoin the assault.

So Marta and the other slaves had been told. Just as they had been told what to do with those among the wounded who, with help, might live but who would not be able to fight again. That reminded her of the knife sheathed at her waist, the one the guard had given her, he and his fellows handing them out to the slaves with smiles as if they were handing out candies. Marta had told herself she would not take the knife, would refuse it. But when her turn in line came she did not refuse, instead accepting the knife quickly lest she anger the guards. And when she *had* taken it, she had told herself that she would throw it away the moment she was out of the guard's sight. When she had failed to do that also, she had told herself that she would by no means use it. Now she walked among the wounded terrified that she would have to discover, in time, whether that last had been a lie or not.

After all, she and the other slaves were being watched by guards stationed on the pickets at the edges of the forest, watched and laughed at, for she and the others had been forced to weather their mocking, crude insinuations as they'd traveled past, some of the older, more developed women being forced to endure pawing grasps which Marta, thankfully, had not.

The guards watched, but of course made no move to help Marta or any of the others, choosing instead to stand and smile from their relatively comfortable positions. Marta had never been the type of person to hate another, had learned early on in life that hate was dangerous. Hate made you start tallying the ways another wronged you, made you start thinking dangerous thoughts, like of revenge. And there were, in her experience, few more dangerous thoughts than revenge, for she had seen a few of the other street waifs, while she was growing up, take it in mind to get revenge on their persecutors. They spoke very strongly about it, described in detail what they intended to do. And then they never spoke again. It wasn't easy, slaying shadows, after all, and any man or woman who took it in mind to step into the darkness had to be careful not to be consumed by it.

Marta paused and stared at the castle walls, wondered if her friends were okay, if they were still alive. Or were they, like so many of these surrounding her, the price of the day's sport? Her breath caught at the thought, and she swallowed past a throat gone suddenly dry, giving her head a firm shake. No. She would not think like that. Despair was another dangerous thing, just like revenge. That, too, the streets had taught her.

She was just about to turn away from the wall to resume the grim task of searching for wounded when something struck her in the back of the head hard. She let out a squeak of surprised pain, stumbling over the corpse of a heavy-set merchant and only just managing to catch her balance.

She spun to see the woman slave, Greta, standing before her. She'd learned the woman's name in the slave tents—hard not to as the forty-year-old woman with tangled hair and eyes like chips of ice had set herself up as the queen of the slaves in all but name. Which, Marta supposed, was just about as useful as being the top piece of trash on a pile of trash. The woman was giving Marta a deadly scowl now, as if Marta had just struck her instead of the other way around. "Back to work, girly," she spat, "before you get us in trouble."

"You're right," Marta said, choking down the anger she felt—much like revenge and shame, that—"gods forbid they get ornery with us. Might be they'd do something terrible to us...like, I dunno. Make us slaves."

"Life can always get worse, little bitch," the woman said, a cruel glimmer in her eyes. "Might be me and some of the girls'll remind you of that tonight back in the tents."

And then she was walking off, just walking, not storming. Likely, she would have liked to, but having to step around corpses put a real damper on storming. As she watched the woman stalk away, Marta cursed herself in her head. That had been stupid, to antagonize the woman. She would have found something either way, of course, women like Greta always did, but that wasn't an excuse to make it easier for her.

Stupid, and a person in her position could not afford to be stupid. After all, it wasn't just her life she was gambling with, not anymore. There was Fermin, too. If she ended up arousing any suspicion because she was too dumb to keep her mouth shut, the manservant would pay for her carelessness just as much as she. Not to mention Sonya—who Marta had still not managed to find, hadn't even really had a chance to *look* for before the army had begun to march to Valeria, and she'd been forced to follow after along with the other slaves.

"And you won't find her standing around here feeling sorry for yourself either," she whispered, then she started moving, following the sounds of moaning. The best thing to do, when a person had a terrible job ahead was just to hop to and get it done. She couldn't save Alesh and the others, couldn't save Sonya either, not right now, but maybe she could save some poor ignorant fool who'd gone and gotten himself filled with arrows. True, that fool was a member of the army who sought to destroy everything she knew and cared about, but she would help him, if she could. After all, the world had already seen enough evil for one day.

Chapter Three

Argush marched through the army encampment—*his* army encampment, despite the fact that some seemed to think otherwise. Men and women leapt out of his way, likely thinking that should they impede his progress, they would suffer his wrath. Which was true. The morning had been off to a great start, his army pouring over the walls of Valeria and once or twice it had even appeared as if they would take the city on the first day, that Alesh and those other fools who followed him would suffer his wrath before the next hateful sun rose upon the world.

He had been watching eagerly, anticipating what he would do to Alesh, how he would make the man suffer more than any in the world had ever suffered or thought to suffer, had been sure that, any minute, the outnumbered, outmatched defenders' lines would break, and his army would swarm over the battlements and into the city. Then, without any order from himself, the army—*his* army—began to retreat, pulling back to the forest like some wounded beast fleeing with its tail between its legs.

The blessings Shira had given him had made him far more than a man, had given him strength and speed, power and cunning far beyond that of any mortal, and it had also bestowed upon him a feral instinct, an understanding. And with this new understanding came the knowledge that, had they pressed the attack instead of retreated, it would only have been a matter of time—very little time, in fact—before the city was overcome, and he was able to set about the taking of his revenge. And, after the city was conquered, his army would march forward, rolling over what little opposition the rest of the country could muster before moving onto to other lands, such as far off Welia, home of the ambassador who was responsible for cutting off Welia's trade agreement with Ilrika.

Argush had made that ambassador suffer, had extracted his vengeance from the man's flesh for his crimes, but his death, as satisfying as it had been, did not change the fact that the Welian king now refused to respond to any of the messages Kale sent. After all, even armies committed to the Darkness took coin to support and Argush had intended to borrow a loan from the rich country of Welia but the king, thinking himself safe in his far away kingdom, had refused to so much as answer.

But he was not safe from Argush's wrath. No one was. It was a truth he would learn soon enough, so Argush promised himself. Then, once Welia fell beneath his influence, he would move on to the rest of the world and within a few years he would be the supreme king of the world itself. But that victory, that conquest had been delayed by some fool who had chosen, despite no orders from Argush himself, to recall his troops. A fool who would soon learn the true severity of his mistake.

He made his way past the healers' tents, ignoring the moans and cries of the wounded. Had they been stronger, had they been faster, they would not have been wounded in the first place. Had they been *better*, he would not be still camped outside Valeria's walls but would instead be marching into the throne room this moment. They had failed, and so it was right that they should feel the pain of that failure.

He stalked to the tent of his captains. He walked inside, none of them so much as noticing him. Half a dozen, each of whom were supposed to be responsible for a different section of the army. Men who worked for him, who *he* had chosen out of the rabble and elevated to a position of authority and power within his army. Now, though, those same men did not so much as even notice when he stepped into the tent.

Instead, they were all gathered around an unmistakably tall, broad figure, one who stood easily a head above any of those men gathered around him. Paren, son of Shira and Amedan, and the God of Conflict. Kale waited for several seconds for them to acknowledge his entrance, but they were listening to the gravelly, rumbling voice of the god. His anger building by the moment, Kale's hands balled into fists at his sides. "Captain Cadish."

His voice came out in a growl, and all of the captains spun to look, their hands going first to the weapons at their sides—most probably not drawn in half a dozen years or more—before they saw who had come among them. Then, their eyes went wide and they all dropped to their knees, bowing their heads low.

"F-forgive me, Chosen," said Cadish, a man with short-cropped red hair and a red beard streaked with gray as he looked up from where he knelt, "we did not hear you approach."

"Tell me, Captain," Argush went on as if the man hadn't spoken as he stepped further into the room, "I heard that you are the one who ordered the retreat of the troops. Is this true?"

The red-haired man's face paled, and all of those around him, while they didn't move from where they were knelt, seemed to shrink away from him. "I...y-yes, sir."

"I see," Argush said, nodding slowly. "Perhaps I am misremembering, Captain..." He paused, standing above the man. "But I seem to recall ordering you to sweep over the battlements, not stopping until Valeria and its soldiers were crushed beneath our mightier force. Am I mistaken?"

Cadish swallowed hard. "N-no, sir."

"Well," Argush said, "it is good to know that my memory is not failing. I only have one question further, Captain, then you may go."

The man did his best to hide his eagerness but was largely unsuccessful. Argush understood, of course. He did his best to hide his appearance, his gifts, wearing hoods and robes that covered his scaled body, but these men were his captains, the leaders of his army, men with whom he spent far more time than anyone else and from whom he was not completely able to hide his appearance or to stop the rumors he knew they passed back and forth between them like sailors might some dockside whore. Rumors of him being disfigured, of being some sort of monster. Yet, those who had seen anything had caught only glimpses, and even the rumors could not come close to the truth, a truth which, he did not doubt, would send them all fleeing and screaming from the tent had they seen it for themselves.

"Y-yes, sir?" the captain asked, glancing up at the shadowed confines of his hood but only for a moment, looking quickly away again as if guilty of some terrible crime. Which—to Argush's mind, at least—he was, though not the one he suspected.

"My question, Cadish," Argush said, doing his best to keep his voice calm, but some small bit of his rage must have touched on his tone, for the man cringed visibly, "is that why, given such orders, would you then sound the retreat, particularly when you had express orders to press the attack and while the city's defenders were hours, perhaps minutes away from being overcome?"

The man's mouth worked as if he meant to say something, and there was no mistaking the way the other captains of Argush's army scooted away from him now, remaining on their knees while they did so, a retreat that would have been comical under other circumstances. "S-sir," the captain began, then hesitated. "I, that is, *we—*" His words turned to a gurgled croak of shock as Argush buried the knife he'd been holding behind his back into the red-haired man's throat.

Cadish looked down, stunned, as if he could not believe what had happened, pawed weakly at the blade, then collapsed on his side. Argush stood there silently, the other captains frozen where they were knelt, wanting to flee but terrified of what he might do if they tried. Paren, the God of Conflict, stood with his hands crossed behind his back, appearing like some statue carved out of stone, a look of obvious displeasure on his features. The only movement in the tent then came from the dying captain as he writhed on the dirt floor in a growing pool of his own blood.

While the man died, Argush stared at Paren, the two of them locking gazes. Shira had sent the god, her son, claiming that he would be a great asset to Argush, that he would share his experience regarding warfare and thereby serve to expedite the process of conquering Valeria and the world. So far, though, he had only served to challenge Argush's authority at seemingly every opportunity, and Argush frowned at him while the dying man writhed on the ground. Writhed and struggled, gasped and croaked, and then, finally, was still.

When it was finished, Argush finally looked away from the God of Conflict and turned to the remaining captains. "I will brook no traitors in my army. You will listen to my words, will follow my commands to the letter, mine and *no* other. Am I clear?"

"Y-yes, Chosen," the captains said in unison.

"You may go," Argush said, "and take the body with you."

The men rose and hurried out, dragging the corpse along with indecent haste and in moments Argush was alone in the tent with an obviously displeased God of Conflict. Some men might have been terrified at the thought, might have quailed and begged, perhaps even prostrated themselves before the undeniably imposing figure. But Argush was no man, was far, far more, Shira's blessings had seen to that, but then even those blessings were not the greatest of Argush's gifts, despite what the Goddess of the Wilds might think. His greatest asset was his own drive, his own ambition, his own *will,* a will which would not be balked. Not even by a god.

"You are dismissed, Paren. I will call on you if I need you."

The god did not react as a man might have, showing his offense by angry curses or threats. Instead, he only raised a single eyebrow. Yet despite his lack of reaction, the air in the tent suddenly felt thick and hot, nearly unbearably so, and it was all Argush could do to keep from fidgeting, to keep from wiping a hand across his suddenly sweaty brow. Such a movement would be a sign of weakness, though, so he only stared at the god in challenge.

"You *dare,*" Paren said in an impossibly deep voice that sounded like some great mountain shifting, "to dismiss *me?* You overstep yourself, Argush. I am a *god,* one who has existed for millennia while you are but a mortal. Were it not for my mother's wishes, I would crush—"

"But your mother *does* wish," Argush interrupted, "doesn't she, Paren? After all, you might have lived for millennia, that's true, but in all that time, you have never managed to destroy the mortals as your mother wishes, have you?"

The god's hands, hands the size of dinner plates, knotted into fists at his sides, the sounds of his knuckles cracking like boulders shattering beneath the force of a smith's hammer. "You have no idea of that which you speak, *mortal,*" he said, using the word as a curse. "For gods, in our true forms, cannot directly influence mortal lives. My father, in his foolish sentimentality to your kind, ensured as much, for to do so would risk our power, our very existence."

"What *power?*" Argush retorted. "It seems that such power as you have has served you nothing, for in a short amount of time I have brought the forces of the Light to the brink, closer than you have ever come in all your *millennia* of existence."

The god took a step toward him then. Only a single step, but it was enough to make his meaning clear, enough that Argush had a thrill of excitement at the thought of combat. For he was a predator now, one fashioned by Shira just as Paren had been, and like all of the world's truest predators, he did not fear combat but welcomed it, welcomed the opportunity to put his newfound strength and speed to the test against the god. In the end, though, the fury which danced in the god's eyes quieted, and he took a slow, deep breath, his massive chest rising and falling.

"You are in my mother's graces for now, Argush, protected at her word, but know that it may not always be so. Should you fail and should Mother rescind her protection, know that we will continue this conversation, a continuation which I will thoroughly enjoy."

"Perhaps you might not enjoy it so much as you think," Argush said.

"You would threaten me?" the god rumbled. "You who know nothing of war? Today, I ordered the retreat because the defenders were ready for us. Today's attack was not meant to overcome their defenses; it was simply a probing so that we might understand their full strength, so that we might take their measure. Now, we have, and we will prepare."

"Fine," Argush said, "I admit that you know more of warfare than I, but from now on you will run such thoughts by me first. *I* am the leader of this army, Paren. Not you."

The massive god bared his teeth in a humorless smile. "As you say, Argush. You are the leader. For now. If there is nothing else?"

"You may go," Argush said.

The god walked toward the tent entrance then paused, turning back. "Only remember: you are not the first creature to go by the name of Argush. There was another before you. He, too, was arrogant, confident in his own abilities, yet confident or not, he was struck down by the Light's Chosen. Beaten, but not killed, not completely, and you cannot imagine what agonies my mother visited upon him when she found his broken body. Remember that. Tomorrow, we will resume the attack."

Chapter Four

Rion had never strangled a man to death. He'd stabbed them—far too often, of late—had thrown them from a wagon rushing at full speed and though he hadn't stopped to check, he thought it likely the tumble had led to a very painful death, though it had to be said that, at the time, he had been too busy trying to avoid an agonizing death of his own to check. Stabbed men, sure, thrown them beneath wagon wheels, but he had never strangled a man to death. Though, the way things were going, it looked like that might change in the next few minutes, yet if the man standing before him—the one who was practically volunteering, *begging* to be strangled—noticed, he gave no sign.

The tailor, a middle-aged rotund man with a face that would have been more at home on a weasel—a particularly weaselly weasel—stood on the other side of the counter, a smug arrogance plastered across his face. His nose, which it had to be said was several sizes too large for his face or, in point of fact, any face Rion had ever seen, was raised high in the air as if he meant to touch the ceiling with it.

In fact, it was far more likely that his nose would be meeting the wall—an inevitable consequence of Rion's growing certainty that strangulation might not be satisfactory and that he would opt instead for slamming the tailor's face into the wall to see which one broke first—than the ceiling. The tailor, though, seemed oblivious of Rion's growing anger, just as he had apparently somehow missed the army camped outside their walls and had failed to notice the four armed men standing behind Rion, Valerian guards there to ensure that even the most reluctant of merchants did their part to help supply the defenders and those healers who saw to their wounds with what they required.

Rion pinched the bridge of his nose, gathering his patience. The problem was that the morning had been a trying one, and what little patience he had left was ragged and threadbare, not enough to cover the tailor's unusually large nose, if it were all picked up and sewn together. Still, he thought he could be forgiven that.

It had been a pretty damned terrible day so far with no signs of getting any better. Though, it had to be said, there were others out there whose day had been far worse, particularly those men who had defended the wall against Kale's first assault, many of whom had died and Rion wouldn't have traded places even with those still among the living.

A dark, bloody morning with a dark, bloody night likely on the way. After all, only a fool would expect an army who served the Darkness to take a break just because the sun was preparing to sink below the horizon.

He had thought, when Alesh had asked—ordered, really, and not in person, for the man could not be found anymore save for on the wall fighting—him to make use of the old connections his father's business had formed to procure wagons and the teamsters needed to drive them, that he had been lucky. Now, though, he thought that luck was in very short supply in Valeria.

Since the early hours of the morning, Rion had been coordinating the transferring of goods from the city to the walls, ferrying weapons and arrows and bowstrings and armor and a thousand other things to make sure that the soldiers there weren't left to fend off the hordes of Darkness with blunt sticks and sharp words.

Those trips had been tiring, speaking with merchant after merchant, blacksmiths for armor and weapons, coordinating the loading and unloading of goods when they reached the wall, distributing those goods to the soldiers there. Those trips had been exhausting trials of logistics and patience, full of a thousand problems that needed solving, all of them contriving to need that solving right at *that very moment*—but those trips, however annoying and however much of a hassle they had been, had been far from the worst.

The worst had been the return trips, trips where the many wagons and carts had not carried swords or arrows or shields but the dead and those whose injuries were so severe that they would never wield a blade or shoot a bow again, men and women largely indistinguishable from the corpses sharing the wagons with them.

The dead were bad, those men and women who had been cut down defending the citizens of Valeria from the army that planned to swallow them up. Very bad. The glassy eyes of the dead staring somehow accusingly, gaping wounds and severed limbs, an absence of life where it had been but moments before, taken so recently that a man could almost see the remnants of life drifting away from their bodies like the mist following a fog bank.

But as bad as the dead were, the sight of the living was far worse. "Living," of course being far too presumptuous in some cases, for those men and women who rode in the back of the wagons, and those still stationed on the walls, had been changed by the day's events, altered in some irreversible way that was as obvious and undeniable as it was difficult to define.

It was not easy to say what was missing, to point out, specifically, what piece of those men and women's souls had been ripped away from them, but the fact that it had been ripped out was obvious to anyone who saw them. It was something in the way they stood, slumped somehow without being noticeably slumped, as if the part of them—courage, perhaps, or more likely, respect for themselves and a belief that they understood some fundamental part of the way the world worked—had been taken from them. It was also visible in something in their eyes or, more likely, something that was *not* in their eyes. They were alive— breathing and moving, shuffling unto the wagons or watching their brethren do so—but at the same time, they were not. The spark of life, the joy of it, had been torn from them by the morning events, carved away by the blades of the men and women who had poured over the walls, most of them not wearing armor and many not even carrying real weapons but intent on bloodlust just the same.

Those men and women were a sight that even a person as cynical as Rion could not help but be affected by, and they had served to darken his already dark mood. And if the plight of those poor defenders wasn't enough, now Rion was forced to endure merchants—the smug tailor standing before him the latest among them—who had never lifted a blade in anger and whose only idea of sacrifice was averting their eyes from the wagons which were already stained with blood from the morning's work, blood that wouldn't come out no matter the amount of effort Rion and the drivers currently under his employ tried.

And now the same fool who refused to even so much as glance in the direction of the wagons which stood testament to the day's tragedy was smugly insisting on charging full price for strips of fabric—strips left over from his labors and ones which would have been thrown out anyway—instead of giving them to Rion and the others so that they might be used to bandage the wounds of far better men, the same men who were sacrificing themselves so that this asshole could continue to peddle his ridiculous fashions to men and women with far more coin than sense.

"Now," the asshole in question pressed, "as I fear I have already mentioned, Lord Eriondrian, while I would love nothing more than to assist in the city's defense in any way I am able, I must insist that even in this dire hour, a man such as myself must be paid for the products of his labor." He leaned forward across the counter as if confiding some great secret. "You, as a business man yourself, must surely understand that should I become destitute by reaching beyond my means and trying to provide assistance of which I am incapable, it will only serve to drive me out of business." He paused, giving a little laugh as if even the thought was ridiculous. "And then what good could I possibly be to the city of Valeria and its citizens if I were no longer able to practice my craft?"

"They're rags," Rion said, doing his best to keep his patience and, judging by the growl he heard in his own voice, largely failing. In truth, he didn't care. He was tired of haggling with pompous merchants and pompous nobles, tired of trying to convince stupid, selfish men that it was in their best interest to help in the city's defense. "Rags you'd most likely throw out anyway. Unless there is some new fashion of which I'm unaware, one which calls for the sewing together of hundreds of multi-colored, multi-fabric strips. The nobles of Valeria have some ridiculous fashion sense, it's true, but I believe that even they would balk at something as hideous as that."

"Rags?" the merchant said in an offended voice. "*Rags?* Forgive me, Lord Tirinian, but these *rags* as you call them are of the finest material available. Now, as I said, I would do anything, of course, to aid in the city's defense, but I cannot, in good conscience simply give away my stock. I've a family to feed, after all, and if—"

"Did you say 'anything'?" Rion interrupted. His father had always taught him that kindness was the surest way to get what you wanted, but while the morning had not affected him as it had those poor, brave men along the wall, it had still affected him, stripping from him the kindness—inevitably feigned—that he might have shown in other circumstances.

The tailor gave him a confused look. "I'm sorry?"

"Did you just say," Rion pressed, "that you would be willing to do anything—short of, the gods forbid, losing profit—to aid in the city's defense?"

The tailor might have been a fool, but he was not so foolish to not see the trap laid out before him. A trap which, they both knew, was unavoidable. After all, Rion had spent his life conversing with far cleverer men than this, had been mugged by cleverer men, in fact, and the merchant's weaselly face screwed up in consternation. "I...that is, of course, I would. Valeria is my city, its people my customers, nay, my brothers and sisters, and I would be remiss if—"

"Very well," Rion said. "We were just about to make a trip back to the wall—our small sacrifice, you see, to make sure that those gallant men and women who are risking their lives to protect us have what they need. Men and women who, thanks to your own brave sacrifice, will have one more man along the walls to help them. Now come, we will get you some armor and—"

"Wait," the tailor stammered. His face had gone ghostly pale as well it might have, for it was a far different thing to know that other men and women were dying on your behalf than to become one of them. "I...that is, I suppose I might dedicate some of my materials to—"

"All of them."

Rion would not have thought, before then, that the man's face could have grown any paler. He would have been wrong. "All of them?" the tailor managed in a choked voice.

"Yes, I think so," Rion said, "but then I think we might need more than that. I mean, I would hate the thought that those men and women on the wall—your brothers and sisters, I believe you said—might suffer or die because the healers seeing to them are only able to bind their wounds with their hopes and wishes. And what better fabric to use as bandages, after all, then what you claim is the finest fabric around? Surely no one would be so callous as to argue that they weren't worth it."

The tailor licked his lips, clearing his throat. "I...that is—"

"Unless, of course," Rion went on, "you would prefer to contribute in some other way. After all, the wall can always use more bodies—what with just today's death toll being so high and—"

"I, of course," the merchant stammered, his skin now a sickly shade of green, "would be pleased, nay *privileged* to donate my excess cloth to the defense."

Rion allowed himself a small smile. "I thought you might." He turned, motioning to the four guards who began to cart out piles of fabric, fine dresses and tunics and trousers, and dumping them unceremoniously into the backs of the blood-slick wagons.

The merchant was fidgeting terribly now, wincing as each item was removed, items which under normal circumstances foolish nobles would have paid a small fortune for. In fact, nobles being who they were, they probably would do so even now, going on about their pitiful, sad little lives, confident as always that their status, one which they had only been born into and which they had in no way earned, would protect them from whatever came. Fools, then, and some of the most dangerous kind.

Rion felt some passing, vindictive satisfaction at the expression of almost pure terror on the tailor's face, but it faded quickly. Some men perhaps deserved to be bullied, and if such men existed certainly the merchant might be counted among them, yet he found no satisfaction in strong-arming someone, selfish bastard or not. The day had made him feel many things, but it had left no room for satisfaction of any kind.

Instead of contempt for the man before him, he felt only pity, and he turned without a word and walked out to where the wagons waited in the street, examining their contents. Weapons and armor, clothes and fabric and medicines. Yet for all his efforts, he felt as if they were already falling behind. Only a day's worth of fighting and already the demand for materials was being stretched thin. The only consolation, if one was to be had, was that if their losses kept up like they had been, all the bandages in the world would make no difference, nor would weapons, for swords and bows, shields and armor were all little good without soldiers to use them and despite the many skilled craftsmen in Valeria—Odrick, his father, and Chosen Larin by far the greatest among them—no one could craft more soldiers out of thin air to replace the many ones they had already lost and those others they would lose as the fighting continued.

It was with a weary body, then, and with a far wearier heart that Rion climbed into the front wagon and motioned the team forward. As the wagons began rumbling down the cobbled street toward the wall where they would once again get to witness the day's tragedy in person, Rion tried to console himself with the fact that, according to the reports, Kale's army had, for the time at least, retreated back into the forest.

Despite heavy losses, they had won the day. The night, though, was coming, and after that, more days, ones likely as bloody as this one. He could only hope that Alesh had some plan for how to deal with the approaching army. A thin hope, maybe, for the man seemed to be fighting a war without as well as one within himself and had been scarcely seen of late, spending all of his time on the wall and not speaking with anyone at the end of the day before retiring to his quarters.

A thin hope, yes, but just then, that was all they had.

Chapter Five

"Lady Sonya, forgive me, but I still do not think that this is the wisest course—"

"Darl, you *promised*," Sonya said, the little girl crossing her arms tightly across her chest in a gesture which brooked no argument.

Darl winced. "Yes, yes, I did, but—"

"Is it that you don't think I'm good enough?" she demanded. "Is it because I'm a girl? Or do you think I'm too little?"

Darl knelt in front of her, draping the two wooden practice swords across his knees as he did. "Lady Sonya, I do not doubt that, should you put your mind to it, you would be a brilliant warrior. As for you being a woman, among my people, some of the best warriors are women. In fact, some of my own training masters when I was a child were women. That has nothing to do with it. It is not that you are a girl...it is only..." He hesitated, watching her face, her jaw set, her eyebrows drawn down in a preparatory frown. "It is only that you are a child, young one, and children should be allowed to remain children as long as possible. There is magic in—"

"Being a child didn't stop those men from taking me," she said.

Darl's breath caught in his throat at the pain and fear and anger he heard in the little girl's voice, things a child her age should never feel, should never be *forced* to feel. "Lady Sonya, your capture was my fault, and I am very sorry. It will not happen aga—"

"But you don't *know* that," she said. "They took me, Darl, and if it wasn't for Tarex, they would have hurt me, I think. They *did* hurt me. Why...why won't they just leave us alone?" she asked, her voice breaking, tears thick in her eyes now.

Darl reached out for her, meaning to hold her, to embrace her and tell her that everything would be okay, but the girl pulled away from him, refusing what comfort he could have given her. He sighed heavily. "Sonya, I understand...I mean only that I am very sorry for what happened to you. But, these men, they—"

"I want to hurt them," she said, the tears flowing freely now. "I want to kill those men. Th-they took Abigail, Darl. Chorin too. And Ale—"

"Sonya, please," he said softly, his heart aching for the young girl. "Violence is not the way to solve problems. Violence only breeds more violence, young one. It is not the right way to—"

"Alesh does."

Darl hesitated. "I...forgive me, Sonya, what?"

"Alesh hurts those people. Tarex did, too. He hurt the people that took me, and he hurt the men in the woods, and I'm *glad*. I'm *glad* he did it. And Alesh is on the wall everyday fighting, hurting the people who are attacking us."

"S-Sonya," Darl said, "Chosen Alesh is...he is in a bad place right now. He has—"

"You said that he is Chosen by the gods. To lead us."

"I...yes. Yes, he is our Chosen, the man who will lead us out of the Darkness."

"Then if he's the one who is meant to lead us...and he's the one Chosen by the gods...how can he be wrong? Besides, those men didn't care that I was just a kid, Darl. They took me anyway, hurt me anyway, and I couldn't do anything to stop them."

Darl considered what he might say to that, but all of his arguments seemed cheap and weak to his mind. Finally, he rose, offering her one of the wooden weapons. "The first thing we will work on is how you should grip your weapon. Come—I will show you."

***

Katherine felt as if she was losing her mind. Or perhaps it was not her mind she was losing after all, but something else. Perhaps she was losing her hope. She had been to the walls—as far, at least, as the guards stationed at the staircases leading to the battlements would allow her to get—and she had seen some small part of the devastation the attack had caused. She knew, too, that Alesh was somewhere up there, had searched for him time after time in the last few days, hoping to talk to him, but he would not see her, would not see anyone, seeming only to speak to Captain Nordin.

It was as if he was pulling away, from her, from Rion and the others, from his own life. She had thought, at first, that she was losing him, though she had no idea why. Now, though, she was beginning to think that she had never had him in the first place. She would have pressed the issue more, would have forced the guards to let her up to see him, but the truth was she had been busy herself, working with Rion and his parents to coordinate the delivering of goods the soldiers needed to the walls, food and water and weapons, working with the healers to try to ensure that no one died because they didn't have the supplies they needed.

Still, as dire as their situation was, she found herself thinking of Alesh again and again, worrying for him, a worry that made it difficult to focus on the many tallies of goods requested and goods received. In fact, she realized that she had been simply staring at the paper in her hands—a report from Healer Malachai, the Chief Healer and scribbled in sprawling text that demonstrated his exhaustion—asking for more bandages, more salves and medicines. Just *more.*

Katherine shook her head, telling herself for the thousandth time to focus, and then set about the task of ensuring that the Chief Healer would get what he needed. Then, when that was finished, she sent the orders off through several runners and rose, stretching. There were a thousand other things that needed doing, that demanded her attention, but she decided that she needed to speak to Darl about Alesh. If anyone knew what to do about the man, the Ferinan would.

It took some time asking around and finally she was directed to the castle training grounds. She followed the instructions the guard had given her and was unsurprised to find the training grounds pretty much empty. After all, if what she'd been hearing of the brutality of the action on the wall was true, it was no wonder that the city's soldiers had little interest in spending their off-shift time training. They'd been doing plenty enough fighting in reality, after all.

She *was* surprised, however, to see Darl and Sonya standing in the center of one of the training squares. The two were facing each other, wooden practice swords in hand. Darl stood tall, his knees slightly bent, his side facing Sonya, in a stance that made his skill apparent. His breath was smooth and even.

Sonya, meanwhile, was in a far different state. The girl's chest heaved with ragged breaths, and she was covered in sweat, the clothes she wore drenched with it. The practice sword shook where she gripped it, pointed in the Ferinan's direction, as if she was so exhausted that she could barely lift the blade. Yet for all the weariness that showed in her slumped shoulders, it was not tiredness that showed in her expression. Instead, it was determination. But not *just* that. There was an expression on the little girl's face that Katherine had never seen there before, one that looked as alien on that normally kind, smiling face as Darl would have looked in a dress: anger. But even that wasn't quite on the mark. The girl didn't look angry—she looked furious, her normally soft features twisted into a hard grimace.

Even as Katherine watched, the little girl gave a shout that would have sounded far more at home coming from some hairy-chested warrior on a battlefield than the Sonya that Katherine knew, brandishing her practice sword and charging forward. Darl moved smoothly and seemingly with no effort at all, bending like a reed in the wind so that Sonya's strike missed him by inches, then his own practice sword lashed out in a blur. A moment later, Sonya's practice sword was spinning away through the air, knocked loose of her hand by the Ferinan's well-placed strike. The girl herself stumbled forward, off-balance, and then fell to her hands and knees onto the hard-packed earth.

She did not look hurt in any way, but instead of rising, she remained where she was, her body tense, and Darl chose that moment to look over at Katherine. There was a world of meaning in the Ferinan's gaze, and Katherine frowned, stepping forward. "Sonya, Darl," she said, "is everything...alright?"

The little girl looked up at her, her jaw clenched and appearing as if she was holding back tears. "I'm *fine*," she said, the caustic tone of her voice belying her words as she rose to her feet and stomped toward where her training sword had fallen.

Katherine walked up to Darl, and the two of them watched the girl. "What's going on with Sonya?" she asked in a voice low enough that the girl could not hear.

Darl glanced over at her, his expression sad. "She is angry, Katherine, and she feels helpless."

Katherine watched the girl scoop up the practice sword, remembering her own reasons for coming to see the Ferinan, specifically being angry and feeling helpless regarding the way Alesh had been risking his life without surcease since the invasion began, as if he was courting death. "I know the feeling," she said, realizing how selfish she had been. For days, she had been only focused on herself, on her own worries and fears, specifically those fears regarding what she thought were Alesh's attempts to get himself killed.

All understandable concerns, but while she had been fretting over them, turning them over this way and that like a spurned lover searching a letter over and over again for some apology or post script she had not seen at first and hoping she would find it for having looked so much, her friends had been hurting. Rion and Darl, Sonya, all of them were dealing with just as many problems as she was. And then there was Fermin and Marta to think about. The young girl and manservant still hadn't been found and Katherine was growing increasingly sure that Marta had gone to the enemy army searching for Sonya.

The thought of that made her wince. Marta, a girl no more than twelve or thirteen years of age, had been brave enough to risk sneaking into the enemy army and in doing so had shown a courage far greater than any Katherine had been able to muster. Katherine had allowed her own efforts to speak to Alesh about what was going on with him to be hindered by something so simple as a guard stationed on the staircase.

No more, she promised herself. She would address her concerns, would make sure Alesh heard them even if Valeria's entire city guard meant to stand in her way. She realized that for too long she had been standing back and seeing problems but leaving them for someone else to address, telling herself, in her cowardice, that here was someone better than her for the task. But Alesh needed help—anyone with eyes could see that. She didn't know what had happened to him, didn't know what darkness plagued his thoughts, but she owed it to herself, to all the citizens of Valeria who counted on him, to find out. She promised herself that she would go and find Alesh, would make him listen if she had to hold him down, just as soon as she left the training grounds.

But first, her friends needed her, friends who she had neglected for far too long. "Darl," she said softly, "I know that lately I've been—"

"I am sorry, Katherine," the Ferinan interrupted, "but Lady Sonya was quite insistent on my training her."

Katherine was going to say more, but then Sonya was there, staring up at Darl, her clothes and arms covered in dust, looking more exhausted than ever but still with that angry, determined look in her eyes, one that reminded Katherine of a similar look she's seen in Alesh's gaze. On the man, that look—one of fury barely contained, of a wish to hurt—had worried her. On the young girl's face, it wasn't just worrying—it was disturbing to the point of shocking.

"Well?" Sonya demanded. "I'm ready to go again."

Darl glanced at Katherine as if for help, and she cleared her throat. "Sonya, look, I—"

"No," Sonya interrupted.

"I'm sorry?" Katherine asked.

"I said no," Sonya repeated. "I know what you're going to say, Katherine. You're going to tell me that a girl, a kid, has no business learning how to fight, but you're wrong. I *do* need to know how to fight. *Everyone* does. And the next time those men or people like them try to take me I'll...I'll kill them."

"Sonya," Katherine said stunned, "that isn't—"

"I don't have to do what you say," the girl interrupted. "You're not my mom. I don't *have* a mom. Abigail was the closest person to it, and men like the ones that took me attacked her. They killed her, and I couldn't do anything to stop them."

Katherine felt her eyes going wide. She had known Sonya for some time, ever since escaping Ilrika with her and Darl, and she had never known her to be anything but polite, to be, in fact, the sweetest little girl she had ever met. But now that sweet, innocent girl had changed—or perhaps more accurately, had *been* changed, changed by those men who had snuck into the city and taken her. And could such a change ever be reversed? Would she ever again be the smiling, carefree girl, the one who had even managed to survive the revolution inside Ilrika? Katherine did not know, hoped so, of course, but she feared otherwise. For if life had taught her anything, it was that some changes, some things, once they were taken from a person, could never be replaced.

"Sweetie," Katherine said, feeling tears in her eyes as she knelt before the girl, "that's not what I meant, not at all." She reached out for the girl with both hands. At first, Sonya recoiled as if she would refuse the embrace but then, after a moment, the practice sword fell from her hands, and she lunged forward, pulling Katherine into an embrace so tight it was almost painful.

The girl was crying, she could feel the wetness of her tears on her shoulder, but Katherine didn't care, was quite sure, in fact, that the little girl felt the moistness of her own tears as well. Katherine decided, then, that while life might often seem like a series of one terrible thing after the other, one terrible *moment* after another, those things, those moments, meant nothing when compared to those rare instances of greatness, of sublime contentment which can come upon a person so unexpectedly, and which, in their coming, made hours, days, even years of the pain that preceded them all mean nothing and amount to nothing, erasing them as if they had never been. The world, she thought, could not be so bad of a place if girls like Sonya lived within it, like flowers sprouting in wastelands, beautiful as they were yet made achingly so by their contrast.

"I love you, Katherine," Sonya mumbled, her words a whisper in Katherine's ear, her soft breath like the flap of a butterfly's wings against her face.

"Oh, sweetie," she said, "I love you too."

She felt a hand on her shoulder then, knew it was Darl, and as always the Ferinan managed to communicate his own feelings, his own love without the use of words, words which, even to

Katherine who spent a large portion of her life singing, perhaps even *because* of it, she knew were no better than a half-knitted net which, when they caught what they fished for did so more by luck than design.

Out of all the many gifts the gods had given her—and there had been many, not the least of which were her newfound powers, ones she still did not fully understand—the greatest she had ever received were her friends, friends she could not help but think she did not deserve. Darl, Sonya, Marta, Rion, and Alesh. People who were tied to her not by blood or duty but by the strongest of connections—friendship. People she would do anything for, would die for if necessary. She had never considered herself a courageous person, a brave person, but she knew that she would make any sacrifice for them.

So why haven't you? a voice inside her head asked, and she found herself thinking of Alesh. The most powerful man she had ever known, the greatest warrior, one she believed better even than Darl, a thing she would not have thought possible until she'd met him. A man who possessed courage and wisdom and strength that he himself did not understand. The Chosen of Amedan, the leader of not just Valeria but of all the Light which stood against the Darkness. And above all—her friend. Whether he was more than that or not she no longer knew, but she knew that he *was* her friend. Just as she knew that he was hurting. She wasn't sure what, exactly, was the source of that hurt, but she saw it in him in those brief instances where she caught a glimpse of him. It was eating at him, that hurt, and how much time was left until there was nothing left inside him but the hurt itself?

She did not know how long she knelt with the girl held in her embrace, knew only that it was a long time that could have never been long enough. Eventually, though, Sonya pulled away, looked up into her eyes, then past her, a surprised look on her face. Katherine glanced around and saw what it was that had caused her confusion, then realized that Darl had vanished sometime without her seeing it, thinking perhaps, and perhaps rightly, that she and Sonya needed some time alone. For both of them.

"Katherine?"

Her voice so low and timid that it made her heart ache. "Yes, sweetie?"

Sonya glanced down at the wooden practice sword as if embarrassed before looking back at her. "I'll quit...if you want me to."

Katherine was left staring, surprised, wondering what it was that she had done to deserve the trust of a girl like Sonya. Nothing, probably, for she knew enough of the world to know that the rain fell and the sun shone on the kind and unkind alike. An inexplicable thing, then, but a fine one. She considered the girl's offer. When she had first seen the little girl with the sword it had struck a chord in her, one that had reverberated wrongly, and Sonya had discerned, rightfully so, that her greatest urge had been to rush forward and snatch it out of her hands. But that had been a foolish reaction, one belonging to the woman she had been long ago. The world was what it was, after all, and much of what it was was dangerous. Ignoring the danger or hoping that it would simply not find her when it never seemed to have difficulty finding anyone was a gamble she thought even Rion would not take.

If what Sonya needed to keep from feeling like just another potential victim was to learn the sword, then who was Katherine to tell her she was wrong? Who was anyone? "No," she said. "Don't quit. You keep doing whatever it is you want to do. Who knows? Soon,"—she paused, winking—"maybe I'll hire you to protect me."

The girl smiled. An innocent expression, one with none of the malice and hate that had been on her face moments before in evidence, and Katherine knew, then, that she was right. That this time, this once, she was right.

"Katherine?"

"Yes, Sonya?"

"How...how do you do it?"

"Do what, honey?"

Sonya fidgeted, avoiding her eyes. "Not...how are you not afraid?"

Katherine laughed, the first real, honest laugh she could remember having. "Sonya," she said, "I'm always afraid."

"You?" Sonya asked, surprised. "But you seem so brave, so...like you always know what to do."

"Oh, Sonya," Katherine said, "I never know what to do. As for being brave...I'm no expert, but I don't think bravery means not being afraid."

"No?"

Katherine shook her head slowly. "I think that courage is getting out of bed every morning, of knowing that anything could happen in the day to come and facing it anyway. Courage," she said, running a hand through the girl's hair, "is deciding not to be a victim anymore, not to sit around complaining about things that have happened to you but to do something about it." She winked. "Something like becoming the greatest swordswoman of the age."

Sonya blushed, obviously pleased, then winced. "I don't think I'm very good. Darl says I'm holding it better though."

"I'm sure you'll be fantastic," Katherine said. "And you want to know a secret?"

"What?" The girl blinked, her eyes wide and solemn.

"I used to be an *atrocious* harp player."

"You?" Sonya asked, frowning in suspicion. "That can't be right. You play beautifully. I've never heard anything so beautiful."

"Want to know how?"

"More than anything," Sonya said.

She laughed then glanced meaningfully at the practice sword still lying on the ground. "Well, it starts with picking it up."

Sonya followed her gaze, looking at the practice sword. Then, she took a deep breath and let out it, reached out, and grabbed the sword.

"Thank you, Katherine," Sonya said, smiling.

"No, Sonya," she said. "Thank you."

The little girl cocked her head quizzically. "For what?"

Katherine laughed, putting her arm around the girl. "How much time do you have?"

Chapter Six

Marta was exhausted. In mind and body, even in her soul, she was exhausted. She hadn't known a thing like that was possible. But several hours spent trudging among the dead and the dying, hours spent checking for pulses, hours spent calling over soldiers—or at least this army's approximation of a soldier, the only requirement being, it seemed, having something pointy they could stab someone with—had proved her wrong. The soldiers, when she or one of the other slaves who'd been given the task of assessing the dead would determine if those men or women were able to be saved. Or, more accurately, if they were *worth* saving, if they might still somehow be useful to Kale and his army.

If this was deemed to be true, those "soldiers" would call over other "soldiers" who would set about the task of lifting the wounded man or woman in question and bringing them back to what passed for healers in the army—these, too, from what Marta had seen, showed an affinity for sharp, stabby things—who then set about what passed for healing. Marta was no healer herself, but the amount of wailing and screaming—and corpses, come to that—that came from those tents made her pretty confident that they weren't either.

Living in the streets of Valeria, she had come as any orphan waif did, to fear the darkness. Or, more accurately, not the darkness itself, not the *night* itself, but those things, those *creatures* which during the day went by the names of men and by night shed the guises which allowed them to walk among civilized society to reveal their true selves. But today was different. *Tonight* was different.

For tonight, the monsters were no doubt still there, but the coming of darkness also meant that her shift and the shift of those other slaves she'd shared the field of the dead with were done, for the day, at least. She and those with her would return to the tents to rest and the second shift of slaves would be sent out to continue the grim work. She didn't envy them, those other slaves, but she also did not pity them. She thought she had probably run out of pity the second, perhaps the third hour into the day's work.

Even thoughts of how she might go about tracking down Sonya or trying to find Fermin, thoughts, *plans* which had served to help get her through the day, to distract her from the grim task at hand, seemed too difficult to contemplate now. There was only the putting of one foot in front of the other, the exhausted, hunched shuffle to the slave tents, her greatest hope, in that moment, not of finding Sonya or Fermin, not of rescuing—but of being rescued. Rescued in the only way that was possible—sleep. Sleep which would pull her away from those bloody corpses, those moans that she thought she could hear even now, moans that she thought she would be able to hear for some time to come. She wanted only to fall into the lice-ridden, lumpy mattress and to sleep. To sleep and not to dream.

The other slaves were waiting, sitting in their cots, all obviously nervous, several guards standing there in the tents, no doubt intending to escort the second shift to the fields as they had Marta and the others hours before. No doubt there to make *sure* they went, to punish any who thought to refuse.

Not that any would. One of Marta's group had thought to do as much and gotten a black eye and a bloodied lip for her trouble. Not much of a shock that the same men who would attack innocent people, who would work with the Goddess Shira and dedicate their lives to the Darkness wouldn't hesitate to hit a woman if they took it in mind to do so, but the slave sure had *seemed* surprised. Then again, Marta supposed a person wasn't ever really ready to get punched in the face. Even bruisers who spent their lives punching and getting punched, even assholes—of which she'd met many—who went around basically begging for it always seemed shocked when it actually happened.

The slaves who had just finished having the worst day of their lives shuffled, half-dead, to their cots while those preparing to have the worst night of their lives walked timidly toward the tent entrance. All, that was, except one. One woman sat hunched on her small cot, her arms wrapped tight around her, her head down so that her tangled mess of hair covered her face. But while her hair might have concealed her expression, nothing could conceal the sounds of her sobbing or the way she rocked back and forth, shaking her head.

In a few minutes, all the slaves were standing at the entrance of the tent, all, that was, save her. "Move your ass, you ugly shrew," one of the guards growled from where he stood at the door.

But if the slave in question noticed, she gave no sign, only continued rocking back and forth, shaking her head and muttering, "I can't, I can't, I can't," in between her sobs. Marta scowled at the crying woman, and she saw those other returning slaves scowling at her as well. And why not? They'd had the worst day of their lives, and now they were watching this woman refuse to do what they'd already had to, to refuse to do her part, and as a consequence of that, she was going to start trouble. And once trouble was started, particularly when assholes like the guards in their tent were involved, it was less like an arrow shot to target than a mad bull let loose on a crowded street, one which—being a mad bull—wasn't very particular about who it ended up goring with its horns, just so long as it gored someone.

Even now as she watched, the guards were muttering to each other, their expressions growing darker and darker, more and more threatening by the moment. Marta didn't want to get involved, didn't want to do much of anything but fall into blissful unconsciousness and forget about the world for a while, to hope, desperately, that the world and all those in it might forget about her as well.

But a storm was coming, as obvious on the expressions of the guards as dark clouds gathering overhead. A storm from which any sensible person would flee at the first sign. Certainly that was the strategy Marta had adopted all her life, was the same strategy which had kept her alive in the streets, which had allowed her to go on keeping her heart beating just the way she liked it while so many others didn't. It had allowed her to keep on breathing, to keep on living. Once, that had been enough, all she could have hoped for. Now, though, Marta found that things were different. She had met Alesh and Katherine, Darl and Sonya, and had realized—despite her best efforts—that there was a big difference between living and having a life. A life full of people who mattered to you, full of things to lose, true, but the thing about that was that having something to lose meant you had something that mattered, and that was a fine thing.

She thought of what Katherine or Darl would do in the same situation, thought of what *Alesh* would do. Didn't take long to think of. What did Alesh do when he saw a storm approach? Well, he walked right into it, thinking, maybe, that he could slay the clouds themselves and save the people he cared about from getting their hairs mussed with rain. And just as likely, he would be right.

So, Marta heaved a big breath, gathered the ragged edges of patience and energy the day had left her, and moved toward the mewling woman. "Hey," she whispered, kneeling down in front of the slave and nearly collapsing from exhaustion as she did.

The woman, though, was so wrapped up in her own tears that she didn't notice, likely wouldn't have noticed had Marta fallen on her, though she bet that she would notice all too well the method the guards would likely choose to get her attention if she didn't stop her bawling soon.

"*Hey*," Marta hissed, giving the woman's shoulder a shake. "Stop that crying. You looking for the fastest way of getting a good beating, that it? 'Cause if so, let me just congratulate you as you're making a pretty damned fine job of it."

The girl—and Marta thought of her as a girl even though from what she could see of her, the slave in question was obviously a woman grown, one that had to be six feet tall at the least—quietened her sobbing for a moment, and Marta had a brief instant to hope she'd gotten through to her. Then the crying started up again, worse, if anything, than it had been before, and the girl buried her face in her hands and shook it as if to deny some question that had never been asked.

But the problem was, Marta realized, that it had been. The guards *had* asked the question, and Marta had asked herself the same one hundreds of times throughout the day. What would a person be willing to do, be willing to give up, if it meant they could avoid the pain of a beating? Would they be willing, say, to traipse through a field of corpses, be willing to lie to themselves and say that they were saving people when it was just as likely that the wounded they found would be killed by the guards or left to die from their own grievous wounds because the guards, in their very finite, very cruel wisdom decided—often on a whim, it seemed—that they weren't worth saving?

For Marta, the answer had been yes. She told herself the answer came as a result of her concern for her friends, for Sonya and Fermin and all the others who she might still help if she were alive. And mostly, she thought that was true. But there was still that part of her—that part which had lived on the streets, which had memorized early on which alleyways were merely dangerous and which were deadly—that had wanted to avoid pain. That, too, she could not deny.

So, instead of screaming at the woman that she was going to get them beaten or worse, Marta breathed a sigh. "Why?" she asked, honestly curious.

Perhaps it was the unaggressive tone of her voice or its sincerity, but the woman did stop her blubbering then, raising her head slowly, skittishly, to meet Marta's eyes. And Marta, finally seeing her, was surprised to find that she recognized her. The woman who had been crying her eyes out at the thought of her task was one of the same women who had held Marta only days before while Greta, the self-styled Queen of the Slaves, had beaten on her. She hadn't seemed much keen on that either, but Marta also couldn't help but remember that the woman had shed no tears on that occasion, at least.

She grunted, surprised. "Farra, isn't it?"

"Y-yes," the woman said, sniffling and running a thick, muscled arm that most men would have been jealous of across her snotty nose. "Oh," she breathed, her eyes going wide, "you're...you're the girl. Listen, about—"

"Never mind that," Marta said. "We'll talk about it later." Or more likely, based on what Greta had threatened her with hours ago, they'd be reliving the event soon enough. "Now, why—"

"I can't," the woman stammered, recoiling as if she expected Marta to strike her, as if such a blow from a girl so much smaller than her would have affected her much at all even if she had. She met Marta's eyes with a desperate, pleading expression. "I *can't.*"

"Sure, sure," Marta said, doing her best to make her voice soothing, doing her best to keep her own exhaustion and ragged impatience out of it. "I'm no genius, but even I can see that much. My question, though, is...well. Why not?"

The woman hesitated, glancing over Marta's shoulders at the other slaves, most staring at her with poorly-concealed hostility, and then at the guards who didn't bother concealing their hostility at all. Then, finally, she met Marta's eyes again, studying her as if looking for something. After a time, she took a deep, ragged breath, and leaned in to speak directly into Marta's ear. "I'm pregnant," she said, her voice so low that Marta could barely hear it despite being only inches away from her.

Marta blinked. "That...that's a good thing, isn't it?"

The woman swallowed hard. "It is my master's child, and he...that is, if he were to find out...he has gotten others of his slaves pregnant...he was...not kind to them."

"But what does that have to do with checking for wounded?"

The woman winced, then her lip began to tremble as if she might break into tears again at any moment. "They say that a child, inside her mother's womb, can feel what she feels...see what she sees. I didn't...I don't want..."

Her breath caught in her throat, and she was unable to finish. But then, Marta didn't think she needed to. Some might have said the woman was being silly to think that her unborn child would feel anything, *could* feel anything even if her mother were to go wading through a river of the dead and dying. Maybe they would have been right—certainly Marta was no midwife or healer to know much of such things. But for her part, she didn't think so. After all, she had grown up on the streets, and it seemed to her that it was all she had ever known since she had known anything. There was no telling what ways it had affected her, ways even she wasn't aware of. She nodded slowly. "And this master of yours...what did he do? To the other women, I mean? And the child?"

The woman swallowed and met her eyes. Once again, there was no need to explain, for Marta saw the truth there in her naked, fearful gaze. Masters looked at their slaves as little more than property, after all, like goods to be used and traded. And what was the only reasonable course of action when a man found himself with goods that had spoiled or become more difficult to keep than they were worth, to his mind? Well, he got rid of them, didn't he?

"But, surely," Marta pressed, "you know that you won't be able to hide this from him forever. Sooner or later, you'll start to show—that much, even I know. And when you do…"

"I'm going to run away," the girl said, a hand going protectively to her stomach, one which Marta quickly took in her own in the hopes of avoiding any of the other slaves or the guards catching on. "I want to protect my baby," the woman said, her voice choked with emotion. "I have to."

Marta wondered, looking at the slave, if her own mother had ever thought as much. Likely, she had not, but there was no way to know for sure as she had never met the woman, or her father come to that. And had she, somehow, been the product of such a union? Stranger things had happened. The last months had taught her that much, at least.

"Well?" an angry voice demanded. Marta and Farra jumped at once, turning at the sound, and Marta felt her stomach knot as she saw that Guardsman Blake, the last person she wanted to see just then, had approached. All the guards were cruel—didn't get a lot of sweethearts signing up for an army bent on destruction, who would have thought?—but Blake was crueler than the others, a man who enjoyed that little power he had, enjoyed wielding it like a blade to cut. He was looming over them now, his scowl well in place, one hand on a club hanging from his belt, clearly eager for a chance to put it to use. "You gonna get up and do your job, woman, or am I going to have to persuade you?"

Farra looked helpless then, little more than a child herself despite her size, one who had woken in the night afraid and alone, hoping that someone would help her but knowing that no one would.

"That's it, off your damned feet, whore," Blake growled, reaching for Farra's arm.

Marta rose, interposing herself between the two of them. "Forgive me," she said to the guard, seeing in his eyes that he was very close to drawing the club at his side. "But…she's sick."

"I don't give a damn if she's got a broken leg," the man snapped. "She'll go out and—"

"It's the monthlies," Marta interrupted, and the guard winced, giving Farra a disgusted look, which was fine with Marta. Let him be disgusted as long as he and the others didn't suspect the truth.

"Well," he said, frowning, "she'll just have to get over it. The boss said to have you lot scour the fields, and so she'll do it, by the gods, or I'll make sure she wishes she ha—"

"I'll go in her place." The words were out of her mouth before she'd known she was going to speak them, but Marta found, as the guard raised an eyebrow, as she heard sharp intakes of breath from those other slaves who had spent the better part of the day at the grisly task and understood just what she was committing to, that she was glad. She hadn't done the right thing many times in her life—the safe thing, nearly always, but rarely the right thing—and it felt good. It felt, really, like the sort of thing Alesh might have done.

"Marta," Farra said weakly, "you can't—"

"Yes I can, now be quiet," Marta said before turning back to the guard. "Your boss won't care, will he, who does the looking, just so long as we do?"

The man grunted what might have been a laugh. "You? Girly, you look as if you're about to fall flat out already."

"I won't," Marta promised, not sure whether it was a lie or not and not much caring. "And if I do...you can always use that club of yours."

The man frowned, considering, then finally gave a shrug. "I don't give a shit. Just get it moving and fast. We've wasted enough time already."

"Yes, sir," Marta said, and she hurried to where the fresh group of slaves waited to set out, Guardsman Blake following closely behind her, maybe waiting to see if Marta would fall down right now and he'd get to use the club after all. Marta wished she knew herself.

"Now enough of all this bullshit," the man said. "Let's go."

And Marta did, shuffling after the other slaves, back toward the field where the dead and the dying waited. She glanced back at Farra only once, and saw the woman studying her with stunned eyes, obviously shocked at what Marta had done. That she understood well enough, for she, too, was shocked. Shocked and, despite her weariness and the hours of soul-eating labor ahead of her, pleased.

Chapter Seven

By the time Katherine, with Sonya in tow, finally managed to speak to a castle guard who would tell her anything about Alesh's whereabouts besides, "the Chosen is busy," it was nearly midnight. She thought of stopping and going to sleep, for there was no denying that she was exhausted and likely Sonya was too, but she decided against it. After speaking with the girl, she realized just how important it was to help Alesh through whatever it was he was going through because that's what friends did. Even if their friend didn't seem to want help—seemed, in fact, to be doing everything he possibly could to avoid it.

After all, men and women rarely knew what was best for them. So instead, she followed the guard's directions toward the castle battlements where Alesh was said to be patrolling with Nordin. She realized, too, that she should have known he'd be there from the beginning. After all, it was the only place he ever seemed to be, and Katherine couldn't even guess when he got any sleep, or even *if* he did.

Two guards were stationed at the stairs leading up to the top of the wall, and although Katherine didn't know them by name, she recognized them well enough as some of those which had turned her away on her near countless trips to the wall. Trips she'd made in an attempt to speak to Alesh and trips which had, inevitably, ended in stymied, frustrated failure. But not this time. This time, she *would* speak to him, no matter what the guards or Alesh himself wanted.

"Lady Katherine," one of them said as he noted her and the girl's approach, glancing with a raised eyebrow at the practice sword Sonya still held in one hand. "Forgive me, once more, but Chosen Alesh has insisted that no civilians be allowed upon the wall."

Katherine had heard the same for the last several days, and her patience wasn't wearing thin—it was pretty well gone. "*I, guardsman,*" she said in the most authoritative voice she could muster, "am no *civilian*. I am a Chosen of the Goddess Deitra herself and, as I recall, one of those who was instrumental in the saving of your fine city from the corrupt Chosen Tesharna. Or am I misremembering that?"

The two guardsmen shifted, obviously uncomfortable. "O-of course, Chosen Katherine. But Chosen Alesh has spoken and we can't—"

"Oh, but you *can*," Katherine interrupted. "Guardsman…?"

"It's Mander, ma'am," the guard said, reluctantly, as if afraid that knowledge of his name might enable her to cast some spell over him. "Guardsman Mander."

"Well, Guardsman Mander," she said, "I'm afraid you have misunderstood this situation."

"Ma'am?"

"Yes," she said. "You see, I'm not *asking* for your permission to be allowed onto the battlements. I am ordering you and your companion here to move aside. Now."

Guardsman Mander winced, glancing over at the other guard who, after a moment, nodded, his eyes slightly wide. Then, as one, they stepped away from the stairs.

Katherine nodded her head in a bow. "Thank you."

"Thank you," Sonya echoed, and the guards smiled at her and the practice sword before bowing. Then she and Sonya were moving up the stairs. It was dark, but the battlements were lined with torches which served to illuminate the guardsmen stationed there, guardsmen who, even in the poor light, looked exhausted and near-collapse and didn't seem to be scanning and protecting the battlements so much as using them as props to keep themselves from falling over.

"We're looking for Chosen Alesh and Captain Nordin," Katherine said, doing her best to ignore the blood, some of it still looking disturbingly fresh, which stained the battlements.

The guards seemed too tired even to respond, sketching hasty bows and pointing down the battlements where she could just make out two vague shadows in the torchlight. "Thanks," Katherine said, and then they were walking.

Alesh and Nordin were walking with their backs to Katherine, but despite that and despite the darkness, she could not help but notice the slumped shoulders and weary postures they both had which made it obvious that they were both exhausted.

Exhaustion which allowed Katherine and Sonya to walk within five feet of them before they finally broke off their muttered conversation and turned. Alesh gave a grunt of surprise and couldn't have looked anymore shocked if an army of nightlings had suddenly materialized on the battlements. "Katherine?" he said, "Sonya? What are y—"

"Alesh," Katherine interrupted, "we need to talk."

Alesh did not move or recoil, exactly, but he seemed to shrink in on himself anyway. "Sorry, but I don't have time to talk. There's a thousand things I need to do and—"

"Like killing yourself?"

This time, he *did* recoil, staring at her with an expression that was haunted and panicked at the same time. "What?"

"You heard me," she said, "and don't act so surprised. Any fool with eyes to see couldn't help but notice how you've been trying to kill yourself, throwing yourself where the fighting's thickest, barely taking any breaks at all, not to mention avoiding all of your *friends.*"

At first his expression was surprised, maybe even nervous, but in a moment it turned to anger. "What do you know about it?" he demanded. "A leader should lead from the front—Chosen Olliman taught me that. He was a better man than I ever could be, and while I'll never be as good as he was, that much, at least, I can do."

"You're right, Alesh," Katherine said, her own anger at being dismissed for so many days, her own frustration at seeing him destroy himself bit by bit coming to the surface. "You're *not* Chosen Olliman, you're not as good of a leader, maybe not as good of a man. But you *could* be!" She realized that she'd screamed the last, that the guards on the battlements, that Nordin and even Sonya were staring at her in shock. She realized it, but in that moment she did not care. "If you would stop feeling sorry for yourself, if you could just *see* yourself as we see you, as your *friends* see you, then you would know that you're better than you think, that the only thing holding you back is *you.*"

For a moment his face was hurt, his expression one so distraught and pained, that she thought he would break into tears. But then, an instant later, that expression changed to one not of sadness or regret but one of fury, a fury so palpable, so imposing, that for a brief instant Katherine was suddenly sure he would strike her. He didn't though, only let his hands clasp into fists at his sides, trembling with barely contained rage. "Y-you think I'm some great man, some great leader, but you're a fool. A fool to trust me, to think I could be anything more than an orphan with scars, inside and outside both, that won't heal no matter how much time passes. You're all fools—Darl, Rion, even Amedan himself—for thinking I was more than I am!"

There was fury in his voice, yes, but there was pain, too, and it was that pain that made Katherine's heart feel as if would break. "Please, Alesh," she said. "Please. We just...your friends, we care about you. We want to help, *will* help, if only you'll let us."

"You can't help," Alesh said, turning away. "No one can—not even the gods themselves," he finished, saying it in such a way that made it clear he meant more than just the words he uttered. Then he was turning and walking away.

"Alesh—"

"*Enough!*" he roared, spinning to glare at Katherine. But it hadn't been she who had spoken. Instead, it had been Sonya, the little girl who cringed away at the unbridled fury in his voice, tucking herself behind Katherine as if he might attack her at any moment.

***

Alesh stared at Sonya, at the little girl who he had always treasured like a sister. He had looked at her a thousand times before over the years growing up in Olliman's castle, but this time he saw none of the love, the *trust* that he had once seen there.

The Age of Men

What he saw, then, was only fear. Fear, perhaps even terror, on the face of a girl who had accompanied Tarex, the Broken, who was arguably the most dangerous and, until recently—at least if he could be believed—one of the cruelest men on the face of the world without being afraid. The deadly Ekirani who stood, even now, only a few feet away, surrounded by the four guards tasked with watching him.

Sonya had weathered much pain and tragedy in her short life, had watched her friends die, watched her city burn, had even been captured by men from the enemy army, an army controlled by the Darkness and led by a man corrupted by it, a man who was not just a man anymore, yet she had come through it all. And now, she was afraid of *him*.

His sister, still, or just a girl scared of monsters and any sensible girl should be, and he the latest one to rise up in front of her? *Gods help me, what have I become?* he thought.

For there was no denying the fear dancing in the girl's eyes, no matter how much he might have wanted to. And not just fear—terror. Since he had been a child stumbling out of the dark forest, his family's broken bodies lying behind him, Alesh had taken a lot of wounds, both small and large, but very few of those approached the agony he felt in that moment. The pain—not just emotional but *physical,* which stabbed into his heart like a shard of ice—rocked him, nearly brought him to his knees.

He reached toward her with a shaking hand. Maybe it was his own sadness at seeing his sister afraid of him, or his own weariness from patrolling the walls, from fighting the servants of Darkness, but his reaching felt more like a lunge, a desperate, almost frantic grab. A grab not just at Sonya, but a yearning reaching for the life he might have had, the life which had been taken from him along with his parents, a grab at the man he might have been, one who could have been so much better than the one he had become. A man who might have understood right from wrong, who might never have come to Olliman's castle, might never have been Chosen and so led a small life. But a small life in which his pains were relatively small, in which the hurt he could cause was small also. A life in which no little girls looked at him in terror, nor recoiled further at the prospect of his touch as she now did, tucking herself behind Katherine so that she was no more than a set of wide, frightened eyes staring at him.

Alesh's breath caught in his throat, and his head began to pound. His hands clenched and unclenched at his sides, his fingernails digging into his flesh, but he was barely aware of it. He did not feel his hands, did not feel even his exhaustion, so much. What he felt, more than anything, was a *slipping.* He felt how a man hanging off a cliff by his fingertips might feel when the loose soil and rock begins to shift beneath his grip, and he realizes that there is no longer a question of pulling himself back onto the ledge, not now, no question of a tragedy occurring or being averted. Now, there was only a question of time.

He would slip. Was slipping already. In time, he would fall. Of that much he was certain. The only question was how much longer he could cling to the cliff face. That, and perhaps who would be there to watch him fall. It would have been better to leave it there, to know that the monster Sonya saw was no more than the truth, a truth he could not fight. He knew that it would be the best thing for him to turn and retreat down the battlements, to put distance between himself and Sonya and Katherine who were watching him. He had been cruel enough to them already; what purpose in adding the cruelty of making them watch him plummet into the darkness which waited beneath that ledge?

But as much as it might have been the best thing, the kindest thing, he found that even this small act of goodness was beyond him, for of all the things he could accept about his life, about himself, he could not have her hate him. That was a burden even his twisted soul could not bear, even his resigned mind could not accept. "Sonya—" he began, but then Katherine was moving toward him, her hand reaching out and slapping him across the face.

"No," she said. "No, you don't talk to her, not as you are. She deserves better. We both do."

Just when he thought he could feel no worse, when the pain of his existence was as heavy upon him as it could be, he was reminded that a man could always lose more, could always have another piece of himself carved away. "Katherine," he began, "I didn't mean—"

"I don't care," she said, but there were tears in her eyes that said differently, "I don't. Just…"

She hesitated then, as if unsure of how to finish, unsure of how to say what she wanted to say, and in that hesitation, Alesh noticed a silence. A silence far deeper than it should have been on the battlements where soldiers patrolled and whispered amongst themselves. They had been quiet since the last few days' tragedy, those soldiers. Quiet but not silent.

"It's only—" she started, but Alesh held up a hand.

"Quiet."

Her face, illuminated in the torchlight, turned crimson. "Don't you—"

"Quiet, damn it," he snapped, and this time she subsided.

"Sir, is everything—" Nordin began, but Alesh held up a hand, demanding silence.

They all looked confused, bewildered, Katherine angry, but they did not speak. Alesh cocked his head, listening. At first, he couldn't put his finger on what exactly had bothered him, but then it came to him. He did not hear the sounds of the guards' footsteps patrolling nearby as he had moments before. Did not hear their quiet exhalations in the darkness or their muttered words—curses mostly. There was only the stillness. The silence. And then, almost too low to hear, a *scraping*. It might have been nothing, that scraping. In another place, another world, Alesh would have taken no notice of it. But here, in this world, he did not think it was nothing. He thought, in fact, that it was the sound claws might make on stone battlements.

He turned to the nearest turret tower, situated on one of the four corners of Valeria's battlements, and noticed something else, something which made his blood go cold within him. The torches of the tower were out. They had been lit moments ago, of that much he was sure, but they were not now, and shadows crouched and huddled against the tower with tangible menace. He turned to Captain Nordin, his heart hammering in his chest. "Get them out of here, Nordin. Now."

The captain frowned, clearly confused. "Sir—"

"Now!" Alesh shouted. And then he was running toward the tower, toward the darkness that waited for him there, that it sometimes seemed had waited for him all his life.

***

The Broken stood with the four guards around him, those which were tasked with keeping him from doing harm, and watched Alesh sprint toward the tower. He had felt the man's pain, listening to him speak, had understood it, understood the place from which it came, for he had been to that place before, had spent years confined within a prison of his own making and had only been able to escape with the help of the young girl now being rushed away by the captain

Alesh was in that place now, that cell of despair and tragedy, but that was a matter for another time. For now, there was the tower and the darkness and the man rushing toward it almost eagerly. That and the guards watching their leader head off alone but making no move to help.

"You have to go help him," he said. The guards, though, only stared at each other uncertainly.

"What should we do?" one asked another.

"I don't—"

But they were out of time, their leader soon to be as well, for the Broken knew all the many shades and textures of the Darkness, and he knew what waited for their leader—knew, too, that the man expected to die, perhaps even wanted to. And with what waited for him, if he did not get help, he would.

So Tarex moved. His hands, manacled before him, knotted into fists and whipped out to the side, striking one guard in the face even as he pivoted, his foot lashing out and catching another. Two down then, and the other two had only begun to turn when he lunged forward, smashing his forehead into one. Pain then, a white hot burst of it, but he was used to pain, had lived a life that held little else since his family was murdered, and he did not hesitate to spin to the fourth, bringing his manacled hands up into the man's chin.

In another moment, they were all unconscious on the ground, and while he would likely be killed for the transgression later, he could not worry about that now. The girl, Sonya, who had been led away by the captain seconds ago, had saved him, and it was clear that she loved the man, Alesh. If his death, then, meant that she would not lose another thing she loved in a world bent on taking, then he would count it a victory.

He ran as fast as he could, but he still lost ground on the sprinting Alesh who seemed all too eager to confront whatever the shadows hid. The man reached the base of the tower and disappeared into the darkness where the Broken could just make out the vaguest outline of the door, one which was meant to be kept shut but that stood wide open and in its silent way destroyed what little hope he'd entertained that he was wrong, that the man was wrong. "Gods watch over him," the Broken rasped as he ran on, although if the gods were inclined to listen to anyone, he doubted it was him.

***

Alesh paused inside the base of the tower, listening. It was quiet, but he found no comfort in the silence. It was still, but he found no reassurance there, either, for the dead were silent and still both. And worse than that, there was the smell. A smell he knew well—blood. It was thick in the air, and he found his mind cast back to a time long ago, to a dark trail through the forest where his parent's bodies lay broken on the forest trail amid the shattered remnants of their cart.

He drew his sword, and the sound of its drawing rang in the air like a chime announcing that the time for blood had come. "Come on, then," he said, his voice shaking not with fear but with rage and with something else, too—eagerness. Eagerness to meet his fate head-on and never mind that he would lose, that he only could lose, for the game was rigged and had been from the start. "Don't keep me waiting."

They came, as he had known they would. They came in a scraping and skittering of claws along the cobbled floor, a wave of darkness rushing toward him, and the air was suddenly alive with the sounds of growling hisses. He did not wait for his destiny to come to him but gave a cry of rage and ran to meet it.

It was dark, but perhaps some small bit of his powers remained, because he could see their forms in the darkness, some scaly, others slick as polished obsidian, their teeth and claws, sharp as razors, flashing in the shadows. And at that moment,

Alesh was not afraid. For the first time in a very long time, he did not feel afraid, did not feel guilty or ashamed, either. With his death charging toward him on taloned feet, what he felt, more than anything, was content.

A creature rushed at him from the left, and his sword flashed out, skewering it. It hissed and spat as it died, and he pulled the blade away, spinning and ducking underneath a swiping claw that would have taken his head from his shoulders. He pivoted, planting his foot in the creature and knocking it sprawling into several of its fellows, buying him an instant of space which he used to turn and lunge in the opposite direction toward the beast waiting there.

A flashing of steel, a spilling of ichor, and the beast fell beneath his blade. And then it began in truth. He was a whirlwind of fury and hate, charging into them and scattering their bodies, leaving a trail of the dead and broken in his wake. But for each creature that fell beneath his attacks, there were two waiting to take its place, and he knew that he could not keep up this pace for long.

A creature pounced at him, its claws spread wide, meaning to knock him off his feet, a fall from which he knew he would never rise. Alesh planted his feet, holding his sword in both hands in front of him, and the creature's eyes flashed with what might have been terror as it realized, too late, where its leap would inevitably carry it. A moment later, he grunted, sliding back a few inches as the creature impaled itself on his blade.

A flash of movement to his left caught his attention, and he tried to pull the blade free only to realize that the impaled beast was clamping onto the steel with both hands, baring its teeth in what might have been a macabre grin. He growled, giving the blade a jerk, and the sharp steel severed the talons holding it, but the moment that wasted cost him, and he was unable to turn in time, cried out as he felt claws slice down his back. He stumbled forward, struggling to keep his balance.

A creature leapt onto his back, scrabbling at him, its claws digging into his shoulders as it fought to gain purchase, and Alesh bellowed in fury as he spun, struggling and finally managed to catch one of its greasy forepaws in his hand. With a growl he pulled the creature free, its claws scoring his flesh as he did. It was surprisingly light, and he spun, hurling it into several creatures which had taken advantage of his distraction to charge at him from behind.

Agony in his back, lines of fire tracing their way down it, but no time to see how bad it was, and he didn't much care in any case. He had known what would happen when he'd come, had hoped for it, but he'd hoped, too, to take as many of the monsters with him as he could.

Everything was a mad melee then as the creatures surged toward him like a tidal wave, coming from every direction. It was only because of the skills Olliman had taught him—skills honed over the last months fighting for his life against all manner of man and beast—that Alesh survived those first few seconds. But, survive he did, and not just that. His sword was a blur flashing through the shadows, slicing through them, cutting them down one after the other as he moved amongst them, never stopping, for to stop was to die.

He did not stop, yet there seemed to be thousands of the beasts, more and more rising up before him as he slew them, and while he did not stop—he did slow. The muscles of his legs and arms were burning, the wounds in his back feeling as if they were pouring blood freely, blood which soaked the rags of his shirt and his trousers, and sapping his strength

He began to slow and as he did, more and more of the darting claws and snapping teeth found their mark. Save the wounds on his back, he had only suffered superficial cuts and scrapes so far, but he knew that it was only a matter of time. A man could not hope to slay the Darkness, and there was not enough light in all the world to find the shadows where they lurked in its deepest, darkest places.

Only a fool would think any other way, only a fool could think to stand against it. Yet for a time he *had* been that fool, and he found that in these, his last moments, he did not regret it. Found that, the being of that fool, seeing the world through his eyes and feeling hope, real, genuine *hope* had perhaps been the happiest time of his life. A time even happier than when he had been a younger fool in Olliman's castle and had begun to believe that he had found a new family, that they would be safe and happy.

Yet even that time did not compare to the weeks spent with Sonya and Darl, with Katherine and Rion. They had become his true friends and for a time he had allowed himself to believe the fiction that he was the man they thought he was or at least that he could be. That he might be the man to carry a light into the Darkness, one so bright and irrefutable that it could only be carried by a hero, so powerful it could destroy the evil which lurked in the shadows once and for all. But such a light did not exist, and if such a hero lived, then he was certainly not him.

Claws scraped across his free arm as he pulled away from his latest kill a touch too slowly, and he cried out. Not a deep wound, but yet another to add to the half a dozen others, each of which slowed his movements, stole his strength. He stumbled and before he could recover something struck him in the side of the head, staggering him. The creatures pursued him, all around, trying to pull him down. His vision was blurry from the blow he'd received, and he backpedaled desperately, evading their claws, slashing out blindly, hoping to buy himself enough time to regain his balance.

He was still retreating when his back struck something, and he spun, thinking one of the creatures was behind him again, but instead of one of the nightlings, he saw that it was only the stone wall of the tower. He had been forced back under the endless assault to the corner of the tower, and now there was nowhere left to go. The door was on the far end of the room, less than twenty feet away, but it may as well have been a thousand miles for all the hopes he had of getting to it to escape, even if he meant to. And he did not.

After all, he thought as he gave his head a shake in order to clear it and gripped his sword in front of him in two hands, *I did not come here to escape.* Neither had he come here to die, at least not as such. He had come for an ending, an ending which, as it happened, one could only reach by traveling the road of death. "Come on then, you bastards," he growled, his chest heaving with his ragged breaths, his body on fire from all his wounds. "Let's finish it."

They started forward again, a wall of darkness in the shadows, and this time, he knew, he would not be able to stand against them. "I'm sorry," he whispered, to Katherine and to Sonya and to all the others who would suffer for his failure. "I'm sorry."

They reared up around him, grim specters of claws and teeth, and he gritted his teeth, determined to at least meet his end with what courage he could. And the creatures did begin to move then—though to his surprise, they did not move toward him.

Instead, they seemed to have forgotten he existed at all. There was a rustling amongst their number, and even those closest to him spun, turning their backs on him as if he were of no consequence. Some of the creatures near the door let out pained howls, but whatever the cause of those cries, it was blocked from his view by the horde of bodies separating him from the entrance to the tower.

He told himself it must be Captain Nordin, the man come back with troops to regain the turret tower, a good thing as should the tower be compromised, they risked losing Valeria itself, and he did his best to ignore the vague feeling of disappointment the thought of being rescued gave him. But whatever—or whoever—it was drawing the creatures' attention, it bought him some time to gain his breath, for the worst of his blurry vision to fade.

Moments later, the line of the nightlings surrounding him broke, several of the beasts being cut down. A figure, what Alesh took for Captain Nordin, appeared in the gap, but the shadows hid his face. The newcomer held an ichor-stained sword in each hand and the creatures nearest him hesitated as he walked toward Alesh.

When he drew near, Alesh was finally able to make out the figure's identity, and his breath caught in his throat. "*You,*" he rasped.

The Ekirani exile gave his head a single nod. "Yes."

"You're behind this somehow," Alesh growled. "Damn me, but I knew not to trust you."

"You are wrong," the Broken said simply. "These beasts are not my allies."

"And yet they aren't attacking you," Alesh said, setting his feet and shifting so that his sword's point faced the Broken.

The Ekirani turned and glanced at the beasts. They still made no further move toward him, but they were shifting, growing more restless seemingly by the moment. "They do not understand."

"Understand what?"

"They are creatures of the Darkness, born to it and therefore can know nothing else. They know me, too, as a creature of the Dark, and so do not understand why I aid you."

There was no arguing that the creatures had stopped their relentless assault, but Alesh was far from believing the man had any intentions of helping him. If he was here, it meant only that there was some motive behind it. "Your defense is that you're a creature of the Dark," Alesh said, eyeing the nightlings who watched the two of them with malevolent eyes that somehow communicated their confusion.

"I was," the Ekirani said calmly, not rising to the bait. "For many years, I was no more than a specter in the shadows, one bent on only destruction, tricking myself into believing that the seeking of such destruction—of *any* destruction—can ever be noble." He raised an eyebrow at Alesh, studying him with eyes that seemed to see right through him. "Perhaps you understand what I mean."

Alesh clenched his jaw, angry. "I don't know what you're talking about."

"Do you not?" the man asked, seemingly genuinely curious. "Is that not the notion which brought you here, alone, when there were guards nearby, allies which might have been raised to aid you in a matter of minutes?"

Alesh did not know what to say to that, how to answer, so he said nothing and after a moment, the Ekirani nodded. "I understand, Chosen Alesh. Perhaps better than any other on the face of this world might. I know what it is that plagues you, what haunts your footsteps, invades your very thoughts turning what few good memories you have sour and bitter so that they serve only as cruel reminders of what you once had, of what you have lost."

"Forgive me if I don't take advice from a man who calls himself 'the Broken,'" Alesh snapped.

"I was the Broken," the Ekirani said, still displaying an unflappable calm, "but no longer. There is no darkness so great that a man cannot find the Light again. It took a young girl—a friend of yours, I believe—to make me understand that. Now, I am only Tarex."

"Damn you, what do you—"

"We must, I'm afraid, continue this conversation later," the Ekirani interrupted, glancing around at the nightlings whose hisses and growls had intensified. "Such creatures as those which serve the Darkness make little effort to understand those things which lie beyond their knowledge. Instead, they predictably choose the path of destruction. They make their choice now."

And then, as if the man's words were a cue, the creatures broke out of their stupor and rushed them. Alesh found himself caught in his own stupor, one of indecision. The Broken—or Tarex, though what he called himself did nothing to change his crimes—might claim to have changed, to have found his way back to the Light, but Alesh had trusted people before. Kale Leandrian came to mind, for while he had never liked the man, he had never thought him capable of the things he had done and had been forced to watch his friends die because of it. How easy would it be for the man to creep up on him when he was engaged with the nightlings and stab him in the back, Alesh far too busy to do anything about it?

But then, if the man only sought his death, why had he come at all? After all, he had arrived moments before Alesh would have been killed. If he wanted him dead, all he'd had to do was wait and the nightlings would have seen the job done soon enough. So why risk revealing himself, risk putting himself in danger? But then, Alesh could never hope to guess what such a man as the exiled Ekirani might think, and in that moment it didn't matter much either way because regardless of the man's intentions, the nightlings were a very real, very present threat. And if the Ekirani *was* being deceptive, he was selling it well, charging forward with that liquid grace Alesh had seen him embody before, darting in and out of the nightlings who, it had to be said, now seemed genuinely intent on killing him. Not that they had any luck, for the Ekirani flowed around their claws as if he were made of wind, his twin swords lashing out with deadly precision, cutting the creatures down in swathes.

Some small glimmer of something—hope, perhaps? Belief?—flared in Alesh's chest like the ember of a flame struggling to catch, but he had no time to think on it, for the creatures were on him now, and his only thoughts were on staying alive for the next few moments. But whether his mind was slow to catch up or not, his body had been trained for years, and his instincts took over. The few minutes of respite he'd gained when the Ekirani arrived had helped, for while he was still tired and hurting, the sharp stitch in his side—as if someone had plunged a knife into it—was mostly gone, and his breathing, while still irregular and rasping, was far better than it had been.

They cut the nightlings down by the score, but there were always more, as if they welled up out of the shadows of the tower itself, emerging from them like the beasts of some damned place charging through a portal intent on slaughter. Alesh took several more small cuts on his arms and chest, his legs and back, until it felt as if his entire body was nothing but one great, throbbing wound...yet he fought on.

At first, he tried to keep his eye on the Ekirani, to see the moment when the man chose to abandon the ruse and make his attack, but he never did, cleaving down creature after creature and soon Alesh lost sight of him in the mad, bloody melee until, after a time, their struggles led them beside each other. They fought back to back, both covered with the blood of their foes which mixed with their own, both with their jaws set, knowing that despite their efforts, the thing could only end one way.

The fight might have lasted for an eternity. There was no way to know for sure, as Alesh had long since lost any sense of time, even place. There was only the moving, only the raising of the sword and the swinging of it, only the resistance, the spurt of blood, and the weary raising of the blade once more.

Alesh wielded his sword in both hands, no artistry to it anymore, no room for feints or parries or footwork. It was butchery, plain and simple, swinging the sword like it wasn't a sword at all but an axe, and he a lumberjack at his trade. A very exhausted, very wounded lumberjack.

A creature leapt at him from out of the throng of bodies, and he barely managed to get his sword up in time. The nightling screeched a terrible *keening* sound as it impaled itself on his blade, but while Alesh had managed to pull his sword up, he had not managed to set his feet properly, and the creature's weight sent him stumbling. His foot slid across one of the many pools of blood staining the ground, and he lost his balance.

He reached out desperately with his free hand, searching for something, anything to grab onto, but there was nothing, only the air, and he fell. He landed on his back, the creature he'd impaled held above him on his sword, and he grunted, straining as he struggled onto his side and tried to work the blade free.

The creature, though, made the task more difficult, thrashing and clawing at him, fighting its way further onto his blade in order to draw close, and he was forced to kick at it, knowing all the while that the nightling's companions would be on him in moments. But try as he might, he could not work the blade free, and in its struggles the creature rolled away from him, ripping the sword out of Alesh's ichor-coated hands.

Alesh scrambled desperately across the bloody cobblestones of the tower floor, trying to catch hold of the sword's handle, but a moment later the creature was gone, rolling into its fellows and disappearing in a mass of limbs.

Alesh was preparing to get to his feet, to launch himself after it, knowing that now, in this place, his life was measured by the distance between him and the sword still plunged into the creature's midsection, when he heard a deep growl. He spun, looking above him at a thick-limbed, red-eyed hulking creature looming there.

This was it, then, the moment in which all the pain and the agony, the exhaustion and sadness...and the joy of his life ended.

I don't want to die.

The thought thundered in his head, seemed to come out of nowhere, but when it came, it came with power. And lying there, moments from his death, Alesh was surprised to find that despite everything, despite all his failures, despite all the pain and agony he'd experienced over the last several months, over his entire life, in fact, it was true.

He did not want to die.

He'd thought he did, had thought it the only way to end the agony inside him. He had been in pain, had been desperate for some answer, and he had found it in resigning himself to his death. He had been a fool. Yes, his life was dark, but there were spots of joy, too, Sonya and Katherine chief among them. And those spots more than made up for all the rest of it.

But it was too late now, the decision had been made, and he the one who'd made it. Now, there was only the ending and—

"Chosen!"

Alesh turned to see that the Ekirani had cleared a brief space around himself and was holding his remaining sword—he'd apparently lost the other somewhere in the fighting—at an odd angle. Alesh expected him to gloat, perhaps, to finally reveal the truth of his deception, and he did not know what the man was up to until the sword was flying through the air at him, not in an attack, but in an arc that Alesh might catch it. And he did, snatching it out of the air by the handle and lashing out with the blade and lopping the head off his would-be killer as it lunged toward him.

He swung about him desperately, forcing the other creatures back, and managed to gain his feet. He spun to check on Tarex and, to his shock, the Ekirani gave him a content smile. Then, without a weapon to defend himself, Tarex was unable to hold off the nightlings who surged forward. A moment later, he disappeared beneath a mass of bodies, and the nightlings claws flashed up and down over and over again.

Alesh watched in shock. Out of all the things he had expected from the man, it had never been that. He had saved Alesh's life, even knowing that in doing so, he doomed himself.

He was running before he knew it. He charged into the creatures with a roar, his sword slashing out again and again and again, but he became bogged down, less than halfway to where the Ekirani had fallen as more and more of the creatures came at him. He found himself desperate to get to the man, calling on the last reserves of his strength to bring the blade up and down and up and down. Tarex had saved him. True, he had only bought Alesh moments more of life, but that made no difference. Moments, seconds, years—the man had, in the end, given up what time he'd had. No, not given it up but traded it so that Alesh could take that time instead.

So Alesh fought to make it to the man, to return to him those few seconds of life he had loaned him, but despite his efforts, he wasn't gaining ground, was instead being pushed back. And then he wasn't just being pushed but fallen to one knee, the creatures all around him, taking cut after cut after cut from their claws and the time Tarex had bought him was gone.

Forms rising above him, his eyes blurry, his head full of fog as the effects of the blood loss took hold. Nothing around him but the nightlings, nothing but the shadows and the claws and teeth and blood. And the darkness.

And then, out of that darkness, light. Light brighter than any he had ever seen before, so bright that it was *felt* more than seen. It exploded into the world, into *him*, like a bolt of lightning. There was a terrible, unimaginable shrieking as the light did to the creatures what all light does to the darkness—killed them.

And in their dying, the cries were so terrible that Alesh found himself screaming too, covering his ears and finding that it did no good. Then, after an interminable amount of time, the light faded. It was over in an instant that lasted an eternity, and Alesh was left panting, not sure, in truth, if he was alive or dead. There was a figure standing above him, a massive figure which seemed limned in golden light, the face obscured by the spots the incredible explosion of brightness had left in his eyes.

"Can't leave you alone for a second."

It was a deep voice, one that sounded like two boulders shifting against each other, and one that, even in his confusion and pain, Alesh recognized. "*L-Larin?*" he rasped. Slowly, the spots which had dazzled his sight began to fade, and his thought was confirmed as the broad-shouldered, thickly-muscled Chosen came into view.

"Aye, lad," the man said, offering him a hand nearly twice the size of Alesh's own. "Well. Up you get, you can get your nap in later."

Alesh took the offered hand, confused and more than a little bewildered, and with a slight flex of the big man's arm he was suddenly standing. Larin let go a moment later and was forced to catch Alesh as he realized belatedly that he had no strength left in his legs, none left in his entire body, in fact. "*Easy*, lad," Larin said. "Easy. It's alright now."

"It's...alright," Alesh said dully, feeling as if he was dreaming, as if he *must* be dreaming or, more likely, that he had died or was dying and the Chosen no more than the figment of his mind as it expired. But it was no dream, and he was not dying—at least not immediately. He was standing on feet he had never thought to stand on again, breathing in air he had thought he'd never breathe again. He was alive. Alive because Larin and—*oh gods*.

"Tarex," he said, his eyes going wide.

"Who?" the Chosen asked.

But Alesh was already turning, pulling away from Larin's hand on his shoulder. The creatures, the nightlings, were nowhere in sight now, the only evidence that they had ever been there at all were piles of ash scattered on the stone battlements. Those, and the body of Tarex the Ekirani, lying on his back, his body and the clothes he wore torn and shredded and coated in blood.

His eyes were closed, his hands—neither of which held a blade thanks to the fact that he had thrown it to Alesh to save him—lying limp and open at his sides. Alesh stumbled toward him, for some reason thinking of Sonya, of the way he had first felt so long ago when he had been at Olliman's castle and Sonya had come to stay there. Sonya, whose innocence and kindness had changed Alesh from a young man who was dark and angry over the loss of his parents and his scarring, over the world itself, into a man who wanted to be better. A man who wanted to be what a big brother should be simply because she deserved it.

Alesh stood beside the body, staring down at the Ekirani. Sonya had brought Alesh back so long ago and he had never understood just how far into the darkness he had gone. So why, then, had he not believed that she had done the same for Tarex? It was clear now that she had, that the Broken had been changed by her the same way that Alesh had been changed. He had been changed, and he had given his life to save Alesh.

"Tarex," he said, his voice little more than a whisper. "I'm sorry. You deserved better. She deserves better."

The Ekirani suddenly moved, breaking into a coughing fit, and his eyes opened slowly, meeting Alesh's gaze. "Yes, Chosen," he said. "Yes, she does."

Alesh would have jumped in shock to see the man still alive after all, but he was too exhausted. Instead, he settled for a surprised grunt. "You're alive."

The Ekirani's mouth twitched in what might have been an attempt at a smile. "I...suppose I am. After a fashion."

"But...why?" Alesh asked. "Why did you save me? Why did you sacrifice yourself for me?"

This time, the small, content smile found its way onto the man's face. "Because it was the right thing to do."

Alesh blinked. "That...that's it? That was your reason?"

The Ekirani gasped in what might have been a laugh. "Our reasons, Chosen, for doing the things we do need not be complicated—in fact, they very rarely are. And the best reasons...the best reasons I have come to believe, are also the simplest ones. It was your Sonya who taught me that."

Simple. Whatever the last few months had been for Alesh, they had not been simple. And as for his reasons, his reasons such as those which had driven him to run to this tower alone and unaided knowing full well what would happen, he realized now that he did not understand them, had not understood them since the beginning. He had accepted his role as Amedan's Chosen without ever really knowing why he'd done it. Perhaps doing the right thing had been a part of it, but maybe not. Certainly, revenge had. He had sought revenge on Kale and the Redeemers and all those others responsible for the fall of Ilrika, for the death of Chosen Olliman.

And recently he had convinced himself that he was useless, a danger to everyone around him, and that had been the reason he'd charged here, telling himself he was ending the danger, telling himself he was doing the others a favor, saving them from himself. But he knew now, had realized during the fighting, that while that might have been the reason he had given himself for his suicidal charge, for his suicidal fights on the wall, it was not the real one.

The real reason was that he was afraid. Afraid that he would fail, afraid that he already had. A simple reason, just as the man had said, far simpler than the lie he'd told himself. And how could he not have been afraid? How could a man walking a path be confident in reaching his destination when he did not even understand why he had set out on it or why he still walked it? He felt ashamed then, but more than that, he felt grateful, for while he was still in the darkness, he thought that the man had been right, that a person could always find their way back from the shadows. Sometimes, they just needed a little help.

But when he turned back to say as much to the Broken—*Tarex*, he told himself, *not the Broken, not any longer*—the man's eyelids fluttered closed, and he let out a slow ragged breath. Then, he was so still that Alesh feared he had actually died until his chest rose once more in a hitching breath. "Healer," Alesh said, blinking. He turned back to Larin. "We need a—" But even as he spoke, more men arrived through the turret entrance, soldiers first, men and women with their swords bared, their eyes scanning the room in search of a threat.

They were followed by several others wearing white robes marking them as healers. At least, robes which had once been white but over the last several days had been stained crimson from their arduous labors, the effect of which could also be seen in the dark, purple circles under their eyes and their shuffling, weary steps which made it seem as if it was all they could do to keep their feet beneath them.

Yet for all their exhaustion, they were kneeling beside Tarex's recumbent form in moments, tending to his many wounds with workmanlike efficiency, an older man Alesh recognized as Chief Healer Malachai speaking in low, urgent tones.

"Is...is he going to be okay?" Alesh asked, shocked by just how much he was desperate for reassurance that the man would live. An hour ago, he would have accepted the Ekirani's death easily, likely would have thanked the man—or beast—responsible for it. Now, though, things were different. *He* was different. Odd, perhaps, that a man might find his way back to the Light while battling beasts in the darkness, but then it was in the shadows that a man could see the light most clearly.

The Chief Healer turned his head. "Doesn't look good, Chosen." He sighed, wiping a hand across his forehead, one that visibly shook in the torchlight. "With the wounds he's taken and the nightling poison...if he lasts the night, it'll be a miracle. Dead before tomorrow, that much is sure."

And with that fatal pronouncement, the man and his apprentices went back to their work. Alesh wanted to say more, to ask more, but the words would not come. He was too stunned to speak, stood trying to think of some way to change things, some way to fix what had been broken. But some paths, once chosen, had to be followed to their conclusion even if a man saw the abyss ahead, the one into which his traveling would inevitably send him.

He wasn't sure how long he stood there in the flickering light of the torches the soldiers had brought, hearing the healer's words in his head again and again and again, thinking of Sonya, of what he would say to her. In time, someone put a hand on his shoulder, and he turned to see Chosen Larin standing beside him, a grim expression on his face. "Come, lad. Best let them be about their work."

"But...he can't...I can't let him..."

He didn't finish, couldn't finish, and the older man began leading him toward the door. "Nightlings," Larin said, shaking his head, a look of obvious disgust on his face. "Gods, but I hate those damned things."

That brought some of Alesh's mind out of the fog. "The light...it was an Evertorch? I didn't know we had any."

Larin nodded. "We didn't, but me and a few of the smiths have been working, though not as hard as you I expect," he finished, his gaze sweeping up and down over Alesh's bloody, torn shirt and trousers.

Alesh paused, turning back to the door of the tower. They were a few dozen feet away now, but he could still hear the healers about their task, the Chief Healer calling for medicines from his assistants. "I tried to save him," he said, feeling guilty, feeling as if he somehow needed to explain himself to the giant beside him. "I tried but..."

"That's alright, lad," Larin said, patting his back, "that's alright. I know you did. It's hard, being a Chosen, few know it better than me. All this power, you think you ought to be able to change the world, to make it how you'd want it. But you can't—even the gods themselves can't, I don't think."

"So...what's the point?" Alesh asked quietly.

Larin grunted. "I wish Brent were here—he'd be far better at telling you than I. He'd say some beautiful words, paint a picture with 'em, and we'd both walk away feelin' better. But I'm not Brent, gods forgive me. Far from it. All I can tell you is that the best a man can do is to do what he can. Protect the ones you can, save the ones you can."

"And the rest?" Alesh asked, his eyes still watching the tower.

"Save the ones you can," Larin said again, his voice low, a harsh whisper that made it clear that while Alesh had his demons, his own personal devils which tormented him—ones which seemed to multiply constantly—Larin had more than his share.

The two of them stood there for a time, both battling their demons, and then the large man spoke again. "It's not easy."

"Being Chosen?"

Larin grunted. "Being alive."

Save the ones you can. Alesh thought of Sonya, of the look she'd given him before he'd charged into the tower, a look of terror. He would have his demons and his regrets—everyone did—but he could not accept her thinking him a monster. Perhaps she had been right to think so, but he realized now that no man could become a monster in truth unless he chose it. Suddenly, he felt a desperate *need* to speak to the young girl, to Katherine as well, to tell them both he was sorry. It seemed like such an empty thing, those words, so small and far too little to fix anything. But it was a start.

He pulled away from the big man's hand, still on his shoulder. "I've got to see Sonya. Now."

"Hold on, Alesh," Larin said, "you need to see a healer first. Foolish, not lettin' them see to you first."

"Later," Alesh said, turning and starting away again. "I'm fine." But he wasn't fine, not even close, and a few steps proved it. He was walking—shambling, really—and then he wasn't even doing that. He was falling, falling down, down, way down into the waiting abyss.

Chapter Eight

It was a saddle-sore, exhausted group which shuffled into what the soldiers had taken to calling "the Tent." It had started as "the tent where some enterprising barkeep had chosen to bring his stock and sell it to weary, thirsty soldiers at a hefty profit," but it turned out that had been a touch too long. From there, some particularly clever fellow—Fermin couldn't remember who, and it didn't matter much in any case—had shortened it to the more practical "Tavern Tent." Then, because why use three syllables when two will do, it had become simply, "the Tent."

At least that was what it went by to Fermin and all the other messengers. As for what the regular soldiers in the army called it, he couldn't have said, for the messengers were kept so busy they didn't often have an opportunity to speak with anyone except those of their own number and even that rarely.

Fermin had learned much of armies, of war, during the last week of his stay among Kale Leandrian's troops. Armies consisted of men and swords, of horses and armor, true, but they also, he'd discovered, consisted of messages. Hundreds, thousands of messages, messages ranging from orders that this captain or that one move his troops forward or back to cooks gathering supplies to make the night's dinner. And all of those messages, without fail, needed to be delivered *right now*.

It meant that Fermin and the other messengers rode their horses to exhaustion through the field and forest in which the army had haphazardly splayed itself like some drunkard fallen half into his bed to pass out. They rode the poor beasts until they could ride no longer, then they traded them with the quartermaster for fresh mounts only to do the same to them. Fermin had pitied those poor animals in the first day. By the second, though, he hated them and never mind that to do so was irrational. The beasts, after all, *were* given rest eventually, once exhausted. The messengers, however, were not so lucky.

Perhaps this meant he should have gone directly to his tent when his day's—and night's—duties were done, should have collapsed on his bed much as the drunkard might have. In fact, for the first few days, he had done exactly that, finding an excuse to give the other messengers who asked him to come out drinking with them. But they had pestered him on and on, practically begging him, and so he had finally come. That had been three nights ago now, and he'd come out every night since.

He knew that these men were evil, that they served the dark goddess, Shira, and therefore served only death and destruction. He whispered it to himself in his mind every time he found himself laughing at one of their jokes or comforting them on a friend lost in the day's fighting. But the more time he spent with the men, the more he came to know them, their names, the names of their wives and children, the quieter that voice became.

Men who served the dark goddess, perhaps, but they were still *men,* after all. Men with hopes and dreams, men who had been wronged, by their friends, their commanders, or their gods. Men angry at the world who had dashed those same hopes, who had crushed those same dreams on the shores of cruel reality. And not just men—his friends.

As he stepped through the tent flap, smelled the familiar smell of alcohol and cooking meat—not sure what, exactly, and it never did a man any good to ask, or so Jale, one of his fellow messengers, had told him half-jokingly—Fermin scolded himself again. He should not be wiling away his time here, should be about the business of finding Marta, for he had not spoken with the girl since that first night when she and the other slaves had been taken to separate quarters.

But now, like the nights past, he told himself that he would do so tomorrow. And some part of him still believed it.

"Well, Fur?" Jale asked, turning around at him and grinning. "You gonna let all the cold air in, or you gonna come have a drink?"

Fermin had never enjoyed ale, had always hated the feeling of abandon it brought, as if part of him were being controlled by someone else. But that had been back when he'd been with the Tirinians in a manor home, and his biggest concerns were that his masters' food arrived on time, that their laundry and sheets were cleaned and pressed. That had been when the worst thing he feared to see upon waking might be a burnt dinner roll or undercooked goose. Now, he spent his days trying to steer clear of Kale and Paren, knowing that to spend too much time near them would be to risk being found out for his and Marta's deception—Paren was a *god* after all. Trying, too, to avoid being shot through with arrows from Valeria's army when his duties demanded he deliver messages to the commanders at the front. As for what he was forced to see...well, it was death. Death in all its forms, the broken, twisted bodies of those who have fallen or been knocked from the walls, the mangled, gaping wounds of those cut through with swords and axes, and the glassy, sightless eyes of all those corpses. In truth, he barely even recognized himself, almost thought that the man who had spent his days tending to the needs of two nobles hadn't been him at all, only a dream he'd once had.

"Shit, Fur," Jale said, slapping him on the back before giving his shoulder a shake. "Come on—if I ever saw a man needs a drink, it's you."

He couldn't deny that much, at least, as the drink had been the main reason, if not the only one, that he had come, that he had come each night, so Fermin, or "Fur" to Jale and the others, followed the man inside. It sounded ridiculous, the nickname—"Fermin" to "Furman," "Furman" to "Fur"—yet he liked it when they called him that anyway. Liked it because in some way he could not define, it made him feel included, made him feel as if he were a part of something.

Fermin had always liked the Tirinians, Rion included, had respected and admired them, and had found it a pleasure to serve them. But in the end, they had still been his masters, he their servant, and whatever else they had been, they had not, *could* not have, been his friends. Jale, though, he and the others, they were his friends, men who understood his weariness, men who had the same quiet despair in their gazes as he did himself. Men who did not question his need to drown the terrible sights and sounds and smells the day had brought him with ale, a medicine that served when no other would.

And, for the most part, it worked. No, those corpses never disappeared from his sight, not completely, and the smell of meat rotting in the sun never completely left his nostrils no matter how much he might try, but the ale helped. It was the only thing that did. And so, just as the three nights previous, Fermin forgot all about Marta and Sonya for a time and followed the man toward a collapsible table where the "barkeeper," a man by the name of Filk who the lads had taken to calling "Filch" on account of the fact that they said his prices were blind robbery, and gratefully accepted the foaming mug Jale handed him.

He took a long pull, oblivious to the ale running down his chin as he did, a state which might have made him apoplectic a month ago, but one he thought nothing of now. Now, there was only the screams of the dying needing to be drowned.

He finished the mug off in another pull and took another. Jale laughed, but there was a harshness to it, a harshness born of understanding—there always was such a harshness among the messengers. "Come on then, you drunk," he said, "let's go have a seat."

"Not drunk," Fermin muttered, staring at the fresh mug of ale he held. "Not yet. More's the pity."

Jale laughed again at that, clapping him on the back hard enough to make him spill some of the ale and a flash of annoyance rose in Fermin, one he quickly pushed back down. Jale was a good friend, if not a good man, and he found that he needed friends just now. "But you're right. We should sit."

"Sure," his friend said, winking, "before we fall, aye?" Then they were moving toward where several of the other messengers sat at another small collapsible table, one barely able to accommodate the mugs of beer—some full, most empty—scattered about its surface.

"Starting early, eh, you bastards?" Jale asked as he pulled up a chair and collapsed into it.

Calden, a man muscular enough to practically rival the God of Conflict himself in build if not in height, gave a hearty bellow—the man never laughed, seemed largely incapable of it, only bellowed—and slapped his knee with enough force to break a man's back, if he'd had a mind. Not that such a thing was likely. Fermin had gotten to know the other messengers over the last few weeks, and Calden was the nicest and seemingly kindest of any of them, save perhaps for Jale. Fermin had often wondered what had brought such a man, who always seemed to be smiling or laughing through his thick blonde beard and eyes that sparkled like a loving father's to join Shira's army, but he had never dared asked.

Such things, for one, were not talked about among the messengers, seemed almost taboo. More than that, though, Fermin feared that the man might tell him and that he might be obliged, in turn, to ask what had brought Fermin here, a question to which there was no good answer. Or, at least, none that wouldn't likely see him murdered badly before the day was out. And while such a thought engendered more than a little fear in him, what it did more than anything was make Fermin feel ashamed. Ridiculous, perhaps, to feel like a traitor when infiltrating an army bent on the destruction of the entire world and everyone in it, but that didn't keep him from feeling like one just the same.

"Well," the big man answered, grinning his usual grin as he responded to Jale, "there was all that ale just sittin' there, wasn't it? Didn't seem right, lettin' it go un-drank. Seemed somebody ought to show it some attention."

Jale snorted. "Tough job."

"Aye," Calden said with another bellowed laugh. "The toughest."

Two of the other messengers who Fermin knew as Pesal and Vardin laughed. The last, the only female messenger and one by the name of Merrilan, did not. Though, to be fair, she never did, choosing instead to scowl at everyone around and her words, on those occasions when she chose to speak, were always cutting. Fermin did not know what choice or tragedy—and weren't they so often the same thing?—had brought Merrilan to join the army, but in her case, at least, he was glad, for it must have been a dark one indeed.

"So, Fur," Pesal said, a thin man with buckteeth, a fact he didn't seem to mind, as now, like always, his wide smile revealed their presence readily to anyone with eyes to see. He leaned forward. "How was it out there?"

That sobered them all up right enough and drew a scowl from Jale. Many things were taboo among the messengers, as if they were their own sort of club, and even Fermin, the newest among their ranks, knew that the "Tent" was for drinking and speaking of inconsequential things, not for speaking of but for forgetting *about* the terrible things they'd witnessed.

"What do you mean, how the fuck *was* it?" Merrilan hissed, each word sharp as a dagger blow, ones which Fermin were thankful were not aimed in his direction. "The same as it always is, you stupid bastard."

Pesal recoiled as if he'd been slapped, his face going pale. Merrilan was a small thing, likely no more than a hundred and ten pounds soaking wet, but the man looked terrified, as if he had just angered some vengeful god. Not that Fermin could blame him—the woman terrified him more than a little himself, and even Calden seemed wary around her, never mind that he could have picked her up and broken her in half with one hand. "Sorry Merrilan," Pesal managed, "I was only asking, that is, I didn't mean—"

"To the Keeper's Fields with what you *meant*. Why don't you just do us all a favor and keep your damned mouth shut? Or is it you don't know the how of it and someone needs to show you?"

The woman had made no move from where she was leaned back in her chair, one arm draped casually over its back, but she might as well have brandished a bloody dagger for the terror in the other man's expression. "T-that's not necessary, Merrilan," Pesal managed, "I'll shut it."

There was a tense several seconds as she studied him with that dangerous scowl, as grim as an executioner's axe. It wasn't the first time, after all, that Pesal had said or done something to anger the woman—everything seemed to, in fact, but the buck-toothed man appeared to have a particular talent for it. Fermin along with the others gathered at the table, held his breath, sure that this time would be the time Merrilan drew one of the sharp, cruelly-curved daggers always sheathed at her waist and made her displeasure known. Finally, though, she gave a sour grunt. "Fucker," she hissed, then took a long drink of ale and they all collectively tried—and collectively failed—to hide their sighs of relief.

The talk went on then, talk and lots of silences. Pesal, after all, seemed content to speak no more for the evening lest he risk Merrilan's anger once more, and as for the rest, well, when you didn't dare speak about your past or about your present, conversation became difficult at best. That was fine with Fermin, perhaps more than fine. He still had the ale, and that was what was important, the remedy which, while only partially successful at healing the scars the terrible events of the last days had brought, was far better than any other.

His thoughts drifted then, or perhaps it was more accurate to say they retreated, retreated away from the stink of the hundreds, perhaps thousands who had died already and the sounds of their screams, but he found himself pulled back to the present when Calden spoke.

"How much longer do you think the bastards can hold out, anyway? The cooks can't fix meals for shit, and I find myself missing my ex-wife's cooking, though the gods know I think it likely she was trying to poison me."

That was as close to talking about their past as the messengers ever got and while Calden asked the question of the table at large, it was Jale who answered. "Can't be much longer," he said, and Fermin didn't think he completely imagined the note of sympathy in the man's voice. Not a monster, no matter what anyone else might think. Just a man.

Jale glanced around as if in fear of being overheard, never mind the fact that what few half a dozen other soldiers shared the tent with them sat on the other side of it and were paying them no attention. "I carried a message from Lord Leandrian himself today, one meant for Captain Wexler."

Fermin found himself leaning forward in interest. "Captain Wexler?"

Jale grinned, an almost childlike expression of joy on his face. "That's right."

Everyone around the table showed obvious interest at that; even Merrilan left off scowling for a moment, raising an eyebrow in anticipation, a change of expression that might have equated to an eager gasp from someone else.

"So what?" Pesal finally asked, speaking for the first time since he'd been called out by Merrilan. "I don't think I know Captain Wexler."

Merrilan scowled at the man, likely preparing to call him a fool, but Calden beat her to it, laughing and patting Pesal on the back with one massive paw. "Don't know him, eh?" the big man asked. "Well, sure, why would you? Wexler's just the man currently given charge of the attack on Valeria, that's all. It's his troops as have been attacking the city."

Pesal's face turned red with embarrassment. "Oh."

"'Oh's right," Calden said. "Anyhow, Jale, you going to leave us all in suspense, or are you gonna tell us what it said?"

Jale grinned, obviously pleased to have everyone hanging on his words. "Well, I suppose, if you're *really* interested..."

Calden barked another laugh. "Go on, you bastard. What's the news?"

Jale leaned forward even further, so much that his chin was in danger of knocking over several mugs of ale. "Well, I'll tell you. The message was for the captain to pull his troops back from the walls by tonight and not launch any fresh assaults."

Pesal frowned. "But why would he do that? That doesn't make any sense..." He paused, glancing around at the others at the table, all with thoughtful expressions on their faces. "Does it? Why would Chosen Leandrian stop attacking the city?"

"That's not what he said," Fermin spoke in a low whisper, the words out of his mouth before he could stop himself. Normally he preferred to stay quiet in such gatherings, to allow others to carry the conversation while he drank and listened, trying—and failing, gods forgive him but always failing—to forget some of the terrible things he had seen in the last week, things no man or woman living in a sane world ever would see. They all turned to look at him and he winced. "I mean, he never said Chosen Leandrian wasn't attacking the city tonight."

"What do you mean?" the bucktoothed man asked. "If Wexler isn't sending in troops then how could he attack?"

Fermin looked to Jale, but the man nodded at him as if impressed, and Fermin felt a surge of pleasure at seeing it, once again satisfied to feel accepted, to feel part of something. "Go ahead Fur," he said. "Enlighten our struggling comrade, won't you?"

They were all looking at him, and he felt his face heat. "I...that is, everyone knows how badly Chosen Leandrian wishes to take Valeria. After all, it is the only thing that stands in the way of his conquest of...what I mean, he would not stop attacking the city for no reason, or at all, as far as I can tell. If he has ordered Captain Wexler to pull his troops back, it can mean only one thing..." He trailed off, unable to finish the last bit. True, Jale and the others had become like friends over the last week, friends driven together by shared tragedy and pain, but all of those he had ever held dear in his life sheltered inside of Valeria's walls, a fact which, should it come to light, he did not doubt would see him dead in moments.

"What?" Pesal pressed. "What is it?"

Jale sighed. "What he means, Pesal, is that Chosen Leandrian will not stop attacking the city. If he has called back Wexler's troops, that can mean only one thing."

Calden grunted. "That he's chosen to send in his *other* troops." All of them seated at the table knew the troops to which he referred, understood too, why the man would not say the words, for they did not like to speak of the nightlings. Fermin had discovered the truth of that early on during his stay in the camp. True, they might have been allied with the creatures of darkness, at least in so much as they all had the same master, but the messengers—and regular soldiers as well, even down to the cooks—aggressively avoided speaking directly about the beasts of fang and claw which roamed the shadows serving Shira's will. Everyone understood what he meant though. Everyone, of course, save for Pesal.

"*Who?*" he asked again, then, finally, realization seemed to dawn, and his eyes went wide, the breath leaving him in a weak sigh. "Oh."

Jale rolled his eyes, but it did nothing to hide the troubled expression on his face. "That's right. I heard it from a friend among Wexler's troops that the...the *others* started for the wall only a couple of hours ago when darkness came." He shrugged. "Can't imagine how anybody would stand up against that. Why, for all I know, the city's already been taken, and we'll be marching inside the walls in a few hours. You know, as soon as they're done..." He cleared his throat. "Well, as soon as they're done."

As soon as they're done eating. That's what the man had been about to say, Fermin knew that as well as he knew anything, and he felt a stab of panic in his chest. Kale had finally grown tired of the assault, it seemed, and had chosen to send in the beasts under his command, the beasts who had been crafted by the Goddess of the Wilds into killing machines. True, Alesh and Katherine and Darl and Rion were all powerful, blessed by the gods themselves, but Fermin thought it too much to hope that they could stand up against such an assault for long. For from what he'd heard of the beasts—mostly from pale, fear-struck soldiers who'd seen them lurking on the edges of the camp—their numbers were endless.

"Damn," Calden breathed. "I know they're the enemy and all, but the gods know I wouldn't wish such a fate even on my ex-wife."

There was a moment of silence then as everyone at the table nodded in agreement. Everyone, that was, except Merrilan. "*Wouldn't you?*" she sneered, her cruel gaze sweeping the men at the table. "Are you all really such big cowards? Or is it that you are more like fat gluttons, more than willing to eat beef but too dainty to wonder at where the slab of meat on your plate comes from? Or are you traitors, then, ones thinking to abandon the army because its commander's methods don't sit well with your delicate sensibilities?"

"Easy, lass," Calden said, but his tone was not one of warning but more of pleading, "no one here's a coward and damned sure not a traitor."

"That so?" Merrilan asked, her eyes sweeping them, and Fermin wasn't sure if he imagined the way her gaze seemed to linger on him for a moment before going back to the big man. "Well. All I can say is you seem like a bunch of chicken shits to me. So what if Chosen Leandrian chooses to send in the nightlings? You know what I say to that? *Good.* Let them feast, let them rip and tear those fools in Valeria limb from limb, let them kill and slaughter and eat until they've had their fill. My only regret is that I can't be there to see it."

There was such venom, such hate in her words, that all those at the table, Fermin included, were stunned by it. Silence followed as each of them considered the woman's words, the poison in them, as no one wanted to speak first, to risk making themselves the object of her anger. Finally, Merrilan gave a hiss of disgust. "Fucking cowards," she said, rising and slamming her beer down on the table before stomping out of the tent and into the darkness.

They all stared after her, and it was Calden who spoke first. "Entirely too relaxed, that girl. Needs a bit more fire in her."

"Sure," Jale said, swallowing. "That way, you can keep her close, the nights get cold. Stay warm."

"Probably not alive, though," Pesal muttered.

They all turned and looked at him at that, and then, simultaneously, they burst into laughter. It was tentative at first, quiet, as no one loved the idea of Merrilan hearing their humor and deciding they were making light of her, but became louder as they each reacted to the other, and soon Fermin found himself laughing too, despite everything. It was good to laugh—sometimes, doing so seemed to keep the darkness back a little, to make the candles and the lanterns shine a little brighter.

"Still," Calden said, running an arm across eyes which had begun tearing up with mirth, "I got to say it again: I don't envy those poor bastards along the wall. They've put up a right good fight, outnumbered like they are. Seems a shame to send the beasts after them."

That sobered them all up quickly enough, and the remnants of their laughter faded away like echoes in the darkness. There was a question in Fermin's mind, one that desperately needed answering and despite his fear of being found out, he cleared his throat and asked, "Do you really think they would beat them? I mean, the walls have held so far..." He trailed off as they all looked at him, sure that they would see his deceit, that they would call him a spy, a traitor, and the men seated at the table—his friends—would kill him.

"Sure they have," Jale agreed, apparently not ready to call him a traitor after all, "but against men. Barely even soldiers, and that's the truth of it. I served for a bit, years ago, and believe me when I tell you that the 'troops' Chosen Leandrian's sent at the walls so far make better corpses than soldiers. Old men and women mostly, who likely would have died to sickness or age in another year or two if not to swords this week. The...the *others,* though, well, that's a different matter, isn't it?"

Fermin's mouth felt dry, his tongue two sizes too thick for his mouth, and it was all he could do to nod. "Yes...yes it is."

"Yeah," Calden said, the big man nodding grimly. "Reckon they've got it pretty bad, that lot. Worse even than the camp slaves and that's sayin' somethin' sure enough."

"The slaves?" Fermin asked, a squeak in his voice, and more than a little shame in his heart, for he had not thought much of Marta. Since the first couple of days when he'd tried to spend what little free time he'd been afforded to find her—and failed miserably in the sprawling, unorganized army encampment—he'd been more focused on ale than on reuniting with the young girl.

"Oh, you hadn't heard?" Jale asked. He shook his head. "The guards have set them to lookin' for survivors." He grunted. "Though the gods alone know how they're supposed to find anything but death and despair in the Red Fields."

The Red Fields. It was what the soldiers in the army had taken to calling the expanse of grassy ground outside the city of Valeria which separated it from the forest. Not that there actually *was* any grass there anymore. There had been, once, but it had long since been crushed underneath hundreds of feet and turned to dirt which had been turned to mud by rain and the blood leaking out of the hundreds of bodies scattered about it. Fermin had read of some battles in his time as Lord Tirinian's servant and knew that it was often customary for two sides, at war, to allow each other the opportunity to collect their dead, but while he'd heard a letter had been sent from Chosen Alesh to Kale for that purpose, the man had blatantly refused. Claiming, according to Pesal who'd carried the message, that the dead were either the corpses of his enemies or the corpses of failures and he cared nothing for either.

So the dead lay where they'd fallen on ground sodden with their own blood and stomped over by their comrades, neglected and left to rot by the leader they had served. The stench alone was unbearable, the sight of so many broken bodies even worse, and Fermin always avoided looking in the direction of the Fields when delivering dispatches. But while the sight and smell of that bloody conflict was terrible, the statement, the *truth* it spoke was worse. The truth that the world had descended into madness where human life was worth nothing, men and women thrown away as if they were the dolls of some careless child. He thought of Marta walking among those fields, among the countless dead, looking for survivors, while he himself was too weak even to look upon them, and fresh shame welled up inside him, so much he thought he must surely choke on it.

"B-but surely they aren't alone," Fermin said, desperately searching for some relief of that terrible, crippling shame he felt. "I mean, surely others are helping them to...to look."

Jale snorted, clearly unaware of his inner turmoil. "Volunteers, do you mean? Men who'd rather pick through mutilated corpses than play cards or have a drink? Not likely. I mean," he said, giving a soft laugh, "would you?"

The words were said lightly, Jale trying to find humor in a dark situation. There was no way he could have known that they pierced Fermin's heart like a blade, no way for him to know that the words made self-hatred grip Fermin's chest and threaten to rip it apart. Marta was out there, perhaps even now, walking among the dead, forced to endure sights and sounds that no adult should ever be forced to witness, let alone a child of only twelve years. Sometimes it was easy to forget that Marta was so young, as clever and knowledgeable as she was, but she was a child just the same. And while she was being treated as a slave, wandering the Red Fields, Fermin was sitting nice and comfortable in a tent, having an ale.

He was out of his chair before he knew it, barely even aware that he had knocked it over in his haste. "I...I have to go."

Jale hastily steadied Merrilan's half-full ale before it tipped over onto the table and looked at him with genuine concern. "Everything alright, Fur? You look like the dead."

No, Fermin was not dead, but in that moment, he almost wished that he was, almost thought that he should be. He had allowed himself to become immersed in his own self-pity at his plight, had allowed himself to focus on nothing but making it through each day, forgetting the reason why he had come here with Marta, to rescue Sonya, forgetting, in truth, Marta herself. "I-I'm fine," he managed. "Just...I'm just tired."

"Sure," Calden said, the big man nodding his head with an unmistakable look of compassion on his face. "Sure you are. Go on then, Fur. Get some rest—we'll all be here tomorrow, the gods know that's the truth."

Fermin suddenly wanted to scream, to rail at himself, at the messengers seated around the table, even at the gods themselves for allowing the world to become as it had, for smearing the painting they had created with darkness black as pitch and blood deep crimson, staining it and everyone in it out of their own hatred, their own jealousies and fighting. He nodded instead, raising a shaking hand to bid farewell.

He turned to go, promising himself, *demanding* of himself that he be better, that he would no longer stand idly by and allow people—his friends included—to suffer. Tonight, he would come up with a plan, any plan to get himself and Marta and—the gods willing—Sonya, away from the enemy camp. He had let them down, had let himself down: he would not do so again.

"Fur?"

Fermin turned back from where he'd started away to see Jale holding up a mug of ale to him. "Forgot your drink—looks to me like you need it, buddy."

Fermin stared at that mug of ale, still nearly full. His third or fourth? No way to know for sure, for he never kept count. He had never thought he'd had a problem drinking. Anyone, in fact, who had ever known him during his life would have laughed at the very thought. But he was not laughing, not now. Only a mug of ale, but it seemed to press at him, to speak to him, to whisper its promises of forgetfulness, of that numb, faux-peace that it would bring.

There was Marta and Sonya to think about now, though, the two children who were counting on him, the children who the Tirinians had tasked him with looking after, with teaching. And what had he taught them? What had he done with that stewardship? He had failed them both, that was what. Was failing them even now, perhaps had failed them already, irrevocably so.

Yet whatever his hopes might be, he was still only a servant, a man who did not plan but followed the plans of others. He had spent his entire life doing as much. What hope did he have of figuring out a way of getting himself and Marta and Sonya out of the mess they found themselves in? None, that was the truth of it. Dealing with dirty laundry or lazy servants, that was what Fermin was made to do, all that he *could* do. Planning and implementing an escape strategy to rescue himself and two others was as beyond him as it was beyond a rock to speak.

So what choice, then? He had failed and would continue to fail just as the rock would continue to be an unthinking, unspeaking rock. The only real option left to him was whether or not to be painfully, soberly aware of his own failure, to feel that terrible gripping shame and hatred inside himself, or…to forget.

"Thanks," Fermin muttered. Then he took the offered ale and left, walking out of the tent and into the waiting darkness.

Chapter Nine

Marta had never much cared for clothes. Certainly, she had always laughed and mocked those noblewomen who spent hours preening in front of mirrors with their fancy gowns and their fancy hats. Dresses that looked more like torture devices, not made for wearing, not really, but made to be *seen* wearing and shoes made for feet she'd never seen, certainly not made for walking but for remarking upon and being asked about.

Ridiculous, all of it. Now, though, as she bent hunched over in her too-big linen "dress" which was really just a fancy name for a sack that chafed and rubbed her skin raw in places, and washed other such "dresses" before hanging them out to dry, she would have killed for some of those noblewomen's gowns. And as for their shoes, well, uncomfortable they might have been, but certainly they could be no worse than going barefoot. After one of the slaves from another tent had attempted an escape, the soldiers had come and taken her shoes along with all the others—the gods alone knew why, as if being barefoot was enough to banish any thought of escape from their minds. Then again, though, the gods alone knew why the soldiers did half the things they did—people in general, for that matter.

All Marta knew for sure was that her feet hurt, her back ached, and she'd long since stopped bothering keeping count of the rough abrasions on her skin that the scratchy dress left. But as she dunked the cleaning rag—far too dirty to make anything clean, really—back into the bucket of water which had started soapy and had long since turned muddy, she told herself that it could be worse. She wasn't exactly sure *how* it could be worse, but she didn't challenge the fact that it could—the world, to her mind, was always far too ready to take up such challenges with an alacrity and eagerness that was more than a little perverse.

She told herself that it could be worse—true. Told herself also that her feet *didn't* hurt, that the sharp ache in her lower back from hours spending bending over buckets or bending over corpses, checking for dirt or checking for a pulse respectively, wasn't there at all. Not true. It was a lie she'd told herself often in the last week, and one that it had to be said was getting harder and harder to believe.

Others, in such a predicament, forced to labor over the dead and dying by men who would do terrible things to her if they found out who she really was—or, simply, if they thought they could get away with it—might have despaired. But Marta was no blushing noblewoman who'd spent her whole life with blinders on, blinders which showed her only good things, like fancy dresses and fancy food and fancy...well everything. No, Marta was not such a woman, was not naïve, for she had seen well what shape the shadows took, had seen the darkness reach out and claim those too slow to avoid its grasp. What she was then—and any of those other street waifs she'd known over the years might have agreed on this, sometimes with a smile, other times with a sneer—was a survivor.

She had survived countless dangers over the years, and she told herself that she would survive this, too. Told herself that, like those other times, she would find some way not only to stay safe from the dangers all around her but to actually benefit from them, to come out the other side of this dark tunnel into a light brighter than the one she had left. And so what if she currently had no idea how she might go about doing such a thing?

Marta did not despair.

But, she did have to admit, that while she did not despair, she felt a bit...itchy. It was an itch that had grown over the last week, seeming to double day by day, an itch that seemed to think she would never make it out of here, that she would be found out sooner or later and even if she wasn't, she would spend the rest of her life—almost certainly a short, painful one—slaving away for the enemy army, watching her own friends and everything she loved being ripped down and destroyed.

Marta did not despair. She simply itched. And washed.

"Careful, lass," one of the guards who she recognized as Guardsman Blake said in a taunting voice as he and one of his companions sauntered past, a thing they did far more often when the women were doing laundry and their thin, itchy dresses clung to their bodies from the wet.

Marta didn't want to answer, but the pair stopped behind her, and she knew that to not answer would be to invite not only their anger—bad—but their attention—worse. So she turned, doing her best to keep the sneer off her face. "Why is that?"

The guard grinned like a child given a treat to see her so easily stumble into his trap—as if she could do anything else. "Well, you see," he said, nodding at the basket of dirty clothes, "from what I hear, you got Dell's laundry."

Marta thought she knew well enough where this was going, but the man was only watching her, waiting for her to play her part, so like a good slave, she did. "Yes, sir. But why does that matter?"

"Well, it *matters*," the guard crooned, taking his idiot time while his idiot companion stared on with a grin on his face, "because Dell ain't exactly the best at holdin' in a shit, when one takes it in mind to leave." Blake's companion actually guffawed at that, a bit of snot flying from his nose as he did. "Particularly," he went on, an arrogant contentment on his face as if he were some fencer who had shown up to the finals of a tournament only to discover that his opponent didn't know which end of his sword to hold, "when he drinks. And, lass, Dell has been doin' him a lot of drinkin' lately."

Blake and his companion burst into laughter at that, and Marta bit back a curse. Few things in the world she hated more than a man who laughed at his own jokes, a crime punishable, to her mind, by a kick in the privates at the least. Not that she was able to administer such a punishment right then, but the thought was one of the first pleasant ones she'd had in a while.

After a minute or so, the two men sobered, and a scowl came over the speaker's face. "What is it, lass? You just gonna kneel there and frown at me, that it? Didn't like my joke?"

Marta winced inwardly. Maybe she'd let a bit too much of her own thoughts, a bit too much of the truth show through—never good when a person did that, not for anyone. True, the man might have chosen not to be offended, but then more than likely he would. It was like he was playing a game, a game in which she was an unwilling participant and one to which she did not know the rules—one which even he did not, only making them up as he went along like a child intent on winning not by skill but by twisting the game so that he could only win. And when playing such a game, Marta knew the best thing was to accept loss graciously. She bowed her head. "Sorry, sir. It was very funny, of course. I...I must have not understood it, that's all."

"You stupid then, girl?" he demanded, warming up to being angry now, enjoying it the same way that selfish child might enjoy bullying another. Always assuming, of course, that the other was considerably smaller and weaker than himself. "Witless?"

"I must be," Marta muttered, but the man's frown only deepened.

"What's that?"

"Yes, sir," she said with more contrition in her tone. "I'm afraid I am."

A cruel grin slowly came over the man's face. "You are what? Let me hear you say it, girl."

Marta's hands were hidden in the filthy bucket of water which was just as well as the man couldn't see that they'd both knotted into fists. Foolish to get angry, to want to get even. She knew that. But then, knowing the foolish thing didn't mean a person was always able to avoid it. She took a slow breath, meeting the man's eyes. "I'm stupid, sir. Witless."

Guardsman Blake nodded his head, pleased, as if he'd just scored a point and to him, at least, he likely had. "I figured as much. Well. I'll let your offense go this time, Witless. After all, I don't fancy giving a beating to someone too stupid to understand why they're getting it. But you make sure those clothes are good and clean or maybe I'll find a way to enjoy it after all." He looked around at the other slave women—a few dozen in all, doing the wash around her. "That goes for all of you, understand?"

None of the other slaves met his eyes, only nodding and murmuring their assent, going about their tasks with renewed vigor, and the guard nodded again, pleased with himself, pleased in the way only a fool can be to be the shitty king of a shitty kingdom. Then he walked away, leading his smiling companion with him.

Marta watched them go, thinking it was stupid to hold a grudge, stupid all the time but even more so in her current circumstances. Thinking, too, that if things came to a point where she knew she wasn't making it out, she'd be sure at least one asshole came along with her to visit the Keeper's Fields.

She had just turned back to her bucket, resuming her labor once more, when she was shoved roughly from the side, and she lost her balance, sprawling on the muddy ground. She ran a hand over her face to clear the mud plastering it away and looked up to see Greta standing over her. The queen of the slaves wore a scowl and her hands flexed furiously at her sides. "Stupid bitch," she spat. "What are you trying to do, get us all beaten?"

A quick glance showed Marta that all the other slaves had paused in their labors to watch. She climbed back to her knees, beginning on the laundry once again. "No," she said. "As for what I *am* trying to do—well, laundry. Seems a bit obvious, doesn't it?"

The wrong thing to say, she knew. There wasn't a right one, of course, but some were more wrong than others and that one, she thought, was pretty far out there. It was a thought confirmed a moment later when the woman slapped her ringingly across the face.

"Witless," Greta spat, her pinched, narrow face growing a furious red beneath her tangled mess of hair. "He was right about that much, at least. And while Guardsman Blake might not enjoy spending his time on fools, I ain't got no problem with it."

"Well," Marta said, "you wouldn't, would you?"

The woman actually hissed at that, and Marta tensed, knowing what was coming. But after several seconds passed, and she hadn't been struck, she looked up to see that someone had interposed themselves between her and Greta. Had, in fact, caught the woman's wrist stopping her from slapping Marta again. Her rescuer, as it turned out, was Farra, the pregnant woman who was over six feet tall and who Marta would have bet money on in a fight against any of "guards" of the enemy army.

"Enough, Greta," the big woman said. "Leave her alone."

Greta's expression showed that she was as shocked by this turn of events as Marta was herself. It had been two nights since Marta had taken Farra's post walking among the bodies looking for survivors, and she hadn't spoken with the woman since.

"The fuck are you on about, Farra?" the queen of the slaves demanded.

"You heard me," the woman said, but while her words sounded defiant, her tone was anxious, similar to that of a child. "Guardsman Blake is...well, he's an asshole. Everyone knows that. He looks for things to be angry about—it's got nothing to do with Marta."

"Doesn't it?" Greta said, her eyes narrowing. "So what, Farra? Do you mean to tell me that you've taken this little shit under your wing, that it? You playing mother to this little runt?"

Farra swallowed, glancing back at Marta, obviously nervous, before turning back and refusing to meet the woman's eyes, never mind that she was over a foot taller than her persecutor. "I just...just leave her alone, Greta. Please."

"*Please*," Greta sneered. "You trying to challenge me, Farra? That it?"

The larger woman fidgeted anxiously, saying nothing, and Marta thought it was a damned shame for a person to have fists the size of dinner platters and be scared of her own shadow. "I'm not...that is, I don't mean..." The woman trailed off, a slightly bewildered expression on her face as if she'd forgotten what she'd been about to say, perhaps forgotten what impulse had brought her to stand against her leader in the first place.

"*What?*" Greta snapped, and while she might have been a small woman, the queen of the slaves had enough anger stuffed into her small frame for three at least. "What did you *mean*, Farra?"

Marta rose to her feet, giving a few swipes at the mud covering her scratchy dress before giving it up as a lost job. "Oh, enough already," she said, and both of them turned to her as if they had forgotten she was there at all.

"What?" Greta said.

"You heard me," Marta answered. "I get it—you're pissed off. Maybe not the way you think life ought to be, you slavin' for folks who mock you and might take it in mind to beat you whenever they feel like it. Maybe you don't like these shitty shifts or this shitty laundry, but guess what—*none* of us do. You're pissed? Gods, woman, we're *all* pissed. So your plan is what, exactly? The world not taken enough from us already, you got to try and take a bit more, that it? Your goal to steal what little bit of dignity we've still got?"

The woman's face was a mixture of emotions, anger chief among them, but there was confusion there too. And maybe, just maybe, a little understanding. "You...what do *you* know of it?" she asked finally. "You're just a girl."

"You'd be surprised what I know of how cruel the world can be," Marta said. "More than any girl should, I can tell you that much, more than anyone should, come to it. I don't like our situation anymore than you do, but what's the point making it worse for everybody by being an asshole? The gods know the world's got enough of them already."

"You little—" The woman started forward, probably meaning to answer the hard questions the way most bullies did—with hard fists—but she came up short as Farra raised a hand in warning.

Greta grunted, clearly shocked, and something like the hurt of betrayal flashed across her face. Marta sighed. "Look, it doesn't have to be this way, alright? Maybe our situation sucks, but we can make it a little better by helping each other, can't we? We're slaves, sure, but that don't mean we have to be monsters, does it?"

The woman stared at her, her hands working as if she would have liked nothing more just then than to wrap her fingers around Marta's throat and choke her—hard to ask tough questions when you can't catch a breath. But with the big woman standing between them, it was no more than a fantasy, and they both knew it. "You're big, Farra," Greta hissed at Marta's protector, "I'll give you that much, but so are cows—stupid and slow and too dumb to know when they're about to be butchered for meat...but big. I'll make you pay for—"

"Oh, come off it already."

This from a new voice, and they all turned to see that another of the slaves, this one an older woman who appeared to be in her fifties with gray hair and a hunched back, had risen from her own tin bucket of clothes and was currently standing with her hands on her hips, shaking her head in disapproval. Marta couldn't remember her name—social gatherings and meet and greets were unsurprisingly few and far between among the slaves. Berta or Betty or something like that, she thought. But though she couldn't remember the woman's name, she'd seen her, had even had her smile warmly at her a time or two, though she'd never before heard her speak.

"What's that, Llanivere?" Greta asked in surprise. "You sidin' with the little whore too?"

Ah, Llanivere, Marta thought, *knew it was something like that.*

"Siding with her for what?" the old woman asked. She held out her hands in a gesture that encapsulated the muddy ground and the muddy buckets tended by muddier women and then spread them wider to encompass the whole filthy army camp, the haphazard, unorganized tents dotting the forest and the dozens of fires and soldiers drinking among them. "Your mistake is thinking there *are* any sides, Greta. The world's a shitty place at the best of times, take it from me, for I've been around long enough to know it. The best a body can hope to do is make their way through it for a while without takin' too many hits—and nobody makes it out alive. What point then in squabbling and bickering like children when the world's just one big boot gonna crush us all like ants anyway?"

Not exactly the most inspiring speech Marta had ever heard, unless the older woman's intention had been to inspire them all to lie down and die, maybe, but it brought the queen of the slaves up short. "I...well, she's going to make it harder on the rest of us with backtalking and acting out!" she finished, and there was no doubting the defensiveness in her words and posture now.

"What's harder?" the old woman asked in a tone that was almost gentle. "Laundry's here, needs doin' just the same as it did, and those assholes"—she nodded her chin at the nearest campfire to indicate the soldiers there—"will still be assholes come mornin'. Naw, Greta, the little lass here ain't the one makin' it harder on folks—you are."

Greta recoiled as if she'd been slapped, looking around at the other watching slaves as if for help. But if help was what she was waiting for, she was to be disappointed, for the women only continued to watch, some even muttering among themselves in hushed whispers, the most life they'd shown since Marta had first seen them. "So what? You all feel this way, that it?"

At first, the women seemed to quail under her withering gaze as it swept across them, but after a moment, one grew bold and nodded. "That's right," she said.

Then others were nodding along, until they were all agreeing, and Greta, once queen of the slaves, had a stricken look on her face as she was forced to watch her throne, such as it was, stripped from beneath her. She looked upset about it, maybe even close to tears, but Marta thought it for the best. She didn't know much about thrones—just that they looked like damned uncomfortable things to have a sit in—but from what she'd seen of Kale, and Tesharna, even Alesh since he'd reluctantly taken over rule of Valeria, they didn't seem to solve any problems, only make more of them and she thought the woman would likely be the better for losing it.

"And if she mouths off one too many times to the guards?" Greta asked, desperately trying one final approach. "And if those guards decide to take out their anger at her at us as they so often do, then what?"

The old woman sighed, shrugging. "Well, lass, then I imagine we'll get beaten. Imagine we'll get beaten anyway, though. And besides," she said, turning to peer at Marta with eyes that seemed particularly clever, "a body can only take so many punches before it starts wantin' to punch back. Most natural thing in the world, slave or no."

"Punch back," Greta said, giving a harsh, humorless laugh, one in which no one else seemed inclined to participate. "And then what? Die?"

"Probably," the old woman said, nodding. "But then, lass, that ain't the worst thing—I'm old enough, I've seen quite a few people take that journey, and it's not so hard, not so hard at all. Your mistake is thinkin' dyin' is the worst thing that can happen to a person."

Greta stared at the woman, her mouth working angrily, then she finally hocked and spat. "Damn you all—do what you want. Be fools, if you want and follow this *child* but don't come cryin' to me when you all end up dead."

"Be a hard thing to do, even if we had a mind to," Marta said, the words coming out of her mouth before she could stop them, and she winced.

Greta let out an angry growl then turned and stomped away—not stomping particularly far, another downside of being a slave was that a person could never stomp very far—before hunching over her bucket and starting to scrub the clothes like she was a torturer and they victims she meant to extract information from.

Marta grunted, surprised, and met the old woman's eyes who only gave her a wink then went back to her own labors. Soon, all the other slaves followed suit and Marta was left standing there with Farra. "Thank you," she said. "Didn't mean to get you involved but...thanks."

The woman smiled, and that simple expression turned her normally plain, slightly-manly face into a thing of beauty. "The least I could do," she said softly, glancing down at her belly that was still not yet showing. "After what you did for me."

"No," Marta said, "not the least—I've seen the least, and believe me, that wasn't it. Thank you."

She smiled. "You're welcome," Farra said, then turned and started back toward her own bucket, and Marta didn't think she imagined the way the woman walked a little straighter, as if maybe she'd just remembered she had a backbone after all and had decided to give using it a go. Marta wasn't sure whether that could be counted a blessing or not—after all, it was about the time a person started showing a backbone that the world started looking for ways to break it.

Marta was still staring at Farra's departing back when she suddenly felt as if someone were watching her. She spun and saw a figure standing behind her in the shadows separating the slave tents and the torches placed around them from the nearest group of soldiers. A short, squat figure, a woman's shape, but she could see little more than that, and did not need to.

The god looked nothing like he had the other times she'd seen him, indeed, had gone so far as to appear as a woman, though the gods—which meant him, presumably—knew why. The woman was short where the man had been tall, the woman fat where he had been thin. Everything was different—except, that was, for the god's eyes, eyes that seemed to see right through her, that seemed to know and understand more about her in a glance than she understood about herself.

"Marta?" She turned back to see that Farra had stopped walking away and was watching her, a concerned expression on her face.

"Yes?"

"Are...are you okay?"

"Sure," Marta said. "Why wouldn't I be?"

"Just...I thought I heard you make a noise."

"A noise?"

"Well." Farra smiled, shyly tucking a piece of her hair back behind her ear. "It sounded more like a growl, really."

"Yeah," Marta said, "sorry about that. I'm uh...allergic. That's all. You know, to the grass."

"Of course," Farra said, "I hope you feel better then." And with that, she turned and walked away again, willing to believe Marta straight away, apparently.

And that, at least, hadn't been a complete lie. She wasn't allergic to grass, true, but to assholes, and any god who would leave his Chosen to rot as a slave in the midst of an enemy army seemed to fit that description nicely as far as she was concerned.

With that in mind, she stomped toward the "old woman" standing in the shadows. If Alcer noticed any of her anger—which he must have unless he was blind—then he apparently wasn't threatened by it, for he only stood calmly, smiling a grandmotherly smile and hunched over a cane which threatened to buckle beneath the weight of his guise.

"Just who in the shit do you think you are anyway?"

"Excuse me?"

"Oh, don't act like you don't know what I'm talking about. You're lucky I don't give you a swift kick in the balls for all the trouble you've caused me."

"F-forgive me, dearie," the old woman sputtered, and even Marta, a connoisseur of lies had to admit that Alcer was doing a damn fine job of appearing like nothing more threatening than an old woman, confused by the sudden, unexpected verbal abuse, "but I don't know what you mean. I only stopped to ask if you knew where Captain Wexler's tent is—I've come to enlist."

Marta snorted. "Very damned funny. And what exactly do you plan to do? Scare the defenders to death with how ugly you are? Or have they hired you as the entertainment—sort of a contest to see what you die of first, old age or being too fat."

"Why I have never been talked to in such a way my entire life," the woman said. "I have only just arrived in camp and am looking to enlist. When I was young—"

"When you were young the world was young," Marta snapped. "Now, enough of—"

"When *I* was young," the older woman said again, "children showed respect to their elders, or else they were disciplined for it."

"Look, enough of the joke, you dirty old bastard," Marta said. "I'm busy, you know, being a slave and all, so if you—" She cut off at the sound of a whistle, a whistle that was almost too quiet to hear, seeming to float along the wind, yet impossible to ignore. She turned and saw a guard standing some distance away by the firelight, motioning for her to come over. A guard whose facial features remarkably resembled Alcer, the God of the Homeless and Destitute. He was staring at her with an eyebrow raised, and Marta froze, staring back, stunned.

After several seconds, he tilted his head to the side, reminding her of the old—old and unnecessarily hurt—woman standing behind her. She cleared her throat and turned back. "I...forgive me, ma'am, but I thought you were someone else."

"Oh?" the old lady asked, and there was a quiver in her voice as if she might start crying at any moment. "Know a lot of fat old ladies, do you? Surprising they haven't all died on you."

"Yes," Marta stuttered, "I mean, no, I...what I'm saying, I didn't mean to offend you."

"I wouldn't worry about it, dear. I'm sure I'll get over it. Still, might be I'll have a word with Captain Wexler, make sure he shows you a bit of discipline."

Marta felt her face heating. She had never been the type of person to be easily embarrassed but then she had never been the type of person to scream at sweet old ladies either and there was no denying that she was embarrassed now. "I'm so sorry and yes, if you think it's best, perhaps I should be disciplined. I didn't mean to—"

The woman leaned in close, so that her face was only inches from Marta's own. So close, the shadows did nothing to hide her features, and Marta decided in a moment that they weren't those of a kindly old grandmother after all. Her face paint was streaked in places, and what was beneath was a pale white. Her lips, too, had been painted in a bright red color that appeared perverse and more than a little disturbing on a woman of her age. Even her eyes—which had seemed to sparkle the way the god Alcer's did, were wrong, so pale that the pupils barely seemed to exist at all yet hard for all that. *"Or,"* the woman crooned in a voice which, coming from another, might have seemed comforting, and Marta could smell the foulness of her breath as she did, "perhaps I'll take it in mind to discipline you myself, how'd that be? I've got a cage back at my manor for little girls like you. It's a tight fit, truth be told, but while I'm afraid I can't make it any bigger, I can certainly make *you* smaller."

Marta hesitated. "S-smaller?"

"That's right," the woman said, smiling widely and giving her another smell of her reeking breath smelling of rot and worse, "you see, while children these days can be so unruly, they can also be quite...sweet."

Marta took a step back. "I don't...I'm not sure what you—"

"Oh, but I think you are, dearie," the woman said, following her with a surprising quickness. "Come on then, how about just a little nip?"

She suddenly lunged forward, the remains of her teeth bared like some beast and Marta jumped back as the old woman snapped her jaws in front of her. Marta gave her a shove, more out of instinct than any conscious decision, and the woman stumbled back but did not fall. The lady cackled at that, a sharp, shrill sound that felt like razors in Marta's ears. "Well," she said, "I've got to go see Captain Wexler but don't worry, dearie—I'll be sure to come back." She grinned, once again putting the few rotten teeth she still had on display, "Maybe I'll come when you're sleeping...wouldn't that be a surprise? My name's Wanda. Remember it, child, for I shall surely remember you."

And before Marta could say anything in response—not that she had any idea of what *to* say as while she'd been threatened a thousand times in her life, this was the first time someone had planned on eating her—the woman turned and stalked off into the shadows in the direction of the front. "Sleeping?" Marta muttered into the darkness. "Not likely. Not for a year at least."

She watched the old woman's form until she could no longer see her then, swallowing, turned and made her way to the god where he still waited, watching her. "I would be wary of that one, young Marta," the god said, his voice somber as he stared in the direction the old woman had gone. "She has fully given herself to my mother, to the Darkness. You would not believe the evil which resides inside her."

"I might," Marta said, her mouth painfully dry, "and more than just evil is inside her too, if I understood her right."

"Oh, yes," the god nodded, a grim expression on his face, "she has consumed the flesh of the living. A most vile practice."

"Speaking of vile practices," Marta said, her annoyance at the god finally beginning to make its way past her fear, "what in the name of, well, you, have *you* been doing? I only ask because, in case you haven't noticed, your *Chosen* has been having a bit of a time of it."

The god winced as if he felt guilty—which he should have, as far as Marta was concerned. "Yes. I am aware of what you have faced—what you still face—and all I can say is that I am sorry. I would help you more if I could, but you must understand that we gods each have our strengths, and mine, I'm afraid, do not lie in open confrontation."

Marta grunted. "Sounds like a good excuse to keep from doing anything, you ask me."

"We all do what we can, young one," the god said. "I, for example, saw your plan to infiltrate the enemy army and have done what I can, in my small way, to aid you in your efforts. Now you are positioned where you might best aid your friends." He glanced over at the slave tents where the others were still busy about their washing, "Already it seems you have made some progress with those other poor souls whom you toil alongside."

"*Progress?*" Marta sputtered. "Sure, if you count progress as managing to keep from getting my head caved in, maybe."

"Oh," the god said in that I-know-more-than-you tone which always made Marta want to give him a good shin-kick, "I think you have managed quite a bit more than that, young one. Considerably more."

"And what does that mean?"

The god shook his head slowly, glancing once more at the slaves. "Seeds sown in the present bear fruit in the future, young one. It is the way, now as it always has been."

"What does that *mean?*" Marta demanded. "And must you always speak in riddles? Things would go on a whole lot better if you just told me what to do. And what good is being Chosen anyway? It doesn't make me stronger or faster—if I were, maybe I could find a way to sneak into Kale's tent and kill him, put an end to all of this."

"Said as if the taking of a life is so easy," the god said sadly. "But no, young one, that is not the way, for your strength, like my own, does not lie in combat but in other, subtler things."

"Yeah," Marta said sourly, "so subtle you might think it didn't exist at all."

The god gave her a small, humoring smile. "Doesn't it?" His head suddenly snapped up, and his gaze locked on a spot behind her. Marta turned, but could see nothing any different than it had been, only the tents spread out around them, only the fires and the shadows.

"What is it?" she asked, turning back to the god and noting his troubled expression.

"Always they search," he said quietly, so quiet he might not have been speaking to her at all, then he raised his hood over his head, casting his face in shadows so that she could see nothing but his eyes, glistening in the darkness. "I must go, young one, or risk being discovered. Already I have tarried too long in this place." The god turned to go and Marta scowled.

"That it, then?" she hissed. "That's all the help you're planning on giving? Damnit, at least tell me what I should *do.*"

He glanced back over his shoulder, studying her. "You know already. Survive, Marta. It is what you have always done."

Before she could respond further, the god took a step into the shadows, and vanished as if he had never been. Marta shook her head, hocked and spat. "Bastard," she muttered.

"Who's that?"

She spun, thinking that the old woman had returned or that, perhaps, one of the guards had noticed her being idle and had come to make her suffer for it. But it was only Farra, the big woman standing behind her. "What?" Marta asked. "I-it's nothing.

No one." She scowled at the place where the god had stood. "The world, maybe."

The big woman nodded thoughtfully as if Marta had just said something profound. "Yes. I...is everything okay, Marta? I thought I heard you speaking but you were alone and..."

"Oh, I'm fine," Marta said, sighing, "just losing my mind." *Or, considering where I'm at, maybe I've lost it already.* "Come on—best we be getting back. The gods know if we don't get the dirt out of those clothes the whole world might come crashing down around us."

Farra laughed and followed her as they made their way back to the slave tent. Marta had barely crouched down over her bucket again and begun her work when she noticed all of the slaves around her looking over her shoulder, expressions on their faces which were even more terrified than usual—no easy feat. She followed their gazes, glancing over her shoulder to see a massive figure stalking down the path between their tent and the nearest soldiers. The figure was at least seven feet tall with a sword strapped on his back that nearly matched him in height. Half a dozen soldiers—looking like children compared to the hulking figure—followed in his wake.

Since coming to the enemy camp, Marta had heard that Paren, the God of Conflict, was present, just as she'd heard it from Fermin the first night, but she had not yet seen him. Now, looking at him surreptitiously over one shoulder, she understood why the manservant had recounted the meeting with such fear and the itch that had been bothering her for the last several days—not despair, damnit, just an itch—grew worse. She didn't need anyone to tell her who the hulking figure was—even a fool could have guessed it. Power and strength and menace seemed to radiate from him in waves as he walked past.

What chance, she wondered, did any of them have against an army among which could be counted the God of Conflict himself, a being bred for blood and violence? One who took it as his trade the way a carpenter took up his chisel or a blacksmith his hammer? The god suddenly came to an abrupt halt causing the six soldiers who'd been following him to stumble and nearly fall over each other then he spun, looking directly in Marta's direction, and she hurriedly turned back to her bucket, going about her tasks.

She did not need to look to know that the god was staring in her direction—she could feel the weight of that stare as an unpleasant pressure on her back, a pressure which grew stronger and stronger with each passing moment. Then, just when she thought she could take no more, thought she would scream, the pressure vanished, and she turned back to see that the god had started moving forward once more only to pause again at the exact spot she and Alcer had stood.

The god frowned, sniffing the air like a hound, slowly turning and looking around the camp. *Gods, he knows,* Marta thought, *he must. In another moment, he'll walk over here, draw that tree-trunk of a sword of his, and that will be that.* But the god did not move toward her, did not draw the sword at his back. Instead, he only scowled and started forward again, him and his followers disappearing further into the sprawling army camp.

"*Gods help us,*" Marta muttered, realizing, even as she said it, how ridiculous it was.

Chapter Ten

Alesh sat slumped over in his chair, staring at the unconscious man lying in the bed, his mind a whirlwind of confused, jumbled thoughts. He had been sitting so for the last several hours, watching the Ekirani's chest rise and fall, and though he had little knowledge of healing, he could not help but notice the man's labored, shallow breaths.

He felt helpless, worthless, wished that there was something, *anything* he could do, any way to save the man who had saved him, but he could do nothing. So he waited for what would come, waited and watched and prayed, that most of all. He did not know if he was still worthy of the gods' attention, but he prayed anyway, prayed for the life of this man who had so recently been his enemy. Partly, he prayed because the man had saved him from death, but mostly, he found himself praying for the man's life because he had saved him from something worse, had shown him that any man could find his way to the Light again.

The curtain which separated the small area in which Alesh sat with Tarex from the rest of the healer's tent opened and Chief Healer Malachai stepped through. If anything, the man looked even worse than he had the day before, his face haggard and drawn, his skin pale, and his white robe bearing fresh blood stains. He shuffled inside and glanced over at Alesh. "Chosen," he said, a touch of surprise entering his weary voice, "you're still here."

"Yes. How is he?"

The old man ran an arm across his forehead. "Sir, forgive my saying so, but you really need to let us look at you. You've lost a lot of blood, and my assistants say you refuse to rest."

"I thank you for your concern," Alesh said.

"But you won't rest."

"Not yet. How is he?"

The man sighed and shuffled toward the Ekirani's bedside. He bent low, bringing his ear directly over the man's mouth. Then, after a moment, he began checking other places, putting his hands on his wrist, the man's neck, bringing his ear down to his chest. Alesh watched silently, willing the Ekirani to be okay, willing him to heal, but when the old man rose and glanced at him, his expression was grim. "Your friend here's in a bad way, Chosen. A really bad way."

No, Alesh thought, *no.* "But...but you can help him?"

The healer winced. "I will do what I can, but I'm afraid his injuries are beyond my ability to heal. He's lost a lot of blood and, what's more, the nightling taint is working its way through his system. Do you see here..." He paused, gesturing to the Ekirani's bare chest where bandages had been wrapped around, then pointing to where black lines crept out of the bandages, spreading out like veins. Alesh knew those lines, those scars, for they were identical to the ones which came from the scar on his shoulder, the one which he had carried with him since he was a child, the one which had never healed. "These lines?"

"I see them."

The man nodded. "They are the nightling taint, a poison transferred to their victims from their talons. A poison which will continue to spread until..." He trailed off, and Alesh sat forward.

"Until what?"

The healer met his eyes with an effort. "Until he dies, Chosen."

"No," Alesh said. "No, there must be some way to heal him, some way to..."

"If there is a way," the man said, "then not I, nor any of those others of my profession within the city, know it. I will do what I can for him, Chosen, will keep him as comfortable as I am able—but this man will die."

"But surely there has to be something, or, or someone who can help him."

The healer shook his weary head, shrugging. "The gods, perhaps, for they alone have the power to do such a thing. Now, will you allow me to see to you? Your bandages need to be changed soon, and you should really rest—"

"Later," Alesh said, staring once more at the Ekirani, watching, once more, as his breath rose and fell with his shallow breaths.

The healer sighed. "As you will." Then he turned and disappeared through the curtain and Alesh was once again left alone with the dying Ekirani and his tumultuous thoughts.

The gods alone have the power to do such a thing.

The healer's words echoed in his mind over and over again as he stared at the unconscious figure. But despite his prayers, no gods seemed prepared or able to answer, so he watched and waited...and prayed.

Some time later, the curtain opened again, and he turned to see Katherine and Rion standing in the opening. "Oh, thank the gods you're okay," Katherine said, rushing forward and pulling him into an embrace. "I thought...when you charged off, I thought you were going to get yourself killed."

Alesh felt his face heat in shame at that, for that had been exactly what he'd meant to do before Tarex had shown up, but he said nothing, only accepting the embrace and the warmth she offered despite the pain it brought to his wounds.

Far too quickly, she let him go and backed away. Rion stepped forward, offering him his hand, and Alesh took it. "Seems you're not such an easy man to kill after all," the nobleman said with a small smile.

Alesh glanced at the recumbent form in the bed, thinking that without him, he would have proven the nobleman wrong quickly enough, but he said nothing, could think of nothing to say past the whirlwind of thoughts still raging in his mind.

In his silence, his two friends shifted uncomfortably. "Alesh," Katherine began, "about what I said, on the wall, I mean, I didn't...that is, I wasn't—"

"No, Katherine," he said, shaking his head. "You were right. It seems that I know less and less as the days go on, but I know this much: you were right, and I was wrong."

Katherine nodded slowly. "I...well, we would have been here sooner, but we've been meeting with Captain Nordin, helping get the walls ready if Kale should push the attack from last night, but so far he's seemed content to wait a day and—"

"A day?" Alesh asked, surprised, for surely it could only have been a few hours since they had come here.

Katherine and Rion shared a troubled glance. "Yes," Katherine said, "or nearly so. Night hasn't fallen yet, but it is no more than an hour away."

Alesh frowned, wiping a hand across his eyes. "That...but that can't be right. Malachai was just here a few minutes ago to check on him and..." He trailed off, suddenly unsure.

"That was nearly twelve hours ago, Alesh," Katherine said softly. "We spoke with Malachai ourselves, and he said he hasn't had a chance to come back yet, not with all those he has to look at. He also said that you refused to let his assistants see to you, refused to sleep, too, when he said that's the best way to heal."

Alesh was shaking his head before she was finished. "I can't sleep, Katherine, not yet. Besides, I'm fine."

Rion barked a laugh without humor. "Fine? Gods, man, I've seen steaks that look more alive than you."

"He's right, Alesh," Katherine agreed. "You really need to get some rest. Otherwise..." she hesitated, a worried expression on her face, not finishing but then not needing to.

Otherwise, you might die. He wouldn't though, not now. A day ago—gods, could it really have been so long?—he had thought he would, had hoped for it, but no longer. That made him think of something else, and he cleared his throat, suddenly nervous, perhaps even afraid. "Did...is Sonya with you?"

The two of them shared another troubled look, and it was Katherine who finally spoke, her voice hesitant, full of compassion. "I...I know she wants to see you, Alesh. But...she was afraid and...maybe she was a little angry, too. Darl's with her now, but I'm sure...I—"

"It's okay, Katherine," he said, not really surprised but surprised, at least, by the pain the girl's absence brought. "I understand."

"She loves you, Alesh. I'm sure she'll come see you soon—or maybe you can go see her," she went on, obviously making an effort to make her voice sound lighter, "when you're well."

"Which you won't get unless you sleep and listen to the healers," Rion pointed out with an eyebrow raised.

Katherine nodded. "We need you, Alesh. Captain Nordin is doing the best he can to organize everything, but the mood is grim. It would help even if you could just be seen, if the soldiers—"

"Not right now," Alesh said. "I need to be here." He turned and glanced at Tarex. "With him."

"But *why?*" Rion demanded, clearly frustrated. "Damnit, man, listen to what we're telling you—Valeria is falling apart. The troops morale is so low I can scrape pieces of it off my boots. They all think you're dead or dying and no amount of us telling them otherwise is going to make any difference—they'll think we're just humoring them! The walls are one, maybe two more attacks away from falling, and if *they* fall, Valeria falls, and here you are playing nursemaid to the single man most responsible for it except maybe for Kale Leandrian himself!"

Alesh winced at the man's anger, wishing there was a way to make him understand why he had to stay, to put into words the feeling in him, the certainty that to leave now, to do anything else, was to doom not just himself but everyone. The problem, though, was that he could not even explain it to himself, so he only sighed. "I'm sorry Rion, I really am. But...but I have to be here."

"*Why, damnit?*" the man shouted, before pinching the bridge of his nose between his thumb and forefinger and taking a slow, deep breath in a visible effort to calm himself. "The city is in danger of falling, Alesh. Don't you care?"

"Of course I care," Alesh said. "But—"

"But you're going to stay here and watch this man—our *enemy*—die," the noble interrupted.

Alesh met the man's eyes. "I have to."

Rion made a frustrated noise and threw up his hands. "Forget it," he said, turning to Katherine, "maybe you can talk some sense into him. I've got work to do—at least somebody needs to try to make sure the city doesn't topple like a house of cards the next time Kale decides to attack." And with that, he turned and stormed out of the tent.

Several seconds passed in silence when he was gone, then Katherine met Alesh's eyes. "You're sure? About being here, I mean? Rion wasn't lying, Alesh. The troops...the city is in a bad place. I don't know how much longer we can hold out even if they see you're alive and well. Without you..."

Alesh nodded. "I know." He turned to look at the Ekirani. "He saved me, Katherine. In the tower. The last person in the world I would have expected it from, a man who I've treated like a nightling himself, and he saved me."

"The soldiers said he threw you his sword, one he'd taken from the guards."

"Yes, but that's not what I mean...or, at least, that's not all of it."

"I know," she said softly.

Alesh grunted, surprised. "You do?"

She gave him a small, sad smile. "You're different, somehow. I don't know how but...different. Better, I think?"

Alesh nodded slowly. "I think so. And I'm sorry, Katherine. For everything. I know it isn't enough—maybe nothing can be. But I want you to know it anyway...I'm sorry."

She gave him another smile. "Sorry's good. Sorry's a start." They met each other's gazes for several seconds then, their eyes communicating some bit of how they felt, some of what their words, at least then, could not. Then she sighed. "I have to go...there are things I need to do but...maybe we can talk more later. When you're...done?"

"I'd like that," Alesh said, giving her a tentative smile of his own before turning back to the Ekirani.

"The healer said no man could save him."

"Yes."

"When I was a girl," Katherine said softly, "I used to love butterflies—every little girl does, I suppose. But I loved them for different reasons than most. It wasn't that they were brightly colored, that they were beautiful—although they are—it was the way they changed, the way they transformed themselves from one humble, plain thing to something better, something greater. You're still changing too, I think. Aren't you?"

Alesh was surprised by an unexpected lump in his throat, but he nodded. "Yes," he managed.

She nodded back. "I thought so. Then I'll leave you to it." She started toward the curtain and paused with her hand on it, turning back. "But Alesh?"

"Yes?"

"Don't take too long, okay? The world doesn't wait on butterflies."

Alesh watched her go, trying to grab hold of the storm of thoughts in his mind, but it was like trying to capture the wind in his hands. The city needed him, he knew that much—and not just the city but the world itself, for if Valeria fell, the rest of the world would soon follow. But the Ekirani needed him too. He did not know *how* that was true, had no idea what he could do to help the man, but knew it to be true just the same. Katherine's words came back to him as he looked at the dying Ekirani.

No man can save him.

And then, on the end of that, the healer's words.

Only the gods themselves have such power.

***

Some time during the night he fell into a troubled sleep. It was not a pleasant one. He dreamed of great waves of shadow and crimson crashing against Valeria's walls, crashing with such power that the stone of the battlements cracked and shattered under the pressure of it, and those hapless men and women standing atop them were sent tumbling over a hundred feet below, swallowed by the pit of darkness which lay at the base of the walls, beyond the torchlight.

They screamed as they fell, as they died. They screamed his name, begged for him to help, to stand between them and the Darkness as he had been meant to, but in the dream—as in life—he could offer them no help. His feet would not obey his commands, so he was forced to stand idly by and watch the tragedy occur. He felt movement at either side and turned, surprised to find Sonya standing there.

He swallowed hard. "Sonya, about before, on the walls, I didn't mean—" But the girl was not listening. Instead, she was staring straight ahead at the battlements in the distance as they cracked and broke and rippled like a wall of water. And not just staring but moving toward them, a grim expression on her face.

"Sonya, don't!" he shouted, reaching out for her, but she was beyond his grasp, drifting away. He turned to his other side and saw Katherine walking past him, her gaze, too, locked on the walls. He lunged at her but was brought up short once more by some invisible force inches away from grabbing hold of her. He shouted for her, begged for her to come back, but she ignored him, following Sonya. And soon, it wasn't just them but dozens, all men and women he recognized, those he called friends—Rion and Darl, Odrick the smith, Larin, Marta and Fermin too, all those he had come to care about, marched toward their doom, and he could do nothing to save them.

He woke gasping for breath and covered in a cold, clammy sweat. There was a hand on his shoulder, and Chosen Larin stood beside him. "Oh gods," Alesh rasped, "I must still be dreaming."

The Chosen grunted, looking between Alesh, down at himself, and then at the Ekirani's unconscious form in the bed. "If this is how your dreams look, lad, then you have my pity."

"No," Alesh said, wiping a hand across his dry mouth as he recalled the dream, remembered those faces, many of his friends and loved ones, and their grim, resigned expressions. "No, not this."

The big man nodded slowly. "That bad, huh?"

Alesh opened his mouth to answer, but he could find no words to describe what had been in his dream, to fully encapsulate the black mood, the hopelessness. What's more, he decided that even if he had been able to tell the man of it, he would not have wanted to. Would have been embarrassed, ashamed by it and more than a little scared, the same way a man going to a healer with an unusual rash fears that he might be judged, and fears even more that it might be a symptom of some inner disease which was far worse than he realized, one for which there was no cure.

Larin, though, stared at him with eyes that seemed to see into his silence, to see the truth of his thoughts, and he nodded, a sad expression on his face. "Alashia—gods rest her—used to always say that dreams were the mind's way of trying to communicate with a person, of trying to make them understand something." He shrugged his massive shoulders. "Likely it's true, as Alashia was always clever, wise, too, as wise as Brent, probably. Problem is, I find that my mind, more often than not, if it *is* speaking to me, does it in a language I don't understand a lick of. Though," he went on, meeting Alesh's eyes, "there are those times, those dreams, where

I understand it clearly enough. Tell me, Alesh, what kind was yours?"

Alesh sighed wearily, staring at the Ekirani. Healer Malachai had been by again, some time after Rion and Katherine had left. After examining the tattooed man's body, he'd shaken his head grimly at Alesh, telling him it wouldn't be long now. Alesh was no healer, but even he could see the way the lines were spreading across the man's body, black, sickly veins that seemed intent on swallowing him whole. "Does it matter?" he asked in a voice little more than a whisper. "They're just dreams, whatever they are."

Larin nodded slowly at that. "Perhaps. Funny, though. When the Six were first formed and Brent was our leader, I remember him telling me that he had a dream of uniting the world against the threat of the shadows, of driving them back and giving people a chance to just live, to create a world where people could walk around at night and not risk their lives to do it. A world where a wife's biggest worry was her husband drinking too much at the tavern, or a husband's was that a wife might fill their bed with another man. Real worries, sure, but *human* ones." He leaned forward, still studying Alesh with those eyes that seemed to know so much, watching him in a way that reminded him of Olliman, "Sometimes, Alesh, a man has to dream a thing before he can do it."

Alesh didn't know what to say to that, for if it was true and all of his dreams were dark ones, what did that mean? Nothing good, surely, and he remained in silence until Larin spoke again. "I couldn't help but notice that in the tower, when all those nightlings were attacking, you didn't use your powers."

Alesh froze at that, feeling very tense, feeling like a child who has been caught in a lie. "No," he managed.

Larin scratched at his chin thoughtfully. "I see." Alesh tensed, expecting the Chosen to ask the question he must be thinking, wondering what he would say if he did. Instead, though, he asked him something he did not expect. "You ever thought about what it really means, lad? To be Chosen?"

Alesh frowned. What did it mean to be Chosen? Oh, he'd thought of that often enough. For him, it had meant a great weight settling on his shoulders, in his soul, one that he had found he was not strong enough to bear, not *worthy* to bear. A weight that he thought would have been better suited to someone else—nearly anyone else, in fact. Being Chosen had felt, to him, like some great joke, though not a very funny one.

Larin must have seen some of his thoughts on his face, for he grunted. "We all have, you know, those of us the gods have picked to give some of their powers. And along with those powers, they don't ask much, do they? Just that we save the world and all the people in it, just that we stand up against forces no man or woman should ever be forced to face, just that we do battle with the shadows, walk among them, and are expected, somehow, to not be touched by them, to not become the thing we fight."

Alesh understood what the man spoke of clearly enough, for he had felt much the same. Still did, in some ways. "It isn't fair," he said, and hated the words as soon as they were out of his mouth, for they felt like something a child might say.

Larin, though, did not mock him or laugh as Alesh feared, did not scorn or scold. He only nodded. "You're right. It isn't fair. But then, life isn't fair, is it?"

Alesh frowned deeper. "What do you mean?"

Larin shrugged. "Obvious, isn't it? Some women go their whole lives trying to have children, women who want nothing more than to be a good mother, to care for something, to love it unconditionally and have it love them in return. Yet, those women are sometimes disappointed, finding themselves old and barren and alone while other women have children nearly as quick as they breathe and plenty of them not giving a shit about them, looking at them only as an inconvenience. Not really fair, is it? Or what of a man born small of stature who finds himself bullied by another of much greater size? True, the man might train, might spend his life in practice so that should the bully attack him, he would be ready. But what if that same bully, gifted with natural talents which have eluded the smaller man, has practiced also, though not to protect himself or others but merely so that he can push around any man he wants to? That doesn't seem very fair to me. Does it you?"

Alesh studied the man, and looking into those eyes, eyes without judgement or scorn, he realized that he had been a fool. A fool in a thousand ways and one of those ways was that he had been so busy wrapped up in self-pity, so busy focused on all that he had been forced to endure, all that he had lost, that he hadn't even considered the thousands of others who had it worse. After all, every man, woman and child in Valeria faced the threat of the nightlings, and all of them save himself and a few others were forced to do so without any powers gifted by the gods, were forced, like the smaller man gifted with no natural talents, to stand against a foe far more dangerous than themselves. And yet, those men and women manning the walls did it anyway, as did those healers and thousands of others who had dedicated their time and energy, their goods and coin, to the city's defense. "I've been a fool," he said quietly.

Larin gave him a small smile. "Yes, you have, but you're not alone in that, lad. The gods know I'm the biggest fool of the lot. After all, you're here, aren't you? You didn't choose to run away and hide in the wilderness like some mad hermit."

Alesh found himself meeting the man's eyes, feeling a love for him in that moment, an understanding. "I wanted to die. In the tower, I mean." It was the first time he'd said it aloud, and he found himself inwardly cringing, afraid of what the man might say, afraid that now, faced with the truth, the man would finally scorn him, would call him unworthy.

Larin, though, only nodded. "I know."

Alesh grunted. "You knew?"

The big man barked a laugh. "Sure I did. Gods, lad, the way you been chargin' into battle, you might as well be wearing a sign says, 'Please Kill Me.' Anyway, fact is, you didn't die."

"No," Alesh said, blinking. "No, I didn't."

Larin glanced at the Ekirani. "You still wanting to?"

"No."

Larin shrugged. "Well. That's alright then."

Alesh wasn't sure what reaction he'd expected from the man, but such a casual acceptance certainly hadn't been it. He followed the man's gaze to Tarex and didn't think he imagined the fact that the Ekirani's breathing seemed even more strained than it had only a few hours ago, that his skin was paler. "He saved me," he said, his voice little more than a whisper.

"So that's the reason you're here instead of being on the walls, then? To save him?"

"I...I guess so," Alesh said.

Larin nodded. "Then why haven't you?"

Alesh felt stunned at that and was unsure of what to say. "I...I mean, Malachai said that only the gods could help him. I don't, that is, I can't—"

"The gods, sure," Larin said, "or..." He paused, meeting Alesh's gaze. "Or a man Chosen by them, and not just any of the gods but the father of them all, the most powerful being in the world."

Alesh shook his head. "I want to but...but I don't know how. I can't."

Larin barked a laugh. "Gods, lad, knowing has nothing to do with it. Babies don't know how to walk, but they do it anyway, don't they? They just, well, they grow into it, that's all. And as for can't..." He laughed again. "Seems to me you were an orphan who became a castle servant, a castle servant who became the apprentice of the greatest of all the Chosen, and an apprentice who became not only the leader of the armies of Light but also Amedan's Chosen. All that from an orphan? You ask me, I wouldn't be making any bets on what you can't do."

Alesh found himself thinking over the man's words, lost in them, as if they were some great puzzle he might solve, and in fact he thought they were—a puzzle which, if he *did* solve it, might help bring order to his unruly thoughts. Might shine a light to drive back the shadows still lingering inside him. "But how?" he asked finally in a voice that was more than a little desperate.

"Couldn't tell you," Larin said simply. "My talents have always lain in the shaping and creating of objects—not with people. Our first meeting likely told you as much. Anyway, best I be gettin' on—a thousand things to do and not much time in which to do them."

He started toward the tent flap then paused with his hand on it, turning back. "Whatever you're going to do, lad, best do it quickly—word is, that bastard Kale's marshaling his troops for another attack, the biggest yet."

And with that, he was gone, leaving Alesh alone with the dying man and a thousand questions. Despite everything that he'd seen of Alesh, despite the fact that he knew he'd sought death in the fight with the nightlings, Larin believed in him. Alesh only wished he believed in himself half as much. Still, he promised himself this much—if he failed to save the Ekirani, if he failed to save Valeria, it would not be from lack of trying.

He glanced at the small nightstand on the bed on which a lantern sat, the flame dancing within it. Was it mocking, that flame, as he had thought when his powers had first failed him? Or was it inviting, instead? Alesh reached his hand out, struggling to clear his mind, to banish the doubts and fears and worries that had nagged at him over the past weeks, to find the quiet center of himself. Then, when he thought he had found it or was at least as close as he was going to get, he closed his eyes, slowly tightening his fist.

For a brief moment, he thought he felt the flame answer, could almost see it, through the backs of his eyelids, as it rose from the lantern, drifting toward him like vapor, answering his call, and he began to grin. But when he opened his eyes, he saw that the lantern still sat as it had, the small flame still inside it.

He might have despaired then, but he had despaired enough in the last week. Now, when the armies of Darkness crouched at the city gates and with his friends all depending on him, was not the time to despair. Now, he told himself as he closed his eyes once more, was the time to hope.

Chapter Eleven

Here, on the beach of the small island, with the ocean softly rippling, the sun shining along its blue surface so that it looked like thousands of diamonds sparkling, a person might fool themselves into believing that the world was at peace, that everything would be, *must* be okay. It was a place of quiet contentment, of peace, not a place for fear or worry, not a place for doubt.

And yet, Deitra, the Goddess of Art and Music, did doubt. She worried and, yes, she feared—that most of all. Her father, the most powerful being in the world, knelt only feet away from where she stood staring at the ocean, a fact that, in normal times, would have given her comfort. But these were far from normal times, and she was afraid.

The island upon which they had taken shelter was one never discovered by the race of men, for it lay deep in the ocean, far away from their settlements and while it was peaceful here, the area around it was filled with rough waters and plagued by frequent storms which would have destroyed any mortal vessel far before its inhabitants managed to discover it. The place was remote, untouched, one of the few still-hidden places in the world. After all, it was why her father had chosen it.

For a week now they had remained on this island, incapable of aiding their Chosen, for Shira, the Goddess of the Wilds, Deitra's mother and author of so many recent tragedies, hunted for them without surcease, and it was only by the aid of Deitra's song—a song she sang even now as her thoughts drifted through her mind like fallen leaves carried on a breeze—that they remained beyond her sight.

Normally, such an occurrence would not have been cause for concern, for at his best, Amedan, her father, was easily a match for Shira's own power and could strike her down easily enough, if he so chose. Now, though, her father was far from his best, weakened by Shira's betrayal when she cast him down to the earth during the burning of Ilrika, a time which felt, even to Deitra's immortal mind, like a lifetime ago.

No, her father was weak, tired. As weak and as tired as she had ever seen him and any direct confrontation between the two, at this moment, could only end one way. So, Amedan squandered what little of his power remained to him trying to reach Alesh, to make it past the barriers the man had erected around himself in his despair. As for Deitra—she sang.

She sang despite her weariness, her exhaustion, for it was a song that had carried on for a week, and she was very, very tired. She did not know how much longer she could continue, how much longer the words she wove might carry enough power within them to ward off her mother's ever-searching eyes, but her father was counting on her, and so she had not wavered. At least, not yet.

The time was coming, though, that much she knew, for even as she stood with her back slumped, her hands knotted into fists at her sides, sweat streaming down her face, she could feel herself weakening, could feel the last remnants of her power carried away over her song as it drifted across the lolling ocean currents.

After another moment, the verse she'd been singing, one of concealment, of forgetfulness, was done, and she turned to her father. Amedan's visage and countenance were celebrated the world over, captured in busts and sculptures and paintings. And in each of these, he always looked kind, but also vigorous, determined, the artists attempting to reflect the quiet power which had shaped the world and everything—and everyone—in it. Now, though, she doubted any of those artists or sculptors would have recognized the object of their art, for he looked weary, with lines of exhaustion etched into his face. His head hung low as he knelt on one knee, his hand, planted on the earth, appearing to be the only thing keeping him upright. His skin was pale and waxy like that of a corpse, and when Deitra approached, he did not look up right away, as if he were too tired even to notice.

"Father?"

Slowly he turned, gazing at her with eyes in which she thought she could see a world of pain and exhaustion, some reflection of what he had sacrificed over the last week to try to protect his creation—of what he still sacrificed.

"Daughter," he said, trying a smile which did nothing to hide his weariness.

"I cannot keep this up much longer," Deitra said, resting a hand gently on his shoulder and hating the way he somehow felt frail beneath it. She had always thought of her father as eternal, a pillar of strength and courage and wisdom that would stand forever as a monument to all that was good in the world. Now, though, she was not so sure. "I can't keep it up and neither can you."

"We will continue as long as we must, daughter," he said, "it is the only way."

Deitra felt a flash of annoyance at that. "You spend too much of your power—too much of your*self*—and for what? Your Chosen has abandoned his duties, Father, how can you not see that? He does not answer the call, does not grasp the power you send, and so it is squandered to no purpose. There must be another way; perhaps if we wait, if you give yourself time to heal—"

"Then Valeria will fall to shadow, and the world with it," he said simply. "You know this."

She felt a tear wind its way down her cheek as she stared at him. "Please, Father, do not do this, not anymore. You torture yourself for nothing. Your Chosen does not answer—perhaps he chooses not to, perhaps he cannot. In the end, it makes no difference. If Javen were here—"

"But he is not here," Amedan said in soft, not unkind voice. "Your brother does what he must, looking over the city as best as he may and so we, too, must do what we can. Without our aid, Valeria will fall—you know this."

"The city will fall even *with* our aid!" Deitra said. "And you—*us*—along with it! Please, Father, reconsider. New cities can be built and—"

"No," he said firmly, some of his normal surety and power shining through. "Do not lose faith in men, Deitra. Do not lose faith in me."

She wanted to scream at that, wanted to cry out and give voice to her anger and her grief. "It is *men* who have brought the world to this—if they were not so easily corrupted then mother's schemes would have ended before they had even begun. Even your Chosen has abandoned the mantle you bestowed upon him, refusing the power and gifts you have offered him. They are a selfish, greedy, cruel race and—"

"Yes," her father answered, "they are. But they are also kind and full of a compassion and willingness to sacrifice themselves that is difficult to fathom. They are cowards, yes, but they are also courageous. They are weak, but they are also strong, daughter. Alesh has closed the door against me, yes, but even now, I sense that he struggles to open it again."

"And has he, then?" she demanded. "Has he opened it?"

Amedan sighed. "Some doors, daughter, once closed, are hard to open and some choices, once made, are hard to undo. Yet, I believe in him."

"But *why?*" she demanded. "Even if he *does* manage to open the door—assuming he even *wants* to—likely, it will not be enough. They face too much now—mother has been given too long to grow her armies, too long to plot. No man, Chosen or not, could stand up against such a threat, even if he wished to do so."

"He is not alone, daughter," he said softly. "You know this as well as I."

Deitra gave a weak, weary snort. "A faithless nobleman, a child raised on the streets, a manservant, a warrior without a people, and my own Chosen. These are who you're counting on to save us?"

He gave her a smile. "Yes, and I am confident that they are more than enough."

She shook her head angrily, but her anger was quickly replaced with sadness as she stared at her exhausted father, somehow shrunken by the events of the last months, somehow *less*. "I wish I had some of your confidence," she said quietly.

"I do not have confidence, daughter," he said. "I have hope. Now, will you sing?"

Her breath hitched in her throat, and she gave a shaky sigh. "I will. As long as I can."

"It is all any of us can do."

Chapter Twelve

Sigan sat as he often did, in the back room of his tavern. Or, at least, one of them. He frowned at that. There had been a time—a very recent time, in truth—when he'd sat just so, had an ale, and gloated to himself over his success. Now, though, he felt no satisfaction or contentment, only a vague, gnawing sensation that he should be *doing* something. Even the ale, a mug of which he currently gripped in one hand, had no taste.

Still, he thought, *that doesn't stop a man from trying, does it?* Then he tipped the mug back, taking a long pull of ale. It didn't help. But then, for the last few days, nothing had, and that gnawing sensation had only gotten worse with each day.

There was a knock at the door, and his frown deepened as he stared at it. He turned to Venner, the only person sharing the room with him, the man currently standing with his back propped against the wall beside the door, playing with one of his knives. Not that the bastard ever did much else. "I told those fuckers I didn't want to be disturbed," he growled.

Venner only gave a single nod, watching him with eyes that always struck Sigan as somehow reptilian. Like a snake's eyes, those. Enough to give a man nightmares—at least, that was, if he was the type of man that was inclined to nightmares. Which Sigan was not.

The knock came again and Sigan grunted. "Best you go and remind 'em, tell 'em I don't mean to be disturbed just now."

The man said nothing, only grabbed the handle and started to open the door, his knife, Sigan noted, still clutched in his other hand. "And Venner."

The man turned back, watching him, and Sigan met his eyes. "You don't tell 'em too hard, understand? I don't want to be buryin' any bodies, not today at least."

What might have been disappointment flashed in the man's reptilian gaze—but only for a moment. Then he was out of the door, closing it behind him.

That left Sigan to stare at his half-empty mug of ale, mate to the five others sitting on the tabletop, and wonder why it was that when a man needed to be drunk the most, it seemed like he never could quite get there. A cruel joke of the gods', maybe.

The door opened a moment later and Sigan grunted. "That was quick."

"Oh, I just got lucky with empty streets, I suppose, what with everyone being so worried about the siege and all."

Sigan frowned, looking at the newcomer. An average looking man with very little exceptional about him. Except, that was, his eyes, one the whitest thing he'd ever seen, the other as black as pitch. "You're not Venner."

The newcomer nodded, taking the seat at the other end of the table before lazing back and propping his feet up. "Ah, and there's that clever wit I've heard so much about. Why, it's no wonder that you've risen so highly, Sigan." He smiled, and his white eye seemed to twinkle. "Or should I say, Glenn Albright?"

Sigan frowned deeper, and he rose from the table. "How do you know that name? And where's Venner?"

The man seemed to consider that. "Venner...Venner. Oh, right. Thin, mean looking fellow, seems to like his knives a bit too much? I wouldn't worry about him—by chance, I think he's decided to take a nap."

Sigan grunted. "Known Venner a long time and while you're right about his knives, I've never known him to take a nap."

"Well," the figure said, shrugging. "I suppose there's always a first time, isn't there?"

Sigan moved closer to the man, looming over him. "You ever been strangled to death?"

But unlike anyone else in the city, the man didn't seem put off by the obvious threat. Instead, he only seemed to consider the question before finally shaking his head. "I don't recall that being the case, and I must admit it seems to be the type of thing someone would remember...or well, perhaps not, them being dead and all."

"Well, there's always a first time, isn't there?" Sigan growled, echoing the man's words. "Now, why don't you tell me who you are and why you're here—and best make it quick. I've got a tendency to start lookin' for answers, I don't get them soon enough, and I do most of my lookin' with a knife."

The man raised his eyebrows. "Impressive. The subtle implication, of course, being that you will search for said answers in my flesh."

"Not so subtle."

The man sighed. "No, no I don't suppose it is. Anyway, you might as well let it go. You and I both know you've committed no crime, not since our dear wounded friend Carlen arrived in the city, at any rate. Speaking of...how is Carlen?"

"Better than you're gonna be, you don't start givin' me some damned answers," Sigan said, getting angry now, and that felt good. Better angry than that vague, confused feeling that had been haunting him for days now. He jerked the man up by the front of his tunic, lifting him off the ground so that their faces were only inches apart. "Now," he said through clenched teeth. "Who are you?"

The man met his eyes, and Sigan stared back, feeling strange, as if there was some great abyss lurking there, in the man's gaze, one he might fall into never to return. "Oh, but you know who I am, Sigan...Glenn, or..." the man paused. "Or is it Ernest? You have known since I stepped foot into this room, I think. After all, you are known for not just your kindness, but your cleverness, too, aren't you?"

Sigan let out a hiss, letting the man—the god—go. "Folks in this city know me for a lot of things, godling, but cleverness ain't all that high up, and kindness don't even make the list."

The god took a moment to brush at an invisible speck on his tunic then shrugged. "Well. Perhaps you're right. Still, the truth and what people believe are, at best, distant acquaintances and usually not even that. And I think you are clever enough to know it."

Sigan walked back to his chair and sat. "What do you want, godling?" he asked, suddenly feeling very tired.

"I think you know that as well," the God of Chance answered. "Just as I believe you know, despite the assurances to the contrary which you ply yourself with daily, exactly what that feeling that's been haunting you *is*."

Sigan grunted, then took another big drink of ale. "Don't know what you're talkin' about."

"It won't help you know," the god said softly. "The ale, I mean. And yes, you do know what I'm talking about. The city—*your* city—is being attacked, and yet here you sit, drinking and trying to convince yourself that feeling plaguing you is no more than a bout of indigestion. It's not, though. It's shame, that's all. Believe me, for I know it well."

Sigan grunted again. "What do you know of shame, godling?"

The god gave a small, humorless smile. "You might be surprised what a god can know of it, crime lord. But I have not come so that we might discuss my own faults, and we have not the time even if I had. Tell me, will you not go to the walls, you and your friends? Will you not help?"

Sigan met his eyes, one black and one white, noted the god's earnest expression then gave a snort. "You might not know much about it, godling—you spending your time sittin' on clouds or whatever the fuck you all do, damn sure it ain't lookin' after us. But crime lords, as a general rule, don't play nice with others, particularly when those others are city guardsmen. As for my "friends," well, they are, one and all, criminals. And criminals don't risk their lives to save anyone else—they risk other people's lives. Often, they're the ones doin' the takin'."

"Perhaps," the god said. "And it may be that you are right—Sigan, the crime boss, would not go to the walls and help. But then, Sigan the crime boss would also not be sitting here moping, trying and failing to drink away the feeling of shame overcoming him. As for Glenn Albright, the Torchbearer, well, he'd be on the walls already, wouldn't he? But you are not Sigan, not anymore. Neither are you Glenn Albright, the Torchbearer. You are Ernest, are you not? So what, then, would Ernest do?"

Sigan sat there, thinking. He wanted to tell the god he was wrong, to tell him to fuck off. The problem, though, was that he wasn't. He was right. The man he had been would not have cared at all about those men and women fighting and dying to defend the city. But he *did* care. No matter the justifications he gave himself, no matter the lies he tried to tell. He cared. "And what?" he said. "You tryin' to tell me that what Valeria's defenders need right now is a bunch of men and women who spend their time robbin' and killin' to come save 'em?"

The god met his eyes, his expression serious. "Ernest," he said, "that is *exactly* what they need."

Sigan grunted at that, and for a time the two of them only remained silent, saying nothing. Then, finally, he sighed. "Fuck it. Might be I can go talk to some of the boys, see if they got any death wishes that'd drive 'em to man the walls."

The god smiled at that, his white eye twinkling brightly. "I knew there was a reason why my Chosen likes you."

Sigan frowned again. "We done here? Don't you got god things to be about? Like kickin' your feet up and watchin' everythin' go to shit?"

"I have another meeting, actually," the god said. "I go to see a certain brother who I have not spoken to in some time."

"Well. Here's to hopin' it'll be fun as this little conversation."

Javen sighed. "I doubt that very much, I'm afraid." He walked to the door, opened it, then paused, glancing back. "You will go?"

Sigan grunted. "I'll go, now fuck off. And godling?"

Javen turned back. "Yes?"

"Good luck."

Javen smiled widely at that. "To us both."

Chapter Thirteen

Fermin woke to a hand on his shoulder, shaking him roughly. He opened his eyes groggily, blinking, and saw that Jale stood above him. "Gods, Fur," he said, "I hope you don't mind my sayin' so, but you look like hammered shit."

Fermin worked his tongue—which felt several sizes too big—around in his mouth, then hocked and spat weakly. "Pity the hammer."

Jale snorted at that. "Nice one, but you'd better get up and quickly—Chosen Leandrian himself has called for all the messengers, and we're late as it is."

Fermin felt a thrill of fear at that, one that did more to banish the drunken, sleepy feeling from him than any amount of the cook's terrible coffee could, and he allowed Jale to pull him to his feet. He glanced around and was surprised to find himself lying next to a burned-out campfire. It was early morning, the sun just peeking over the horizon, and a few soldiers milled around, some passed out drunk, while most still slept, the smoke of their dying campfires from the night past drifting into the air in dozens of lazy gray columns.

Jale grunted. "I know that look—had it a few times myself, when I woke up from a night's drinkin' and had no idea where I was or how I got there."

And that was true enough. Indeed, Fermin had no idea how he had ended up here, the night's events a vague blur. He remembered leaving the Tent with the ale Jale had given him, remembered walking out with the intention of finding Marta. But he also vaguely remembered going for a drink only to find his cup empty and deciding that, to make a plan to escape with Marta, he would need what courage the drink provided and so had stopped by a campfire, meaning only to have a sip or two, to prepare himself. After that...there was nothing. He had not found courage after all, only oblivion, and had been thankful for it.

Jale shook his head. "Damn, but you really did a number on yourself, Fur. I'll fix you a tea later, one a friend of mine used to recommend for hangovers—tastes like sewer water, but it'll do you up right. First, though, we'd better get moving—a hangover is bad, but pissing off Chosen Leandrian will be a damned sight worse. So be confused, Fur, but be confused while we walk, eh?"

Fermin gazed around, trying to center himself, to bring some order to his chaotic, drunken thoughts. It wasn't easy, and if there was a center, he could not find it, had lost it some time during the night or maybe before then. Self-loathing, though, that he found easily enough. He had left the Tent so motivated to find Marta, driven to help her any way he could and to get them out of this mess—with Sonya along, if it was at all possible. But somehow, in the few minutes it had taken him to walk away from the Tent, the whole thing had become too big, too much, and he had sought the dubious comfort the ale offered—sought it, and found it.

Still, Jale was looking at him, watching him, and he nodded. "We'd better go."

The walk was not a pleasant one. Fermin spent it hating himself, scolding himself for being a coward and a fool, and doing his best not to puke out his dinner from the night before—one that he suspected consisted exclusively of ale. And being afraid. Since first arriving in the camp and being given the role of messenger by Kale Leandrian himself, Fermin had seen neither him nor the god, Paren, and had counted himself lucky. Now, though, it seemed his luck had run out.

An uncomfortable walk, to be sure, but one he would have extended indefinitely if it meant he didn't have to come face to face with the Chosen and the god—both of whom he thought were bound to see through his charade and easily understand the real reason he'd come—again. But despite his wishes, they arrived at the tent in short order, and Jale paused in front of the four guards stationed there, giving his and Fermin's name and showing their messenger badges.

The men stared at them, and Fermin wasn't sure whether or not he imagined the way their gazes lingered on him as if they wanted nothing more than to pull the swords sheathed at their sides and drive them into his flesh. In the end, though, the commander of the guards only grunted. "You're late."

"Yeah," Jale said, "sorry about that, but—"

"Inside," the commander interrupted as he pulled the tent flap open. "Now."

Jale met his eyes, swallowed, then stepped inside the tent, Fermin following reluctantly behind him. It was the hardest thing he'd ever done for he was convinced that they knew of his deceit already and that he had been called here under the pretext of his role as a messenger to ensure he would walk into a trap. But, if it was a trap, it was an elaborate one, for as he stepped into the tent he saw several other messengers, Pesal, Merrilan, and Calden among them, standing at attention and facing the other end of the tent where a desk stood. As with the first time he was called here, Fermin saw that Kale sat behind the desk and, like the first time, shadows seemed to cling to him. And beside him stood Paren, the God of Conflict, his head only inches away from brushing the top of the tent as he loomed over everyone present.

They all turned as Fermin and Jale entered, and despite the shadows obscuring his features, Fermin could feel Kale Leandrian's anger coming off him in waves as his hooded head rose from several papers he'd been studying on his desk to regard them.

"Forgive us, Chosen," Jale said, "for being—"

But before he could get the rest of the words out, Kale Leandrian suddenly rushed forward with impossible speed, striking him across the face, and Jale's words turned into a cry of surprise as he fell to the ground. *"Silence,"* the Chosen growled down at him, and Fermin felt his breath catch in his throat.

Jale stumbled his way to his feet, blood leaking from his mouth, his lip obviously busted, but he said nothing. Only a foot away from the Chosen, the air felt thick to Fermin, and he was overcome by an unpleasant feeling, as if he were fevered or coming down with something. He wanted to help Jale, to say that it was his own fault, for the man was only late because he had come to find him, but it was all he could do to breathe in and out, all he could do to keep from turning and running from the tent as fast as his legs could carry him. Not that it would have made any difference. No matter how fast he ran, he knew it wouldn't be fast enough to escape the God of Conflict and Shira's Chosen.

He glanced over at Jale, expecting his friend to say something, to point out that he was only late because he'd been gathering Fermin, but he said nothing, only accepting his punishment in silence, and Fermin loved him for that. He tried to risk a glance at him, to meet his eyes in the hopes of conveying some of his guilt and gratitude, but Jale only stood facing forward and in another moment, Fermin gave up the attempt.

Finally, Kale grunted and turned back to walk toward his desk and sit once more, taking with him the air of oppressiveness, and Fermin struggled not to breathe a sigh of relief. "If any of you show up late again, when I have summoned you, you will be long in dying. Do you understand?"

"*Yes, sir,*" they said in unison.

Fermin risked a glance at the god who had remained silent during the exchange. Paren stood with his massive arms crossed in front of him, an almost bored expression on his face.

"Now then," Kale growled, "since the rest of the messengers have decided to grace us with their presence, we can get on to business. I have summoned you all here because, tonight, I intend to finish the threat of Valeria once and for all."

He moved toward the side of the tent where something which appeared the size and height of a wardrobe stood, covered in a large drape of cloth. Kale paused beside it, grabbing a handful of the fabric, and turned back to Fermin and the others. And although he could not see the man's face—the shadows, now, like always, contriving to hide his features—Fermin got the distinct impression that the man was grinning underneath his hood. "One of our pickets on the outer edges of the army discovered a messenger trying to sneak past toward the city, a *Welian* messenger."

With a flourish, Kale pulled the cloth away revealing what wasn't a wardrobe after all but was in fact a small cell. A cell in which a naked figure huddled. A figure which was covered in bruises and scrapes, his back scored from what appeared to be the repeated lashes of a whip, and though the man was a stranger, Fermin felt his heart go out to him. The man trembled, curled up into a wounded, bloody ball, his arms wrapped tightly around his legs, his head buried in his knees. Fermin was also struck with the smell of blood and that, coupled with the terrible state of the man, made his stomach roil threateningly.

Kale, though, seemed to feel nothing but pleasure at the man's current state, turning back to them and speaking with obvious contentment in his voice. "We have since asked him a few polite questions and it seems that the Welian bastards are on their way, meaning to offer aid to the doomed city, and I mean to ensure that they arrive to burned buildings and corpses, nothing more."

Fermin felt a brief flash of hope at that, but it was one tempered with the terrible sight of the messenger, and as Kale spoke on, the hope faded then vanished altogether.

"I will send the full weight of my army at the walls at once. Already, my men are in place, having used the cover of darkness last night to position all around the city. The defenders are weak, afraid, and far too few in number to be everywhere at once, so we will coordinate our strikes so that we attack from all sides at the same time. It will be your jobs, then, to relay my orders to my commanders in the field. Captain Wexler will remain in charge of the troops and so you are all expected"—he paused, his gaze lingering on Jale and Fermin—"to be at the command tent and prepared to do your duty as soon as darkness falls. Am I clear?"

"*Yes, sir,*" they said again in unison.

"And should any of you be tardy this time," he growled, his voice full of menace, "then you cannot fathom the agony you will experience before I allow you to die."

Fermin felt terror roll through him, but not at the man's threat. Instead, he found himself fearing for Eriondrian, for the Lord and Lady Tirinian, and Alesh and all the others. Terror and, of course, a fresh wave of shame.

The people of Valeria had spent the last week risking their lives to defend the city and now, it seemed, the night would bring them no peace, would instead only bring a challenge greater than any they had yet faced, great enough, perhaps, to overwhelm them. Meanwhile, Fermin had done nothing but spend his days carrying messages back and forth like a good slave, his nights selfishly drinking himself into oblivion.

Kale dismissed them with a wave of the hand and he and the others flowed out of the tent eagerly. When they were out of the tent and past the guards, Fermin walked up to Jale, putting a hand on his shoulder. "Thank you," he said.

The man turned to him, running an arm across his mouth and smearing the blood there before giving him a smile that was only half-convincing. "Don't sweat it, buddy. What are friends for? Anyway, I'm going to get some rest—sounds like it's going to be a long night. See you later, huh?"

"Yeah," Fermin said. "See you later."

Jale turned and walked away and Fermin watched him go, thinking.

What are friends for?

Yes, he was a servant, he decided, but he was more than that—Alesh, Katherine, Rion, Marta, Sonya, they *were* his friends, not just his employers, as he had convinced himself over the last days. And what were friends for, if not to watch your back?

He felt terrible, as if he might be ill at any moment, and the only thing he wanted to do just then was to find a nice, quiet, dark place to lie down and fall once more into oblivion, but if he did that, he would be disappointing his friends. Again.

No, let Jale get his rest—Fermin had work to do.

***

Several hours passed before he finally managed to make his way through the sprawled army encampment to where the slave tents had been set up. It should have been an easy enough job, but he'd realized less than an hour into his search that the slave tents were no longer in the same spot they had been when he and Marta had first arrived, and he had been too obsessed with drowning his own sorrows in ale to even have noticed.

By the time he finally saw the tents in the distance, it was early afternoon, and he fancied that he could feel each minute slipping away like sand through an hourglass.

He breathed a relieved sigh and started toward them before freezing realizing that, fool that he was, he'd spent the entire trip here trying to come up with some way of warning Alesh and the others, of helping them, and had given no thought to how he would actually speak to Marta without both of them getting found out. Now, he stood awkwardly, staring at the several guards patrolling the tents, there, he supposed, to make sure that none of the slaves got any crazy notions in their mind—notions like freedom or no longer being someone's property—and chose to make a run for it.

He wanted to turn around then, to accept that he had failed, tuck his tail between his legs and shuffle his way back toward the relative safety of his tent, perhaps have an ale or two to soften the shame he felt. But if he did that, he knew that Alesh and the others would have no warning of what was coming at them, no idea that the Welians were on their way to help, so he took a slow, deep breath, doing his best to banish the fear gripping him. He thought of what Marta had told him when they'd first arrived in the enemy camp, that he would have to lie, that he would have to be clever.

"Excuse me, sir."

"Of course," Fermin said, stepping aside as a soldier passed by him in the small avenue between the staggered tents, then froze as an idea struck him. Kale Leandrian's army had very little organization to it, perhaps unsurprising in a force made up largely of soldiers without any actual training. Unlike many armies, the hierarchy of troops—a hierarchy upon which many forces relied—was largely nonexistent. However, messengers, as a whole, were seen as higher up the army hierarchy than a regular soldier as they were individually more important to Kale and his mission than the soldiers were.

Which meant, theoretically, at least, that Fermin outranked any of those soldiers who were currently patrolling the slave tents. Of course, in an army full of criminals, full of murderers and thieves, there was no guarantee that such a hierarchy would be observed. Still, it was something.

But should he walk up to the soldiers looking nervous and afraid—which, of course, he was—they, like other predators such as wolves, would sense his weakness and pounce upon it. So Fermin took a slow, deep breath, straightening his back and doing his best to ignore the clenching in his gut as he marched toward the nearest guard.

"Soldier."

The guard paused, turning around to look at him. "Yeah?"

Yeah. Not *sir.* It wasn't a good start, but Fermin was too far in now, and there was no way out but forward. *"Yeah?"* he repeated in a demanding voice. "Is that how you address your superior, boy?" he asked, and never mind that the man was at least as old as he was himself.

The soldier frowned, and Fermin thought he could see the man considering whether to accept the rebuke or to challenge him, perhaps drawing the blade at his side and attacking Fermin with it. After all, it would have been far from the first killing that had happened among what were supposed to be allies, and Fermin did his best not to let any of his nervousness show as he stared at the man with a sneer on his own face.

Finally, the moment passed, and the man bowed his head slightly. "Sorry, sir. Didn't see your insignia."

Fermin glanced down at the badge on his shoulder, the one marking him as a messenger, and fought the urge to breathe a heavy sigh of relief, frowning deeper instead. "You blind then, soldier, or just stupid?"

A look of anger flashed across the man's face for a moment, and he opened his mouth to speak, but Fermin beat him to it. "I've come for one of the slaves, a young girl."

"Ah, that right?" the man said, a slow, knowing grin spreading across his face. "And just what might you be wantin' with such a girl? That is, if you don't mind my askin'. *Sir.*"

Every instinct in Fermin's body told him to run then, told him that the man had seen through him, but he knew that to do so would be to doom himself and, worse yet, to doom Marta too. After all, he was honest enough with himself to know that if anyone was able to hold their tongues once the torturers started asking their questions, it was not him.

So instead of running, he raised his nose in what he hoped was an imperious gesture. "What is your name, *soldier?*" he sneered, mimicking the emphasis the man had used.

The soldier suddenly looked uncomfortable. "Don't matter none—"

"Oh, but I think it does," Fermin said, leaning in now, sensing the man's resolve giving way. "You see, Chosen Leandrian is very particular about the way his messengers are treated. I think he'd be most curious to learn that one of his soldiers had chosen to obstruct one's path when said messenger was on a mission given personally by Chosen Leandrian himself." He shrugged as if considering. "Perhaps I'm wrong. What do you think?"

The guard licked his lips, his face going pale. The average man and woman in the army might not have been fully aware of Kale's evil nature, of what he had become, but there were rumors, of course, and those rumors came remarkably close to the truth, rumors which included the wrath the Chosen visited on any—including members of his own army—who got in his way. "T-that won't be necessary, sir," he said, in his voice a note of contrition to replace the one of challenge that had been there moments before. "A young girl, you say?" He nodded slowly. "Well, there's a few of 'em, I guess. Anything you—that is, anything Chosen Leandrian is lookin' for in particular?"

Fermin frowned, confused by the man's question, then he realized what the guard was asking him, and he didn't have to feign the sneer that came onto his face, not this time. "I'm looking for a *specific* little girl."

"Sure," the man said, shrugging, "whatever you like, ain't no business of mine."

"Damnit," Fermin said, "I don't...I wouldn't..." But he saw, staring at the man, that it was pointless. Here, then, was the distinction, if one needed to be found, between the forces of Kale's army and those beleaguered defenders manning the walls of Valeria. This man, this guard, had come to expect the men and women around him, those who were supposed to be his allies, of any possible atrocity. He lived in a world where men in their forties came to slave tents looking for young girls, where such a thing was normal.

Fermin found himself feeling an even greater desperation to warn Alesh and the others, for he did not want to live in a world where old men asking after young girls was acceptable, where everyone saw only the shadows in each other and none of the light. Where there was only darkness. "Forget it," he said, knowing there was no changing the guard's mind. "I'm looking for a girl around twelve years of age..." He went on to describe Marta in detail, the guard listening, his eyes growing slowly wider as he did.

When Fermin was finished, the guard grunted. "Real specific on what you're lookin' for, sir."

Well, I would be, wouldn't I, Fermin thought angrily, *since I'm looking for a specific person.* He didn't bother saying so though, only nodded. "Yes."

The guard nodded thoughtfully. "Might be I've seen such a one wanderin' around the tents. A slight thing, she is, a bit of a waif, if I'm bein' honest. Matter of fact, sir, you don't mind my sayin' so, why don't I show you some other of the...*goods* we have on offer, eh? Might be I can find you somethin' a damn sight better than that mite of a thing. Someone's got a little meat on their bones, maybe."

"In fact, I *do* mind," Fermin managed through gritted teeth. "Just find me the girl I asked for."

"Sure, okay," the man said, "take it easy, alright?" He glanced around thoughtfully at the tents. "Can't remember exactly which one she's in. I'll fetch her, but it might be a few minutes. That alright?"

"Fine."

***

The rest of the slaves in the tent were asleep or doing a fine job of pretending to be at any rate. Marta, though, had no such luck. It wasn't that she wasn't tired—in fact, she was exhausted from a day spent washing clothes and helping the cooks prepare what could only loosely be described as food for the army's soldiers. She was also sore in places she had never been sore before never mind that she had spent more than a few nights of her life sleeping in one of Valeria's hard-cobbled alleyways.

She had always thought it was ridiculous when she'd heard the housewives in the common quarter complaining about being sore from cleaning their house or washing their clothes, had always wanted to ask them how they thought it would be if they owned no house to clean and the only clothes they possessed were the ones—tattered and frayed and with few days left in them—currently adorning their person. Now, though, she was beginning to feel a bit of sympathy, for her own lower back ached from hours spent bent over at washing, and her hands were calloused and blistered from the scalding water—and scalding pots—in the cooks' tent.

All in all, she felt pretty wretched, likely the most wretched she'd felt since arriving at the enemy cam—and the memory of Alcer's visit the day before did nothing to console her. After all, the god had told her no plan, given her no idea of what she should be doing, instead seeming under the assumption—a very dangerous, very *wrong* assumption—that she already knew. No, she felt terrible, the lowest she had felt since coming to the camp and, considering what she'd been through since arriving, that was saying something, and what it was saying was not a good thing.

The word despair came to mind, but she fought it down with an effort. Despair was a luxury for other people, for noblewomen worried the tailor wouldn't be done with their new dress in time for the ball or for noble fathers concerned that their philandering sons would never find good brides. It was not something a slave girl from the enemy army could afford.

And yet, it was there, crowding her thoughts, making it difficult to see a way clear of her situation. The only escape she could see was the temporary oblivion which sleep might provide, yet as tired as she was, she was also scared, filled with a nervous, restless energy and so even that simple pleasure was denied her.

So she lay there in her itchy straw cot, fighting the urge to scratch—for each itch she scratched only seemed to birth three more—missing those relatively simple, carefree days of growing up on streets full of muggers and murderers and worse. She lay and listened to the sounds of the others breathing in their sleep, wishing she could join them but knowing that she would not, not, at least, until after several hours of tossing and turning. And worrying. That most of all.

She was so engrossed in the problems before her—all of which seemed largely unsolvable—that she didn't notice someone approach until she felt a hand on her shoulder. She choked down a scream, spinning to the side to find a vaguely hunched form which she could not identify in the darkness. At first she thought it was the woman from before, the old woman who had threatened to eat her, but then the figure leaned in closer, and she choked off a scream as she realized it wasn't the old woman after all, but a different old woman, Llanivere.

Llanivere must have seen some of the terror in Marta's face, for she gave a small smile. "Sorry, love. Didn't mean to frighten you, though I suppose if I was confronted with a face like mine in the dark of night I'd want to scream too," she said, a humorous note to her voice as if she was holding back a laugh.

"I-it's not that," Marta said. "I...that is, you're lovely."

The old woman gave a soft snort. "Been a long time since anyone could ever call me lovely with a straight face, little one. I'm a far way past my prime, that's the truth, and the fact of the matter is I was no great prize even then. Still, I appreciate your sayin' so."

"My mother used to say that there were a lot of different kinds of beauty," Marta said, "the temporary kind that resides on the outside, changing as easily as the seasons, and the inside kind, the kind that lasts." A lie, of course, for Marta had no mother, at least none that she knew. Still, it seemed the type of thing a mother would say, if she'd had one. But either she was out of practice, or the old woman was particularly keen at telling lies from the truth, for she gave a knowing smile, as if she recognized the lie for what it was.

"Well," the Llanivere said, "she sounds like a sweet woman, your mother. A shame the world doesn't look particularly kindly on sweetness, I suppose."

"And what *does* it look kindly on?" Marta said, surprised by the desperation, by the frustration in her own voice.

The old woman winked. "I find out, I'll let you know. Anyway, I hope I'm not botherin' you. Just thought I'd come pay you a visit, what with you not sleeping and all."

Marta frowned. "How did you know I wasn't asleep? Were you...I mean..."

Llanivere gave a soft laugh. "Spying on you? Oh, nothing so provocative as that. I simply don't sleep much myself—being old, you understand—and so I spend most nights listening to others sleeping. I could just tell you were awake, that's all."

"I see..." Marta said, not sure what was expected of her. "Well..."

"And now, you're wondering why an old hag like myself is bothering you while you're...well, not sleeping, eh?"

Marta remembered all too well how the woman had helped her with Greta and the other slaves, and the last thing she wanted to do was offend her. She shook her head. "No, it isn't that, ma'am, I just—"

"Please, gods, not 'ma'am,' young one," the woman said. "Makes my old bones ache just to hear it."

"Sorry," Marta said, "what I mean, Llanivere, is that I didn't know if you needed something or—"

"Llanivere is dead and gone," the woman said, "the woman who wore that name was an altogether different sort than the one you see before you now. A bitch, if you want to know the truth, one who didn't care about anybody but herself."

"So...what should I call you?"

The woman gave a wry smile. "Hag doesn't work for you?"

Marta felt her cheeks flush at that, and the old woman gave another soft laugh. "Oh, relax, child. Llany will do me fine. Better than 'slave' anyway, isn't it?"

"Yes," Marta managed. "Yes, it is. So...what can I do for you Llaniv—Llany?"

The old woman considered that for a moment then leaned in, speaking in a tone barely loud enough for Marta to hear despite her being only inches away. "I'm thinkin', love, that it's more about what I can do for you. You and your messenger friend."

Marta's breath caught in her chest at that, for she and Fermin had been careful to avoid any unnecessary contact, hoping no one would link the two of them together. Up until that moment, she had been sure they'd been successful, but it seemed that she had failed in even that much. "Llany, I'm not sure what you mean. Messenger? I don't—"

"Save it, love," the woman said. "And relax—you're pale as a ghost. I'm not going to tattle, if that's what you're frightened about. The gods know the woman Llanivere might have, but then, as I've said, that woman's dead and gone. The woman I am now wouldn't tell on you for anything, even if she didn't quail at the thought of the steps it would take—and the aches and pains in her knees she'd feel—if she took it in mind to go traipsing out into the camp looking for a guard to tattle *to.* No, lass, I know about you and the messenger, saw the two of you come into camp. Just as I know"— she paused, glancing around at the shadowed forms where the other slaves lay sleeping before leaning in closer still, so that her lips were nearly touching Marta's ear—"that you are not a slave. That, in fact, you have come from a very particular city."

Marta froze, fighting the urge to jump out of the cot and run. Running had saved her before, too many times to count, but she didn't think it would do any good, not this time. If Llanivere took it in mind to tell the guards that Marta was an impostor, to tell them about her and Fermin's relationship, then she wouldn't be fast enough to outrun an entire enemy camp, and that was before one factored in the nightlings. She'd be caught, likely killed, long before she made it even halfway back to Valeria. *Besides,* another part of her, the part which had grown up on the streets, the survivor, thought, *if she had wanted to tell the guards, she already would have instead of coming up to you in the middle of the night.*

So, then, the woman had come to bargain, and had shown Marta her hand so that she knew exactly where she stood. No use denying it—it was clear the woman knew the truth. The only thing now was to discover what, exactly, they were bargaining *for.* "What do you want?" she asked, unable to keep all of the anger, the fear out of her voice.

The woman seemed to consider that for a moment. Then, "Llanivere's a rather fancy name for a slave don't you think?"

Marta frowned, not sure where this was going. "I guess?"

The woman nodded. "A fancy name, the kind noble parents might bestow on their child. Which, in fact, they did."

"Wait a minute," Marta said, blinking, and surprised despite herself. She had met many noblewomen in her time—most often when she was begging them for enough money to buy some moldy bread to eat—and from her way of speaking and her bearing, not to mention the fact that she was currently a slave, she would not have taken the other woman for one. "Are you saying you're a noble?"

The old lady smiled, her eyes twinkling in the near-darkness. "Perhaps it's better to say I *was* a noblewoman. But that was a lifetime ago now. Oh yes, I was born into a very wealthy family with very handsome prospects. My parents were middle-aged when they had me, and I must admit that they spoiled me terribly so that all I had to do is reach out my hand and could rest assured that whatever it was that I wanted—dresses and face paints and other frivolous things, mostly—would be placed there in short order."

"Sounds nice," Marta said, because it seemed that she was supposed to say something.

"It does, doesn't it?" Llanivere said. "And maybe for some people it even would be. But for me, dear Marta, it spelled ruin. I can't speak for everyone else, understand, but in my case, being given everything I wanted only made me want more. Do you understand?"

Marta didn't understand about dresses and shoes, about balls and courtly manners, but she thought she understood that much. After all, it had been much the same for her, when scratching a life out for herself on the street, thankful for the moldy half-loaf of bread, sure, but always wishing it was a full one, maybe with a touch less mold on it too. "I...think so."

Llanivere smiled. "You are wise beyond your years, love. Has anyone ever told you that?"

"Maybe," Marta said, "but I don't feel particularly wise."

"The wise never do," the old woman said simply, "while fools, in my experience, feel nothing else. Certainly I thought I was wise, preening and batting my eyelashes at men who smiled and flirted only because of my parents' money. A useless, wasted existence, but it was, at least, an easy one, though I didn't know it at the time."

Despite the many worries and fears roiling through her mind, Marta found herself curious. "So...what happened?"

The old woman shrugged. "Life, I suppose. Though, it is probably more accurate to say that *I* happened. As I've told you, my mother and father doted on me, their only child, and would have done anything for me. Instead of being grateful, I always asked for more, *expected* more. Clothes and dresses, sure, but not just that. It came to a point where I expected more from everyone, expected them to be slaves to my every whim." She shook her head. "Ironic, then, that I should end up a slave myself, in the end."

She smiled. "Ah," she went on, "I can see by your face that I have still not answered your question. Very well, though it shames me to remember it—even more to say it, I suspect. But I deserve far more than shame for my crimes, that much is sure. As for the crimes themselves, well, it is enough to know that while my parents' fortune was vast, it was not infinite. Not enough even, as it turned out, to satisfy a willful, ignorant young woman who thought the world should—and did—belong to her. So I bought on credit and bought on credit from this store and that, dresses I never wore, shoes I never even took out of the packaging, all the while ignoring my parents' soft words when they tried to explain our situation to explain, too, that father's business had not been doing well for some time, and that money was growing tighter. 'We have to be careful, love,' they told me, 'we have to be frugal.' And what, young Marta, do you think that selfish young woman did?"

"Ignored them?"

The woman gave a soft laugh. "If only. No, I was far worse than that. Instead of heeding my parents' advice—or even ignoring it—I chose to take it as a challenge. Instead of lowering my spending, I increased it two-fold, three-fold, each handbag or bit of jewelry assuring me that all was right with the world and that I was being treated to the lifestyle I deserved. This went on and on, my parents' pleas, my spending, until there was nowhere in the city which would sell to me on credit any longer, until shopkeepers locked their doors at my approach, eager to avoid the scene I would cause."

She paused, and Marta thought she saw what might have been tears gathering in her eyes. "I saw those shopkeepers soon enough, though. Or, at least, I saw the men they sent. Big men, mostly, with hard, cold eyes, ones who seemed completely unaware of the amount of respect, no, *admiration* I thought I deserved. My father and mother did what they could—they always did, you see. They sold what they could, not my belongings, of course, for even then I wouldn't hear of it, but of their own, until they both wore little better than rags while I walked around in my fancy dresses and face paint and scolded them for letting my life come to such a point. You see, even then I didn't understand what was happening, not really, just assumed that what we faced was no more than a minor upset to my way of life, and that any day now the universe would realize my true worth and right itself in my favor."

Marta frowned. "I know something of the universe...don't seem to me it does that too often."

"You see?" the woman asked. "You *are* wise, no matter what you may think. And, as it happens, you are correct. The universe most certainly did *not* right itself in my favor, and even after my mother and father had sold nearly everything they owned, it was not enough, nowhere near enough, in fact. The creditors continued to come, my father begged and pleaded, told them that business would pick up, was *bound* to."

"But it didn't?"

"No," the woman said softly. "No, it didn't. And eventually, the men who came were no longer satisfied only to use words. One night—I was asleep in my fancy bed with my expensive sheets and quilts—they came, and this time they did not knock. They chose instead the expedient of breaking the door down. I heard my mother scream, heard my father shout as he was jerked out of bed. I, though, remained in my room with the door locked, well and truly frightened—perhaps for the first time in my life. I sat against the bed, weeping silently, not fearing for my father, for as I said I was a selfish creature who cared only for herself, but fearing that those men might come into my room, might break the door down and find me in my night clothes and, finding me so, feared what they might do. But they did not come into my room, not that night, at least. Instead they only beat my father to death as I listened, as my mother screamed."

The woman paused then and Marta let go a breath she hadn't realized she'd been holding. "Gods, Llany. I'm so sorry."

The old woman barely seemed to hear her, so absorbed by the memories of that time long past. "My mother killed herself that night," she said in a voice so soft Marta could barely hear it, "after the men left. By the time I'd gathered up the courage to leave my room, they were both dead. Perhaps my father put up a fight—perhaps they both did—but while they were kind, my parents, they were not strong."

"What...what did you do?"

"The same thing I ever did," Llanivere answered. "Nothing. I only remained in that shell of a home, the broken bodies of my parents still dead on the floor and felt sorry for myself. The next day, the men came back and found me." She heaved a heavy sigh. "I have been a slave ever since, have been forced to endure things that spoiled child could never have even imagined and, in many ways, I think I am even better for it."

Marta blinked, unsure of what to say. She had always envied the noblewomen their lives, always mocked them—never to their faces, of course—for their frivolous purchases, for all the gifts their lives had given them without them having to earn them. She realized now that she had never paused to consider that while money could be a blessing, it could also be a curse. And here, then, was a victim of that curse. "I'm very sorry, Llany."

The woman waved a hand dismissively. "It was a long time ago. Do not pity me for my struggles, for I brought this doom upon myself. My only regret is that my parents were made to suffer for my sins. Still," she said, after pausing to wipe a tear from her eye, "there is nothing to be done—nothing, that is, except to try to do better, to *be* better. Anyway..." She sniffled. "I do not tell you this for pity. I tell you instead to make you understand. You asked me, before, what I wanted, and now I will tell you. I want to help."

Marta blinked. "Help?"

"Yes. This army is an evil thing, Marta. Perhaps one needs to have been evil to know it when one sees it, but I know it clearly enough. I see it. And I know that you and your friend have come to do something about it, though what that something is I am still not clear on. I have lived a bad life, Marta, a selfish, evil life, and I do not kid myself that there is not much left to me. I only want to do something good before the end, to feel the light on my face once more. Do you understand?"

Marta nodded. "I understand. But...how do you know? About me and Fermin, I mean. How could you?"

The woman shrugged. "No great trick, that. I saw the two of you come into the camp, that's all. Just a bit of happy luck or maybe it is the gods giving me this final chance to redeem myself. Who knows?" She grinned, leaning forward. "But then, maybe you do. After all"—she paused, glancing around to make sure no one was listening—"you are one of their Chosen, are you not?"

Marta grunted in surprise, and the woman laughed again. "Oh yes, I know that, too. I saw you, when you spoke with him. Alcer, unless I miss my guess."

Marta was at a loss for words as she studied the old, unassuming woman. "I thought...but no one else—"

"Noticed?" Llanivere smiled, nodding. "If you live the life I have, love, you learn to pay attention, to notice the things others wouldn't. Besides, I'm a slave, aren't I? And slaves learn to pay attention—it's the best way to keep from angering your master and being beaten. Not a guarantee, of course, for sometimes there is nothing to do but take the beating and move on. Still, it helps. You and your man have done an admirable job of hiding it but, well, I was ignorant, as a youth, and I promised myself I would never be so again."

"So...what do you know?"

The old woman shrugged. "Only what I've told you, little else. But I know that you and your friend have come here for a reason, and whatever that reason is, I don't expect that Kale Leandrian or that big-shouldered god would like it very much, would they?"

Marta could have lied—the gods know she'd done it before—but she didn't want to. For one, she thought that this woman would know a lie the moment she heard it but, more than that, she found that she didn't *want* to lie to Llanivere. The woman had been nothing but honest with her, direct in a way so very few people were, and she wanted to show her the same respect if she could. So instead, she shook her head. "No. No, they would not."

"I thought as much," the old woman said, nodding. "Well, as I've said, I'd like to help."

"I don't know if anyone can help me," Marta said, allowing herself, in that moment, with this woman who felt like the sweet grandmother she'd never had, to show, to herself and another some small part of her despair. "I came here for a reason, to save my friend, Sonya, who was taken. But I haven't been able to find her, have barely looked."

"Oh, you'd be surprised what help an old woman can be," Llanivere said, patting Marta gently on the shoulder. Marta hadn't had a lot of gentle touches in her life, and she found herself feeling better, even before the woman spoke on. "In fact," she continued, "I might be able to help you just now. The girl, the one you came looking for, how old is she?"

Marta sighed. "Six, I think. Or...seven? She's young. Just a kid."

Llanivere smiled. "I see. Well, I can tell you with some confidence that your friend is not here anymore."

Marta felt her breath catch in her throat. *Oh gods, no.* She'd feared it, of course, since coming to this place. Had wondered what chance there was that the Broken and Kale would keep Sonya alive once she had served her purpose, whatever purpose that might be. "You don't...I mean, she was just a child. They didn't—"

"No, no, dear," Llanivere said, waving a hand in dismissal, "it's nothing like that. Only, the little girl left. Escaped with that Ekirani fellow, if you can believe it, the one as calls himself the Broken."

Marta frowned. She'd heard some mention, of course, of the Broken leaving the army. Specifically why, or what had occurred, though, she didn't know. It wasn't difficult to *get* specifics in an army camp—the problem was getting far too many different, conflicting specifics so that a person had no idea what was the truth and what an invention of some soldier trying to impress his fellows. "Why, though?" she asked.

Llanivere shrugged. "I'm sure I couldn't say. I only know that they left together—she not his prisoner, I don't think, but his fellow fugitive."

Marta felt her face heat with shame. She felt like a fool. Here she had come to save Sonya, thinking herself capable of it, and not only had she not found the girl, she hadn't even so much as known that she'd left the camp. "Gods, I'm an idiot," she said.

"No, dear, not an idiot," Llanivere said, patting Marta's hand. "A very wise young woman who was very brave to come here searching for her friend."

"Lot of good it did," Marta said, knowing she sounded sulky but unable to help herself.

"Well, it's not over yet, is it?" Llanivere said. "Might be, there's still some good you can do here. As for your friend, I'm sure she's fine. I don't know much, but everyone in the camp knows that that Ekirani isn't the sort to be trifled with. Why, I wouldn't be surprised if he they made it away without incident, who knows, perhaps even to Valeria itself. Now, about—"

The old lady cut off at the sound of a man's voice from outside the tent, accompanied by the light of a lantern which outlined two forms moving toward the tent flap. "Think it's this one here, sir. She's young, like you said, seems to be what you're lookin' for."

Young. What you're looking for. Marta felt a thrill of fear run through her at those words, for she was by far the youngest slave in the tent, all the others being grown women, and it didn't take long for a girl who'd grown up on the streets to figure why a man would appear in the middle of the night searching for a young girl.

A moment later, one of the guards assigned to the slave tents stepped through the flap, followed by a second figure still hidden from view by the guard's form. The guard glanced around the tent at the sleeping forms, some of which were beginning to stir in the lantern light, with a perverse grin, something about his manner reminding Marta of a man at market, shopping for livestock. Finally, his eyes settled on her, and his grin widened. "You, Witless, isn't it? Get your ass over here. Now."

Marta was not often afraid. Or perhaps it was that she was *always* afraid, a product of growing up as she had, so that normally she could operate within that fear, was used to it, at least as much as someone could *be* used to such a thing. Now, though, she felt that subtle undercurrent of fear that always thrummed within her rise to a frenetic pitch. She had dodged such men as this before, had always escaped their clutches. Not all of those other children she'd known on the streets had, and those few who she saw again—often, those who were taken vanished without a trace—always seemed as if they had partly died inside, as if some vital piece of them had been carved away somewhere out there in the darkness.

So while she knew the guardsman would punish her for her insolence, she did not—*could not*—move. "You heard me, you little bitch," the guard growled. "If I have to come get you, I promise it'll be a damned sight worse."

Marta was looking for words, trying to find some way out of this, when Llanivere stepped in front of her, the old woman putting her hands on her hips. "I'll be thankin' you for leavin' the girl alone. We've had a long day of work with another ahead of us. We need our rest, and ain't none of us got time to be gallivantin' off in the night with some stranger comes callin'. 'Less you want to haul yourself out there tomorrow and go pickin' around the dead and dyin'.'"

The guardsman sneered. "Sit down, you old bag, before I sit you down."

Llanivere did not though, only stood her ground, and Marta loved her for that. For the guard, though, it had the opposite effect, and with a growl he marched forward, his hand already raised in preparation of a slap. Just when it looked as if he were about to hit the old woman, the second figure—who'd been hidden in the shadows behind the man and who Marta had largely forgotten about—stepped forward and caught his wrist. "That will be enough, guardsman."

To Marta, the guard looked as if he were just getting started. He turned with a growl. "Ain't no concern of yours, sir. It's my job, mine and the others, to watch the slaves, make sure they don't start gettin' mouthy, start thinkin' they can do what they want. Sometimes, they get out of line, you gotta give 'em a bit of a beatin', set 'em back right again. No different'n the way you might take a switch to a hound, it starts pissin' on the floor."

"They aren't animals," the newcomer said, and although he was still blocked from view by the guardsman, there was something familiar about his voice. "They're people."

"Yeah?" the guard sneered. "Some of 'em even children, ain't that right? As I said, my job—"

"Your *job*," the authoritative voice said, "is to keep your damned mouth shut and do exactly what I tell you when I tell you to do it. And what I'm telling you to do now, is get out of my way."

The voice was strong, powerful, sounding like the voice of a king demanding his rightful due from one of his subjects, and the guardsman complied immediately, stepping to the side. Marta couldn't blame him—with such a voice, she would have done the same. She expected to see Paren standing there, or Kale or perhaps some other high-ranking army official, for only those with great power, in her experience, had mastered such a tone as the one the newcomer had used. She was more than a little surprised, then, to find that the visitor wore the simple uniform of an army messenger. Was even *more* surprised, when the figure stepped forward enough that his face was revealed in the lantern light, and she realized with a shock that it was Fermin.

At least, she thought it was Fermin, but there was such an authoritative expression on his face, an almost imperceptible sneer that looked so strange that Marta began to think she'd been imagining things after all. His eyes traveled between Marta and Llanivere with a cold disregard that reinforced the idea that this was not, *could not* be the manservant, no matter how much it might look like him. The newcomer studied them for a moment then turned back to the guard, glancing at him as if surprised he were still there. "You may leave now."

"But sir—"

"Leave," the newcomer growled. "Now."

"She got to be back by mornin'," the guard said in an unmistakably sullen voice, then he turned and walked out.

"F-Fermin?" Marta asked, anxious despite herself. "How did y—"

"Shut up, slave," the man growled, meeting her eyes pointedly then glancing behind her. Marta followed his gaze and realized that nearly all of the slave girls had sat up in bed now—no surprise, as past, often painful experience had taught them that when someone speaks with such a tone, they'd better be ready to obey quickly or be slapped just as quick. They were all watching her and the newcomer, and she realized how foolish she'd just been, speaking to him as if they were friends instead of he a cruel soldier and she a cowering slave. Which, she had to admit, he was doing a fine job of pretending to be just then.

"F-forgive me, sir," she said, licking her lips, surprised to find that she was nervous. She had often thought of the manservant as a sort of fumbling, silly man, kindhearted but clumsy to the point of hilarity. But there was nothing silly or fumbling about him now as he studied her with a look of pure disgust on his face. Terrifying, maybe, but certainly not silly.

"Damn your apology," he spat. "Now, come with me."

Marta swallowed, glancing back at Llanivere and at the other slaves before following him. She did not have to feign the anxiety she felt, for this man seemed far removed from the manservant she knew, did not seem like the same person at all.

Outside, the darkness was lit by dozens of blazes while soldiers sat and drank outside their tents. Marta noted the guard who'd escorted Fermin a short distance away, a frown on his face as he spoke to another of his number, and it didn't take a genius to figure out what he was talking about. But if Fermin was bothered by it, he didn't show it.

"Fermin," Marta said in a whisper, "you've really—"

"Not here," he said quietly. Then, louder, "This way, slave," he growled as he grabbed her by the arm and practically dragged her after him as he marched further into the army camp.

Marta resisted the urge to talk, to ask him if everything was alright, if for no other reason than to make sure that this *was*

Fermin, not some man who shared characteristics with him, for surely there was nothing about the way he acted that was similar at all to the manservant, and she felt a stab of fear as he started leading her toward a small tent, practically dragging her sliding across the ground.

"Fermin," she said, close to panic now, "what's wro—"

He ignored her though, throwing the tent flap aside and giving her a rough shove so that she lost her balance and nearly fell. A moment later, he stepped inside, closing the flap. "Fermin," she said, "look, I don't know what I did, but—"

"Oh, but it is good to see you again, Lady Marta," the manservant said, and he was no longer the angry, authoritative—and more than a little frightening—man he had been moments before. Now, he was only Fermin again, a sweet, gentle man who she would have laid odds was incapable of intimidating a lady bug, let alone one of the guards. "Sorry," he said, "about..." He paused, waving a hand. "You know, all that. I just didn't want—" But he never got a chance to finish what he was going to say.

Before he knew it—before *Marta* knew it, come to that—she had lunged across the intervening space between them and pulled him into a tight embrace. The manservant grunted in a surprise to match her own, but a moment later was hugging her back, just as tightly. "Gods, but I've missed you, Fermin," she said.

"And I you," he said in that soft voice, the one that she had always thought didn't really belong on a man his age, perhaps one twenty or thirty years older, but one that she hadn't realized how much she'd missed until she'd heard it again.

Then she was crying, with no idea why or no idea where the tears had come from, wetting his shirt where she'd buried her head in his chest. "I'm s-sorry," she said, sobbing quietly, and with just as little idea as to what, exactly, she was sorry for, only that she was. For bringing him along, perhaps, for just trying to survive and not searching for Sonya, she did not know for sure, only that she was.

"No," he said, running a hand over her hair and the gentle touch was almost enough to set off the sobs again, "I am sorry, Lady Marta," he went on in a low, tortured voice. "I have...the things I've seen, the things I've *done,* I haven't—"

"No, Fermin," she said, stepping back and meeting his eyes, surprised to find tears gliding their way down his own cheeks. "No. Let's not talk about what we've done or not done, okay? Please."

He let out a watery, shaky sigh and nodded. "Very well. But I am still sorry, for the way I acted. I had to find some pretense to get you alone." His face flushed. "I am quite ashamed of what the guards and the other soldiers must think, what the women in your tent must think. It is abominable and—"

"Damn what they think," Marta said, surprised at the feeling, the anger in her voice. "Listen, Fermin, about Sonya—"

He winced, turning away, and she was sad to feel his hands go away from where they had gripped her shoulders, sad to lose that small comfort. "Lady Marta, I know you said not to speak of it, but I fear I have been a fool and a coward, too. I have barely even begun to sear—"

"She's not here," Marta said.

The manservant turned back to her, a surprised expression on his face. "What?"

"She's gone already, gone with the Broken, if you can believe that. They both escaped."

Fermin's face twisted in an incredulous expression. "With the Broken? But why—"

Marta was shaking her head before he was finished. "I don't know why, only that they have. From what I've heard, the Broken is no longer following Shira and for some reason he took Sonya with him."

"Hoy there, you bastard!"

Marta and Fermin both spun toward the tent flap from where a voice had come. By the light of the lantern Fermin held, she could make out a man's outline through the canvas. She tensed, unsure of what to do, what she would say, when the man stepped inside.

"Save some of that drink for me, eh?" the man asked, and then instead of coming into the tent, he stepped away, no doubt heading toward one of the nearby campfires.

They both let out a ragged sigh, and Fermin turned back, his face pale and looking as scared as Marta felt. "We don't have much time, Lady Marta. I came to tell you—Kale called all the messengers to his tent earlier. He's planning an attack on Valeria today, the worst yet, but that's not all. Apparently, the Welians will soon land and—"

"The Welians?" Marta asked. She had heard of the Welians, of course, but knew little of them other than that they made fine wine and were said to be the richest country in the world. "But why are they coming? Gods, the last thing we need is another enemy to fight—"

"Not enemy," Fermin interrupted quietly, glancing behind him at the tent flap before going on. "According to Kale, the Welians have come to help us—that is, to help Valeria."

Marta's eyes went wide and she felt the despair which had settled in her begin to shift as hope, or something very much like it, kindled inside her. Over the last weeks, she had grown increasingly sure that there was simply no way Alesh and the others could win, that there were far too many who had chosen the Darkness for them to hope to stand against them. But the Welians were rich and were said, she'd heard, to possess an ample army of skilled mercenaries. With their help, it wasn't outrageous to think that they could actually win.

"But...where are they landing?"

"That's the problem," Fermin said. "I don't know. Kale didn't say."

"Damn," Marta said, the flame of her hope flickering. Flickering, yes, but not gone out, not yet. "We have to find out more, to figure out exactly where they're landing or when." She grunted. "Perhaps Alesh and the others will know, will have gotten news or—"

"No," Fermin said, shaking his head sadly. "I don't think so. Kale's commander in the field—Captain Wexler—has the entire city surrounded. A messenger was sent, but he was caught, was in Kale's tent and..." He swallowed hard, growing paler still. "He has been ill-used, Lady Marta."

"Damn," Marta said again with feeling. "Well, surely this man would know something. We have to find a way to talk to him, to get him out of Kale's tent."

Fermin winced. "Actually, I think I may have an idea of how to do that."

Marta grinned. "Well, that's great! Why are you looking like you just ate something that had gone off, then? All we have to do is get to him out, find out what he knows and—"

"And I know a way we may be able to do that," Fermin said, wincing, "but..."

Marta felt a sinking feeling in the pit of her stomach. "But what?"

"Eriondrian told me about many of your adventures," Fermin said softly. "About...some of the things you were all able to do. He spoke of one particularly pertinent detail, one in which you used your...powers to hide yourself and the others from the Broken. And I was thinking...well, Kale's tent is heavily guarded. There's no way anyone would be able to sneak in to such a tent, not unless...well..."

"Unless that person were invisible," Marta said, the words coming out in a croak.

Fermin winced again. "Yes."

Marta wanted to scream then, wanted to tell him that hiding herself and the others from a few soldiers versus hiding herself from an entire army camp—not to mention the God of Conflict himself—were two very different things. She wanted to tell him that, before, she'd had help, that the others had believed the lie with her, and that now she had no one.

"It's a bad plan," Fermin said, "forget I even mentioned it. I'll think on it. Perhaps there's some other way—"

"There's not," Marta said. "You know there's not. You know it and I know it too."

The manservant said nothing, avoiding her gaze, and finally Marta sighed. "Fine, I'll try. Can't promise I won't end up being very visible, or at least my head which will likely wind up on a pike."

The man turned pale at that, and Marta immediately felt guilty. He had come trying to help, that was all, and she was making him feel bad about the only possible solution to their problems. "I'm sorry, Fermin—forget I said that. I'm sure it will be fine. Still, even if I do find out more and get a chance to talk to this messenger, what then? It isn't as if Kale and his army will just allow me to ride to up to the front lines and hold up a big sign saying 'The Welians Are Coming!'"

Fermin gave a small, shaky smile at that. "No, I don't expect they would. But a messenger is expected to make such trips regularly, at least to the front lines."

Marta blinked. The Fermin she had known weeks ago blanched when he saw a spider, and a speck of dust on the Tirinians' dinnerware was enough to make him go running for the hills. Now, that same man was wanting to make it to the front lines of Kale's army under false pretenses and risk being executed at best—likely, he would not be that lucky. "It will be dangerous," she said, studying the man.

He was pale, that much was certain, and there was an undeniable tremor in his hand as he raised it and ran it through his thin hair, but he straightened his back and nodded. "Yes, I expect it will be."

"And even if you reach the front lines, how will you get a message to Alesh and the others?"

"With great difficulty, I expect."

Marta laughed. She couldn't help herself. And in another moment, the manservant was laughing two, both of them doing their best to be quiet. It went on probably longer than it should have since they ran the risk, at any moment, of someone walking in and wondering why a man would ask for a slave only to sit around and tell jokes, but Marta didn't care. It felt good to laugh, felt good to feel something besides the gnawing sense of dread which had been eating at her insides for over a week.

Finally, the laughter trailed off, and Fermin's smile slowly faded, his expression growing sober once more. "Do you think you can do it?"

Marta winked. "Sure, no sweat. Just leave it to me. I'll go tonight." A thought struck her then, and she frowned. "But how will I tell you what I find out?" If, that was, there was anything to find out except for that they were as screwed now as they had been. Still, she didn't think that would help either of them to say so.

"Just leave that part to me," Fermin said, giving her a wink of his own. "No sweat. Anyway, we'd better be getting you back. That guardsman seemed like a bit of a jerk, and I doubt he'll be content to stand idly by without trying to raise a fuss."

"Asshole," Marta corrected. "Where I come from, we call them assholes."

Fermin sighed. "Sometimes, Lady Marta, I despair at the progress of your etiquette lessons. Still, given our current situation, I suppose some allowances must be made. Besides," he said, giving her a small smile, "he is an asshole."

Chapter Fourteen

Winter was coming on, and the air here, in the castle's inner courtyard, was cool—freezing really, cutting through his thin clothes like daggers of ice. But Alesh did not notice. He had been kneeling before Tarex's covered, recumbent form where it lay on one of the stone benches once used, in better times, for visitors to the castle to sit and enjoy the gardens which now lay dead from the frost. Soreness crept up his back, and his knees throbbed from sitting so long on the hard cobbled path of the courtyard but that, too, he did not notice.

Night was coming on, the sun sinking low so that shadows danced and capered around the courtyard mockingly while his breath plumed in front of him in great clouds, but Alesh paid none of this any attention. He only had attention for the man lying before him, for the candle set carefully on the ground beside him, its flame sputtering fitfully in the breeze.

Somewhere, within the city of Valeria, the great bell rang, calling its beleaguered defenders to their stations, an indication that another attack was imminent, perhaps underway already, and men and women shouted in the distance, commanders getting their troops in order, and there was the distant yell of *"Loose!"* as Nordin or one of his subordinates called for another hail of arrows to be launched. But like the cold and the shadows, these sounds meant nothing to Alesh.

He saw only the man and the flame, both weak and fading, heard only the Ekirani's shallow breaths as they rose and fell in his chest, almost imperceptible now as he drew closer to death. And, in time, he was not even aware of these things. Instead, he closed his eyes, shutting off the world, shutting the door to the many fears and uncertainties that threatened to unman him, that tried to convince him that he would fail, that he *must* fail. He closed his eyes, and he looked.

He looked not for someone to save him, as he had, nor for someone—mostly himself—to blame. Instead, he looked for understanding, looked for that power which lay deep inside him. Looked, in truth, for himself. But it is not so easy a thing for a man to find himself once he's lost himself, not so easy at all. He let his mind drift, away from the worry, away from the besieged city, away from Kale and those others who sought only to destroy.

For a time—just how long at time he would not know, then or later—his mind drifted like a fallen leaf held aloft on a gentle breeze, carried forth this way and that with no apparent rhyme or reason. He drifted past himself, past memories of his life, one after the other. He found himself remembering a voice, his mother's perhaps, singing to him when he was very young. He could not hear the words, not quite, but that did not matter for he could hear the love in them, could *feel* it, a profound, unquestioning love which neither time nor death could diminish. And then he was past, and he could smell bread cooking in Abigail's kitchen, a smell that was fresh and somehow warm, comforting, could see her smiling at him, giving him that special wink as if the world was some great joke and only the two of them understood it.

Then he was sitting in a tavern with Chorin, laughing at some jest his guardsman friend had told, one likely at his own expense as was his way, but laughing mostly because of his friend whose features were open and honest and full of joy. And before the laughter had ended, he was gone again, echoes of it following him as he came to where he and Katherine sat outside Valeria what felt like a lifetime ago, stealing a moment for themselves as darkness approached, holding and being held, comforting and being comforted.

There were a hundred other memories, thousands of them, moments in time where he had not feared failing, had not worried that he was different, or that he was not enough, times when there had been only joy and love and laughter. The world was like a dark, endless room, and within it, it was easy for a man to lose his way, but should he search for lights in the darkness, he would find them. It might take time, and he might stumble along the way, but if he looked long enough, if he did not give up, he would always find them.

In the end, the errant leaf that was his thought, his *self* came to rest in another place, another time, one many years removed from the besieged city of Valeria, and a self much younger than the one now knelt in the castle courtyard.

His face hurt where one of the other boys had punched him, and there were bloody scrapes on his back from the gravel where he and the other boys had fought, rolling around and struggling against each other. His right hand was swollen, the knuckles there raw and bloody, but the worst hurt came not from his hand or his face, but his pride. Pride and, most of all, fear. Fear that the boys had been right to taunt him, that he was a nightling spawn, a monster. Fear that all he had ever brought to those who loved him was grief and pain and death as he had his parents.

The door to his small room in the castle opened, but he did not turn to look, instead continued staring out the window sullenly, weeping silent tears of frustration and loneliness. "Leave me alone, Abigail."

But when a hand came to rest gently on his shoulder, it was not the hand of Chosen Olliman's head cook, but instead that of Chosen Olliman himself. Alesh looked at the man and felt his eyes go wide. "Forgive me, Chosen," *he said, sure that the man would now finally realize his mistake in taking him, an orphan, into his home and would banish him.* "I didn't know...I mean—"

"Peace, Alesh," *the man said softly. He motioned to the bedside.* "Be at peace. May I sit?"

The child Alesh knew that he was in danger of being kicked out, of being alone again, but part of him, a very large part, just then, thought that he deserved no better, and he shrugged. "It's your castle. Do what you want."

Instead of the angry rebuke he had expected, the man only sat beside him, saying nothing, and for a time, they only stared out of the small window in his room. Alesh sat tensely, knowing that the man was searching for the right words to tell him he was no longer welcome, but when Olliman spoke, it was not to exile him. "Are you happy, Alesh?"

The question was so unexpected that it caught him off-guard, threatening, for a moment, to pull him from his anger, anger at the boys, yes, but at himself as well. Stubbornly, he held on to that anger like a man underwater refusing to surface despite the ache in his lungs demanding air. "No."

"Why not?"

Alesh made a frustrated sound in his throat. "Why not?" he said, for the moment, forgetting, in his anger, that he spoke with the most powerful man in the city, likely the most powerful man in all the world. "Isn't it obvious? They make fun of me, they laugh at me. Kale's the worst. He's always calling me names when no one's looking, throwing rocks at me or tripping me. They hate me. All of them hate me."

"So?"

Another unexpected question, one that nearly left Alesh at a loss for words. Could the man not see? Could he not see that Alesh was mistreated, hated by all the other kids in the castle? Proof of that could be found easily enough in his black eye or on his bloody shirt which he still had not changed out of pure stubbornness. Or was it that the man did see and simply did not care? "Forget it," Alesh said finally, crossing his arms over his chest, a motion that made him aware of the hateful burning of the scar on his shoulder, the one that would never heal, the one the children said marked him as cursed. "You wouldn't understand. Everyone loves you. Even the gods love you—after all, you're their Chosen," he said, and even he was surprised by the amount of bitterness in his voice.

There was a soft sound from Olliman then, one that might have been a laugh. "I have been very blessed, Alesh, to find great friends, to find a great family. But it may surprise you to know that a Chosen has his fair share of enemies."

Alesh was only a child, one currently absorbed in his own hurts, his own anger, but even a child could not have helped but to hear about Olliman's many exploits during the war, his battles against the creatures of the darkness, his victory over Argush, the nightling king, and some of his anger gave way to shame. "Sorry," he managed, choking the word out.

"For what?" the Chosen asked, genuine curiosity in his voice. "Being human? We all hurt, sometimes, Alesh. We all grow angry."

"Even you?" Alesh asked, turning to look at the man.

Olliman laughed louder this time. "I expect there are some men—some gods, too—who would say especially me. What you have to understand, Alesh, is that anger and hate, jealousy and doubt—and yes, before you ask, I have entertained more than my share of doubts—are just places that a man or a boy goes inside himself. They are doors that we ourselves open. Doors that no one else, no matter what they say or do, can force us to enter, not unless we choose it ourselves. Do you understand?"

Alesh frowned, not really understanding and not really wanting to, wanting to be angry, to feel what he felt was righteous anger against his antagonizers, against those boys who called him names and laughed at him, whispering behind his back. "No."

Olliman, though, either did not see or chose to ignore Alesh's sullenness. "That is okay. It is a truth that most adults—men and women both—do not understand." He gave a soft laugh. "Even I, knowing it, often forget. But the sun still rises whether a man is there to see it or not, and the truth remains the truth whether or not we acknowledge it."

"I don't understand what the point of this is. Why bother telling me? I'm just a kid, a cursed, nightling spawn kid."

"No," Olliman said, and for the first time there was emotion in his voice. Anger. "No, do not say that, Alesh. You are what you are and are far greater than you know. The world will find enough ways to try to beat us down, lad. There is no reason to help it. And the point is that while anger and sadness are places, rooms we ourselves walk into, so too, then, are joy and peace. A man, then, is not the sum of the doors that are closed to him—doors behind which are those things he has lost or had taken, those things which he might never get back except in his memory—but a product of those doors which he chooses to open, those rooms which he chooses to enter."

"But what does all of that *mean*?" Alesh asked.

Olliman smiled. "What it means, Alesh, is that if a man finds himself in a place—in a room—he does not like, it is up to him to leave it, to find another. You are not evil, Alesh, not cursed. You, me, all of us, are lights in the world. And remember, when times get tough, when you feel as if you are alone, lost in that room and that there is no way out, remember that you are the light. And lights, Alesh, shine brightest in the darkness."

The scene faded then, that memory he had forgotten until that moment, blurring and vanishing, and he was back in the courtyard once more, back with the dying man he had taken from the healer's, for they had needed the bed and had said there was nothing more they could do for him. Back, yes, but he could still hear the echoes of Olliman in his mind. *Lights shine brightest in the darkness.*

It was the answer to a question he had not asked, the answer he had been searching for without knowing it. A man, Olliman had said, was not a sum of the doors which had been closed to him, his losses, but instead of those he chose to open himself. And now, if he was going to protect his friends, if he was going to be the light he needed to be, then he would have to open those doors. Doors of hope, yes, but not just that—doors of belief.

Alesh's eyes traveled away from the wounded Ekirani, away from the scrawl of black veins radiating almost to the tips of his toes, covering his cheeks and forehead as if meaning to consume him. Instead, he turned his gaze to the candle, to that small flame. It was dark outside now, what little light there was coming from the fitful flame, though how long it had been so, how long he had been visiting that memory from long ago, he could not have said, and it did not matter in any case. All that mattered was what Olliman had told him—lights shine brighter in the darkness.

So Alesh put away his doubt and his fear, left the rooms and closed the doors behind him, locking them tight. He stared at that candle, at that flame. Stared at it then, reaching out a hand, he called a question to the flame, to the light coming from it.

And this time, the flame answered.

Chapter Fifteen

Katherine sat and watched as Darl and Sonya practiced, their wooden swords *clacking* in the still air of the otherwise empty training yard. Empty because those soldiers who might have made use of it were getting their training now fighting for their lives instead of listening to swordsmasters correct their form. She thought that if a single image, a single moment, could ever encapsulate all the wrongs of the world, all the darkness in it, then it was the little girl holding her wooden sword as she faced off against the Ferinan.

It was not that Katherine felt there was anything wrong with a girl—or anyone—learning to defend herself. Instead, it was the look of quiet desperation on the little girl's face, in the anger that flashed across her eyes each time she was too slow to block one of Darl's blows. Blows which had left their mark on her arms with several bruises. Darl was a master warrior and the kindest person Katherine knew, but no matter how good or how kind, when people started swinging weapons around, someone was bound to get hurt, even if those weapons were made of wood.

And every time one of those hits landed and Katherine heard the sickening sound of wood smacking flesh, she jolted, starting toward Sonya, but the girl did not cry as she might have done. Instead, she would only snatch up her sword from where she had dropped it and reset her stance, obviously angry with herself. It was that anger that bothered Katherine the most. Anger that showed that the girl expected too much of herself, *demanded* too much, but no matter how much she—or Darl—tried, Sonya refused to quit or even take a break. It was not right, Katherine thought, to see such desperation in one so young, wasn't right, in fact, to see it in anybody.

When Sonya was struck yet again, this time in the wrist with a blow that sent her practice sword spinning away from her, Katherine rose, starting forward with the intention of telling the girl they were done for the day.

That was when she heard the bell.

She'd heard the bell often over the last couple of weeks, ringing as it did each time Kale's forces came at the walls again, but this time, there seemed to be a frenetic, panicked quality to its ringing that she hoped was only in her mind. And if it *were* only in her mind, then it was not only hers, for she saw soldiers—who'd taken the opportunity to catch a few hours of desperately needed sleep—rushing out of their barracks, tugging on armor and fastening sword belts as they started toward the walls at a weary jog.

Katherine turned and saw Darl watching her, a troubled expression on his face to match the worry she felt shifting inside her. "We'd better go see what's happening," she called.

The Ferinan nodded. "That's enough for today, Sonya."

"But—" the little girl began, then cut off and glanced in the direction of the city's bell tower as if she had only just noticed it, her young face going a little pale. "Oh. Okay."

As they made their way toward the walls, past crowds of people who all seemed to be scrambling in different directions but all of whom looked equally terrified, Katherine tried to tell herself it was fine, that the sinking feeling in the pit of her stomach was just her imagination, nothing more, and that this attack was no different than the others. The problem, though, was that it *felt* different, that something inside of her was telling her that it *was* different and that this attack might well be the last one.

She was sweating by the time she, Darl, and Sonya made it near the walls. Even before they'd reached the steps leading up, she could see that it wasn't going well. Up to now, Kale had been content to attack one part of the city or the other, sending in relatively small forces, likely with the thought—terribly accurate, thought, Katherine feared—of weakening the city's defenders, slowly chipping away at their energy and their resolve. This time, though, was different.

All along the battlements in every direction she could see, a mad melee waged. Men and women fought in struggling, desperate knots, and in the chaos it was nearly impossible to distinguish friend from foe. Nearly impossible, but not completely, for though the attackers often wore no armor and were dressed in little better than filthy, stained rags, and though they displayed little skill in actual combat, they fought with a frenetic, bestial energy that the weary, beleaguered defenders could not match.

Looking for only an instant as she rushed toward the stairs leading to the battlements, Katherine saw several defenders who should have been able to get their weapons in front of them in time instead fall or be overwhelmed by their less-skilled attackers as they either lacked the strength or the will to raise their weapons in their own defense.

Finally, after what felt like a lifetime, she reached the battlements and with a quick search found Captain Nordin in the midst of half a dozen other defenders currently locked in combat with roughly the same number of attackers. Even as she watched, Nordin and his fellows managed—with great difficulty, it seemed—to push the attackers back to the wall and, in another moment, to send them hurtling over.

All around her was madness, the screams of the dying, men and women hissing and growling and spitting, cursing and wailing. *What am I doing here?* She thought wildly. *What are any of us doing here?* She glanced back at Darl and realized in her own haste to get here she had unforgivably brought Sonya along. "Sonya," she said, "get out of here. Go back to the castle to the Tirinians, do you understand?"

"But, Katherine," the girl said, "I want to help."

Katherine felt her heart breaking for the girl, her face so earnest as she studied her, and she knelt down, cupping her face in her hands. "You can help, sweetie. You can help me by getting away from here. It will help me to know that you're safe, do you understand?"

The girl's mouth worked, clearly wanting to argue the point further, but just then the sounds of fighting grew louder around them, and Katherine felt that sense of urgency, the sense that all that she and the others had fought for now hung by a thread. They were running out of time, that much she knew, if, that was, they weren't out already.

"Sonya, there isn't time," she said. "Go now while you can."

"But Katheri—"

"*Go.*"

The girl winced at the shout, and Katherine immediately felt guilty, but before she could say anything, could try to make it better, Sonya turned, a hurt expression on her face, and fled down the battlements. It was painful, watching her leave, but Katherine consoled herself with the fact that at least the girl would be safe. She turned back to the battlements where the weary defenders were still struggling with a seemingly insurmountable number of enemies that continued to stream over the battlements while they themselves barely seemed to have the strength, the will to lift their blades in their own defense, and another thought struck her. Sonya was safe, yes. For now. But for how long?

The defenders were flagging, that much was sure. And why not? They had faced long odds for days. In truth, it was nothing short of a miracle that they had survived this long, had managed to raise their swords over and over and over again. But how long could a miracle be expected to last? Against such long odds, they could be forgiven for thinking—indeed, it was hard to imagine them thinking anything else—that it was not a matter of *if* they would lose, only when. And even for Katherine who knew little of battles and sieges, that time did not seem far away now. Not far away at all.

Katherine wished then that she was someone else. Alesh, perhaps. He would have known what to do. With his talent, his skill, he would have been a great asset on the walls, but even that wasn't the best of it. The best of it was that the men respected him, looked on him in some ways as if he weren't a man at all but some god or the closest thing to it. With him here, they would have found a strength, a will that they would not have known they possessed.

Chosen Alashia, if she were here, would have no doubt have had some plan, for she was always wise had always, it seemed to Katherine, been able to see solutions to problems no one else could. But Alashia was not here, nor was Alesh. There was only

Katherine and Captain Nordin, Nordin who was currently engaged in a life or death struggle with a thick-shouldered man that looked as if he could have crushed a boulder in his massive hands, if he took it in mind to do so.

She glanced to Darl, but there was no help there, for the Ferinan was only staring back at her saying nothing, only waiting for what she would do, waiting for her to make a decision. He would follow her lead, she knew, would commit, without question, to whatever choice she made. The problem, of course, was that she had no idea what that choice might be. But then, a moment later, she did.

Katherine was no great warrior like Alesh, no leader to inspire courage in his troops. Neither was she wise like Alashia, a woman among whose gifts had been counted the ability to sometimes catch glimpses of the future. And even if Katherine could do such a thing, she doubted, given what they faced, that she would like what she saw. No, she had no skill with a sword, no talent for discerning the future, for staring into it the way another might stare through a window.

What she could do, though, what she had *always* been able to do, was sing. Most people would have wondered what possible use such a talent might have in a situation like this one, but Katherine did not. Her music and the music of others had gotten her and her family through tough times. The toughest of times, in fact, including her mother's death, and she thought that their current situation qualified for that, if nothing else.

"I'll need my harp," she said to Darl. "And a stool."

Darl had known her for years, had worked with her as Alashia's agent long before the world had gone mad and Darkness had begun to spread across it like some plague carried on the breaths and in the hands of those who had let their own pain turn to hate, their own fear turn to rage.

He had known her, had been her friend, for years. He did not ask her what she meant, did not ask her what possible use the instrument might prove given their current plight, he only nodded and, without a word, turned and sprinted back toward the stairs, moving with that smooth, feline grace he always displayed.

Katherine loved him for that, for his faith in her. She only hoped it was justified. She looked back to the battlements, the situation grim and growing grimmer by the moment. She hurried toward Nordin who had, with the help of the six men with him, created a small space of brief tranquility in the midst of the mad melee raging around them.

"Captain."

If anyone needed to know how desperate their situation was, they need only have seen the man's face as he turned to her. Hard lines were etched into his pale face, and there were great dark circles under his eyes like bruises. Katherine didn't know much about wars, didn't know much about commanding troops in the field, but she knew that the expression on the man's face wasn't the expression worn by a man who expected to win. It was the set, resigned expression of a man who saw his doom—and the doom of all he loved—coming and was only doing his best to meet it standing up, a task which seemed to be taking all of what little strength he possessed.

"Lady Katherine," he said, a note of surprise audible through his exhaustion. "You shouldn't be here—Leandrian has renewed the assault, and it shows no signs of slowing. You should go to the castle, lock yourself in and—"

"And what, Captain?" Katherine said, all too aware that that was exactly what she had told Sonya only moments ago. "Sit in my room and wait for Kale's troops to break the door down, wait for them to find me huddled in the corner in fear?"

"Forgive me, Lady," the captain said, wiping a slightly-trembling hand across his sweaty brow, looking older, in that moment, than he ever had before. "I did not mean to offend you, I meant only—"

"Forget it, Captain," Katherine said. "No offense caused."

"Thank you, Lady. So what can I do for you?"

"Actually, Captain," she said, "I have come hoping that I might do something for you—for all of us, really."

"Oh?" he asked, and Katherine did her best not to note the doubt in the man's voice. After all, she felt that same doubt herself. But there was an idea running through her and not just an idea—a melody. Or, at least, the beginnings of one. A note, ringing softly in her mind, a low hum almost too quiet to hear. But she *did* hear it, and she had heard it before, one time, at least, that she could remember clearly. She had heard it when she and the others had been attacked in the inn, and her song had frozen all of the men—or nearly all, she could not easily forget the blow she had received to the head—in their places.

But then, she thought she had heard that note entire life. Sometimes, the note was lower than others, times when her doubts and her fears crowded around her—doubts and fears which were trying their best, even now, to force their way into her thoughts, to cloud her judgment and make her believe that Nordin had been right and that she should flee to the castle, close the door, and wait for her doom to come upon her. She had listened to those doubts before, many times, but she promised herself that she would not listen to them now. After all, if she did, if she allowed herself to doubt, to fear, then there would be no other chances. The Darkness would win, Valeria would fall, and that would be the end of it.

So she focused on that hum, and she met the captain's eyes with as much confidence as she could. "I'll need some room."

"Lady Katherine," he said, "are you su—" but he cut off, looking over her shoulder, and she turned to see that Darl had returned, her harp case in one hand, a stool in the other.

"I...don't understand," Nordin said.

Neither do I, Katherine thought, but she didn't think that it was only her imagination that the note, the humming, was growing louder in her. "Just clear me some space, Captain. And hold the walls—as long as you can."

The captain clearly had more questions, no doubt involving what she thought she was doing here, and why she, a woman who was, admittedly, as far from a warrior as anyone could be, was demanding space on top of the walls where even now a battle raged, but he only nodded wearily, too tired or too distracted to bother asking them. "As you say, Lady," he said, then he turned and began barking orders again, sending those men with him in every direction to help their struggling companions.

As the captain departed, Katherine found herself growing uncertain again. She had expected the captain to order her off the battlements. After all, here, on the walls, he was the authority unless Alesh showed up—an occurrence that wasn't looking as if it would happen anytime soon—and it would have been understandable for him not to have wanted a musician playing and singing while his men were fighting and struggling for their lives. If he had, she would have had no choice but to listen, and with that lack of choice, no responsibility. But he had not ordered her down, and she took a slow, nervous breath turning to Darl. The Ferinan watched her, a small smile on his face, one that instantly made her feel better.

In the years they had known each other, Darl had always been her rock, one she held onto when storms of doubt and worry lashed about her. No matter how bad the situation in which they found themselves—and there had been a few bad ones over the years, though admittedly none as bad as their current one—the Ferinan had never seemed to experience the doubts and fears which so often plagued her. He had always been there with that confident smile, trusting that everything would work out, in the end. Trusting *her*.

Darl sat the stool in front of her, and Katherine took a slow, deep breath before sitting down, then waited as he opened the latches of the harp case. He got it open a moment later and offered her the harp. Katherine did not hesitate, for even a second's hesitation now, in this moment, could cause years of pain and suffering.

She took the harp.

"Please, Deitra," she whispered, "help me."

Then she began to play. The first note, to her ears, sounded uncertain, tentative, but the second was clearer, better. By the third, the doubts and fears which had plagued her began to fade, carried away in the same manner that all of her problems were when she began to play.

In their place, confidence and courage rose within her. Not just courage and confidence either, but power. A deep well of power. Music—it was not just tavern songs about prostitutes and drinking. It was more than just entertainment. It could touch people, could cut past their own worries, their own concerns, and lift them up to a different place. A better one. And they all needed to be in a better place just then, a place where they could hope for more than death, where they could see, could *believe* in something besides blood and more of it, could experience something besides pain and grief.

Then she began to sing. Carrying her confidence, that feeling of contentment that always came upon her when in the grips of her music, out on the notes of her harp and her voice, sending it out to those exhausted defenders on the wall, those men and women who fought so bravely. Power—waves of it—radiated out from her voice, her harp, lending strength to arms which had moments before been too weak even to lift the blades they clutched, and she *felt* more than saw the battle begin to shift in the defenders' favor.

For while the defenders grew stronger, while their wills grew greater, those of their opponents grew weaker, their movements slower, more uncertain, and they began to be cut down in droves despite their greater numbers, as Valeria's brave soldiers fought with a renewed vigor.

They fought like warrior gods, standing where others would have fallen or fled, each of them better, in that moment, than they had ever been before, than they ever would be again. The music, by the magic exclusive to art, brought out the best in them. They did not fear, did not doubt—they only fought, only stood.

Yet for all their efforts, there were simply too few of them to keep up with the amount of enemy soldiers climbing over the walls. Enemy soldiers who, soon, seemed to take note of the woman sitting on the battlements playing her harp, seemed to understand that it was her song which posed the greatest threat. And, perhaps unsurprisingly, they began to charge toward her, meaning to end the song which to them was so hateful by the expedient of killing the woman singing it.

But Katherine did not dare allow her song to waver or falter, for the power of the song was like a tapestry she continued to weave, note by note, and should she stop, even for a moment, she knew that power would fade, the tapestry unraveling before she could pick it up once more and the spell her music wove would vanish as if it had never been.

So she closed her eyes instead, ignoring those men and women rushing toward her, screaming their fury and rage. She focused only on the music, for there was nothing else, could *be* nothing else. And those enemy soldiers who rushed toward her did not find a vulnerable musician awaiting them. Instead, they found Darl, one of the greatest warriors on the face of the world.

The Ferinan held his spear in his hands, gliding around her in a circle like a dervish, his weapon lashing out and cutting down those who came at her with brutal, elegant efficiency. Yet for all those soldiers he cut down, more were coming all the time, dozens of them, and despite his skill, she knew that even the Ferinan could not hold out against such a tide forever.

There was nothing to do then, nothing to do but hope. Darl could not hold out forever—*she* could not hold out forever—but perhaps they could hold out long enough.

Chapter Sixteen

Marta lay in her bed, waiting for the others to go to sleep, listening to the sounds of their breaths slow and grow softer as they drifted off. She lay there, thinking, as she had for the entire day since Fermin's visit the night before, of some way that she might sneak into Kale's tent—possibly past Paren, the God of Conflict—without getting her head lopped off. And now, like then, she had no answer, could come up with no scenario that didn't end with a terrible death.

She had thought of it while she delivered bowls of stew—the contents of which she didn't like to spend much time considering—from the cooks' tent to the soldiers around the camp. She had continued to think on it while bent over a tin bucket scrubbing at clothes that should have been discarded—or at the least, mended—long ago. But while Kale's army had no shortage of people who wanted to kill someone—anyone, really, they weren't too particular on that count—it had, as it happened, not a single tailor.

She had stared at that bucket while her calloused, wrinkled hands scrubbed away, as if she might divine some answer, might find some solution in the muddy suds. She hadn't, though, found only mud and clothing that the girl she had once been, the girl who had grown up living on the streets, sleeping in alleyways, would have been ashamed to wear.

She had not found her answer in the stew, had not found it in the bucket, and she did not find it now in the dingy canvas of the tent looming over her head. What she found, mostly, was terror.

Terror that she would fail, terror that Fermin and Sonya, that Alesh and Katherine, Rion and Lord and Lady Tirinian, all of those who were counting on her, would be let down.

She told herself it was no big deal, that fear. After all, she'd been afraid before, had spent the better part of her life afraid of one thing or another, one shadow or another. But she could not kid herself—this time was different. Those other times, she'd had to only worry about herself, and if she hadn't been fast enough or clever enough, it would have only been her who would suffer for it. Now, though, she had others to think about, a whole city of others who were counting on her, whether they knew it or not. A heavy weight to carry, one she felt crushing her even as she lay there, making her breath come in short, tight gasps.

"You know," a voice said from beside her, and she nearly screamed, turning in her bed to see that the old lady, Llanivere, was there. "Sometimes, when I'm nervous or anxious about something—whether or not I'll make it to the privy in time usually, have I mentioned that old age has a myriad of challenges?—or when a problem seems too big to handle, I have a little thing I like to do."

"Llany," Marta said breathlessly, "what are you—"

But the old woman spoke on as if she had not heard her. "What I do, see, is break it down into bits. One—don't pee myself. Two—get up from the bed, walk to the privy. Small bits, you see? That way, if you've got some big, tough thing ahead of you, you can take it one step at a time, get it done one step at a time."

"I...I don't know what you're talking about," Marta said.

Llanivere smiled. "Well sure, 'course not. Why would you? I'm just an old lady talkin' that's all. That's another thing about gettin' old—sometimes, a body just says things. Anyhow, I think I'll just go lie down. Who knows? I might even manage some sleep. You know—if the gods are watchin'. And something," she said, leaning in, "makes me think they just might be." She winked at that then turned and walked away.

And while Marta thought the woman needed to work on that whole creeping up on people while they were—well, not *sleeping* exactly, but pretending to at least—she also found that, despite the fact that her heart was only now beginning to slow down, she felt better. Short of breath, sure...but better.

She couldn't sneak into Kale's tent and speak with the Welian prisoner, then get that information to Darl without any being the wiser. Of course not. That was too much. What she *could* do, though, was get out of bed and walk out of the tent. That much she could do. And after that? Well, she'd worry about that when she got there.

She glanced around, making sure that the slaves in the beds around here were still sleeping. Then, quietly, she rose from her cot and started toward the tent flap. First small step almost done then and as it turned out Llanivere was right—she felt better. Now, she would just have to—

A figure suddenly stepped in front of her when she was only feet away from the exit. Her heart threatened to burst from her chest, and she was beginning to think it must be Llanivere again, was preparing to scold the old woman about surprising people. Unfortunately, she wasn't so lucky.

It was not the old woman standing there, but Greta, blocking the tent flap and doing a more imposing job of it than many tavern bouncers Marta had seen. The woman's hands were on her hips, and she was scowling at Marta like she'd just stolen something. "And just where do you think you're going?"

Blame it on exhaustion—the gods knew she hadn't slept much lately—or blame it on Marta's own anxiety. Normally, in such situations, lies came easier to her than the truth. Now, though, she could think of nothing. Nothing, that was, except the fact that she was currently planning on sneaking into the commander of the army's tent, past not just any god but the actual *God of Conflict* himself. And that, just then, the absolute last face she wanted to see—except, perhaps, for that of Kale or the god—was currently standing directly in front of her, looking like trouble waiting to happen.

"I..." Marta stalled, "that is..."

"Well, what is it, girl?" Greta said. "Or are you really witless after all, like Guardsman Blake claims?"

"Oh, leave it alone, Greta, for the gods' sake," a voice came, and it was Llanivere, the old woman standing and matching the younger with a scowl of her own. "The girl's got to use the privy, that's all. Or would you rather her just squat and do her business right here? Just because they treat us like animals don't mean we are, does it?"

Greta's face colored. "No, of course not. I didn't—whatever. Do what you want. But if she gets up to something out there and pisses the guards off then that's on you."

"The guards being pissed off about something?" Llanivere said, rolling her eyes. "Imagine."

Greta frowned. "Forget it." And with that, she turned and stomped away toward her cot.

Marta watched her lie down and turn away from them then glanced back at Llanivere. The woman gave her another wink before moving to her own bed. Marta breathed a heavy sigh of relief. First hurdle crossed then, so that was something. Her relief lasted right up until she stepped out into the night. Campfires burned all around her, lighting up the darkness and illuminating dozens of soldiers scattered about the camp. By some trick of the flickering light—and no doubt mostly her own fear—their faces looked demonic.

"Relax, Marta," she told herself, "one step at a time." She glanced around and saw several guards—Guardsman Blake among them—patrolling the area around the slave tent. Right now, she was hidden in the darkness of the tent's opening, but should she move much further out, she would be forced to step into the light of the torches scattered about the area. Then, the men would have to be blind not to notice her.

Unless, that was, she was invisible. Marta considered that. She had done such a thing before, as Fermin had said. True, she'd had help and, true, she'd been hiding from a few gate guards instead of from an entire army at the time, but she thought that, maybe, she could do it again. Or at least she hoped. Otherwise, this was going to be a very short trip with a very painful destination.

She closed her eyes, taking slow, deep breaths in an effort to quiet her rapidly beating heart. She told herself that she was not Marta, not now, not a spy come from Valeria to impede the enemy army. She was no one. Just another anonymous soul in a world full of them, one of those many—the poor and the destitute—who were invisible to the others around them. Invisible, it had to be said, mostly because those around them preferred not to notice them, preferred not to see their desperate plight, for seeing it, acknowledging it, reminded them of how easily all that they had could be taken away from them.

You can do this, she said and then, since she didn't believe it, *You can do this. You* have *to do this.* And that was better. She took a slow breath and started toward the center of the army camp where Kale's tent stood. She drew close to one of the patrolling guards and wanted to hesitate. Instead, she forced herself to go on, focusing on being invisible, telling herself that the guard's eyes would simply skim over her the way the people of Valeria's had so often done when she'd crouched with a tin cup begging for spare coin.

She held her breath, sure as she moved past that the man would challenge her, would shout at her to ask her why she was out of her tent. It was a tense moment that lasted a lifetime, but then, a second later, she was past.

The slave tents were not so far away from the center of the camp, an hour's walk, no more than that, yet it was the longest walk of Marta's life. But as she continued on without challenge, Marta grew more and more confident, began to feel more like herself, like the girl who had grown up on the streets, who had survived when so many others had not. It was a good feeling, a feeling of returning to herself, one that slowly began to push away all the fear and doubt that had plagued her over the last weeks.

Soon, she was no longer doing the tentative walk which she had started with but a walk more reminiscent of that girl who had not only survived on the streets of Valeria but had also thrived. At least, that was, as much as anyone could ever be said to thrive in such a place.

It was nice, feeling like herself again, feeling confident again. It was just unfortunate that it was only to last for a few minutes, just as long as it took her to come within sight of Kale's tent and, more specifically, the four guards stationed there. These four were a far cry from the disheveled, unprofessional guards stationed around the slave tents, barely guards at all really, just men with hate in their hearts who'd been given enough authority—and a blade— with which they might express that hate.

These guards were large and muscular and did not bother sneering or scowling around at those that passed to show how tough they were, not the way Guardsman Blake and the others did.

Instead, they only stood, waiting, slightly-bored expressions on their faces, but a look in their eyes that made it clear that they were more than ready to pull the blades at their waist should anyone provoke them.

Anyone, say, like a slave girl who was planning on sneaking into their commander's tent and having a chat with a Welian prisoner. A slave girl who, as it happened, would have to pass within inches of them to enter the tent. But what choice did she have? Already, she knew she would not be able to maintain this lie, not forever, for with each minute that passed it was growing harder and harder to hold onto the belief, the lie, that she was invisible. And should it fail, should her power fail, she would appear in front of the guards as if by magic, a slave girl peering suspiciously into their commander's tent.

Somehow, she doubted they would bother asking too many questions, would likely choose to practice swinging the swords sheathed at their waists instead, practice she doubted she would enjoy very much.

Still, she consoled herself with the dubious comfort that, as close as she was, if they could see her they would have cut her down already. She felt the urge to stay there, frozen, but she knew that she was running out of time, so she took a slow, shuddery—and please, gods, *silent*—breath and started forward, moving slowly and on the balls of her feet. There was very little space between the two guards nearest the flap, less than a foot, in fact, as if they somehow knew what she planned and intended to bar even any invisible intruders from accessing their commander's tent.

Not enough space for a grown man to move between them but, she hoped, enough that a slim girl of twelve might slide past. Maybe. It would be a close thing, but there were no other options, so she took a deep breath and, thinking skinny thoughts, she started to ease her way in between the two guards. She was just about past and was starting to think about what she would do next, particularly if Kale was inside the tent. She shouldn't have, of course. She should have, instead, done as Llanivere had said, focused on taking one step at a time. It was foolish to allow yourself to become distracted at the best of times but particularly when doing so meant it was likely you were going to wake up the next day—if you woke up at all—missing some fairly important bits.

She was so focused on thinking about the tent, about the Welian prisoner inside of it, that she didn't pay enough attention to where her feet were going, one of which struck that of the guards, and she barely managed to stifle a scream as she stumbled, falling to her hands and knees and barely catching herself.

The guard spun immediately, and there was the unmistakable—and unmistakably terrifying—sound of a sword being whipped from its scabbard. Marta froze, then slowly turned her head to look back and see that the guard had spun and was looking directly at her. Looking at her but, judging by the fact that his sword was remaining still instead of cleaving into her, not seeing her. He frowned as if someone had just posed him a particularly difficult question, one he was mulling over intensely.

"What?" one of his fellows asked as he scanned the darkness around them, his hand on the hilt of his sword as were those of the other guards.

"Felt somethin'," the first guard growled. "On my foot."

They might have trusted their companion, but then trust could only go so far, particularly when there was nothing to see, and the second guard grunted what might have been a laugh—if laughter was as terrifying or menacing as a hissed death threat. "The bogeyman, was it?"

The first guard grunted. "Fuck off," he said, then, to Marta's relief, he turned and looked away, taking his penetrating gaze—and the worst of her blood-curdling terror—with it. He and the other guards went back to watching the darkness.

Which left Marta to cower on her hands and knees, struggling to get her breath back without panting like a terrified animal—which was exactly what she felt like just then. Slowly, so very slowly, she began to ease her way to her feet once more, sure that the guards could actually see her after all, that they were just playing some cruel game with her and that, at any moment, they would turn and cut her down.

They didn't, though, and she finally made her way to her feet and was left staring into the darkness of the tent flap, a darkness which somehow seemed deeper, more menacing than that of the night surrounding her. Nothing left to do but to go inside, to walk into the shadows, something she had made a point of avoiding all her life. *You're stalling*, she told herself. Then, suddenly angry at her own cowardice, she stepped inside.

It was dark inside the tent, the air thick, oppressive. Yet that was far from the worst of it. The worst of it was the smell—blood and sweat and worse. The smell was more unnerving because, at first, she could see nothing, only darkness. But slowly, as she stood there, her eyes began to adjust and she began to be able to make out vague outlines in the darkness.

There, a vague rectangular shape that could only be a foldout desk, a chair that she was gratified to see was empty sitting behind it. In the center of the room, a table on which what appeared to be a map lay stretched out. But what caught her gaze—and held it—was what sat at one of the tent's edges. A cage, the type of cage a person—at least, that was, the type of person who thought it okay to put a person in a cage in the first place—might use to hold, say, a captured Welian messenger. An assumption that was supported by the muffled, quiet sounds of pain—whimpers, really—she could hear coming from inside it.

Now that she was here, in the tent, Marta found that much of the gut-wrenching terror which had gripped her was gone. She was already here, after all, in the most dangerous place in the world she could imagine, and when you were already *in* such a place, how much worse could things really get? That or, maybe, she was just about all terrored out for a while. After all, how much time could a person spend being scared to death? Not forever certainly.

Not long at all, if you keep dawdling, she scolded herself.

Marta walked to the cell. Fermin had warned her that the messenger had been ill-used, but even his warning had not prepared her for what she would see, and her breath caught in her throat. A naked figure huddled in the corner of the cage. His arms were wrapped around his legs, his back to the rest of the tent as if trying to forget about its existence, to will away his newfound reality the way a child might try to will away the monster under her bed or in her closet by hiding her face under the coverlet. But reality, like those monsters, was a stubborn, cruel thing and once it gripped something—or someone—with its claws, was loathe to let it go.

The man wept, sobbing quietly, and as her eyes continued to adjust to the darkness, Marta understood, for it was clear, even in the poor light, that the man's short time among Kale Leandrian's army had not been a pleasant one. Proof of just how bad that time had been could be seen in the bloody welts and slashes—that looked as if they'd been made by a whip—which criss-crossed the light-brown skin of the man's back and legs, weeping crimson even as she watched.

"*Hello?*" Marta asked in a whisper.

The prisoner did not turn around, only let out a loud moan which made her wince. "Please," he said in a breathy rasp, "please, no more. I've told you everything...everything I know. Please—"

"*Quiet,*" Marta hissed, "or they'll hear us."

The man stopped trembling at that and, after a moment, his curiosity seemed to get the better of his fear, and he slowly unfolded his arms from his legs, turning as if each movement was a terrible agony which, no doubt, it was. "W-who are you?" he asked. "W-what do you want?"

"I want a lot of things," Marta said, "but we don't have time to go into that, not now. My name's Marta...what's yours?"

The man looked surprised by the question, blinking as if he was having difficulty producing his own name. "I...that is, my name is Efial Tarnes, Royal Messenger for my king and the mouthpiece of his wi—" he paused then, giving a watery, shuddering sigh, as if he did not have the energy or the will to finish.

Staring at the man, seeing the obvious agony he was in, Marta felt a wave of shame wash over her. For the last weeks, she had spent most of her time pitying herself, her terrible plight, focused exclusively on her own suffering. But her ordeals, such as they were, were nothing compared to what this man had been through in the last several hours. She noted, too, that while he was naked, he still wore several large golden hoops in his ears as well as one in his nose and that his hair—long and dark and with a thick luxuriousness that any noblewoman would have killed for—was adorned with a variety of charms containing precious gems and stones. Had Kale somehow not noticed these adornments or had he not known their value? No. More likely, the man had left them out of some perverse and convoluted intention to show the man just how far he had fallen.

She knew that she needed to hurry, could feel the time wasting away as she stood there, yet just then, she could not bring herself to ask the questions she needed to ask as she watched the man sobbing silently, likely expecting that her presence was just another twisted form of torture devised by his captors. Instead, she made her way over to the cell and knelt, reaching through the iron bars and laying her hand gently on one of the few patches of his skin which was left unscathed from Kale's attentions.

The man jumped at first, cringing away from her touch. Then, he stopped, and she felt his entire body shudder beneath her hand, continue to shudder as he quietly sobbed. For a time, Marta only crouched there, her hand on the naked man's back, transferring what warmth, what compassion she could, doing her best to make the beaten animal he had become into a man again.

Finally, his body stopped the worst of its trembling, and he turned to her, his dark brown eyes shimmering with tears. "T-thank you," he said. "Even if you are some torturer or only a figment of my imagination, thank you. Yours is the first kind touch I have felt since leaving my homeland."

"Why...why did you leave?" Marta asked. "Why are you here?"

The man studied her and despite his obvious discomfort, there was an intelligence in his gaze. "I do not know that I should tell you."

Marta gave him a small smile. "Got a lot else goin' on, do you?"

The man gave a soft laugh at that, smiling back, and Marta felt prouder of herself in that moment than she could remember feeling in a very long time. "I...I suppose not," he said softly. "My king sent me ahead of our force. News of the troubles here reached us, and at once he began mustering his forces, hiring the best mercenaries in the world. He sent me with a message for Chosen Alesh, ruler of Valeria, Son of the Morning and hope of all those who love the Light. My king entrusted me with this task..." He trailed off, tears coming to his eyes once more. "And I will fail him. It is that which grieves me most."

"When?"

"Excuse me?"

"When will the king be here?"

"He...the bulk of our forces will arrive in two days' time. I was meant to give notice to the Son of the Morning to ensure that he would be able to cover our arrival." His face twisted in grief. "Now, I fear what will happen, and I am ashamed. Worse, I deserve to die, for I told Kale Leandrian everything. I did not mean to, you understand, but he...it..." His mouth worked then, and tears began to stream down his cheeks.

Marta did not know what to say, did not know what a person could say to such naked grief as that which twisted the Welian's features. "You...it's not your fault," Marta said.

"Then whose fault is it?" the messenger asked, meeting her eyes with a tortured gaze.

Marta could think of nothing to say to that, so she only remained silent. The man nodded. "It is my fault and mine alone. I have betrayed my king and my country, and so deserve whatever punishment this Kale Leandrian and his legion of Darkness might visit upon my flesh. Now he knows the exact day, the exact hour of my king's coming. He will be waiting, I am sure, for them to make landfall. And when they do..." He trailed off at that, once more breaking into great, wracking sobs.

"Listen..." Marta began, "it isn't...that is...what if you were able to deliver your message after all? What if...what if you *could* reach Ale—that is, the Son of the Morning?"

The man ran a bruised arm across his nose, meeting her eyes with a faint glimmer of hope in his own. "Then...if such was the case then, perhaps, the worst might yet be averted but...but no," he went on, shaking his head. "It is too late. There is no hope. My only wish now is that they will kill me as I deserve to be killed. Perhaps..." Again, he met her eyes, but this time with a dark hope glimmering there in his gaze, one that she did not like at all. "Perhaps...you are young, but I wonder, could you do this thing for me?"

"What?" Marta asked, scared that she knew all too well what the man meant.

He waved a hand. "You need not do it yourself. Only, bring me a blade—there is one there, on the desk. A thin blade used for opening letters. Thin but sharp—I know that better than anyone. If you will but bring it to me and leave, I can—"

"No."

The man blinked, recoiling at the rebuff. "B-but, please. You must. Believe me, I pray, it would be a kindness. I have failed and there is no hope left. Please, do this for me. Let me end it."

"You're wrong, Efial," Marta said. "I may not know much, but I know that. There is always hope. For the living, at least, just as there is always a chance for a girl—or a man—to make up for her mistakes. To be better, to *heal*. The living can heal, Efial. They can hope. The dead, though, stay dead, and the worms eat the hope along with the rest." And Marta found that though she was speaking to the Welian, she was also speaking to herself, at least to the self that had spent the last two weeks in despair.

But Efial's head was hung low, his shoulders slumped. "Please, Marta. Pl—"

"No," she repeated. "And that's the end of it. I will not help you kill yourself, Efial. I will, however, make sure that your message is delivered to Chosen Alesh in Valeria. *We* will make sure of it. Together."

"But...how?" the Welian asked.

"I find that, when faced with an impossible task, it is best to take it one step at a time—" She paused as the man let out a breathless, sobbing sound that might have been laughter. "First, then, let's get you out of this cell. Then we'll make it back to the slave tents. I can hide you there, I think, if we're careful. There's a friend coming to see me later tonight and—"

"Forgive me, Marta, but I fear that your plan is bound to fail. You see, I cannot take the first step, neither great nor small."

"What do you mea—" Marta began, then cut off as the man, with obvious pain, stretched out his legs so that his feet—or what was left of them—were visible. She was unable to keep the gasp of shock from coming to her, for the man's feet were a mangled, bloody ruin. The darkness and blood made it difficult to see, but it appeared to Marta as if the man only had three toes left between both of his feet, and she was forced to jerk her gaze away as she felt her stomach roiling dangerously.

"They have finished me, Marta," he said. "So, you see, there is no way out, no escape for me save death. Now, please, will you do this thing for me? You need not stay for it. Only slide the knife through the bars of my cell and leave, with my thanks."

Marta felt that despair begin to creep in again, as if grief were a contagion that might be passed from one person to another. But, then, wasn't it? After all, it was a sickness that she and the other slaves in the tents had been passing around for the last weeks, a sickness that had stolen her hope and her confidence, turning her into one of those cowering, terrified wretches that she had seen so often on the streets, the ones she had promised herself she would never become. "No, Efial," she said. "No, I will not pass you the knife. Neither will I leave you here, in this place, in the dark. You are coming with me."

"Please," the man said in a desperate voice which broke with his grief and pain, "please. Can you not see? I am unable to walk. It is all I can do to sit here and not scream with the pain. I only want an ending, it is all you can do for me, all anyone can do now."

"*Enough,*" Marta hissed, her frustration getting the better of her. "So you failed—get over it. We *all* fail, Efial. You ask me, it's what we're best at. But that doesn't give you an excuse to sit there and pout. Imagine where the world would be if we all did that. You have a mission from your king, if I recall, a mission to deliver a message. And you will not give up—I won't let you. I won't let *us*. Do you understand?"

"But—"

"No buts," she interrupted. "If you can walk around with that hoop in your nose and believe that no one is going to give it a good yank the first argument you get in then you can believe me about this. If you can't walk, I'll carry you. Now, get up."

The man looked like he wanted to argue but perhaps he saw some of Marta's determination in her eyes, determination she was thankful to have finally found. For in the end, he grasped the cell bars with trembling hands and slowly, painstakingly, began to clamber his way to his feet. After what felt like a lifetime, he was finally standing, though Marta didn't miss the way his hands trembled where they held the bars or the way he swayed uncertainly, obviously off-balance.

She realized, then, that she had no way of opening the cell and wanted to curse herself for being a fool. She looked around and sighted the key immediately, left sitting on the desk in plain sight of the cell and the prisoner therein. Another perverse form of torture or just carelessness? Though perhaps it wouldn't have mattered. What were the chances of the man somehow managing to get the key and, even if he had, what was he supposed to do then, when he couldn't even walk?

Marta moved to the table, grabbing the key, and a moment later she was back at the cell, wincing at the metallic creak as the door swung open. She took one of the naked man's arms and draped it over her shoulders, doing her best not to groan from the weight of it. "Alright," she said. "So we just have to get you out of here and—"

"But the guards, Marta," the man said, panting. "They'll—"

"Never see us," she answered. "Just so long as you stay quiet."

"But...how? They are waiting right outside the tent, I saw them when I was brought here. I cannot even imagine how you managed to get inside without—"

"Leave the guards to me. You just focus on putting one foot—" She cut off, an image of the man's mangled feet flashing into her mind. "You just stay quiet, alright?"

"As you say, Marta," he said, "but I will not forgive myself should you be caught trying to rescue me, and I fear that nothing short of the intervention of one of the gods themselves could get us out of here unseen."

Marta grunted. "Interference, more like."

"What?"

"Nothing. Anyway, Efial, I know a little bit about the gods"—*a sight more than I'd like, if you want to know the truth*—"and in my experience, not all of their help is flashy and incredible. Sometimes it's a bit more subtle than that." *Sometimes,* she thought with a frown, *so subtle that, if a person wasn't paying attention, she would almost think it didn't exist at all.* "Now, enough talk. We'll be fine—it's past time we left. Kale could be back any—"

She cut off as she heard a voice from outside the tent.

"Chosen, welcome back."

Marta's skin suddenly broke out in a cold sweat, and she froze.

"Marta," Efial began in a whisper, "get out of here, while you still can. I'll tell him that I escaped, somehow, that—"

Marta didn't bother pointing out how ridiculous that was, for the man couldn't walk without help, let alone somehow contrive to retrieve the key from where it had been placed and make his way halfway across the tent. Partly she didn't say so because it was obvious, but mostly it was simply because they did not have the time. She gave her head a hard shake. "Quiet," she hissed, then led the man toward the edge of the tent.

"But he'll see that the cell is empty and—"

The man cut off then as the tent flap was thrown open, and a hooded figure, one which could only be Kale Leandrian himself, stormed inside.

We are not here, Marta told herself, fighting down the panic bubbling up inside her. *You do not see us. How could you? We are not here.*

But Kale did not even so much as glance in their direction. His hands were gripping his head as if he were in great pain, and he half-stumbled, half-ran to his desk where he collapsed in his chair. *"Mistress, please,"* he croaked, *"no more. I'm here."*

Marta was beginning to think the man had gone insane—though maybe it was more accurate to say, given the things he'd done, that he'd always been that way—when, suddenly, there was a crash of thunder overhead, so loud that it made her jump, and it was all she could do to keep from giving a shout of surprise.

Then suddenly, a figure materialized in the tent. One moment, there was nothing there, only Kale slouching in his chair, gripping his head like he meant to crush it, and then there was a tall woman looming over him. Her hair was long and dark, the darkest hair Marta had ever seen, hair which shifted and swayed in a sudden heavy wind, one which had seemingly come out of nowhere and whistled outside the tent.

Even before Kale spoke, Marta knew who this newcomer was, who it must be. Icy fingers of terror gripped her heart in a cold fist, and she trembled as she focused on being invisible.

"Mistress," Kale said, panting. *"I did not know you meant to come in person. Forgive me, I—"*

"You will not keep me waiting so long again, Argush," Shira, the Goddess of the Wilds said in a voice that reverberated in Marta's mind like thunder.

"Please, I did not mean to—"

"Enough. I do not have time to speak of that. The Welians are only two days from shore and still you have failed to conquer Valeria. You have failed me, Argush. You have failed me greatly."

"T-there is still time, Goddess," he said, and though Kale Leandrian was a powerful figure, one thought by nearly the entire world—certainly that part of it that didn't count murder and torture as their favorite pastimes—to be one of the most dangerous, if not *the* most dangerous person now living, he did not seem so now. Now, cringing before his chosen goddess, he seemed like little more than some frightened child waiting to be punished. "The orders for the attack will begin shortly—in less than an hour's time—the greatest attack we have yet sent. The defenders are weary and what few remain will not put up much of a fight. Why, they can barely stand. Victory is assured, if only you will give me a little more time—"

"*You are out of time, Argush. The city must fall, and it must fall tonight. You have failed me several times, but you will not fail me again. I have made sure of it. I have chosen to send you help.*"

"Made sure of it?" Kale asked. "Forgive me, Goddess, but what do you mean? What kind of help?"

"*The sort that ensures there will be no more problems. A...child of mine, one only recently come into this world.*"

"Please, Mistress," Kale said, his voice hesitant, "already, Paren causes more problems than—"

"*Oh, you need not worry, Argush. This child will be very, very different. Perhaps 'child' is not the right word. Perhaps...'creation' will serve. It will come and, when it does, you will have no more need of siege ladders or tunnels underneath the city, for it will destroy the gate as if it never existed.*"

"Yes, Goddess," Kale said, and even through her near-panic, Marta could hear the reluctance in his voice. "And when might we be expecting this...creation?"

"*Very soon, Argush. Tonight, in fact. Though...*" She paused, glancing around the tent with a haughty expression, "*you may want to meet it outside. It will not fit in this tent. For you see this new creature is quite large and—*"

Marta wasn't sure whether the strangled noise of panic came from her or the Welian, and in the end it didn't really matter. What *did*, though, was that both Kale, evil Chosen and commander of an army bent on world destruction, and Shira, the Goddess of the Wilds who sought to destroy all mankind, spun to stare directly at the shadows where she and the Welian stood...or maybe cowered was a better word.

The guise which her powers had created, which her *lie* had created was still around them, but Marta could feel it faltering beneath the penetrating stares of two of the most powerful beings in the world. She concentrated, calling on all of her years living in the streets, all those years of wearing cast-off clothes and eating cast-off food in alleyways, hiding in places decent people refused to go, refused to even *look* when they could help it. And immediately, a thought entered her mind.

I'm not good enough.

How could she be? How could anyone be good enough to best a Chosen of the Gods and, even worse, the Goddess of the Wilds herself? A person could not hide from a storm, after all, and any shelter she might seek would be blown away on powerful gusts of winds, would be set ablaze by bursts of lightning from the sky.

She forced the thought down though, for it would do her no good, not now. And to her surprise, she found her thoughts—which were desperately seeking anything but pure terror—drifting not toward her years as a street waif but toward her days and weeks as a friend, a friend to Alesh and Katherine and Sonya and Darl, even Rion. Better friends than an orphan like her deserved, friends who needed the message the Welian carried, needed, too, to be told of this latest threat to Valeria, the one Shira had told Kale about. It was *they* who would suffer should she fail—so then, she would not, *could not* fail.

She gritted her teeth, her hands clenching into two tight fists at her sides, so tight, in fact, that the nails of them dug into her palms, but she did not notice the pain of it, noticed nothing, in that moment, except the stares of the two as they looked. Her magic was like a shield, their questing, narrowed gazes like blades seeking to penetrate past her defenses, and it was all she could do to hold those sharp points at bay. Yet she *did* hold, held even as she felt her grip on the magic, on the lie, begin to falter in the face of that relentless assault. She held until her muscles shook with the effort, until her body was soaked in sweat, and her eyes ached where she squeezed them shut, concentrating only on making it through the next moment, then the next.

She knew that she was failing, that no matter how much effort she put in, it was not enough, not for such powerful foes as this. Perhaps Efial, the crippled Welian standing beside her, understood some bit of her struggle or perhaps he simply sought to offer solace before the end. Either way, he reached out and put a hand on her shoulder, gently, kindly. Marta had not been touched in such a kind way often, and she was not sure whether or not she imagined renewed strength flowing into her from the contact. Was the man Chosen as she was? But no. She realized that was not it. There was not magic in the man, only in the touch, a touch born of kindness just as there was magic in all good things, rather big or small.

It was not much, maybe, but it was enough, enough for her to hold on for a few more seconds and hold she did. Then, suddenly, there was movement at the tent flap and a guard stepped inside.

"Forgive me for interrupting you, Chosen, but Captain Wexler has sent a messenger asking for—" The new voice cut off, and so, too, did the relentless pressure that Marta had felt as both Chosen and goddess turned to regard the new arrival. Marta, having so recently felt the pressure of that gaze herself, understood the newcomer's sudden discomfort.

"Forgive me, Chosen," the man said, his voice breaking as he noted the goddess in their midst, "I did not mean..."

"Forget it," Kale said, casting one more frowning glance at Marta and the Welian's hiding place before turning back to the guard. "Come in—bring me what news you carry and be quick about it. Tonight is to be a busy night."

Marta breathed a silent sigh of relief and glanced at the Welian who was staring at her in what she might have taken—had he been staring at someone else—as awe. She inclined her head to the tent flap, putting a finger to her mouth as she did—probably not necessary, given their circumstances she thought it unlikely Efial was planning on breaking into a song and dance routine anytime soon. But then, given their circumstances, she figured a person couldn't be too careful.

As the messenger droned on, recounting troop numbers—depressingly high—and the estimated number of defenders still manning Valeria's walls—depressingly low—Marta and the Welian made their way toward the tent opening. It was a trip that lasted forever or at least seemed to—terror had a way of making time do strange things—but finally they made it to the entrance.

The four guards were still stationed there as they had been, but she couldn't help but notice that they stood farther away from the tent entrance than they had before. Marta supposed that the arrival of an evil goddess had a way of wrecking a person's professionalism. But unlike the trip into the tent, she found herself far less worried this time. After all, she had just weathered the stares of Shira and Kale. After that, four men with swords weren't as threatening as they might have been.

They were passing the guards, walking through the gap their fear had provided, when she heard Kale's voice from inside the tent. *"Very well. Tell Wexler to finish the probing attacks. The real invasion begins now."*

Marta winced at that and continued away from the tent, quickening her step. As it turned out, things weren't as bad as she had feared. They were worse.

They weren't running out of time.

They were out already.

Chapter Seventeen

Katherine was tired; she wasn't sure that she had ever been so tired in her life. She had sung many times, of course, in many places, had sung far longer than she had now without any signs of exhaustion. This time, though, it was different, for what she did was not just sing or play the harp. What she did—what she was doing—was nothing less than magic, a magic granted her by the Goddess of Music and Art, Deitra herself. And a magic that, she feared, was fading.

She did not know how much longer she could keep it up, for already her fingers felt uncertain on the strings of her harp, and it was becoming more and more difficult to keep her voice on key. She wanted to stop, to rest, but she dared not, for she knew that, should she do so, the magic which was buoying up the defenders, the magic which was granting strength to the their weary arms, the magic which was giving the courage and determination which overrode their fear and weariness, would fail. The spell would end and, with it, any hopes of Valeria's—of the world's—future.

Some might have thought it odd, perhaps, that the fate of the world hung on the words of a song, on the crisp notes of a harp, but not Katherine, for she knew well the power of music, the spell that it might cast even with no gods involved. Still, she did not know how much longer she could keep it up, and that was far from her only worry.

For all his skill, for all his martial prowess, Darl was beginning to falter, displaying a sluggishness in his movements that, while they still would have seemed incredible coming from anyone else, were for him, an obvious sign of exhaustion. And for all those that the man cut down with his spear, more and more attackers came on. Many of them, feeling the difference Katherine's song made, recognizing that it was stealing their strength while granting more to the defenders themselves, rushed toward her, intent on cutting down this woman who dared sit in such a place of violence, singing and strumming her harp. They charged at her with hate and fury in their gazes, their faces twisted with it, some even ignoring the defenders in front of them, spurred on by their rage to kill her and her only and being cut down from behind for their efforts.

The bodies of those who were cut down by the Ferinan's spear spread around her in a broken circle, splattered with crimson, a circle which was growing all the time. And despite Katherine's efforts, hers was not the only losing battle happening on the wall, for while the spell her music cast might grant the defenders strength and courage, it did not keep the blades of their enemies from finding their targets. For every defender that fell, three or four of the attackers did, but if the enemy army had anything in abundance it was more soldiers to send into the fray, and spell or not, those far greater numbers were beginning to tell.

It was only a question then, of who would fail first. She—and her song—or those brave defenders risking—and giving—their lives for the city they loved. Katherine sang on, played on, and watched the night grow darker.

Chapter Eighteen

By the time the slave tents came into sight, Marta was trembling, her body numb with fatigue. She had often felt, in her life, that she was invisible. She was reminded of it every time a noblewoman turned her nose up and hurried past, ignoring her pleas for spare coin or on those rare occasions when she'd scraped together enough money to purchase food on her own but was summarily ignored by bakers and butchers who wanted none of "her kind" in their shops. Such as those, when they noticed her at all, made their disgust clear by then summarily kicking her out of their shops.

A lot of practice at being invisible then, more than most people got in a lifetime in her short twelve years, but she had never been *so* invisible for *so* long, and the effort it took—a surprising amount—could be seen in her pale face and shaky hands, in the way each step was more difficult than the last. It was as if someone were following her, strapping weights onto her ankles as she walked. It didn't help, of course, that for all her own weariness, Efial the Welian, had it far worse. After what Kale had done to him, the man could barely stand, let alone walk, and what little strength the man had left was flagging with each passing moment, a fact noticeable by the way he was forced to rely more and more on Marta until she was finally slumped nearly double under his weight.

He had asked her to leave him at least half a dozen times, begged and eventually demanded, but each time she had refused him and continued on, assuring him that they would make it, that it would be okay. Still, despite her assurances, she was beginning to doubt they would ever reach the slave tents. She had lost all sense of time or place, and was relieved—and more than a little shocked—when her drifting gaze settled on their shapes in the distance.

"Not far now," she whispered, adjusting the man's weight on her shoulders in an effort—a useless one it had to be said—to make the pain in her back go from horrendous to simply agonizing.

The Welian said nothing—maybe still sore over her having the nerve to save his life, maybe too exhausted to speak—and Marta started forward again. The guards were still patrolling though there seemed to be less of them than normal. Marta barely noticed, was too tired to focus on anything but putting one foot in front of the other and, at any rate, none of them gave a shout of alarm as she and the Welian hobbled past.

They reached the tent flap and stepped inside and, immediately, Marta let her magic slip, let the veil she had cast over herself and the Welian falter and fail. Not so hard a thing, really, not so hard at all as it had been about to happen whether she'd wanted it to or not. Still, it was a great relief to let the power go, and she took a slow, trembling breath, looking at the Welian who met her eyes with a vague, exhausted stare. "See?" she said in a harsh whisper. "No sweat."

"Not yet maybe, Witless," a voice hissed from behind her, "but I imagine you'll be sweating soon enough. Screamin' too, come to it."

Marta spun, nearly falling in her weariness, and saw Guardsman Blake standing at the tent flap, his sword in his hand. Marta knew she should be terrified, but mostly she was just tired, still too glad not to have to hold the spell any longer to worry about much else. She stared at the sword in the man's hands not out of terror but out of mere curiosity, thinking idly about how many times she'd feared him drawing that blade, feared what would be a cruel man's instrument with which he would execute his will upon the world the same way a hammer was a smith's.

"So, Witless," the man said, grinning evilly, "where have you been?" He glanced at the wounded Welian. "And who's your new friend?" His stare roamed down to the Welian's mutilated feet. "He looks...fun."

"Oh, you know how it is," she said, shrugging, "you go out, meet people. Such is life, right?"

"And death, too," the guardsman said, no doubt thinking himself incredibly clever despite the fact that it made no sense at all.

"How did you know I left?" she asked, still not scared—she didn't doubt that would come later, once the torturers had begun their work—just curious.

Then a figure stepped out from behind the guardsman and Marta was disappointed—not surprised, just disappointed—to find that it was Greta, the Queen of the Slaves, smiling a very unqueenly smile of malice and cruelty. "Hi there, Witless."

Marta sighed. "I'm shocked, Greta, us being such fast friends and all. Still, I'm sure he promised you some great reward for tattling. Let me guess, an extra load of clothes to launder? Who knows, you've been so good, maybe he'll even put some extra food in your bowl."

"Go ahead, make your jokes. Can't just go missin' for over an hour and not have folks wonderin' where you got to, girly," Greta said, still smiling.

"Alright, enough talk," Guardsman Blake said, moving toward Marta and the Welian, "you been bad, Witless, and bad girls get punished, don't th—" Abruptly, Blake's words cut off. His eyes went wide, and his entire body went rigid, his back arching.

Marta stared on, confused, thinking it far too much to hope that the man had chosen that moment to have a seizure and die—after all, she wasn't the Chosen of the God of Luck, that was Rion. But Blake dropped his sword and continued to paw at his back, a confused look on his face as if he'd just heard someone whisper his name in an empty room. Then he spun to look behind him, and Marta saw what the problem was.

Said problem, namely, being a knife in the back, a guarantee to ruin anyone's day. "What?" Blake asked, as if trying to understand that unseen speaker, "what was..." He trailed off then, his eyes rolled up in his head, and he collapsed to the ground in a heap, revealing a smiling Greta who hocked and spat on his unmoving form.

"Never did like that bastard."

It had been a strange, terrifying night, and Marta thought it didn't look like it was going to get any simpler anytime soon. "I...don't understand."

Greta rolled her eyes. "Catch up, Witless," she said, not with malice but only exasperation. "Guardsman Asshole, here, came by to do a head count. It was only a matter of time before he would have found you missin' and sent up the alarm. I gave him the idea that maybe he should see to your punishment himself. Wasn't so hard—he was a sadistic bastard and that's a fact. Anyway, it's done now."

"But...but you hate me," Marta said. "Why would you help me?"

The woman sighed, shifting and displaying a discomfort that she had not shown when stabbing a man in the back or, for that matter, beating Marta on her first day in camp. "Because Llanivere was right, that's why. Farra too. We're slaves, but that don't mean we're animals."

"That...thank you," Marta said, suddenly at a loss for words.

"That son of a bitch has dragged me to his tent a few times. Believe me when I tell you, it was a pleasure. Now, what's the plan, Witless?"

Marta blinked. "Plan?"

Greta snorted. "Sure. Sneaking out and coming back with a Welian that looks worse than some corpses I've seen, I figured you've probably got a plan. I want to help..." She glanced around the tent. "All of us do."

Marta turned and surveyed the tent, realizing for the first time that all of the slaves were standing. And not just standing. They were all watching her, nodding in agreement with Greta's statement, all of them waiting for what she would say.

She blinked. Surprised to still be alive, surprised, also, that all the women present—including a smiling Llanivere—would trust her to come up with some plan. Thankfully, as she stood there, one came to her. Or, at least, the beginnings of one. "Alright," she said, giving a wink at the Welian standing beside her as if she'd expected this all along—she had not, had expected something like Guardsman Blake's ambush, sure, but not this—then moved to the nearest bed, sitting Efial down and taking a seat beside him. She leaned forward, her arms on her knees. "Here's what we're gonna do."

Chapter Nineteen

Rion had never considered himself much of a fighter. A gambler, sure—not that he'd ever intended to gamble with his life, or at least not as much as he had lately, anyway. He had never considered himself a warrior or a defender of anything—except for maybe his own life when he won a bit too many coins and their erstwhile owner wasn't particularly pleased. Yet, anyone watching him doing his part in the mad melee upon the battlements would have thought differently, for he fought and growled, hissed and cursed and bled along with all the rest. Maybe he hadn't ever considered himself a warrior, but then he'd never considered himself much of a *die-er* either, and if it came to killing or being killed, well, a man didn't have to spend a lifetime sleeping in a barracks and polishing his sword to make that decision.

A decision he was forced to make even now as a man old enough to be his grandfather charged at him brandishing what looked suspiciously like a fire poker and screaming wordless sounds without meaning. Except anger, maybe, and a man didn't need words to see that, though what the man was angry at—and why he seemed to direct that anger at Rion in particular—only the gods could say.

Rion could have waited for the man to approach, could have engaged him in a sword-fight—a sword-and-fire-poker-fight at any rate. It would have been the sporting thing to do, the type of thing some straight-backed, no-nonsense swordmaster might have trained his pupils about regarding honor. The thing was, though, Rion had never had a swordmaster and the dead lost everything—

honor included—when they lost their lives. So instead, Rion slipped his hand inside of his tunic, withdrawing a knife—unable to avoid noticing that there were very few left from what he'd started with this morning as most were currently sticking in one body or another. With a practiced flick of his wrist, he sent the blade hurtling through the air to plunge deeply into the old man's thin chest.

His attacker's mad rush faltered, and he stumbled, staring down at the knife sticking out of him. Then, in another moment, he did what all men do, sooner or later—sooner with a knife protruding from a vital organ. He died.

Rion took the brief moment of respite this afforded him to glance over to check on Katherine and Darl. He'd meant to help them, but the furious fight on the walls had led him away from them no matter how hard he'd tried to fight his way back. They both looked exhausted—everyone did, of course, but the two of them in particular. But they were still alive, so that was something, and Katherine was still singing her song. A beautiful, sweet melody that—while not Rion's particular brand of music when given a choice—had had an undeniable effect on the defenders as well as himself.

Woman and man were covered in crimson splatters. Darl's spear, Rion saw, had been broken some time during the fighting, and he now held the two separate halves in either hand, making use of them as skillfully as he had the spear itself on the latest person to charge toward Katherine, meaning to give her a very scathing—very *cutting*—critique on her music.

And then, that was the last, and Rion saw to his shock that no more bloodthirsty attackers clambered up ladders onto the walls. Now there was only him and the other defenders of Valeria—their numbers woefully diminished in the last week. And, of course, there were the corpses. Corpses that, though they did not speak, made their presence known by the stink and the terrible, horrific sight of their battered, bloody bodies.

Rion didn't think he could ever remember, could even *imagine*, a worse night, a night in which the only light to be seen, the only light in the *world*, or at least so it felt, was the lights of those flickering torches and lanterns placed in regular intervals along the battlements. He couldn't imagine how things could get any worse than they already were.

That was when it began to rain.

And not *just* rain, for that would have been bad enough, turning the terrible night into a sodden, uncomfortable, chafing nightmare. But there was wind, too, great, powerful gusts of wind that seemed to rise out of nowhere and which threatened to sweep Rion off his feet, so that he was forced to reach out a hand onto the grime-slicked battlements to keep his balance.

There was something unnatural about all of it, a storm coming out of nowhere, and the sky which had been clear moments before was suddenly choked with dark clouds which churned and seethed like the countless, amorphous bodies of some nightmare creatures. A great, wailing *keening* rose in the air as the wind whistled past, buffeting him and the others, so powerful that it seemed as if it threatened to rip the very stones out of the walls, and he turned to Katherine and Darl.

They, too, looked confused, but if something unnatural *were* occurring—which all signs, including the helmet which was whipped past his face, nearly braining him, seemed to point to—he could think of no place he'd rather be than with the two of them. Except, that was, curled up in bed under thick blankets, barred away from the world by a locked door, but he didn't think such a paradise was on offer just now.

He heard shouts of panic and saw one of the defenders lose his feet under the heavy gusts. The man was thrown onto the ground then tumbled across the hard stones the way a leaf might be carried on a breeze. Except for the fact that the leaf didn't end up slamming with bone-breaking force into the crenellated stone wall of the battlements.

Rion had experienced a lot of panic in his life—the vast majority, as it happened, having taken place in the last year or so—and had thought he had become somewhat inured to it, had begun to face their increasingly desperate plight not with terror but with a weary resignation, the type of resignation often seen on soldiers after years spent at war. But he realized, in that moment, that he had been wrong, and that there was some terror left in him after all. Quite a bit, in fact.

After all, their enemies, to this point, had been terrible indeed, shocking in their brutality, distressing in their hate. But those enemies had, at the very least, been human—or, in the case of Kale and his other nightling creatures, something more like beasts. He had known, of course, as they all had, that they fought not just men and beasts but the gods themselves. But he discovered now that knowing a thing and actually *seeing* it, being *confronted* by it, were two very different things.

For of this much he was sure—the power that was now being brought to bear on the weary defenders, the power currently buffeting wall and soldier alike, could be nothing short of the furious wrath of Shira, the Goddess of the Wilds.

Gritting his teeth, the wind howling furiously in his ears like some beast roaring its anger, Rion began to inch his way down the battlements, gripping the damp stone desperately like a drowning man seeking purchase on a slick, muddy river bank. Katherine and Darl were less than a few dozen feet away, but they might as well have been miles, so slow was his progress.

He heard another scream as he walked, one loud enough to rise even over the thundering rain and wind, and he glanced to the side in time to see another poor defender knocked from his feet by the powerful gusts. This one, though, was not as fortunate as the first—if being knocked unconscious by a stone wall to lie at its base in a heap could be considered fortunate. Still, unconscious was better than dead, and Rion, still gripping the battlements desperately, was unable to do anything but watch, helpless, as the second guardsman was flung over the battlements by the wind as if he were an ant being flicked away by some petulant child.

In a moment, his screams vanished, swallowed by the storm, and Rion said a silent prayer for the man as he started working his way down the wall toward Katherine and Darl once more. Not that he thought it would do him much good, for how could this be happening at all? How could Shira be free to vent her wrath on the city's defenders without worrying about reprisal from Amedan or Javen or one of the other gods on the side of the Light? The only answer to that was that either they were too weak—or too busy—to help. If the first were true, then they were all screwed anyway. And if it were the second, then they had better hurry and finish whatever it was they were doing or else it would be too late.

The Age of Men

Chapter Twenty

Deitra did not know how long she had been singing, her words, her song, acting a shield against Shira's will, a will which sought to find them. She knew only that every part of her being was exhausted, yet she knew also that should she stop, even for a moment, should she let the defensive net of the spell her song created falter, then her mother would find them. And with her exhausted, her father in his weakened state, and Javen nowhere to be found, she knew that if that happened, they—and the entire mortal world—would be doomed.

But then, just when she thought she could sing no more, the roiling storm clouds over head began to lift and clear, and the approaching storm—which had seemed to be gathering all around them and which had been growing more and more powerful no matter her efforts—suddenly vanished as if it had never existed at all.

Immediately, Deitra let out a shaky sigh of relief and collapsed onto her knees on the wet sands of the small island's beach, her breath ragged, her hands trembling. "Thank the Light," she muttered in a hoarse voice.

But her relief was short lived, for something did not feel right, not at all. And she had some sense as she knelt there struggling to get her breath back, that the storm had not vanished, not in truth. It had moved. And if it were not here, there was only one other place that it could be. *"Oh no,"* she breathed.

A rustling of cloth caught her attention, and she turned to see that her father had stood, though "standing" was far overstating the case. In truth, her father's face was etched with exhaustion and pain, and it looked as if it took all he could just to keep his feet beneath them, as if even that small, normally simple task was a trial. But while seeing her father so weak, so frail, shook Deitra to her core, worse was the other thing she saw in his face, saw carved into his stare and his pale skin. Fear.

Seeing such an emotion writ plainly on his features brought cold terror into her own heart. "Father," she said, "what is it? What—"

"Your mother," he said, his words a harsh croak. "She brings her power against the city. I must..." His eyes grew distant then, as if he was unsure of what he had been about to say. Then he gave himself a shake and some focus returned to his gaze. "I must help them."

"Father, no," she said, "you can't. You're too weak. If you go, mother will find you and—"

"There is no choice, Deitra. Without help, the city will fall."

"But...what about your Chosen?" she asked, desperately casting about for any other solution. "Perhaps he could—"

"No," Amedan interrupted, shaking his head. "He is not ready, not yet. There is no choice, I—"

"Then I will go," she said.

Amedan gave her a sad smile. "That is kind of you, daughter, but no. You are weary. Perhaps if you were at your full power, you might be able to counter your mother's strength, but now—"

But Deitra did not give her father enough time to finish. In the normal course of events, she would have never been able to overpower her father in any way, for her strength, her magic was a pale shadow of his. But now, her father was not at his best. Was the weakest she had ever seen him, probably the weakest he had ever been, and Deitra stepped forward, placing a hand on his shoulder. Then she began to sing. A soft, lullaby song, a song of peace and contentment, a song in which there was no fear and no darkness, only warmth and kindness and love.

"Daughter..." he began, then his voice trailed off, his eyes slowly closed, and he would have fallen had she not caught him and laid him gently on the beach. In sleep, his face seemed to regain its nobility, its majesty, and he was her father once more, not the broken, incomplete wreck he had been since her mother betrayed him and cast him down during the fall of Ilrika. Deitra suddenly felt an overwhelming love for him, for this being who gave all of himself for those mortals he loved so much, who was willing to even risk destruction to keep them safe.

Deitra bent and gently kissed him on his brow. "Thank you, Father. For everything." Then, slowly, Deitra rose. She took two steps to the beach, the third of which would take her to that place, to that storm where her mother's will raged against the world of Light, and she paused. She knew what her going would mean, what it *must* mean, and she turned once more to gaze upon her father's recumbent form. "Goodbye, Father," she whispered. "May the Light guide you always."

She wished she could say goodbye to Javen, to tell him that though they had quarreled and disagreed, she loved him, for his loyalty and his kindness and yes, even for his humor which she had so often scorned. She wished, too, that she had been kinder to him. But there was no time left, and she could only hope that he knew.

A storm was raging now, one that threatened to shake the very foundations of the world itself, to tear down all that her father had built, to make of it a ruin. Most times, when such a storm came, a person could only hide and wait it out, but this storm would not fade in the morning and give way to clear skies. This storm, if not checked, would last forever. Sometimes, a person—or a goddess—could hide from the storms and, sometimes, she must go out and meet it.

And so she did.

Chapter Twenty-One

Rain fell around her in sheets, soaking through her clothes and chilling her. It was not a natural rain, this, that much Katherine knew immediately, just as the buffeting wind was not natural. There was malice in this storm, a hatred she could feel in each rain drop, could taste in the air. This storm, she knew, came from the Goddess of the Wilds, was her answer to the lives she would destroy, a small taste of what she would make of the world, if she succeeded in her conquest.

"What's going on?"

She turned to see that Rion had approached. The man was soaked, his hair hanging limply around him, and although he had screamed, his voice was only just audible over the storm's wrath.

"*The Goddess of the Wilds exerts her will,*" Darl answered in a shout of his own.

Rion opened his mouth to speak, but just then the world was lit up by a terrible bolt of lightning, one which struck the wall, shattering stone and sending the lethal debris flying into several of the nearest defenders who screamed as they were struck, more than one falling under the deadly barrage.

"*What does this mean?*" Rion shouted. "*What do we do?*"

Darl glanced at Katherine, and she saw the helplessness in his gaze, this confident warrior who had been by her side for years. Perhaps the greatest warrior in the world, certainly one who stood his own with Alesh and Tarex, the Ekirani. But no matter how great a warrior was, he could not slay a storm. Katherine did not know what it meant that Shira was able to unleash her fury unchecked by the other gods. Perhaps, seeing Valeria's defeat imminent, Deitra and Amedan had given up on them, had decided that it was a lost cause. Perhaps even Javen, the God of Chance, knew that no amount of luck could alter the outcome of this battle. But no, she would not believe that. She must believe that whatever reason the gods had to leave them, unaided, to the storm, was a good one. Yet that did nothing to answer Rion's question, nothing to answer the question she could see in Darl's gaze as well as the gazes of those bewildered, frightened defenders clutching the battlements and staring at her, looking for a miracle.

She could not tell Rion what it meant, but she thought that perhaps she knew what they must do, what *she* must do. She only hoped—doubted, yes, but *hoped*—that she would be strong enough. She looked down at her harp, the harp she was clutching desperately to her as if it were a shield that would protect her and those others around her. And...perhaps it was. She met Darl's eyes and, as in so many other times during their years together, the Ferinan seemed to know, without needing to be told, exactly what she was thinking. He smiled, nodding as the rain poured down his face, and Katherine felt some of her strength, some of her courage return to her at seeing his confidence. She only hoped that it wasn't misplaced.

She began to sing then, to play, but her voice sounded thready and weak before the roaring storm, and her fingers were fumbling and uncertain on the slick strings of the harp which seemed to cut into her.

I am not strong enough.

The thought popped into her mind unbidden and unasked for, but she knew it was true as soon as she had it. How could she, a mortal, hope to withstand the will of a god? How could anyone? She redoubled her efforts, focusing on a song that would bring peace to the raging world around her, a song of hope, that the light would come out again even after the darkest of nights.

And still it was not enough. No matter her efforts, no matter her wishes and desires, she could not escape one undeniable fact.

She was not strong enough.

She looked at Darl, and he must have seen some of her despair in her face, for he gave her a single nod, accepting her failure without judgment—which only made her feel worse.

Then, suddenly, inexplicably, her voice began to sound more sure, and she was able, then, to find the notes she had sought. Her fingers—numb with the cold—became nimble and quick as they had ever been, *quicker,* in fact, and though she sat alone on the chair on the battlements, she felt as if someone were there with her, as if a presence stood just behind her, hands on her shoulders, lending silent support.

You are right, dear Katherine, a familiar woman's voice said into her mind. *You are not strong enough. Neither, I'm afraid, am I. But...perhaps,* we *are.*

Deitra? Katherine thought back, not daring to pause in her song long enough to say the word aloud for fear that she would not be able to find the notes again.

I am here, Katherine, the goddess said, and though Katherine could not see her, she could hear sadness in her tone, as if she held some great, terrible knowledge, some knowledge which Katherine did not understand.

I am here.

***

Argush stood at his tent flap, staring in awe at the roiling storm clouds, at the lightning strikes which constantly lit up the world around him and which had already killed more than a few men and women of his army, searing them to ash. Several tents blazed nearby with fires so intense even the driving rain did not seem capable of putting them out. It was the greatest storm of his time, perhaps any time, one which dwarfed all other storms that had come before it.

Here, then, was the power of his goddess finally revealed, and he could only stare on in wonder as men and women scrambled to find shelter, as if tents, as if anything, could protect them from such a spectacle. There was no safety, not here, so Kale only stood, watching in awe. Here was true power. Had he really thought, not so long ago, that he might one day usurp the Goddess of the Wilds? That he might somehow grow in power until he was greater than she, until it was *she* who answered to his bidding? He knew now that he had been a fool. No one could stand against this—no one. The world itself could not. At least, not for long.

It seemed as if it would go on forever, one great endless storm...but then, Kale heard something. At first it was difficult to make out. A moment later, though, he realized that it was a voice, one that seemed to be carried on the wind that roared around him. A woman's voice. And not just one but two, two voices entwined so tightly together and in such perfect harmony that he could barely tell one from the other. And, with that realization, he noted something else that was strange. The storm was beginning to weaken, the flashes of lightning and roaring of thunder becoming less and less frequent.

"Damn her," came an angry hiss from behind him.

He spun and was shocked to see Shira standing in the tent. The Goddess of the Wilds looked furious, her hands knotted at her sides, her eyes flashing as if the storm itself was reflected in her gaze. But she did not *just* look angry. She looked tired, strained, as if she were carrying some great weight.

"Mistress," he said, surprised. "How can...the storm...it is your doing?"

"Of course it's my doing, *fool*," she snapped.

"But...it seems to be weakening."

She snarled and, for a moment, Argush thought that he was finished, that she would let her wrath—so pointedly shown in the storm's power, even if it were waning—loose on him and end it. Instead, she only stared past him, through the tent flap. "It is my daughter, her and that *bitch* of hers."

"I...I don't understand, Mistress."

"Do you not *see?*" she demanded. "She is fighting me. *They* are fighting me. Deitra, the fool girl, has given her life to the effort." She moved to stand beside him and, now that she was closer, Kale was surprised to see water running down her face. Were they tears, he wondered? Or were they no more than streaks of the rain which had already soaked him through?

"But surely, Mistress," he said uncertainly, "they are not powerful enough to—"

"Send in your troops, Argush," she growled, hissing the words out of clenched teeth. "Now."

"But Goddess," he said, hesitating, "you said to wait, for the other, your creature—"

"It will be here soon," she snapped, "but there is no time. The walls must fall tonight! Send some of your troops up the walls, tell them to find this *Chosen* of my daughter's and kill her. The bulk of your forces, though, are to gather at the forests' edge, facing the gate."

"But...the gate is reinforced, Mistress. We have tried to break it down with battering rams, but it will not—"

"Do as I told you, Argush," the goddess growled. "Send in your troops. *All* of your troops, Argush—my children as well."

Kale was angry and wanted to argue. For one, the nightlings would not do well with the soldiers who were terrified of them. Rightly so since in the past weeks several men and women who had wandered too far away from the campfires at night had been killed. Putting the two groups together would ensure that many more would suffer a similar fate, for the nightlings, while powerful, were not very particular on whose flesh they feasted on, just so long as they did.

Shira looked at him as if she could read his thoughts. "Casualties are inevitable in war, Argush, and they are irrelevant so long as the city falls. Do what I told you—now."

Kale did not like being ordered about as if he were some servant, had not liked it when Olliman had done it and so had taken great pleasure in seeing the man dead. This, though, was different. The goddess before him had none of the mercy which he had always thought weakness in Olliman, none of the kindness. There was only fury there, only rage.

He did as he was told.

Chapter Twenty-Two

Fermin was afraid. It wasn't a particularly new experience for him—he had come to realize, over the last couple of days, that he had lived most of his life that way. Afraid of letting down Lord and Lady Tirinian, afraid of disappointing Rion or more recently Sonya and Marta, those put in his charge.

But this time it was different. Partly, the source of that fear was the unnatural storm—and there, at least, his fear was shared by everyone in the camp—but it was not just that. Marta had not shared all of the details of her experience in Kale's tent with him as she'd told him what the Welian, Efial, had told her—the man, at the time, getting some much needed rest. But then, she hadn't needed to. He had seen the truth of her ordeal writ plain on her face. She had sacrificed much, that young girl, had risked much to get the information they needed.

Now, it was up to him to make sure that she had not suffered what she had—that Efial, the poor man, had not suffered what *he* had—for nothing. They had all done their part. It was up to him, now, to ensure they had not suffered in vain. So, instead of doing what his fear wanted him to do—what nearly every cowardly fiber of his being was *demanding* he do—and hide inside his tent, he was riding his horse toward the front line.

Or, at least, he was trying to. His progress was slowed greatly by the many troops marching the same direction he was traveling, toward the frontline—not that the soldiers of Kale's army did anything so organized as "march." Instead, it was sort of a mad scramble in which people seemed to be running in every direction without any clear reason why they were doing it while the army's various sergeants and commanders bellowed commands, trying and failing to bring some order to the chaos. A chaos which was, it had to be said, made dramatically worse by the terrible storm raging around them.

Lightning rained from the sky in great bolts of fury, striking tent and soldier alike and setting them ablaze. Most of those unfortunate enough to be struck by the bolts were at least fortunate enough to die instantly. Others, though, were not so lucky. Their clothes were set ablaze, and they sprinted madly around, human infernos, all their hatred for the Light and the people who served it forgotten in their agony as they screamed for someone—anyone—to help them before finally collapsing in death.

It was chaos, the worst kind, and Fermin was forced to knock several men and women who got in his way aside with his mount, for he knew that he was running out of time. The enemy was marching on Valeria in force now—or would be, once the commanders managed to bring some semblance of order to their wild, directionless charges—but that wasn't the worst of it. The worst was that, according to the Welian messenger and Marta, the Welian force would arrive soon. And without help, they would be set upon in ambush as soon as they reached the shore.

Everything was riding on his success, on him getting a message to Alesh and the others in Valeria that the Welians were coming, not to mention whatever creature Shira had told Kale about. The problem, of course, was that he had absolutely no idea how to go about doing that. So, as he forced his mount through the crowd, he wracked his brain, all his thoughts focused on how he would get the message to Valeria's defenders.

He was so focused, in fact, that he did not notice the figure moving in the distance behind him, regarding him with narrowed eyes. A figure who moved amongst the chaos, following him without fail. A woman, this figure, one who followed in his wake, an evil scowl, as always, plastered on her face.

Chapter Twenty-Three

It was the strangest thing.

One moment, the winds were so powerful, the rain so thick and driving, that Rion felt as if he would be swept from Valeria's battlements. Indeed, several of the defenders who had been too slow or too tired to grab hold of the walls had suffered just such a fate. But in another instant, the rain slowed down to a trickle that was no longer freezing where it touched him but almost pleasant, the way a summer shower sometimes felt when a man found himself caught in one and, to his own surprise, found that he was not upset but pleased to be standing beneath that gentle rain. The winds, too, had changed so that now they felt like a cool autumn breeze against his skin, not an enemy seeking to hurl him over the battlements any longer, but a playful entity giving him a playful hello.

But as strange as it all was, Rion did not need to wonder at the source of this abrupt change, for he, like all the rest of Valeria's defenders manning the walls, knew well enough. And he, like those others, stared now at that source, feeling a mixture of awe and inspiration, of gratitude and appreciation that words could not express.

Katherine sat in her chair, her long hair flowing in the breeze, and she played her harp, creating such beautiful music that to even call it "music" seemed to cheapen it. For the song she played was not just music, not just art. It had risen above both, had become something grander, something greater. This was no barroom ballad sung by men too drunk to be on-key and too drunk to care.

The Age of Men

It was not a martial hymn that might be played by an army on the march or a subtle tune strummed in some great hall, quietly so as not to disturb the guests.

This song was different, was greater than all of those. And yet, this song had parts of those songs within it, the joy felt by those men and women hoisting their cups of ale in some tavern or another, the inspiration, the camaraderie, the *closeness* felt by those soldiers sharing hardship and triumph alike, even that soft insistence of those courtroom ballads. This song was none of those and yet it was all of them and as such was greater than them, greater, in fact, than any song Rion had ever heard or had ever thought to hear.

It was a song of courage and beauty, of peace and contentment and honor and love. It was a song which gave answer to the worst the world had to offer, that shed light on those dark figures huddling in the closets and underneath the beds of cowering children. It was a song which proved, beyond doubt, that the world's countless fallen had not died for nothing. It was, in the end, an answer. An answer to all those many worries and concerns, those fears and doubts which plagued any man or woman living in the world.

Katherine's harp, its notes clear and precise, wove the shape of that answer, and her words gave it meaning. It was the most beautiful thing Rion had ever heard, more beautiful than anything he had ever expected to hear, and he, like those others on the battlements, could do nothing but stare in wonder at the woman as she sang.

It was dark on the walls, the torches aligning it sputtering and many of them already gone out, yet he could see her clearly, for Katherine seemed to glow like some beacon, not like the blazing of some great torch, but instead like the soft glow of an early morning sunrise, when a man finds himself awake to see it and, in that moment, can believe—can hardly *help* but to believe—that the world, in all its beauty, had been made for him and him alone.

It was beautiful and wonderful and...it was strange. For while Rion had heard Katherine's voice before and even he—who had never cared much for music—could not claim that it was anything but beautiful, this time, it sounded different. It sounded, in fact— perhaps by some trick of his weary mind—as if two people were singing together, their voices raised in perfect harmony, a harmony that seemed to thrum through him.

But even stranger was that from time to time, Rion seemed to see two people sitting in that seat, Katherine and another, a woman of profound beauty who, at first, he did not recognize. And then he did. How could he not? For he had seen her likeness often enough on statues adorning city squares or great halls. Deitra, the Goddess of Art and Music, and however beautiful the song, there was something about her demeanor, something about a sadness he could see in her gaze, that unsettled Rion.

Katherine, too, looked troubled, and even as she sang tears ran down her face. Rion glanced up at the sky, roiling moments ago with great storm clouds through which bolts of lightning danced but clearing even as he watched. What did it take, he wondered, to stand against the fury of the Goddess of the Wilds? He did not know, could not imagine, but he knew that such a standing, that a refuting of so much power would have a cost. And though he did not know the exact details, he felt—he *knew*—that Katherine, and Deitra along with her, were paying that price even as he watched.

Darl, too, seemed to understand the sacrifice the mortal and goddess were making, for he met Rion's eyes, a profound sadness in his own, and Rion was forced to turn away, unable to stare at the spectacle any longer. He regretted it immediately. For there, in the distant fields, the enemy army was beginning to gather once more. Hundreds, thousands, of shapes stood just outside of the forest edge, well out of bow shot. Yet, a small consolation—and in such times, a man must take what he could get—was that, for the moment, at least, they were not charging to renew the attack, only standing as if waiting for something.

Were they waiting, he wondered, for Katherine's song to fail, for the magic to be overcome by Shira's own? Or was there some other matter which prompted their unusual reluctance when the last weeks had proved the members of Kale's army—and Kale himself—all too eager to throw their lives away?

Chapter Twenty-Four

Katherine's fingers felt numb and uncertain on the harp's strings, strings which were cold and wet with the rain and seemed to bite into her fingertips with each strum. Her hair hung about her in lank strips, and her throat felt raw from her song, yet all of these things seemed like only minor nuisances compared with the terrible, heavy exhaustion which had seeped into her. An exhaustion which was continuing to grow with each passing moment, an exhaustion not just of the body but of the mind, one which threatened to steal her concentration, to rob her song of its power.

The song was faltering beneath the terrible power—power of the Goddess Shira herself—arrayed against it, and how could it do anything else? How could anything stand against such might as what she felt pressing against her, tearing at the magic her song wove like a dagger thrusting at a fine dress, meaning to make of its beauty a farce.

I cannot do this, she thought desperately, *I cannot.*

And yet you must, a voice said inside her head, and she knew that it was the goddess, Deitra, speaking to her. *We must.*

The goddess sounded tired, an exhaustion in her voice to match Katherine's own, but that was not all. She sounded...weak. As if she were somehow getting farther and farther away and her voice came from some great distance, yet Katherine knew that was not true, knew that the goddess was with her still. With her and yet...fading.

You're dying, Katherine thought, the realization striking her like a hammer blow. *It...it's killing you.*

When the goddess answered, her voice was weak, frail. *Yes, Chosen Elar. My mother's power is...vast.*

Even as she sang on, Katherine's mind raced with panic. *But what...what can we do?*

We are doing it already, Katherine Elar. We do it even now.

Katherine felt tears gliding their way down her cheeks, mingling with the rainwater soaking her, for she knew, she *felt* the goddess fading, felt her dying.

All things which live must die in their time, sweet one, the goddess said in her mind, and though she still sounded tired, she also sounded resolute. *It has been my privilege to know you. Now, do not cry. Instead, let us sing.*

And so Katherine sang.

She sang as she felt the goddess with her begin to weaken, felt her begin to fade. She sang until she no longer felt her at all. And then she sang some more.

Chapter Twenty-Five

Rion felt it happen. One moment, the song was drifting in the air, over everything, everyone, the song of two voices mingling in perfect harmony. Then, there was what he would only recall later as a sort of thunder without sound, and it seemed that some heat, some warmth that he had not realized he'd felt until it was gone, vanished, was torn away.

He spun on instinct, not knowing why, exactly, and looked at Katherine. The woman's face was covered in tears, her skin pale, but still she sang on, her fingers thrumming the notes of her harp, a terrible grief writ plain on her face. At first Rion wondered what it was, but then he noticed that the song had changed. There were two voices no longer, and he saw no second form sitting with Katherine as he had imagined he had moments ago. It was only her, and the song she sang was hers and hers alone.

The air was suddenly split with a terrible, shattering roar of thunder that almost sounded like a cry of anguish and, a moment later, the enemy forces began rushing forward again. He was still trying to understand, to piece together what had happened, when they were climbing up siege ladders, weary defenders turning to meet them.

But even Rion, who knew little of warfare and sieges, could see that what few of the defenders remained were nowhere near enough to turn back the tide, not this time, not even with the help of Katherine's song. But with no choice left him, Rion rushed toward the nearest ladder.

The cobbles were slick with rain and blood, treacherous footing, and by the time he managed to make it to the ladder, one of the attackers had already gained the battlements. Not an old man or woman this, not someone who would have looked more at home bouncing a grandchild on his knee. No, this was a killer born, a man with wide shoulders and thick, muscled arms. There was a ragged scar across his face, and the man was missing an eye. He bellowed a roar, his one remaining eye gleaming with madness, but that was not drew Rion's attention as the man charged toward him.

Instead, his gaze focused on the battle axe in the man's hands, one that, just then, looked big enough to split the world in half, one that didn't appear as if it would have any problems chopping up a fool nobleman. Panicked, Rion stumbled away from the man, narrowly avoiding a vicious, two-handed swing of the axe which would have put an end to all his worries in a hurry, had it connected.

"Come here, little bug," the man growled, grinning madly. "Come and play."

The man growled, swinging his weapon again, and Rion stumbled backward again until he struck the battlement wall. "No thanks," he said, "I'm far too tired to play. Or get squished, as far as it goes."

The man hefted the axe, moving closer to him, his insane grin still in place. "Think so? Let's test that, friend."

He brought the axe he held down in a vicious arc meant to split Rion in half, bellowing as he did. Rion, left with nowhere to run, did the only thing he could do. He lunged forward, underneath the descending axe, and plunged his knife into the man's stomach.

The big man's body went rigid, and he stared down at Rion in disbelief. "You silly little fucker," he growled, dropping the axe and foregoing any other conversation, choosing instead the expedient of making his feelings known by wrapping his thick hands around Rion's throat and squeezing.

Rion fumbled at the hands on his throat, trying to break the man's hold as he wheezed for breath that would not come, but he might as well have been trying to push a mountain for all the good it did him. His vision began to dim, and he gurgled and hissed as his attacker pressed him against the hard stone of the battlement wall, as if he was trying to decide whether to choke or crush him to death.

Rion flailed desperately, his hands lashing out and striking the man but to no avail. That was when, by chance, one of his hands struck the handle of the knife still protruding from the man's gut. Desperately, his vision dimming rapidly by the second, his chest feeling as if it were on fire, he grasped the handle and with a breathless grunt, gave it a hard tug so that the blade traveled through the man's stomach and cut upward, toward his chest.

The man gurgled, blood pouring from his mouth, and his hands came free of Rion's throat. Rion breathed in desperate, choking breaths as the man stumbled backward, staring at the crimson rent in his stomach and chest as if he couldn't believe it. Then he gave Rion an accusing look. "You...silly...fu..." The man trailed off, wavering, and a moment later collapsed to the ground at Rion's feet.

Rion wanted to say something in return, some rejoinder, but the man was dead. More to the point, he was too busy gasping for breath, falling to his knees as a terrible wave of vertigo swept over him.

"Hi there, dearie."

The voice sounded almost kind, far more out of place on the battlements than the big man's roar had been—or Rion's wheezing, as far as that went—and he raised his head to see an old woman standing before him.

She was heavy-set, with a hunched back and gray hair, her teeth, as she smiled at him, all black with rot and, perhaps most strange of all, both of her hands clutched a cane which seemed to be the only way she was standing upright, so hunched was her posture.

Perhaps from lack of oxygen or from nearly dying, Rion felt confused, and he could think to do nothing but nod his head wearily. "Hi," he wheezed.

"My name's Wanda," the woman said, smiling and giving him another unwanted peek at her ruined teeth and a whiff of foul breath.

"Well, Wanda," he said, staring to climb his way to his feet, "it's a plea—" He cut off, his words turning to a squawk of pain as the old woman moved with a speed he wouldn't have expected, bringing the cane around and striking him full-on in the face with a blow that made stars dance in his eyes.

The next thing he knew, he was lying on his back, the hunched form of the old woman standing over him, somehow reminding him of a vulture regarding some recently dead animal. "Easy there, lad," the woman said, smiling. "Wouldn't want you to tire yourself out, not if I'm to have you for dinner.

"I'll pass," Rion said, trying to spin away but, again, the woman's cane met him, this time giving him a ringing strike across the upper arm that made it go numb, and he cried out.

"Oh, I'm sorry to say that's not an option lad," the woman said. "You see, you're a guest." She laughed, a cackling, screeching sound. "In fact, you might go so far to say you're the guest of honor. The one," she leaned forward, producing a knife from somewhere within her filthy shift, "that I'll be having. For. Dinner."

Rion was hurting all over, feeling even dizzier than he had been, and so he was forced to watch, helpless, as the woman raised the knife over her head, cackling madly. Rion had a brief moment to think that out of all the terrible things he'd faced in recent weeks, it was a shame that he would finally be killed by an insane old woman. But then, suddenly, the woman seemed to hover into the air, floating one foot above the ground, then another, a confused look on her face to match the confusion Rion felt. And then she wasn't hovering at all but flying, hurtling through the air toward the stone crenellations of the battlements, and not just toward them but *over* them, and Rion thought he heard her let out a scream before she vanished from his view to plummet down somewhere into the fields outside the city far, far below.

"Mad bitch," a voice growled, and Rion looked up to see Sigan standing over him, the crime boss frowning after where he'd thrown the old woman as if he wanted nothing more than to go retrieve her and do it all over again.

"W-what are you doing here?" Rion said, noticing just then that the crime boss was not alone but that there appeared to be several dozen men and women—criminals, many of which Rion recognized from one dark alley or another—standing behind him.

The crime boss turned and frowned at him. "You mean on account of we didn't get an invite? I'm still a bit hurt about that, you know."

"Sorry," Rion said dazedly, shocked to still be alive. "Must have slipped my mind."

"Well," Sigan grunted. "Better slipped than eaten, eh? 'Less I miss my guess, that old hag meant to take a bite out of you."

"Doubted she would have cared for it," Rion managed. "Probably taste like fear and failure."

"Fear sure," the crime boss said. "But not failure—not yet, anyway." He held out a thick-fingered hand. "Now enough lyin' around on your pampered noble ass. We've got fightin' to do."

"Seriously," Rion said, taking the hand and trying to fight down the panic at how easily the crime boss hoisted him to his feet, "why are you here?"

Sigan grunted. "Like we got so much else to be about? Anyway, I had a talk with some of my...friends here." He paused, glancing back at a group wholly made up of people Rion didn't think *anyone* could call "friend" with a straight face, then back to Rion. "We figured that it weren't much good, robbin' and killin' if the folks you aim to do it to have already been robbed or killed by someone else." He shrugged his massive shoulders. "Might say we're protectin' our interests, as it were."

Despite everything, Rion found himself grinning, and the crime boss grinned back. "Thanks," he said.

Sigan grunted. "Don't thank me yet. There's plenty blood left to be spilled—enough, I imagine, that we'll all have our fill 'fore it's done."

Rion couldn't argue with that, and he never got the chance to in any case. Seconds later, a great roar—an earth-shattering, ear-splitting roar—shook the air, shook the very stones beneath his feet. He turned to the regard the distant tree line from which the sound had come, and his blood went cold in his veins.

Something moved in the shadows of the trees, some unimaginably large form, and even as his mind was trying to understand what his eyes had thought they'd glimpsed, trees began to fall, the sound of their trunks shattering and cracking punctuating the words of Katherine's song.

Fear trilled through him despite the power in the song, for what could possibly cause such destruction? What could brush aside great towering trees as if they were blades of grass giving way before a heavy trod? A moment later he got his answer, too, and like the first, he wished he had not.

The figure that emerged from the woods was unlike anything Rion had ever seen or thought to see before. It was massive, standing twenty feet tall at the least. Great, hulking muscles squirmed and writhed underneath the creature's ebony skin, visible in the moonlight like eels wriggling in some twisting knot. Its shape was similar to a man's but seemed somehow in mockery of it, with arms and legs as thick as tree trunks and fists bigger than some wagons Rion had seen. Its facial features were scrunched, flat and revolting.

"*Oh gods, help us,*" Rion breathed.

"Friend of yours?" Sigan asked, and Rion noted with more than a little dismay that even the crime boss's normally menacing voice sounded unsure.

"What *is* that thing?" one of the nearby defenders, a young man who could have barely been twenty years of age, asked in a quavering voice.

"Our doom, lad," another answered, this one a man who appeared to be in his early fifties with a gray beard flecked with crimson stains from the day's efforts.

Rion meant to dispute that, to tell the man that he was wrong, but just then the creature let out a thundering roar and whatever he had been about to say was pushed out of his mind. He turned to Darl and Katherine, meaning to find some solace there. They would have a plan, they had to. But they didn't look like they had any plan, not then. Katherine's shoulders were slumped, clearly exhausted, and she looked as if she would have collapsed if Darl had not been holding her shoulders to keep her upright.

There would be no help from that quarter then, for he knew that the song was the only thing holding back the storm rushing at them. Rion stared back at that great hulking form, struggling to fight down the budding panic growing inside him. "What do I do?" he asked in a whisper. "What do I do?" The answer came to him out of nowhere. *Captain Nordin.* Of course. The man had been leading the city's defense since Alesh had vanished, had managed to hold the walls against all odds. Surely, he would have some answer.

He turned back to Sigan. "Hold the walls," he said, then motioned to Katherine and Darl. "Protect them."

Sigan stared at him for a moment, perhaps thinking about finishing the job the big man had started and strangling him to death for giving him orders. In the end though, the crime boss just nodded. "You heard him," he growled at the others around him. "Spread out—there's killin' needs doin'."

Feeling a little better, Rion rushed down the battlements in search of the captain.

He found Nordin surrounded by several of his sergeants, and even before he reached them, the slight flicker of hope he'd been entertaining began to wither and die. They stood in a quiet circle, gazing over the battlements at the forces—and, particularly, at the great hulking beast—with expressions of quiet dread. Their faces were those of men preparing to give up, men who saw their death coming and were only waiting for them to arrive. They did not, in short, look like the type of men who had a plan. Unless, of course, that plan was to lose.

Still, seeing no other option, Rion moved toward them. "Captain," he said.

Nordin turned away from the spectacle with a stunned expression on his face. "Oh," he said in a weary, lifeless voice, "Lord Tirinian. How can I help you?"

"Just Rion is fine," Rion said, waving a dismissive hand. "So anyway, what's the plan? Do we send out a sortie or—"

"A sortie?" Nordin asked with a dry, humorless, somehow *old* laugh. "Against that?" he went on, indicating the creature. "Forgive me, my lord, but we don't even have enough soldiers to man the wall. Who would we send? And what would such a sortie ride? Donkeys or bulls? For we have little else."

Rion winced. "Well. So what then? What do we do?"

Just then, the creature let out another great roar and began moving toward the gate with surprising speed. The men and women of the enemy army scrambled out of its path—at least mostly. Those too slow or too oblivious to notice its approach were crushed beneath the creature's feet or swept aside by its massive arms like dolls discarded by some cruel child.

"What do we do?" Captain Nordin asked, drawing his battered blade from the sheath at his side. "We hold."

Perhaps not the most inspiring words Rion had ever heard, but not the worst either. At least, that was, until the man finished. "As long as we can."

"But...there's got to be something we can do," Rion said, "some way..." He trailed off, for if there was a way to defeat that great beast, he could not see it.

Nordin met his eyes, a weary resignation in his own. "You should go, Lord Tirinian. There is nothing left for you to do here." *Nothing but to die, at least.* The man did not say it, but Rion heard the words as clearly as if he had.

He turned back to look at the creature. Already its surprising speed had brought it a third of the distance across the field as it moved unerringly toward the city gate. The great, reinforced city gate which had, up to now, withstood the relentless assault of Kale's soldiers. But this was no soldier carrying a battering ram. This was something else. Something far worse. Compared to the great beast, the gate seemed like nothing.

It means to break its way through, he realized and, in that moment, he realized also what it was that the enemy soldiers—at least those who had not yet been crushed by the creature's passage—were waiting for. They were waiting for the moment when the gate which had barred their passage for the last weeks fell to the creature's assault, as it must.

Rion looked around for someone, anyone to tell him what to do. But Katherine and Darl were busy, and Alesh was still nowhere to be seen, would likely still be huddled over the dying Ekirani when the city fell. As for Nordin, the man only watched the oncoming creature grimly, seemingly lost in his own thoughts, thoughts which, judging by the expression on his face, were dark ones. There would be no help from that quarter either, then.

There was no one then, no one to step forward and save the day. There was only him. "Very well, Nordin," he said, the words sounding as if they came from someone else, "I will go. To the gate."

Nordin turned to look at him, a terrible knowledge—knowledge which Rion did his best not to notice—in his visage. "May the gods watch over you, Eriondrian Tirinian," he said softly.

Rion gave him a single nod. "May they watch over us all, Captain."

Then he was turning and hurrying toward the stairs leading down to the gate with no idea of what he would do when he got there. What he did know, though, was that the time had finally come. The time which he had feared for his entire life. The time, in short, when he would be forced to look after himself, to make his own decisions, and could count on no one but himself. He was a gambler, true, but he was a bet even *he* wouldn't take. At least, that was, under normal circumstances, but circumstances, just then, were far from normal.

He had only just reached the top of the stairs when he heard Nordin's voice raised from behind him. *"Ready—loose!"*

Firing arrows into the charging beast no doubt and also no doubt knowing, just as Rion did, that they would do no good, that arrows against such a creature as this would be no more than a minor nuisance, like a mosquito bite might be to a man.

Rion barely paid it any mind, though. He only rushed to the gate. Likely, he rushed to his own death, for he could not imagine how such a creature could be defeated, and if it *could* be, certainly he wasn't the one to do it. Only, there was no one else. And he told himself that things might still work out. There was a *chance,* after all, always a chance. He just wished, as he took the steps two at a time, that he believed it.

Chapter Twenty-Six

The darkness lay heavy upon the land, and what little he could have seen in the perpetual moonlight was coated in waist-high fog so thick he imagined he had to force his way through it, brushing it aside like a curtain as he walked.

He did not like this place. He never had. It was a serious place, and Javen hated serious things. His brothers and sisters, even his father, his mother before she had become what she was, had always told him that he needed to take life more seriously, and many were the arguments with his siblings because they grew weary of his constant jests and mockery. They believed he did it because he simply did not care about the way the world was, thought his taunts and mockery were symptoms of a life led without a care.

But they were wrong.

Even his father, who knew so much, was wrong. Those taunts, those jests Javen so often made to his siblings' consternation were not symptomatic of him not caring enough. They were, in fact, the desperate, grasping attempts at levity for a being who cared too much. None of them understood that, understood *him*, save, perhaps, for Deitra.

He told himself that was okay, that love was not dependent upon understanding and a good thing, too, lest no one feel its warmth. How could he expect them to understand him, after all, when he hardly understood himself?

Mortals thought of him as fickle, mercurial, unpredictable, but he thought that, in truth, he was none of those things. What he was most of the time—all the time, nearly—was scared. Sometimes without even knowing what it was that had aroused his fear, and his jokes and taunts, such as they were, were only the whistling of a child in the darkness, trying to assure himself there was nothing to fear and knowing it for a lie even as he did.

And so, for a god who feared so much, so often, it was no real surprise that he did not enjoy coming here to this place, to these Fields. For there could be nothing more serious, he thought, than those forms—seen only as vague, indefinable shapes through the thick blanket of fog—walking around him.

Hundreds—thousands—of forms, it seemed, wraiths in the mist. Were there always so many, he wondered, or were recent events contributing to an increase in their number? He thought he knew the answer to that, but it was a very serious answer, and so, as he did so often in his life, Javen chose not to pursue the question.

He did not know how long he walked in the perpetual twilight of that place, the only sound the hiss of the grass beneath his feet, grass he could not see for the thick fog which swirled around him. He did not know how long he journeyed with those others, those wraiths in the mist. He knew only that he walked. He walked without searching for anything, without looking for it, for here in this place, a man—or a god—could never find anything. He could only be found. That much he remembered.

In time, he caught sight of the orange glow of a distant fire, and he made his way toward it. As he drew closer, he saw a familiar, white-haired figure sitting on one side of the campfire, holding an iron rod in his hand. An old man sat on the other. They did not speak. Tears glided down the old man's face, and the white-haired figure watched, an expression on own, lit by the firelight, that could only be compassion.

In time, the old man's sobbing quieted, and he looked up at the figure sharing the fire with him. "I can't...that is, I can't go back?"

"No," the white-haired figure said softly. "You cannot. No one may turn back on the path they have traveled, Yallen Hargrove, not the living nor the dead, for it is a path they themselves chose, one they chose to set their feet to."

The old man sniffled, running an arm across his face. "Wish I'd have done some things different. Picked a different path, maybe."

"So do all," the white-haired figure said, "man and god alike. Now, are you ready?"

The old man swallowed, his eyes studying the iron rod the figure held, the tip of it glowing with heat. "Will it hurt?"

"No," the white-haired figure said. "You are done with that, Yallen Hargrove, and will hurt no more."

The old man gave a rueful laugh. "Well. I guess that's a good thing, isn't it?"

The other figure said nothing, only gave him a small smile, and after a moment, the old man nodded, rising. "Well. Guess I'm ready then."

The white-haired figure stood, and though Javen knew he had told the truth when he'd claimed it would not hurt, still he found himself looking away as brand met flesh. When he turned back, the old man was walking toward the edge of the firelight, the white-haired figure watching until, a moment later, the walking man vanished into the shadow.

"Come then, brother," the Keeper of the Dead said, turning to stare at where he stood in the shadows. "You wished to speak to me—I am here."

Javen cleared his throat, fighting back the urge to hesitate, and stepped into the firelight. "Hello, brother."

The Keeper studied him with eyes that seemed to see through him. "Have you come, brother, to sit at my fire?"

Javen grunted. "N-no," he said. "Not that. Not...I wanted to talk to you."

The Keeper gave him a small smile. "Very well. Then speak. I am here."

Javen knew what he wanted to say, what he wanted to ask, but now that he was here, in this place of the dead, he found that he was having difficulty bringing it up. Instead, he glanced in the direction the old man had gone. "He seemed...upset."

"Yes."

"But...well, I mean, he was old, wasn't he? I'd have thought the old would be ready for...well, you know, for *it.*"

Another small smile from his brother. "For death, you mean?"

Javen found that he could not speak, so he only nodded instead.

The Keeper knelt, placing the end of the brand he held gently, almost reverently, in the flames. "Men—and gods—make their lives out of their habits, Javen. And the old have lived for a long time—it is not so easy a habit to break. Not so very different, then, than the habit you have formed of not coming here, to this place."

Javen grunted. "I've uh...well, I've been meaning to visit, but..."

"But you do not like this place." It was not a question, not really, only a statement.

Still, Javen found himself answering it anyway. "I mean, it's nice and all but...well. I suppose there's places I'd rather be."

The Keeper smiled again at that. "So say all men and gods who come to this place. Do not fret, brother, for I understand."

Javen fidgeted, feeling guilty, somehow, as if he needed to explain. "It's pleasant in a way...you know, the fire and all. It's just...well, it's a lot of walking, isn't it?"

The Keeper cocked his head to the side, watching him. "Is it?"

Javen frowned, realizing then that he couldn't guess at how long he'd walked. A minute? A year? In this place of perpetual twilight and fog, time seemed to have no meaning. "I...I don't know."

The Keeper nodded. "The walk matters, Javen. It *all* matters. The finding of the fire and the leaving of it. The shadows and the fog and the brand. It is all part of it."

"Part of what?"

"I think you know."

Javen winced. "Part of death, you mean."

The Keeper nodded slowly. "Yes. And part of life. But enough of that—tell me, why have you come? What is it you seek here, in this place?"

Javen had come for a very specific reason, to ask a very specific question, but now that he was here, he found that his mouth was dry. "I...I come to ask a question."

"Very well," his brother said. "Then ask it. I am here."

"I...that is, you know some of what is going on? In the world, I mean."

The Keeper smiled. "You mean that a battle now rages, one which threatens the very world of which you speak?"

"Right," Javen said, clearing his throat. "That's it."

"Yes, I may have heard some tale of it."

Javen glanced back at the log sitting beside the fire, the one which had, moments before, been being used by a dead man and how many other countless dead before him. "Right," he said slowly, "well, I guess you would have, wouldn't you?"

His brother said nothing, only watched him, and Javen took a slow, deep breath. "The thing is, Father is weak now, weaker than I have ever seen him. And Mother...well, she betrayed him, and he cannot stand against her, not as he is. I was wondering...that is...if you knew some way..."

"To kill her," the Keeper said flatly, without any trace of emotion in his voice.

Hearing his thoughts echoed so bluntly, without garnish, Javen winced. "I...I mean, we have to do *something* don't we?"

The Keeper sighed. "Know, Javen, that despite the stories told of me, I am no grim figure in hood and cloak who comes at darkness to steal the life from the living."

Javen fidgeted. "I didn't mean—"

"Forget it," his brother said, waving a hand. "It does not matter. I made my peace with how I am perceived long ago. Yet for all that, I am not an executioner. Instead, I am a guide, my purpose not to kill but to help those who find themselves in this place. To show them the way."

Javen sighed. "Right. So you don't know how. Sorry, I—"

"I did not say that I do not know how, brother," the god interrupted. "And know that I understand what it has cost you to come here, what it has cost you, further, to ask what you have."

"So...you do know," Javen said slowly.

"How do you kill a god, Javen?" the Keeper asked. "You, having suffered what you did so recently at the hands of the brother we knew nothing about, the one our mother raised in secret, surely you must know this better than most."

Javen remembered all too clearly the time spent writhing with fever as the shadows consumed him, and he nodded, fighting back the dark memories. "Their will," he managed. "You destroy their will."

"Yes," the Keeper said softly. "In that way, we are not so very different from mortals, for many who come to me come for that exact reason."

"But...Mother's will," Javen said, "it...*she* is so strong."

"Even the greatest castle, might tumble, brother, should you but steal the foundation from beneath it."

"And you know what that is—Mother's foundation, I mean?"

"Don't you?" the Keeper asked, watching him.

Javen frowned. "I don't...I mean, no. No, I don't."

His brother nodded, motioning to the log. "Sit, Javen. Sit and we will talk, brother to brother."

Javen raised an eyebrow at the iron rod, still sitting in the fire. "That's not for me, I hope."

His brother smiled. "Not today."

Not exactly the most comforting answer, but Javen nodded, starting toward the log. "I'm sorry—for not visiting more, I mean. And thank you, Valaz. For your help."

"Please," his brother said, "call me the Keeper."

Chapter Twenty-Seven

Marta paused in scrubbing the dried, crusted food off the bottom of the large iron pot and glanced toward the opening of the large cook's tent in which she now stood. Soldiers milled about outside, the shouts and orders of the officers audible even over the talking and steaming pots inside the cook tents. Something was happening, she knew, something big, the attack that Fermin had warned her about, no doubt, and she took a moment to say a silent prayer for her friends in Valeria as well as the manservant.

By now, Fermin should have reached the frontline and, with any luck, had been able to somehow get a message to the others, though how he would accomplish such a thing she had no idea. It seemed near impossible to hope that—Marta grunted in surprise as someone struck her a ringing slap in the side of the face, and she looked up to see the head cook frowning down at her.

A heavy-set woman with gray hair, matronly in appearance. In another place, in another, better world, she might have been someone's favorite aunt, but now she was scowling, her hands on her wide hips. "Ain't got no time for you to be daydreamin', girl. The soldiers got to eat before they go in for the second wave. Without food, they'll be too weak to fight"—*we can hope,* Marta thought—"and without clean dishes, we won't be able to make the food. And who do you think will have to answer for it if those soldiers go unfed?"

"Sorry, Mistress Shay," Marta said, bowing her head. "I'll do better."

"Best you do," the woman said, nodding in apparent satisfaction. And then she was gone, wondering through the tent critiquing the other slaves who were busy cooking food or cleaning the dishes or at one of a dozen other tasks.

Marta rubbed at her smarting cheek, sparing a quick glance at Farra who tipped her a wink that was about as subtle as...well, a slap in the face. Marta shot a look at Mistress Shay and was relieved to see that the woman was too engaged in demeaning one of the other slaves for her stirring incorrectly—a thing Marta wouldn't have thought possible—to notice.

Farra was a good woman, a kind one, but subtle she most certainly was not, and Marta went back to scrubbing her own dish lest the woman take her continued regard as an invitation to brag aloud and give them all away.

An occurrence which would, undoubtedly, lead to all their deaths. After all, here, in this cooking tent, as well as the half a dozen others scattered throughout the army encampment, all of the slaves were currently busy preparing a meal for the soldiers meant to reinforce the lines once the first wave of the assault had been finished. A meal which was meant to keep up their strength and ensure that they could fight long enough to kill some of Valeria's defenders before they themselves died. Not that they would ever get the chance to make it to the front lines—at least, that was, if Llanivere was right about the herb she and the other slaves had spent the last day and night sneaking. An herb which, the old woman had said with a cackle, would ensure that the only fighting the soldiers would do the next day would be fighting not to shit themselves. A battle which, she had assured Marta and the other slaves, they would inevitably lose.

If the plan worked, nearly half of the enemy troops would spend the next few days moaning and clutching at their pained abdomens. Marta didn't feel particularly good about it—but then, she didn't feel particularly bad about it either. After all, each enemy soldier focused on not loosing their bowels was one more soldier that couldn't be sent against her friends. A difference which could make *all* the difference.

Not exactly a timely rescue by a great knight on a white horse with a sword shimmering in the sunlight, maybe, but she decided it would do.

She went back to scrubbing her pot.

Chapter Twenty-Eight

Rion reached the city gate to find a dozen men already there. Apparently, Nordin had seen fit to reinforce the gate with as many troops as he could spare. A good thought, as it had turned out, but thoughts, as good as they might be, could not create soldiers out of thin air, nor did they give energy and strength to men who had long ago run out or courage to those who knew their deaths charged toward them, carried in the form of a beast that, in a right world, would not exist at all.

Still, the men were there, staring pale-faced at the gate, their swords clutched in their hands, so at least that was something. Rion thought that, without Katherine's song, the same men would have either fled or passed out from exhaustion long before. "Sergeant," Rion said, moving toward the man who was marked by the insignia on his uniform and offering him his hand. "My name's Rion."

The man scratched at his beard. "Aye, I know you, Lord Tirinian. What can me and my men do for you? Though, I warn you, it seems we'll be busy presently."

"Actually, sir, I'm hoping I can do something for you."

"Oh?" the man asked, raising an eyebrow. "What'd that be, then?"

Rion shrugged, affecting as much nonchalance as he was able. "Well. I heard tale that some mongrel dog was wandering this way, thought I'd see if I could help you put it down."

There were a few laughs from the men at that but not many—impending doom had a way of stealing the funny out of life. Still, it was something, and the sergeant even favored him with a weary smile. "That so? Well, can't say I ain't thankful for the help." He paused, leaning in so that only Rion could hear him. "Though I also can't say that I think it'll be any help. You've seen it? The thing as is comin' this way?"

"Aye," Rion said, adopting the man's manner of speech without even realizing it, "I've seen it. A great big mongrel sure enough. Still, I suppose we'll give it a good kicking, send it on its way."

The sergeant did bark a laugh at that. "A good kickin', is that so?" He glanced meaningfully down at Rion's booted feet.

Rion smiled. "They're bigger than they look."

The man laughed again. "Aye, well, they'd have to be, wouldn't they? Anyway, if you mean to help, we'll do what we can for you, won't we, lads?"

There were answers in the affirmative to that, and Rion tried his best not to notice the weariness and fear in them. The man gave Rion what might have been an apologetic look for the weak response then nodded his head. "Right. So, you got a plan?"

"Something like that," Rion hedged.

"And what do you aim to do?"

"What do I aim to do?" Rion asked, meeting the man's eyes. "Well, Sergeant. I mean to kill it."

The man nodded slowly as if giving it a good think. "Well. Unconventional, maybe, but why not? Anyway, what do you need from us?"

Rion shrugged. "Oh, nothing much. Only perfection." Another bout of scattered laughter, this one a bit more lively than the first. "And one other thing," he went on. "A crossbow."

The sergeant blinked. "From what I've seen, arrows ain't been doin' a whole lot to this beasty, you don't mind my sayin' so."

"I don't mind at all," Rion answered. "Anyway, sergeant, that's only because those arrows haven't hit in the right place."

"Really?"

Gods, I hope so, Rion thought, but the truth was he was making it up as he went along, just as he'd done the rest of his life. He told himself that wasn't such a bad thing. After all, making it up as he went along was exactly what had gotten him this far. But then, when he considered where exactly "this far" meant—currently looking in imminent danger of being mauled or eaten by an onrushing monster—that feeling of reassurance vanished. "Sure," he said. Maybe not the most confident response, but it was the most he could manage just then as he was feeling short of breath and his skin had broken out into a cold sweat.

The sergeant, though, either did not notice Rion's discomfort or chalked it up to simple terror, one his soldiers shared. He gave a grunt, motioning to one of his men. "Alright, Flint. Let's have it."

The soldier in question stepped forward, frowning and obviously reluctant to relinquish his crossbow. Clearly the man had been hoping to do his fighting from a relatively safe distance, shooting bolts at the monster and foregoing getting beaten to death with his comrades. Rion couldn't blame him, but could have told him that it didn't really matter. If the gate fell, then they would all be the meal of some gods-blasted creature sooner or later. Likely sooner.

The sergeant grunted as if he knew clearly enough what the young man had been thinking as he took the crossbow, then passed it, along with the equally reluctantly offered quiver, to Rion. "Know how to use one of these, do ya?"

"Sure," Rion said, no more convincing this time, at least to himself, than when he'd said it a moment ago.

He was eyeing the crossbow with a frown when the sergeant offered him something else: a metallic hook the use of which he couldn't imagine. Some of his confusion must have showed in his gaze, for the sergeant grunted what might have been a laugh. "For the string. But," he said, giving Rion a small grin, "I'm sure you already knew that."

Rion cleared his throat. It was ridiculous that a man facing imminent death—a terrible, bludgeoning death—could be embarrassed, but he was. "Sure," he said again, thinking that maybe saying it a third time might sound more convincing now that he'd had a few rounds to practice...it didn't.

The sergeant opened his mouth, perhaps getting ready to call Rion out or, perhaps, to give him some tips that would have no doubt proven invaluable. But whatever the man had been about to say, he didn't get a chance to finish, for the world chose that moment to intrude—as it so often did—and this particular intrusion came in the way of a thundering crash, one which shook the gate and sent trembles running through the ground that nearly knocked Rion from his feet.

The sergeant was barking orders then, the soldiers, terrified or not, showing their discipline as they took up their stations. Everyone then, moving with an economic, practiced efficiency. Everyone, that was, except Rion himself who was left staring blankly at the crossbow and quiver he held in one hand and the hook he held in the other. He started going over in his mind the ways in which he was a fool but decided there simply wasn't time. He used the hook, pulling back the string of the crossbow, and loaded a bolt into the device, doing his best not to accidentally shoot himself or one of the defenders in the process.

That done, he slung the quiver across his back, tucked the hook into his pocket and fished into his other pocket. He had a panicked, terrified moment when his fingers touched on nothing but the lining of his trousers and then, a moment later, he let out a shaky sigh of relief when his clammy hand closed around a coin. But not just *any* coin. This was Javen's coin, proof of the god's favor. There was power in the coin, that much he knew. Though how much—and if it would be enough to keep him from getting beaten into a bloody pulp—he had no idea. "If you're there," he muttered, "it's time to get to work."

The coin seemed to warm in his hand, though whether that was real or imagined he didn't know and didn't dare think about for long. Either the God of Chance had heard him or he had not, either he was able to help or he was not, and either Rion would die in the next few minutes—along with the guards at the gate and soon followed by every living person in Valeria—or he would not.

A moment later there was another crash at the gate, and the unmistakable—and equally unwelcome—sound of the reinforced wood splintering from an incredible blow. This was followed quickly by another, equally loud crash, and Rion watched in shock as a massive fist broke its way through the center of the gate. A fist which opened up, grabbing hold of the gate—a gate which had stopped the enemy advance for weeks, one which Rion knew had stood for years which, he had thought, would stand for years more—and with one vicious tug, ripped the entire thing away as if it were nothing, revealing a creature out of nightmare.

Rion had seen the beast, of course, from where he'd stood with Nordin on the castle walls, and seeing it from a distance had been nothing short of terrifying, a sight to freeze the blood in a man's veins. Now, though, up close, the thing was even more terrifying, and his breath caught in his throat. The guards, too, shared his terror, though one of them, the one the sergeant had called Flint shared it only for a minute. And then demonstrated to Rion and the rest that while some of them might have felt frozen with terror, he was most certainly not, doing so by using the expedient of charging away with a scream of terror into the city.

Rion couldn't blame him. In fact, had his feet not felt rooted to the ground, there was a fair chance that he would have joined him. It wasn't just the creature's height—which could not be overstated as it was quite simply incredible, standing at least twenty feet tall, perhaps more—so great that the beast was forced to hunker over, folding almost double in order to work its way through the gate. Neither was it just its size which meant that as it forced its way through, its great, perversely large shoulders broke the gateway itself, tearing chunks off the frame.

Those things were bad—enough, surely, to send anyone with the sense the gods gave him running in any direction, just so long as it was away—but what was worse was not the creature's size or height but its skin. Or, more accurately, what was *beneath* its skin.

Shapes writhed underneath the creature's ebony skin, all over its body, a terrible, perverse writhing which was shocking and unnerving to behold, yet from which Rion could not seem to pull his gaze. For those shapes, the longer he stared at them, looked more and more like...people. People trying desperately to break free of the flesh prison in which they found themselves, and even as he watched Rion saw what could only have been a human face pressed up against the creature's stomach, its mouth opened wide in what might have been a scream.

Rion's own stomach roiled in protest, and a wild, panicked terror flickered in his mind, one that threatened to steal his reason, to send him screaming and running wildly away from the gate and those men he had come to help. What had he been thinking? He could not fight such a thing as this—*no one* could. Even Alesh himself would have cowered before it...but no. That wasn't true.

Whatever else the man was—maddening came to mind, particularly of late—Alesh was no coward was, in Rion's opinion, brave to a fault, for surely he had gone to confront Tesharna and the Broken without any sign of the terror Rion was now feeling. No, the man would not have fled, neither would have Darl. But Rion was not Alesh, and he was not Darl—he was no great warrior, no man to inspire hundreds with the sounds of his voice, to stand, to display such an overabundance of courage that those around him might take some for themselves like bread handed out to the hungry. What he was, then, was a nobleman—only in the very strictest sense of the term—a gambler and, when he managed it, sometimes a womanizer. He was not a warrior, no great hero out of legend. But he *was* here.

Maybe he wasn't a great man. Likely, he wasn't even a good one. But he believed—*had* to believe—that even normal men were capable of moments of greatness from time to time. He was still trying to convince himself of that when the creature seemed no longer content to stand there and scare the shit out of everyone and chose, instead, to bellow a roar that made Rion's bladder weaken before charging.

And just like that, there was no time left, no time for worry or doubt, no time for anything at all. The creature rushed at the nearest guardsman who, to his credit, did not turn and run at the approach of a beast that dwarfed him the way a grown man might a child. Instead, the man fought back the obvious terror plastered across his face, gripped his sword in two hands, and with a growl that sounded dangerously like a scream, swung his blade at the onrushing creature. The creature did not try to dodge or evade the blow. Instead, it took it directly across the chest. The blade carved a deep furrow across the beast's flesh, but it didn't seem to notice. At least Rion thought as much, considering the fact that the creature did not react to the blow except to wrap its hand around the waist of the brave guardsman and lift him up as if he weighed nothing. Then, its pig-like face split into a cruel, perverse grin, and the insane muscles of its great arm tensed.

The guardsman screamed—but not for long. There was a terrible cracking, *squishing* sound and the man's body crumpled like a paper doll as the beast crushed him in its grip then tossed him away as if he were a bit of refuse. The remaining guardsmen shouted in terror and fury, and Rion could only stare at the corpse in awe. He turned to the beast then who stood there still smiling maliciously and saw to his shock that the huge, bloodless furrow in its chest began to mend before his eyes until, moments later, the wound was completely gone.

Faced with such a terrible, unnatural sight, the guardsmen understandably retreated back a few steps to where Rion stood. The sergeant glanced over at him. "Chosen," he said, "what...what should we do?"

How in the name of the gods should I know? Rion thought. It was preposterous that the man should be asking him. But the man was asking, and though the soldiers with him did not speak—at least except for the occasional whimper of terror—they, too, were looking at him, waiting for what he would say. *Chosen,* the man had called him, not *Lord Tirinian.* It was well-known throughout the city now, that Rion, along with Alesh and Katherine, even Marta, had been Chosen by the gods to be their champions in the fight against the Darkness. Now, the man was calling on Rion in that capacity, hoping that what abilities the gods had given him would be enough to somehow answer this monster before them.

Rion wanted to say that he was not the right man for this—that he was, in fact, just about the worst possible man for it. What would they do? Die most likely. But that was not the answer the man needed. As the creature gloated over its kill, a thousand thoughts rushed through Rion's mind, most of them just variations on his own terror, his own fear. The guardsmen's blades would be no use against the creature, that much seemed certain, and by standing against it they would only doom themselves to a death as bad as their fellow whose broken body lay crumpled and leaking blood onto the cobblestones of the street.

Rion was not a great man. Likely, he wasn't even a good one. But just maybe he could have his moment. "Sergeant," he said, his voice surprisingly calm, "order your men back. I'll take care of this."

The man opened his mouth as if he might argue but then seemed to remember that when one was faced with a massive beast out of nightmare and someone was giving him an out, he'd be a fool not to take it. "You're...you're sure?" he asked instead.

Absolutely not. "I'm sure."

The man swallowed hard, nodding. "Very well. Good luck, Chosen."

"Thank you, Sergeant."

The men moved past him, shooting grateful glances at him as they did, and Rion felt guilty for that. Likely, all he had done was postpone their gruesome deaths for a few seconds, for the time it would take the creature to do to him as it had to the guardsman. Still, this was why he had been Chosen. Rion had been selfish often in his life—always, truth be told—worrying only about his own welfare or that of his family's. He had lived a wasteful, self-absorbed life. At least he knew that whatever else happened, he would meet his death doing the opposite.

The creature's piggy eyes slowly moved to regard him, its smile widening. He did not know how much actual thought went on behind those terrible features, but there was enough, he saw, that the creature had some inkling of what he had said, of the fact that he meant to face it in one on one combat—or one on one massacre, as the case may be—and was pleased at the thought.

That makes one of us. "Come on then, you ugly fucker," he said.

The creature's smile faded at that, and it bared its teeth in anger. It let out another roar—not much of a conversationalist, this one—and charged forward. The very ground shook with its coming, and Rion forced himself to take a slow, calming breath, aiming the crossbow at the creature's chest. He wasn't sure what good it could possibly do, only had some vague thought that perhaps the bolt might penetrate the beast's flesh enough to reach its dark, corrupted heart.

But just then, the creature's oncoming rush—which made the cobbles buckle beneath him—made Rion lose his balance, and even as he pulled the release lever to loose the bolt, he tripped, falling backward, and the bolt went wide of its mark, though just how far he didn't manage to see as he was busy landing on his back on the hard cobbles.

Shit.

Rion fumbled, trying to get up while also trying to disentangle himself from the crossbow string which had somehow become wrapped around his arm when he'd fallen. He was panting, sure that any second the creature would be on him, would grab him up in its great paw and he would feel the pressure of his insides becoming far too close with the *rest* of his insides as he was squeezed to death like the unfortunate guardsman.

He was more than a little surprised, then, when he managed to clamber to his feet, his arm still hopelessly caught in the crossbow, and remained—for the moment, at least—decidedly uncrushed. He looked up at the creature and saw that its mad charge had faltered, and it had a confused look on its face. A confusion which was likely caused by the crossbow bolt sticking out of one of its eyes.

Rion blinked, aware of the coin, a warm disc in his pocket. "Damn," he muttered. The creature pawed at the crossbow bolt in its eye then, suddenly, fell to its knees, shaking the ground as its full weight struck. It wavered, drunkenly, then collapsed on its face.

Rion regarded it, stunned, was still doing so when there was a great roaring cheer from the guardsmen behind him. A moment later, they were surrounding him, patting him on the back and laughing like men who had just been given a pardon from execution at the last possible instant. Which, it seemed, they had.

The sergeant laughed, clapping him on the back. "Can't use a crossbow, eh? That was a fine shot, Chosen. Damned fine."

"What?" Rion said, turning. "Oh, right. No...I mean yes. Yes, it was. Thank you."

The soldiers continued to laugh and whisper excitedly amongst themselves. Rion, though, only stared at the beast's form. He should feel good, shouldn't he? After all, he had risen to the occasion, had had his moment of greatness after all. But he didn't feel good. At first, he couldn't decide what it was keeping him from it, but then he knew. The creature's skin was still writhing, the forms inside of it still moving. Rion didn't know much about dark magic—didn't know much about a lot of things, but certainly that was on the top of the list. Still, it seemed to him that if the beast were dead, its skin wouldn't be moving so much.

Seconds later, his worst fear was realized as the creature began to move, one of its hands twitching and pawing at the debris of the cobbles it had shattered when it fell. Then more of its arm began to move, and it raised its head from where it lay, regarding him, the broken shaft of the crossbow bolt still sticking out of its eye.

"Sergeant," Rion said softly, "best pull your men back once more."

"Eh?" the man said, cutting off in his mirth, then he slowly turned, following Rion's gaze. "Oh gods."

"Not exactly," Rion said, reaching into his tunic and meaning to grab a few of his knives as the creature began to heave its massive bulk off the ground. A crossbow bolt to the eye had not killed it, but it was clear by the mask of rage and pain on the creature's face that it had not enjoyed it either. Perhaps, if he were lucky, and if it sat still long enough for him to try to throw several more blades at it, he could manage to sink a blade in the creature's other eye. Not a great plan maybe, but a plan anyway, one that fell apart immediately as his grasping fingers brought a most unwelcome realization to his mind—he only had one knife left.

A simple knife might not be much of a weapon against such a creature as this, yet he was loathe to waste it in a throw that would almost inevitably fail. The soldiers might have faith in him—certainly they were not watching with terror now but with confident, patient expressions like they'd hired a man for a job and were only waiting for him to get it done—but the problem was that he didn't have any in himself. The crossbow bolt had been a stroke of luck, a fluke, and he did not know how much such luck he could count on.

The creature regarded him, its expression furious and then, perhaps unsurprisingly, it charged once more. This time, though, there was a halting uncertainness to its charge—Rion supposed mad rushes were made more difficult when you had a crossbow bolt through one eye. Still, it was on him with surprising quickness, and Rion just managed to duck a swipe of its massive arm, one that, had it connected, would have no doubt done a thorough job of ending all of his worries and his doubts with incredible speed.

Rion spun then, taking advantage of the creature's slowness, and plunged his knife into the creature's side, dragging it around as he moved behind it. The creature seemed no more put out by this than it had the swordsman's strike, and it spun with surprising speed, bringing its massive fist down to splat him like a bug. Despite what he'd seen, Rion was taken off-guard—when you carved into someone's stomach with a sharp blade, you expected at least a bit of hesitation on their part—and only just managed to leap out of the way.

But while the creature's blow might not have struck him, it struck the cobbles, and they rippled beneath Rion's feet, making him lose his balance once more, and he grunted as he struck the ground hard.

The creature, though, did not lose its balance—how could it, standing as it was on legs thicker than most trees Rion had seen?—and it proceeded to use one of those legs to kick out at him. Rion scrambled, trying to get out of the way, but did not completely manage it, taking a glancing blow from the creature's foot on his arm. From a normal person, such a small strike would have been next to nothing, but a great, terrible pain rushed into Rion's arm before it promptly went numb, and he was sent rolling across the shattered cobbles, crying out as he suffered several bruising impacts until he finally fetched up against what was left of the gate frame.

He was in terrible pain, his entire body aching, and if his arm wasn't broken, it certainly wasn't in good shape. Part of him—the part that had always counted on his family to bail him out of problems, the part who had refused, quite pointedly, to ever take any responsibility for his own actions—wanted to give up then, wanted to lie there and let the beast do what it would. No doubt it would be painful, but it wasn't as if you could crush a man to death twice. Sooner or later, it would be over, the hurting would be over, and he could finally rest.

The problem, though, was that the men were counting on him, all of Valeria was counting on him. So, the other part of him, the part he had often tried to smother into silence—his conscience—prevailed, and he groaned as he grabbed hold of the gate's frame and worked his way to his feet. To his surprise, he found that he still clutched the knife in his other hand. The creature was grinning again, a particularly macabre expression on its face, and it started toward him, taking its time, enjoying the game of it.

Rion watched it come, thinking that he had spent most of his life letting others deal with his problems or, at the very least, putting things off until the last possible moment. That, after all, was one of the main reasons—if he was being honest with himself, something he largely struggled not to do—why his father's business had failed. Rion had seen what was happening—what was coming—but had simply thought that it would take care of itself. It hadn't, though, just as the creature wasn't likely to up and vanish just because he wished it. Ever since he had become Chosen by the God of Luck, Javen, he had largely just relied on the god to take care of everything, waiting for him to use him like a tool the same way a sculptor might use a chisel or a blacksmith his hammer. But he couldn't continue to rely on others to solve his problems.

None of the soldiers would be able to help and he held up his hand, stopping them as they started forward, meaning to creep up behind it. They could do nothing but die, and Rion thought he could handle that much by himself. The fact was, he was tired of standing still, tired of waiting for his fate to come to him. So he did not wait any longer. Instead, he transferred the knife to his good hand—all things being relative as it was not quite as bruised and battered as the other—and with a shout of his own, he rushed toward the creature.

The most damning bit of it, he thought as he charged headlong, was that this might not have even been the dumbest thing he'd ever done. The creature paused in its walk, surprised—or more likely amused—that the object of its ire might dare rush to come to grips with it. Not much of a hesitation really, but a bit of one, and that was more than Rion could have hoped for. He'd once heard a soldier say that the best thing to do in war—or battle—was the unexpected. Or at least, he thought he had. Maybe he'd read it in a book.

Either way, seeing the creature's hesitation gave him courage, confidence, and so he did something then that neither it—nor he—expected. He leapt at it, bringing the blade he carried down in a two-handed grip. The creature was too slow to react, thrown off-guard, likely, by his suicidal leap which put him in easy range of its massive fists, and it didn't move out of the way in time to avoid the blade from plunging into the top of its head.

Rion kept hold of the handle, not daring to lose his only weapon, which meant that he was left hanging off it, his feet dangling somewhere slightly below the creature's midsection. The creature reached for him, but Rion kicked off its stomach, his legs narrowly avoiding its grasp, and he used the momentum to bring both of his legs back down and into the creature's gut.

The beast stumbled, off-balance, and Rion struggled to hold onto the knife's handle with hands slick with sweat. It reached for him again, growling furiously, and once more he kicked off its stomach, using the blade, still stuck in its head, as a lever to swing himself up and away from its grasping hands. He swung back, kicking it with all the force he could muster once more, and this time the creature didn't just lose its balance—it fell. Rion felt a moment of triumph—one which, it turned out, was decidedly brief as he realized that his grip on the knife was dragging him along with it to strike the ground with an earth-shattering crash.

The creature was down but not out, and it reached for him again, its movements sluggish and uncertain. Rion was not afraid, not now. What he was, more than anything, was angry. Angry at this creature for the way it had so carelessly killed the guardsman, snuffing out the brave man's life with no more thought than a man might give to crushing a bug. He was angry, too, at Shira and Paren and the other gods as well as the people who had chosen the Darkness, who had decided that the only way they might be happy was to make others suffer. Mostly, though, he was angry at himself for his fear, for spending his life being afraid of one thing or the other and of being too lazy to make a difference when he could.

He ripped the knife free, bringing it plunging down into the creature's face. He was aiming for its eye, but it was thrashing in its confused struggles, and the blade punched into its cheek instead. Rion did not let himself be disappointed. After all, when a man failed, there was nothing to do but try again. And so he did, lifting the blade and driving it down again and again into the creature's face, making its gruesome features even more gruesome as he tore hole after hole in them. The wounds were healing, slowly, but not fast enough to keep up with his wild attacks.

"Die, you fucker!" Rion growled, bringing the knife down over and over and finally, more by the law of averages than skill or luck, the blade found its mark in the creature's remaining eye and Rion leaned over it, putting all his weight on the blade and bearing down. The beast didn't roar, not now, for it seemed its roaring days were done. Instead, the monstrosity let out a sort of gasping wheeze and its weak, ineffective struggles finally ceased.

Rion stabbed it a couple of more times for good measure and then sat back, panting heavily, staring at the creature's mutilated features. The broken shaft of the crossbow bolt protruded from one eye, the knife was still stuck in the other—which just went to show that when a man couldn't count on skill or luck, sometimes he just had to fail enough until he finally succeeded. Unfortunately, the frenzied attack had taken a lot out of him, and he was exhausted. Worse, his arm which the creature's foot had grazed was throbbing painfully now, an agony so powerful it seemed to spread all the way through his body.

He was covered in a cold sweat also, and he ran his arm across his forehead, still struggling to get his breathing under control. That was when the cheering started, and he raised his weary head to see the soldiers hooting and clapping. Only twelve of them—ten, really, since the one soldier who had fled was still well and truly fled, the other still a corpse—but Rion thought he had never heard anything so fine.

His exploits had been celebrated before, of course—if anyone in the world was ever a target of undeserved praise it was a rich nobleman's son—but largely it had been empty celebration, one he had known even at the time that he did not deserve. This time, though, was different. He had done it. Not Alesh, not Katherine or Darl. Him. Eriondrian Tirinian.

A moment later, the soldiers were on him, clapping him on the back and laughing, exultant to still be counted among the living, no doubt. Rion understood it, but he was too tired—and too, dare he think it, *proud* of himself—to think much on it. The soldiers hoisted him to his feet which was good considering he wasn't sure if he could have managed it himself just then.

And as they went on praising him, telling him how great he was, Rion found that he was grinning from ear to ear. Rion was still smiling when the soldiers suddenly stopped laughing, staring over his shoulders with expressions that were far from celebratory. That were, in fact, inarguably fearful. Rion considered not turning to look, thought maybe he'd just lie down, take a nap instead. In the end, though, he sighed and turned to see what had caught the soldiers' attention. He didn't have to look for long. After all, it wasn't easy to ignore a stampeding army racing toward the gate. Or, that was, what was left of the gate. Which was, thanks to the monster, absolutely nothing. An army of angry men and women, their faces twisted with insensate rage and wielding weapons ranging from broken-off broom handles to clubs with nails sticking out of them. "Oh," he said, remembering the entire enemy army. "Right."

***

His hand lay on the Ekirani's shoulder, but Alesh was not aware of it. His muscles were cramped from so long sitting but this, too, went beyond his notice. For him, there was nothing but the place inside himself, that place of contentment, of peace, a place where there was no room for doubt or fear, no room for worry or self-loathing. He did not search for that place, not anymore, for he had found it, had found it within himself.

There was warmth there, warmth and no pain, and while there was no room in that place for fear or doubt, there was also no room for sickness, such as the sickness now running through the Ekirani's body, a sickness brought on by the wounds the man had taken to save Alesh's life. So, through his touch, he began to transfer that warmth into Tarex's body. He did not think of how he would do it, did not worry about the mechanics of the thing. He just did it.

He closed his eyes, and let the warmth, the peace that he felt, that he *finally* felt, flow out of him and into the Ekirani. He did not worry about stealing the warmth from himself, of taking it away to give to the unconscious man, for the warmth of that place was limitless, the peace infinite.

He was not sure how long he sat there, for time had no meaning to him, not in that place. All he knew was that the black vein-like lines covering the man's body began to recede, and eventually the Ekirani began to stir beneath his hand. Then, suddenly, the man's eyes snapped open, and he stared at Alesh. For a time, he said nothing, only stared, his eyes slowly widening. "You healed me," he said, his voice not coming out in a croak or a whisper as one might have expected from one who had come so close to death, but coming out strong and full of life.

"No, Tarex of the Ekirani," Alesh said, pulling his hand away and offering it instead to the man to help him up. "You healed me."

The Ekirani smiled and took the offered hand, rising to a sitting position in the bed. Then his expression sobered. "How fares the city's defense?"

"Not well." Alesh wasn't sure on the details, for while he received reports regularly, sometimes spoken through the door, sometimes slipped underneath on a hastily scrawled note, he had been distracted with his efforts at healing the Ekirani. More than that—at healing himself. Yet he needn't have communicated with Nordin or have read the latest reports to know by the sounds— and the chiming of the city bell which had been ringing almost constantly—that there was not much time left. They were out there, even now, the city's defenders, Katherine and Darl and Rion and all the rest, fighting for the city.

Alesh stood. "I am glad that you are well, Tarex, but I must go."

"I am coming with you."

Alesh turned back from where he'd stood at the door. "You need to rest. I mean, can you even stand?"

"Oh, yes, Chosen," the Ekirani said, rising from the bed as if he had only lain down for a brief, energizing nap and moving to where his weapon, the weapon the God of Conflict had given him, sat propped in a corner. "I can stand," Tarex confirmed, taking the weapon in his hand and turning back to Alesh. "In fact, Son of the Morning, I can do far more than that."

***

An army of men and women bent on destruction rushed toward the gate where Rion and the guardsmen stood. That was bad. What was worse, though, was that, at their head, rushed hundreds of the night's creatures, their claws and teeth flashing in the moonlight. None of them were as big as the one lying at Rion's feet, but what they lacked in size they made up for in numbers, numbers enough to get the job done, that was sure.

Rion watched them come, the pride, the hope he'd felt at defeating the massive beast waning as he realized that, in his exultation, he'd forgotten one minor detail. Namely, the enemy army camped outside Valeria's gates. Or, that was, the enemy army which *had* been camped outside the gates and which, just now, was charging toward the gate opening.

"Chosen?"

Rion glanced at the sergeant standing beside him, saw the question in the man's eyes. At first, Rion felt offended. It wasn't fair, that question. But then, maybe it was. After all, the men had just witnessed him perform one miracle—it was not so unreasonable that they might hope for a second. The problem, though, was that Rion was fresh out of miracles. He looked for something to say, the words that might somehow make it better, but if there were such words, he did not know them.

The sergeant watched him for another moment then grunted, giving a nod which said he understood clearly enough. "Alright, lads," he said, "time to earn our pay."

He and the other soldiers moved toward the gate opening, and Rion stared on with something like wonder. Less than a minute ago, they had been cheering him on, celebrating Rion's accomplishment, but he thought that, in truth, they were the ones who should be celebrated. These men who faced the evils of the world without any special gifts or powers given them by the gods, who relied, who *could* rely on nothing and no one but themselves.

Rion hesitated, trying to decide what he should do, but it did not take long. He could think of things he'd rather do than die—that was a particularly long list—but if he was going to die, and that seemed pretty much inevitable, then he thought he could do far worse than to die among such men as these.

He reached down and ripped the blade out of the dead monstrosity's eye then moved to the gate opening where the other soldiers were. The sergeant looked over at him and gave him a small, knowing smile. It felt good, that smile, as well as the simple wink the man gave him. He felt accepted. Accepted not because of who his father was or because he was rich or at least *supposed* to be rich. Accepted simply for who he was. It was a really good feeling. Probably the feeling wouldn't last once the beasts started giving him a good chew, but that was alright.

At least, it had better be, for the army was close now. Their mad dash had carried them at least two-thirds of the way across the field, close enough that Rion fancied he could see the glimmer of madness in the eyes of those men behind the beasts, close enough that he could hear the snorts and growls of the nightlings.

Rion glanced down at the small knife he held, then back at the approaching army of beasts and mortals, all of them bent on destruction. He wished he would have brought a bigger weapon—a cannon, maybe. But there was no time left to find another, even if one could be found, which was unlikely, for he knew all too well how short on supplies the defenders had become over the last week. Maybe it was a good thing, he told himself, that it was about to be over. Certainly if the battle had gone on for another few days, the city's defenders would likely have been doing their defending with angry words and shaken fists.

Or small, pitiful knives which, the more he looked at the one he held, appeared more like something a man might use to pick his teeth with than to defend himself against ravening madmen and beasts made by the Goddess of the Wilds herself. A part of him thought then that there was still time to flee, to turn around and leave these men to their deaths. It wasn't as if him dying with them would change anything.

No. Maybe him being here would make no difference, but he had been running pretty much all his life, often figuratively and, lately, physically. The truth was he was tired of running. Sometimes, a man had to stand for something, even if that standing meant that he would die. After all, if a man was not willing to die for the things he believed in, then did he really believe in them at all? And if he did not, if there was nothing in his world that he would sacrifice himself for, nothing that he held more important than his own personal well-being, then was he even a man?

No. Rion had run plenty of times, was just about as practiced at it as any man could be. He had done it for years, knew the place that running would take him, even if he did not know the exact location. He'd given running its fair try—more than that, truth be told. It was time to stand.

"Rion."

He was so tense that he jumped and nearly screamed at the sound of his name. He turned then, and stared, slack-jawed, at the speaker. "A...Alesh?" he asked, thinking he must be imagining the man standing there, a small smile on his face.

But if the man were a figment of his imagination, he was a particularly stubborn one, for he nodded. "I'm here, Rion."

I'm here. Two simple words, but Rion had never heard anything so wonderful, something which filled him with so much hope, chasing away his despair the way the sun chased away the shadows in the early morning. "Well," he managed, "it's about time."

Alesh's grin widened at that, and he nodded his head at the corpse of the great beast Rion had slain. "Your doing?"

For reasons he couldn't explain, Rion suddenly felt embarrassed. "Well...yes."

Alesh nodded, clapping a hand on his shoulder. "Well done."

Rion found himself smiling widely, his face flushing with a mixture of embarrassment and pleasure. "Thanks," he said, then he sobered. "I don't think it really matters though." He waved a hand at the onrushing force which would be on them in the next few minutes.

"Oh, it matters, Rion," Alesh assured him. "It always matters."

"And the Ekirani? Seemed like a bit of a bloodthirsty bastard, but I can't say I'd mind having his skills just now."

Then, as if he'd been waiting for just such an invitation, the tattooed man stepped out from behind Alesh, smiling. "And so you shall, Eriondrian Tirinian, Javen's Chosen. So you shall."

Rion coughed. "About the bastard, bit, it was just a, well, a joke, you know? I didn't mean—"

The man took one of his hands away from his weapon and waved it dismissively. "A man should never regret speaking truth, Chosen. Indeed, I have been a bastard and far worse. But perhaps there is time yet, time for me to right some of those many wrongs which I have caused."

Rion blinked, his gaze traveling between the two men. One of them, last he'd seen, had been swallowed by despair, looking as if he were already dead, only waiting for his body to realize it. The other had been very nearly there in truth. But gone were the black, vein-like lines which had covered the Ekirani's body and gone, too, was the despair which had seemed to radiate from Alesh's every pore. The two men stood there now, confident and healthy, looking as if they had no idea what fear or despair or pain even was.

"Well," Rion said, "what...what's the plan?" All too aware, even as he asked it, how he was now, like the sergeant and guards had been moments ago, the one looking for a miracle.

Alesh glanced at that onrushing army, no fear in his expression, only determination. "We will stand, Rion, and we will fight. Sometimes, it is all a man can do, to stand against the shadows."

Before Rion could respond, Alesh was turning to where the sergeant and his soldiers stood. "Sergeant Weller," he said, offering the man his hand, and Rion was surprised that Alesh knew the sergeant's name.

The sergeant, too, looked surprised, taking the offered hand. "Chosen. It's good to see you back."

Alesh grinned. "It's good to be back, Sergeant. I'd like for your men to stay on our flanks, to deal with any that get by us. Do you understand?"

"Of course, sir. It'll be our privilege."

"No, Sergeant," he said. "The privilege is mine." With that, he turned away from the blushing sergeant to Tarex and Rion. "Ready?"

"We are with you, Son of the Morning," Tarex said.

Speak for yourself, Rion thought, but he sighed. "Guess we'll be standing at the gate then?"

"Of course," Alesh said with a laugh. "We wouldn't want to leave our guests ungreeted, would we?"

The sergeant and his soldiers spread out on either side of the gate, and Alesh moved to the center, followed by Tarex and a very reluctant Rion. "Rion," Alesh said, "stay between us and a little behind. And relax, will you?" he went on, clapping Rion on the shoulder again. "Everything will be fine."

Everything didn't look like it would be fine to him, not at all, but Rion wasn't going to argue. If he had to face an onrushing army of deranged maniacs and monsters out of nightmare, he could think of no place he'd rather be than standing behind two of the greatest warriors he had ever known. If only Darl were here, he would have felt as safe as a baby tucked in its crib. Relatively, of course. "How do you know?" he asked instead.

"That everything will be fine?" Alesh asked. He shot a meaningful glance at Tarex before looking back to Rion. He shrugged. "I know, that's all."

Rion wanted to argue that, to say that if the man was so certain he ought to lend a bit of that certainty to Rion. But the army was on them, the nearest of the nightlings only seconds away now, and there was no more time.

He stood, waiting for them, his hands sweaty and trembling. Alesh and Tarex, though, did not wait. Instead, the two men glided forward as if of one mind, or twins sharing the same mind perhaps. The Ekirani wielded his familiar—and terrifying—dual-bladed weapon, the one which Rion had seen the man use to devastating effect. Alesh held a simple, unadorned sword in one hand, but as he moved forward, he held up his free hand and suddenly the torches bracketed near the gateway flickered, their flames drifting toward Alesh's hand and a moment later it was wreathed in fire.

The nightlings closest screeched, hesitating at that, but only for a moment. A second later, they rushed forward, lashing out with their claws and teeth. But for all their efforts and all their unnatural speed, they might have well been fighting the air, for the two men shifted and swayed as if in the midst of some great dance and none of the creatures' blows landed. But while they moved like the wind, the two men struck with the power of lightning strikes, with the precision of master archers. And everywhere their steel was, creatures fell. They fell in droves, their bodies scattering about them in great, ever-growing heaps, so that the men were forced watch their footing as they moved among them.

Rion was left standing with his knife clutched in a trembling hand, his eyes wide, feeling fear, yes, as any sane man would given his circumstances, but feeling, too, an overpowering feeling of awe as he watched the two men, masters at their work.

***

Alesh felt stronger than he ever had, *faster* than he ever had, and he dodged the creatures' attacks easily, weaving in and out of their clumsy strikes with little effort, his blade reaping a bloody harvest.

Tarex was a reassuring presence at his side, the Ekirani fighting with an incredible skill, his gods-blessed weapon sending beast after beast back to the Darkness, while the soldiers and Rion cut down those few of the nightlings which managed to get around or between them.

Yet despite their efforts, despite the terrible casualties among the attackers, more were coming on all the time, hundreds, thousands of them rushing toward the gate opening as if the entire world had lined up and waited in queue for their chance at Valeria's defenders. As he and the others were forced to slowly give ground beneath the relentless pressure, Alesh came to an unwanted conclusion.

They could not win. Yes, they would fight and take many of the creatures—and those mortals which had chosen the Darkness—with them, but in the end, they would fall. He knew this, yet he did not despair, for he had been healed there, in the room, as much as the Ekirani had been healed. He had learned something, had come to understand that men did not stand, did not fight because they knew that they would win. He knew now that doing the right thing was standing even when you knew that you might lose.

So he stood and he fought, for some things must be fought, must be stood against even if there was no hope of victory. He would stand until he could stand no longer, would fight until there was no strength in his arm left to swing the blade he carried. He would do so just as a light, guttering and weak, would continue to push back the darkness until it could no longer.

He would stand.

Chapter Twenty-Nine

Fermin was working his way through the bustle of the soldiers near the front line, trying to find some way around, but there did not seem to be any options. Everywhere he looked, men and creatures of the night were charging toward Valeria's broken-down gate. Even if he somehow managed to make it past the pickets placed regularly along the army camp's edge, he would likely be shot by arrows from the city's defenders before he ever reached the gate or, even if he did somehow accomplish that small miracle, be cut down before he could explain himself.

He felt ashamed, for Marta had risked herself to get him the information he carried, and now it looked as if he was doomed to fail to deliver it. Certainly he had failed to get a message to them regarding Shira's latest creation in time, the one which had so easily destroyed the gate, though what had become of it he could not say, for he could see nothing past the troops pouring into the city.

Had Valeria fallen already? Was the great beast, even now, leading a rampage of destruction and mayhem through the streets of his home? Fermin decided that he didn't just feel ashamed—he felt angry. But that anger brought with it an idea. A wild, dangerous idea that began to take shape in his mind.

He grabbed the shoulder of a soldier hurrying past, stopping him. The man turned on him with an angry frown, pausing as he saw the insignia on Fermin's shirt, the one marking him as a messenger. "Soldier," Fermin said, "I seek Captain Wexler. Where is he?"

The man jerked a thumb behind him. "Captain's at his tent—that way. You can't miss it."

Fermin nodded, letting the man go, and then he was riding, pushing his horse as fast as he could through the throng of soldiers. It didn't take him long to reach the tent, and the soldier had been right—there was no way to miss Captain Wexler's tent, for it was surrounded by several guardsmen with men and women filtering out of it as Fermin watched.

Fermin took a slow, deep breath to calm his nerves, then ushered his mount toward the tent. As he approached, one of the guards stationed at its front held up a hand, stopping him. "What's your business?"

"I carry a message for Captain Wexler," Fermin said, forcing the words out past a suddenly terribly dry throat.

"Very well," the guard said. "Give me your message, and I'll make sure the captain gets it."

No, that wouldn't work, not at all. Fermin thought he was already taking a chance, a great risk, and it would be for naught if the guard got lazy and did not deliver the order or, worse yet, if the captain did not believe it. "Sorry, Sergeant," he said, noting the man's own insignia, "but I cannot. I was tasked to carry this message by Chosen Leandrian himself."

"And carry it you have," the man said, frowning. "Now, if you'll just tell me—"

"I was ordered, in fact," Fermin pressed, "to deliver the message to Captain Wexler personally. Chosen Leandrian was most firm on this point, Sergeant, and I would most certainly not wish to be the man who stood in the way of his will. I do not think, given what is at stake, that Chosen Leandrian would be very forgiving of such a person. Do you?"

The sergeant frowned. "This is highly irregular but, as you say, Chosen Leandrian's will must be obeyed. Only do not take long—the captain is very busy with the assault."

"Of course not," Fermin said, climbing down from his horse and handing the man the reins, "I will take as little time as possible." And that much, at least, was nothing short of the truth. The guard motioned him inside, and Fermin went, doing his best to look like a messenger carrying a message instead of a spy on a mission to save the city he loved.

He had not seen Captain Wexler before, as he had not been one of the messengers tasked with carrying messages to the front, but although there were half a dozen men standing around a small table on which figures denoting the army's ranks sat, it was not difficult to pick the man out. He was the one the others kept speaking to, the one who looked harried and exhausted and in danger of losing his temper any second.

"Captain Wexler," Fermin said.

All of the men—commanders in the army—cut off from their steady stream of talk to look up at him. "Yes?" the man he'd taken as Captain Wexler asked.

"I've got a message, sir—" Fermin began, but didn't get a chance to finish.

Captain Wexler waved a hand, dismissing him. "Leave it with the guards outside, and I'll get to it in a moment. Now..." he went on, his voice lowering as he resumed his discussion with the men around him.

Fermin fidgeted, clearing his throat anxiously. Then spoke louder. "Forgive me, Captain, but this message cannot wait."

The man turned a scowl on him. "Is that so? Tell me then, messenger, what is it that has brought you here, that you deem a better use of my time than coordinating the attack on the city?"

Fermin felt his face heat with his anxiety, felt the eyes of the men in the tent boring into him like daggers, but he took a deep breath to steady himself and spoke on. "I carry a message from Chosen Leandrian himself. He sends order for you to pull your forces back from the city of Valeria."

There were sputters of disbelief from several of those in the tent at that, but Wexler held up an angry hand, silencing them. "What?" he demanded.

Fermin fought the urge to shift on his feet, meeting the man's gaze. "You heard me right, Captain. Chosen Leandrian has deemed the attack not worth pursuing at this moment and has sent me to tell you to sound the retreat. He means to...to enter into peace negotiations with the city."

"But that...that's ridiculous!" the captain barked. "The gate is down, man. Even now our army is forcing its way inside. It's only a matter of time before the city falls! Why, we are only an hour, perhaps even minutes away from victory! If he waits but an hour, he could be having his peace talks over the corpses of his enemies. What could the Chosen be thinking?"

Fermin met the man's gaze with as much confidence as he could muster. "I do not think to question my Chosen, Captain. Do you?"

The man's mouth worked angrily, and Fermin was forced to stand there, waiting to see if the captain would order one of his men to cut down this willful messenger or, perhaps, draw the blade sheathed at his side and take care of matters himself. Finally, his fists clenched where they rested on the table, he turned to one of the men near him. "You heard him," he growled. "Sound the retreat."

The man blanched, looking incredulous. "But, sir—"

"You heard me," the captain snapped in a voice that left no room for argument. "Chosen Leandrian has spoken—sound the retreat. Now."

"Yes, sir," the man answered, and then he rushed out of the tent flap to do as he was ordered. Seconds later, a great horn began to sound, three notes the meaning of which Fermin did not need to ask about and probably would have lacked the breath for even if he'd wanted to.

He stood there, shocked that his hastily-created plan had actually worked, shocked, too, to still be counted among the living. He was so stunned, in fact, that, in a very large way, he forgot where he was. At least, that was, until the captain turned to regard him once more, his face red and blotchy with his anger. "Is there anything else, messenger?" he said through clenched teeth, not so much a question really as a challenge. "Perhaps you'd like for us to all lay down our arms and march toward the Valerian square, maybe fight to see who gets to get executed first."

Fermin swallowed. "That...no, Captain. That is the only message I was given."

The man grunted. "Better for us all if you were dead, messenger."

Fermin felt his blood go cold in his veins. "What...I don't know what you mean..."

"Then let me make it clear for you. I wish that great beasty of the Chosen's would have picked you to stomp on when it was chargin' the gate. If it had, we'd all be celebrating our victory within the hour instead of making one of the most colossal military blunders in recent memory. Now, get the fuck out of my tent."

"Y-yes, sir."

Fermin, not daring to push his luck any further, hurried out of the tent flap, hardly able to believe that it had worked, that *his plan* had actually worked. He wanted to collapse with relief and exhaustion—mostly brought on my anxiety—but he knew that he could not. Yes, his plan had worked—at least so far—but getting the captain to sound the retreat had only been the first part of it. He still had to get to Valeria and warn Alesh and the others of the Welian's arrival. Everything hinged upon it, for if he failed, the Welians would land without any form of help or reinforcement, and it would only be a matter of time before they were surrounded and cut down.

And if *that* should happen, it was not just the Welians who would be doomed, but the entire world, for even Fermin—a man who knew far more about dining etiquette and ballroom manners than war and battle strategies—could see the way the battle was going clearly enough. Valeria's defenders had accomplished the impossible already to have stood for as long as they had against the forces arrayed against them, but even those brave men and women manning the walls—those lucky, or perhaps unlucky few who were still left after weeks of fighting—could not stand forever.

Which meant that Fermin's work for the night had only just begun, and some of the relief he'd felt moments ago slowly dissolved away as he regarded the task before him. Still, he thought he had an idea, one that rose easily enough from the lie he had told Captain Wexler. He had told the man that Chosen Leandrian had called for a parley, for peace talks—ridiculous, of course, as the very last thing a man like Kale Leandrian sought was peace—but it did open up some interesting possibilities. After all, if there was to be a white flag carried to the castle then, by necessity, someone—a certain, manservant turned messenger, perhaps—would need to carry it.

So, as the troops who had been at the back of the attack on Valeria began to filter back into the camp, confused and angry looks on their faces—and why not, as they had just been called back only minutes from victory and looting—Fermin retrieved his mount and pushed through them, searching for a launder's tent. There they would have white sheets—or at least sheets that had started their lives as white and perhaps still retained enough of it to be counted as such—white sheets that could, with some small bit of attention, become a white flag.

He had only taken a few steps when a figure emerged out of the chaos around him, stopping to stand directly in his path. "Hi, Fur."

There was a strangeness to Merrilan's scowl, one which made Fermin decidedly uncomfortable. Nearly as uncomfortable, in fact, as the perpetually angry messenger finding him here, only minutes away from Wexler's tent while a horn still sounded the army's retreat.

Then, Fermin realized what it was about the woman's scowl that struck him so strangely. Particularly, the fact that it wasn't a scowl at all. For the first time since he'd met her, the woman was not scowling at all but smiling. A smile that, it had to be said, was in many ways far worse, far sharper than the scowl she normally wore. There was no mirth in that smile, and if it held any joy it was of the kind felt by cruel children throwing rocks at mongrel dogs or by jealous merchants pleased to witness the downfall of their business rival. Not joy for its own sake, surely, but joy brought on only because of someone else's suffering.

"M-Merrilan," Fermin managed, swallowing hard, hoping that the darkness would hide the sudden, fevered flush which had come to his cheeks.

"What'cha doin', Fur?" she asked, a sing-song, mocking quality to her voice that Fermin did not like at all.

"I was...that is..." He cleared his throat, forcing himself to stand straight. "I was delivering a message."

"Oh?" she asked, retrieving one of the knives sheathed at her waist and beginning to pick her nails with it as if distracted. Then, suddenly, her gaze rose from her nails, and she pierced him with her eyes as if they were twin daggers. "To whom, I wonder? And what did it say?'

"F-forgive me, but that isn't any of your business. The messenger code states—"

"No, you're right," she said, sighing, "I don't know what came over me. Still," she went on, stepping closer. "We're friends, Fur.

You can tell me, can't ya? After all, we share plenty in the Tent, don't we?"

Fermin nodded, scrambling for thought. "Right. Well, it was, that was, it was nothing. I was only sent by the chief laundress, that's all, to ask after sheets." He gave a soft, breathless laugh at that.

"Sheets," she repeated.

"That's right," he said, giving a shrug. "The gods know why—I guess maybe they're running low on them in the center of camp. Anyway, you know how it is. It isn't our job to question the message, right? Just to deliver it."

"Right, right. I suppose that makes sense. Well, good luck, then. I guess I'll let you get back to it."

Fermin fought the urge to breathe a heavy sigh of relief at that, only nodding. "Alright. I'll see you in the Tent later?"

She nodded thoughtfully, as if she was distracted by some errant puzzle. "Sure, sure."

With that, Fermin started around her, doing his best not to break into an out-right run. He was nearly past her when she suddenly reached out and grabbed his arm with a hand that felt like a claw. "Just one more thing, Fur," she said, meeting his eye. "Sorry, but you know how it is—my curiosity's been roused, and if I don't put it back to bed, I'll get no sleep tonight."

"S-sure," Fermin said, hating the squeak in his voice, "what, what is it?"

"Well," she said, giving a soft laugh and a slight, self-deprecating shake of her head, "it's nothing, really. Silly, I'm sure, something easily explained. Only, if you were heading toward the laundry tents as you claim then why, I wonder..." She paused, the grip of her hand on his arm tightening until Fermin had to fight the urge to squirm beneath it. "Did I see you go into Captain Wexler's tent? And while your story—about the laundresses, I mean—is a good one, Fur," she went on, leaning in close so that he could smell the reek of soured ale on her breath, "it is not, to my recollection, the same one you told to the guards outside Wexler's tent."

Fermin's breath caught in his throat. "It isn't, I mean, I'm not...there's an explanation for this, Merrilan."

She gave him that humorless smile again. "Now that, Fur, I believe might be the first true thing you've told me. But wait—

don't give it away. How about I guess? Hmm...what could it be? How about, that maybe, you are a spy sent from Valeria, a spy sent to sabotage us wherever he could? How would that do for an explanation?"

Fermin winced. "That...that's ridiculous. I, I'm as much as part of this army as you are."

"That so?" she asked thoughtfully. "Well. See, the thing is, Fur—I don't like you. I don't, as a general rule, like anybody, of course, but there has always been something about you that's bothered me. I couldn't ever put my finger on it exactly, but there was something about you that struck me as off, wrong, you know? Still, I thought maybe it was nothing, just a weird feeling caused by the gods alone knew why. But then you did something strange."

"S-strange?" Fermin asked.

"Sure," she said, winking. "You see, Fur, it's clear to anyone who spends any time around you at all that you're soft, that you're not built for this sort of army. So soft, in fact, that the only way you can make it through the day is knowing that ale, enough for you to get drunk beyond belief, is waiting at the end of it. And don't think I haven't seen you sneaking nips during the day, either."

"A-all the messengers drink," Fermin said.

"Sure," she agreed, "but not all of 'em do it with that desperate, thankful look on their face that you do, like they're not sittin' in a tent at all but drownin' and the ale's not ale but air. No, I've seen your like before, Fur, men too weak to exist in the world as it really is, men who are forced to dull the hard edges with drink. My father—the prick bastard—was such a man."

"I...I don't know what that has to do with anything," Fermin managed, "even if it is true."

"Well," she said, "you see, that's the interesting bit. My father, as I said, was like you, Fur. Weak, soft, a man who could only get through the day—and the night, particularly the night—with the help of drink. So I know a bit about people like you, and what I *know*, Fur, is that that sort of man will do anything to make sure he gets his drink, do anything to keep the world's hard edges away. But you have not been to the Tent—the only reasonable place to get a drink in this camp—not for two days. I saw my father—as much a drunk as any, as much a drunk as *you*, Fermin—go one night without his drink from time to time. But I never saw him go two. Made me wonder, you'll understand, what was keepin' ya. Suppose I could have just asked," she went on, her grin widening, "but sometimes, when you ask, people lie, don't they? They say a thing even though they know it isn't true. In that way, I find it better just to figure out some things for myself. Imagine my surprise, then, when I saw you slinking away from the slave tents."

Fermin felt despair begin to creep through him. Had he really thought that he could make a difference? Had he really just been celebrating his own cleverness? How stupid of him. How stupid to think that he could be anything but what he was—a failure. "Y-you followed me," he said.

"Yes," she said, "but not *just* me. You see, as I believe I said, I asked myself what could possibly keep a drunk from his drink not for one night, but for two and I came up empty. So then, I decided to ask some other people."

And as if they had only been waiting on their cue, several people, ones Fermin recognized all too well, stepped forward out of the shadows. There was Calden, the big man with a frown on his face, Pesal, looking equal parts confused and terrified, and Jale, staring at Fermin with a hurt, wounded expression.

"Tell me it isn't true, Fur," Jale said. "Tell me you wouldn't pretend to be our friend only to backstab us. You're not a traitor, surely. You wouldn't...I mean, you *couldn't*..." The man trailed off, shaking his head as if unable even to finish.

"It...it isn't like that, Jale," Fermin said. "I mean, I'm not a traitor, really, I—"

"Oh, enough of your bullshit," Merrilan snapped, her voice as cutting and as sharp as the blade she still held—the blade Fermin could hardly take his eyes away from. "There's an easy enough way to find out, isn't there? Seems to me"—she paused, glancing around them at the troops still returning from the front—"that someone here has sounded the retreat. Odd, don't you think, for Captain Wexler to do that when it was clear the city was going to fall? I, personally, can't think of a single reason why he would. Unless, that was, he received a message from his superior, perhaps from Chosen Leandrian himself, and if he *did* receive a message, then surely it must have been carried by a messenger. And I, myself, think I've a pretty good idea who that messenger was."

"N-no," Jale said, shaking his head. "You're wrong. Fur wouldn't do that. Tell her, Fur."

Merrilan smiled, the smile of a snake or a vulture, it seemed to Fermin. "You're probably right," she said. "I mean, a man would have to be absolutely mad to risk sneaking into this camp, knowing, after all, how Chosen Leandrian deals with his enemies. Of course," she continued, tapping her chin with her index finger, "there's an easy way to find out. We can settle this quickly enough, prove that I'm being nothin' but a paranoid bitch, and all go and get us a drink at the Tent. All we have to do, see, is go ask Captain Wexler if he's received any messengers in the last hour or so, particularly ones resembling our friend, Fur, here. What do you say, Fur?" she asked, grinning her humorless grin. "You ready to clear all this up?"

His mind raced then with a thousand thoughts, a thousand fears, but not a single excuse. Then, suddenly, the storm of his thoughts cleared like the skies after a summer storm, and he was surprised to find that now the worst had happened, he was not afraid. Not surprised, either, really, for he had expected to be caught the whole time, hadn't he? He knew that they would torture him, that he would be forced to endure incredible pain before he came to his end, yet still he felt no fear.

What he did feel, though, as he turned to look at Jale, his expression a mixture of hope and hurt, was regret. "I didn't mean to hurt you," he said softly, his gaze traveling to regard those others, "not any of you."

Jale's eyes went wide at that in an expression of surprise and disbelief he saw mirrored on the faces of Pesal and the big man, Calden. "Y-you mean the girl's right?" Calden asked. "You a traitor, Fur?"

Fermin considered that then finally shook his head. "No. I'm not a traitor, or, at least, if I am, I'm not in the way you're thinking. I haven't betrayed Kale or Shira or all the rest, for I never served them. Though, perhaps," he said softly, "it could be said that I betrayed the others, my friends. You see, I did not come here to hurt your army, to trick or lie. I only came here for my friend, a young girl by the name of Sonya. She was taken from Valeria when the army first arrived. I came to see that she was safe, to rescue her, if I could."

"*See?*" Merrilan hissed, her voice sounding remarkably like the way a snake would sound, should a snake be able to talk. "I told you all," she went on, regarding the other messengers. "A *spy.*"

"So you said," Calden said in a thoughtful voice. "But seems to me that if he's telling the truth—about this at least—the man ain't a spy. After all, he didn't come to spy, did he? Only came to save a young girl. How old is she, Fur—this girl o' yours?"

Fermin's mouth felt incredibly dry. "I...six? Maybe seven? Certainly no more than that. She is young."

The big man grunted. "I had a daughter 'round that age, once upon a time. A good age, when they're all full of questions and sweetness and innocence, 'fore the world takes hold of 'em and wrings it out of 'em like dish rags. So. Did you find her?"

Fermin winced. "I'm afraid no—"

"Who *cares?*" There was such hate, such simmering rage in the voice that anyone who knew her might have been forgiven for thinking it came from Merrilan despite the fact that it was most obviously a man's voice. And not just any man's voice but Jale's, and on his face a furious rage which twisted his normally amiable features into something monstrous. "You *lied* to us, Fermin. You lied to *me.* I thought—" He waved his hand at the others. "*We* thought you were our friend. Now, it turns out you're a *spy.*"

"Jale," Fermin said, feeling a terrible, heavy guilt, "you are my friend—all of you are. I did not mean—"

"Damn what you *meant,*" Jale hissed with more anger than Fermin had ever heard or would have thought to hear from the man.

Fermin recoiled at the fury in the man's voice, on his face, and Merrilan spoke again, her voice sounding sweet and deadly at the same time, the woman sounding more satisfied, happier than he had heard her sound. "Oh, but you will suffer for this, spy," she hissed. "I can only hope that Chosen Leandrian will allow me to stay to watch."

They were all staring at him, their expressions a mixture of anger and confusion and hurt. The old Fermin would have said nothing, would have only stood and taken whatever was coming to him, would have been too scared to say anything in his own defense. But he had changed over the last few days—over the last hour, in truth—perhaps had *been* changed by the events surrounding him. "You're right," he said softly, his gaze roaming those messengers, those who he had called his friends. "I did lie. I lied to all of you, and I'm sorry for that. But I would do it again, if I had to, would risk my life again. Sonya needed my help. My *friend* needed my help, and I could not call myself her friend if I had not done all that I could, all that was within my power to help her, to try to save her. The same as I would do for any of you, if I could."

"More lies," Merrilan hissed. "Enough, *spy*," she went on, starting toward him, "it's time you took what was coming to you. Now—"

"Hold off, Mer," Calden said in a harsh, gravelly voice so at odds with his usual jovial tone.

"You can't be serious," Merrilan said. "Calden, he—"

"But I am serious," the big man said, holding up his hand, a tone in his voice that showed he would accept no argument. "I want—I think we *all* want an explanation. He owes us that much, at least."

Her face twisted with rage and for a moment Fermin got the distinct feeling that the woman would refuse the big man, that she would attack him with the dagger she held. In the end, though, she subsided, her eyes flashing with promised retribution, though whether on Fermin or Calden—perhaps on the world itself—it was unclear.

"You want an explanation?" Fermin said, eyeing them all. "Well, I don't know what to tell you. I did what I did, knowing it was dangerous, knowing that likely I would die in the attempt. But if a friend isn't worth risking your life for then I don't know what is. I could tell you that she is a kind soul, a good soul, perhaps the kindest, the best that I have ever known, but what would be the point? That doesn't matter. The truth is that the world is a cruel place—I think all of you know that much. After all, it's why you're here, isn't it? All of you have been hurt, have had things taken from you, and so you would hurt in return, would *take* in return. But it does not have to be that way. The world might be a cruel place, but it can be changed—*we* can change it. After all, it only takes one light to drive back the darkness, and no man can travel so far into the shadows that he cannot find his way back out again. I think..." He paused, shaking his head. "No, I *know* that there are things worth saving, *people*," he went on, meeting Jale's eyes, "worth saving. And—"

"Oh, *enough already*," Merrilan hissed. "I don't have time for this bullshit, now let's—"

"Wait, Merrilan." And to Fermin's surprise, the voice was not that of Calden but of Pesal, the small man looking nervous and withering under the woman's stare but speaking on. "Let him talk. I...I want to hear what he has to say."

"Oh, stow it, you fucking coward," she said. "Unless, that is, you want to be executed right along with him." She moved toward Fermin, grabbing him roughly by the arm. "I'm going to enjoy this, you prick," she said, grinning wickedly. "I'm going to enjoy it immense—" Suddenly she cut off, her eyes going wide, and her hand slowly fell away from his shoulder.

Fermin shared the confusion on her face until she turned, revealing the knife protruding from her back and Pesal, the small man not looking scared, not now, but angry.

"Maybe I am a coward," the bucktoothed man said, "but even cowards will fight back, you kick 'em enough."

They all stared, shocked, Pesal seeming at least as stunned as any of the rest, as Merrilan moved, her hand reaching out in a furious claw as if to grab the small man by the throat, but instead she collapsed a moment later at his feet.

Fermin felt as if time froze then, all of them stunned with disbelief, until a flash of movement caught his eye, and he saw Jale rushing toward Pesal, his face a mask of rage.

"*No,*" Fermin blurted, "*don't—*"

But it was too late. The smaller man had just started to turn, alerted by Fermin's voice that something was wrong, when Jale's sword slashed across him, cutting deep into his shoulder and arm instead of his back where it had been aimed. Blood spurted, and Pesal screamed, falling to the ground, his arms held up to defend himself.

"Please, Jale," Pesal whimpered in obvious pain, his hands raised above him as if to ward off a blow, "don't—"

But Jale wasn't listening. His normally kind face was twisted with madness, and he hefted the sword over his head in two hands, preparing to bring it down.

"Jale, don't!" Fermin screamed, lunging forward and catching the man's wrists.

"Get *off* me, traitor!" the messenger screamed, trying to brush him aside, but Fermin did not let go. They struggled for several seconds, stumbling around, until Fermin tripped on the writhing Pesal, and they both went down.

He felt the blade turn, felt it slide into waiting flesh, and Jale cried out, Fermin echoing the cry as he stared in disbelief at the sword piercing his friend's flesh.

"N-no," Fermin said as Jale's eyes went wide with shock and disbelief, "oh gods, please no."

But the damage was done and could not be taken back no matter how much Fermin wished it.

Something—regret or shame? Confusion, perhaps?—came over the other messenger's face then. "*Fur...?*" he rasped, but he never got to finish what ever he'd been about to say, for the light, the *life* left his eyes, he breathed a heavy, shaky breath, and then was still.

"Oh gods," Fermin breathed, "oh gods. Jale? Jale—"

"He's gone, Fur."

It was Calden's voice from above him, but Fermin ignored him, shaking his head furiously. "No, no. He's just hurt, that's all. He'll be okay. He has to be." Fermin gave his friend a shake. "Wake up, Jale. Wake up. *Wake up!*"

But the man did not wake, and then there was a hand on his shoulder, a big hand, surprisingly gentle. "Come on, Fur. Get to your feet." Fermin felt limp, numb, and he allowed the big messenger to pull him toward his feet. He didn't know what would happen, what torture or painful death was in store for him and, staring at the corpse of his friend lying there dead by his own hand, he found that, in that moment, he did not care.

"Listen, Fur," the big man said, "you've got to listen to me now. You hearin' me?"

Fur felt empty, hollowed-out, and he regarded the big man—noted, too, that several soldiers had paused and were frowning at the scene, confused. "H-he's dead," Fermin said. "I killed him."

"He killed himself, lad," the big man said. "He, like most of us here, chose his path a long time ago. There's nothin' to be done; it's too late. What matters now is that you get out of here quick."

Fermin blinked, some small bit of surprise making its way past the fog that had settled in his mind. "You're...helping me?"

Calden gave him a small smile, shrugging. "Maybe you're right, Fermin. Maybe a man *can* find his way back to the Light. My daughter..." Tears gathered in his eyes, and he gave his head a brisk shake as if to banish whatever memory had come to him. "You would have liked her, I think. She was a sweet soul. Much like your Sonya."

"I'm sure she was wonderful," Fermin said softly, watching the tears roll down the big man's cheeks.

"Aye, she was," he agreed. "A light better'n this cold world deserves. But who knows? Maybe it ain't got to be cold. Maybe we *can* change it. Now you go, lad, and you change what you can, alright?"

Fermin felt a sense of wonder rising in him. "Come with me. If you stay, they'll know you helped me and—"

"No, Fur," the big man said, shaking his head. "My place is here, at least for now. After all, someone'll need to explain all of this. So go, with my blessing."

Fermin stared at the man, saw his resolve. He knew that Valeria was still counting on him, the Welians counting on him too. Still, he turned to Pesal writhing on the ground. "I should help him, I—"

"I'll take care of little Pesal," the big man said. "I used to know a bit about healing, a long time ago before...well. I'll take care of him. You just go, lad, go and do what needs doin'."

Fermin spared another moment, staring at the man then, finally, he offered his hand. "You're a good man, Calden. A good friend."

The big man grunted, clearly embarrassed but, judging by the smile on his face equally pleased. He took his hand, giving it a firm shake. "Go on then, you bastard. Who knows? Maybe we'll see each other again."

"I hope so," Fermin said, meaning it. Then, he took a deep breath, saddled his horse, and went to find a sheet.

Chapter Thirty

Alesh's body thrummed with energy, with power greater than any he had ever felt before. And even as he fought, his blade flashing out to cut down first one nightling, then spinning to impale a bloodthirsty man who had been rushing toward him, he realized something. He realized that the power had been there all along, had never abandoned him as he had feared. Instead, it had been *he* who had abandoned *it*.

Yet no matter how much power was rushing through him, no matter that he and Tarex and all those others gathered at the gate fought as well as they could, he knew that it would not be enough. Knew that despite their efforts, they would fall, soon, and the city would fall with them.

That was when a horn sounded, one he could hear even over the shouts and screams, the growls and hisses of the enemy. Three notes, carried on the wind, and suddenly, the onrushing horde of attackers—the horde which had been ready to sweep over them in minutes—began to dissipate.

And as he cut down his latest opponent, Alesh was left panting for breath while he, Tarex, Rion, the sergeant and the three gate guards that remained watched the enemy army retreat toward the forest. He turned to regard his companions, all of them looking exhausted, bloody and battered, but still standing, expressions of relieved confusion on their faces to match his own.

He frowned, thinking it must be some needless cruelty Kale might have construed to better crush the spirit of the city's defenders, yet that seemed ridiculous, even for the malicious nobleman, and the army did not turn to renew the attack but instead continued to retreat back toward the tree line.

"Well," Rion said from beside him, "that was unexpected. Do you think...is it some trick or...?"

Alesh frowned off at the distant tree line where he could see a figure emerging, one riding a horse and carrying what looked like a white sheet tied to a pole. "I don't think so," he said softly.

Rion followed his gaze and grunted. "He wants to parley? But *why?* To gloat? Gods, but if he'd waited a little while he could have done all the gloating he wanted with no one to argue—corpses don't have a lot to say, do they?"

Alesh couldn't fault the man's logic, and he shook his head, having no answer to give him. He glanced at Tarex, but the Ekirani only gave a weary shrug to show that he, too, was confused by this strange turn of events.

So they were all left to wait and watch while the man on the horse carrying the white flag approached. At first, the figure was too far away to make out any specific features, but he continued to ride closer, and Alesh felt a shock as he realized who it was. The last few months had had a lot of surprises in store—most of them bad—but Alesh was left breathless by this surprise which, in many ways, was the greatest of any he had yet seen.

"What?" Rion said, frowning, noting Alesh's shock. "What is it? What do you—" But then he cut off, letting out a grunt of his own. "Is that..."

"Fermin," Alesh confirmed. To his shame, Alesh had spent little of the last few days thinking about the manservant, had been so absorbed by his own worries and fears that he had barely had time to consider anyone—or anything—else.

"He looks...different," Rion said as the man reached the halfway point between the forest and the city.

And although Alesh had not seen the man much since coming to Valeria, he had seen enough to know that in this, at least, Rion was right. The Fermin he remembered, the one who he had only seen and spoken to briefly, had reminded him of a mouse, one that lived a frightened, timid life and who was prepared to flee at the slightest sign of trouble. Now, though, he did not remind Alesh of a mouse, not at all. He wasn't sure *what* exactly the man put him in mind of, but it was certainly no mouse.

True, there was a tenseness to his posture that bespoke of some great emotion—fear perhaps—yet he rode with his head up, his shoulders squared, the pole with the white flag held aloft.

"What do we do?" Rion asked.

"Sometimes, Rion," Alesh said, "there is nothing to do but wait."

And so they stood at the gate, weary and bloody, but standing still. They waited for what would come. And the city of Valeria, the entire world, waited with them.

Chapter Thirty-One

"What is *happening?*" Kale demanded. He stared in disbelief at his army, the army which had been only moments away from taking the city, now retreating in chaotic fashion, men and women flowing into the camp in an unorganized mob.

"Treachery," a voice growled beside him with a gravelly sound like two great boulders shifting against one another, and he was reminded of the god's presence.

Kale let out a hiss of rage, turning to one of his guards. "Where is Captain Wexler?"

The man fidgeted as he weathered Kale's furious scowl. "He is on his way, Chosen. He should be here any—"

"He had *better* be," Kale snapped. "I will have an explanation for this, this *folly,* or I will have his head. Perhaps I will have it anyway."

Just then, the flap to Kale's command tent swung open, and Captain Wexler stood in the opening, his face looking haggard and tired and scared. *As well it should,* Kale thought. "Captain," he said, "I demand to know the meaning of this. Why are my troops retreating? Under whose order?"

The captain's eyes went wide, and on his face was a mixture of confusion and fear. "Y-your orders, Chosen."

"*What?*" Kale demanded. "What are you saying? I gave no such order. Speak, man, or you will suffer such a fate that your children will weep for the rest of their lives."

"I-I received a messenger, Chosen," the man stammered quickly, "one bearing a message carried from you personally. He wore the insignia of the messengers, and I had seen him around before so..."

"So *what?*" Kale snapped. "So you thought that I would be so foolish as to order a retreat when victory lay only minutes away?"

"I...I did not think to question your order, sir," Wexler said, pointedly avoiding his gaze, his shoulders hunched as if he expected to be struck.

Kale waved a hand angrily. "Forget it—I will deal with you later, Captain. Now, order the attack and send the troops back to the city gate. Valeria falls—Valeria *must* fall within the hour, for the Welians will arrive any moment."

The captain winced, his face growing paler. "Sir, when the retreat sounded...that is, the soldiers have not been trained, and they have scattered. I have my commanders in the field now trying to bring some order to them, to regroup their units but...sir, it is chaos."

Kale was at the man in a moment, jerking him up by the front of his shirt, his body trembling with unvented rage. "*Chaos?*" he demanded. "*Chaos?* I will show you chaos, Captain. I will show you such chaos that you would think your life but some terrible nightmare, one from which you will never waken. Now, if the first wave is unable to be sent, then send the second. It is why we kept them in *reserve,* after all, is it not?"

"Y-yes, Chosen, only..." The man trailed off, and Kale gave him a shake.

"Only *what?*"

He stared at the man's face as his mouth worked, and he felt it all falling apart. They were so close now, so very close to the victory, to the *revenge* which he had sought for so long, the revenge which would make all that had happened to him—all that he had *become*—worth it, and now everything was going wrong.

"T-they're sick, my lord."

"Sick?" Kale demanded. "What do you mean *sick?*"

"I-I don't know," the captain said, shaking his head desperately. "Only, all those soldiers who were still in the camp, who were not part of the original attack, seem to have come down with some terrible illness. Some have died already and the rest...I am afraid that they are not fit to fight, Chosen. They are overcome with sickness, with stomach cramps and vomiting blood, it is…it is a most terrible thing to see."

"Then get the healers to look at them damn you!" Kale screeched.

"We have, Chosen," the captain stammered, "but there are far too many sick and far too few healers. Perhaps if we had brought more—" The man's words cut off as Kale slashed his taloned hand viciously across his throat.

Blood spurted onto Kale's robe and face, and the captain collapsed at his feet, his head nearly severed from his body. Kale's taloned hands worked in fists at his sides, and he licked his lips where some blood had splattered, taking a slow, deep breath in a vain effort to calm himself.

"That was foolish."

Kale spun, furious, then hesitated to see the god, Paren, watching him. "What did you say?"

"You heard me, *Argush*," the god said, "and my mother's creation or not, I will not suffer you to take that tone with me, do you understand?"

Kale stood there trembling, his chest heaving with rage, possessed of an almost irresistible urge to attack the god, to flay the flesh from his body with teeth and claw. In the end, though, reasonable caution overcame his fury.

Paren smirked as if he knew well what thoughts had gone through Kale's mind and was amused by them. "As I was saying," the god went on, "it is a foolish commander who blames his subordinates for his own failings, and you *have* failed, Argush. You have failed terribly. My mother will be here soon, that I do not doubt, and she will not be pleased. I wonder if, given yet another disastrous failure such as this, her patience for you will have finally worn out, for my mother, you see, is not known for her patience."

A bubbling cauldron, a mixture of fear and rage, steamed inside Kale, and he was just about to speak when someone else appeared at the tent flap. One of the soldiers who had been entrusted with guarding his tent. "Sire—" the man began, but cut off, growing pale, as he noted Captain Wexler's corpse lying inside the tent.

"*Speak,*" Kale hissed.

"I-I was sent, sir," the man stammered, "to inform you…that is, it's the Welians."

"What about them?" Kale roared.

"They're…they're here, sir."

Kale let out a growl. He wanted to hurt someone, to rend and tear, but there was no one there, no one except for him and the god, and the guard who had already vanished outside the tent flap. *No,* he told himself, *no. This can still be salvaged. Somehow.*

Yes, that was right. Armies suffered setbacks, that was all. He still had the far mightier force, was still far more powerful than Alesh or any of those others who stood against him, and he promised himself that he would hunt down the messenger who had betrayed him, whoever he was, and ensure that he suffered. But later. First, he would deal with the Welians and then he would take the city. Yes, the cowards huddling inside the walls of Valeria had been granted a short reprieve, but it would not last.

"*Enough,*" Paren growled. "It is enough. Go, Argush, nightling king, and destroy the Welians."

Kale frowned. "And the city? Without our forces—"

The big god turned to meet him, his eyes dancing. "I will deal with that, will make sure that my mother's soldiers are prepared to fight. If you do not hurry in dealing with the Welians, it is likely you will return to see the city conquered while you were away."

And with that, he stomped out of the tent.

Chapter Thirty-Two

As Fermin approached the broken-down gate, the guards moved forward to intercept him. "That will not be necessary, sergeant," Alesh said, smiling. "This man is a friend."

The sergeant turned to look at him with surprise then grunted. "As you say, Chosen."

The manservant rode to the opening of the gate, picking his way carefully around the dozens, perhaps hundreds of corpses littering the ground, his face pale as if he might grow sick at any moment. Then, he looked up, reminded that they were watching him, and gave an embarrassed look, dismounting from his horse. "H-hello," he began, but cut off with a grunt as Rion charged forward, enveloping him in a tight embrace.

"Damn, Fermin, but you had me worried," the nobleman said, no artifice or sarcasm in his voice, not now, only pleasure, "thank the gods you're alright."

The manservant stood stunned for several moments, as if he had no idea how to react then he smiled widely, returning the embrace. "Ah, Lord Eriondrian, but it is good to see you again."

"And you," Rion said, finally pulling away, and Alesh did not think he imagined the tears in the man's eyes as he did. "But tell me, what's happened? How did you make it back?"

"That..." Fermin winced, an embarrassed expression on his face. "Well, I fear that is a story that will take some time in the telling."

Rion stared at him then laughed, clapping him on the back. "Well, I'll be pleased to hear it later. I'm just glad you're alright, man. Now, what of Marta? How is she? Did she make it out already?"

Fermin winced again, but this time it was not embarrassment on his face. Instead, it was shame. "I am afraid not, Lord Tirinian. I wanted to bring her...but there was no way to do so without being caught. She is with the enemy still and it is at her behest that I am here. That I have...done what I have."

"What do you mean?" Rion asked. "What did you do?"

"Isn't it obvious?" Alesh asked, grinning.

Rion frowned, turning to him. "What do you mean?"

"What I mean, Rion," Alesh went on, "is that, unless I miss my guess, we have Fermin here to thank for the enemy's retreat."

Rion blinked, his gaze traveling between the two of them, and the manservant fidgeted as if embarrassed once more. "Fermin?" he asked. "Is that true?"

Fermin studied his feet. "That...I did, perhaps, play some small part. Though, I fear it will be a short reprieve. Soon, Kale will muster his troops once more."

"You have given us time, Fermin," Alesh said. "That is no small thing, and I will not listen to you downplay it. Without your intervention, it is likely that we would all be dead already."

The man grinned widely at that, his face flushing with obvious pleasure. "T-thank you, Chosen."

"No," Alesh said, "thank y—"

"Alesh?"

The voice came from behind him, the speaker not in his sight, but he knew it at once, and a flood of emotions ran through Alesh. Shame and fear, yes, but mostly love. He turned to see her standing there. She looked exhausted, as if it was all she could do to keep her feet and only that with the help of Darl who stood beside her, one of her arms draped across his shoulders.

But even with her face lined with exhaustion, her clothes stained with blood, she was beautiful. The most beautiful thing Alesh had ever seen, and while she looked as if she might collapse at any moment, her being there, her being part of the world meant that it could not be so bad as he sometimes feared. That for all the violence and tragedy, for all the darkness, there was greatness in it too. "Katherine," he said, finding himself out of breath in a way he had not been when fighting back the attackers.

"You're...here," she said.

"I am," he said. "But...are you okay? What's happened?"

"I'm fine," she said, waving a hand dismissively. "You know, sometimes playing music takes it out of me, that's all."

Alesh could see that there was far more to it than that, but he would have to get the details later, for he knew that while Fermin had bought them time, they could not afford to squander it. Still, he took a moment, turning to the Ferinan. "Darl," he said. "It's good to see you."

"And it is good to be seen, Son of the Morning," the man said, smiling widely.

"We were on the wall," Katherine explained, "we saw the army retreat. What happened? Did you...did you do something or—"

"Not me," Alesh interrupted, turning to gesture to the manservant who was pointedly avoiding everyone's eyes. "Him."

"Fermin!" Katherine said, and in a moment she was rushing forward, finding some strength after all, and embracing the smiling manservant.

Then, his expression slowly grew somber. "Forgive me," Fermin said, "but I have not only escaped...I brought news. Marta has learned—"

"Marta!" Katherine said. "Is she with you? Is she okay?"

"She...is not with me," Fermin said, "but she was well last I saw her."

"It will be okay," Alesh said, meeting Katherine's gaze. "We'll find her. Now, tell me, Fermin, what news do you bring?"

"It's the Welians," Fermin said. "They're on their way with their army, and Kale means to intercept them before they make it to the city. He captured the messenger meant for Valeria and means to surround and trap them before they make it off the shore."

"The Welians?" Rion asked, clearly confused. "But what are they doing here?"

Fermin shook his head. "According to Efial—the Welian messenger—they heard of our plight, have heard, too, that the Son of the Morning has come to the land, and they mean to aid us."

"So...what do we do?" Rion asked.

They were all staring at Alesh then, waiting for what he would say, for some solution. But while they were faced with many problems, it seemed that solutions, for him at least, were in short supply. They could stay in the city, he supposed, stay and allow the Welians who had come to help them to be ambushed by Kale's forces while they cowered behind walls which had no gate. Or..."What do we do?" he asked, the answer coming to him. "Well, the Welians have traveled far, across the ocean, to meet with us. It would be rude not to provide them an escort."

"Wait a minute," Rion said, "you mean..."

Alesh met Tarex's eyes, and the Ekirani smiled, bowing his head in acknowledgment. He turned to regard Darl, and the Ferinan smiled, winking. "Yes, Rion," Alesh said. "If we are to have any hope of victory, then we need the Welians. And though they know it not, they need us, too. We will go out to meet them."

The nobleman's eyes went wide at that, and his mouth worked as if he might argue but then finally he only shrugged. "Well. Suppose a man can only wait on his death to come to him for so long before even that gets boring. Might as well go out and meet the bastard."

Alesh turned to regard the soldiers still left standing. "Sergeant," he said, "I need you to send a runner to Captain Nordin on the wall, tell him what we intend and to send all of our forces who are willing here, to this gate. We leave within the hour."

"Of course, Chosen," the sergeant said, then he motioned to one of the soldiers who went rushing toward the stairs leading up to the battlements.

"If we are to do this, Chosen," Tarex said, "then you will, perhaps, need a better weapon."

Alesh frowned, glancing down at his sword and was surprised to see that the blade, which was coated with the blood of those foes—mortal and nightling alike—which he had cut down, was battered and bent, twisted out of shape from countless blows.

"I think we might just have an answer for you."

Alesh turned and was surprised to find Chosen Larin standing there, the big blacksmith, Odrick, beside him, a long cloth bundle in his hand. "Good to see you up and about, lad," Larin said. He paused, glancing at the broken bodies of the dead scattered about the gate opening. "And not a moment too soon it seems."

"Well," Alesh said, smiling, "I had a bit of help. But how did you know—"

Larin waved a hand. "Well, the first clue is the fact we're all still breathin'. Anyway, I went to check on the walls and saw the enemy army retreating. Figured something was goin' on so we came here. And a good thing we did too," he went on, eyeing the bent blade in Alesh's hand, "if, that is, you mean to go chargin' into battle with that thing." He turned to Odrick who shifted nervously as the collective gazes of those gathered at the gate regarded him. "Go on, lad. Show him."

The blacksmith cleared his throat, clearly uncomfortable with the attention. He undid a tie fastened about the cloth bundle and pulled the fabric aside to reveal a long blade. The grip and cross guard looked the color of burnished gold, reminding Alesh of an early morning sunrise, and indeed, something which looked like a sun, lines of its light radiating outward, had been etched into it. The steel of the blade glistened in the orange light of the torches of the gate, so that the blade itself seemed to shine with some inner fire.

"You...you made this?" Alesh asked, unable to keep the awe from his voice.

Larin grunted. "The lad did it, mostly. I only added a few...well, minor touches, we'll call 'em."

"A fine weapon," Tarex observed. "Tell me, Son of the Morning, what will you name it?"

"Name it?" Alesh said, finding it difficult to takes his eyes off the blade, losing himself in the way the light played along its length.

"Oh yes," Tarex said. "Such a fine weapon as this should be named."

"Very well," Alesh said, taking the offered blade in his hand and, as if by magic, thought he could feel some of his strength returned to him along with it. "Then it will be named...Dawning. A reminder that no matter how dark the night gets, morning will come again."

Tarex nodded. "A worthy name for a worthy blade."

"Thank you, Odrick," Alesh said.

"It isn't much," the blacksmith said, meeting his eyes for a moment only to shyly look away again, "not a weapon blessed by the God of Conflict, certainly, but—"

"No," Alesh interrupted. "It's better. For this blade was not made and will not be used to bring conflict, Odrick, but to end it. Truly, thank you."

The man smiled, clearly pleased, and moments later Nordin and his troops began to arrive. Alesh knew well the numbers of defenders Valeria had left, and he was surprised to note that it seemed that, along with the captain, every defender was accounted for. More surprising, in fact, when one considered the others—shifty-eyed men and women, mostly, who looked like nightmares waiting to happen. He stepped forward, offering the captain his hand. "Nordin."

"Chosen," the man said, looking exhausted as he took it, but smiling.

"You have done well, Captain," Alesh said. "Better than anyone could have ever expected. But perhaps it was unclear—I meant only for those men and women who are willing to volunteer to go out and help the Welians to come."

Nordin nodded. "Yes, Chosen. These men and women here—they all volunteered."

Alesh stared at the soldiers and criminals arrayed behind the captain. They all looked exhausted, tired, but there was something in their eyes—determination, perhaps—that gave him heart. These men and women had spent the last days fighting an enemy who knew no mercy or compassion, who sought only destruction and unmitigated slaughter, yet instead of taking time to rest, of relying on someone else, they were here, all of them, and all of them watching him for what he would say.

Alesh took a slow, deep breath, feeling a sense of awe at what they were willing to sacrifice, at what they had sacrificed already. He did not know what a man should say to such courage, what a man *could* say. But he knew that he owed it to them, at the very least, to try. "Chosen Olliman," he said, raising his voice so that they would all hear him, "was like a father to me. A man greater than any I have ever known, a man who sacrificed everything for his people, who led the Torchbearers in a battle against the Darkness, saving the entire world from the evil of the nightlings. I am no Olliman, but you, I can tell you, are as great as any of those Torchbearers, and whatever comes, I want you all to know that I am proud to stand with you."

They gave a cheer at that, and Alesh turned back to the small group gathered around him, Rion and Katherine, Darl and Tarex. "Okay, if you all will go to the gate, I'll meet you in just a second."

They all nodded, turning and moving that way, but Alesh grabbed Katherine's arm. "Not you, Katherine. I need...that is, I would speak to you."

She met his gaze, a world of meaning in her own. "Okay, Alesh."

"I know..." He hesitated, frowning. "I know that I haven't been a good man, a good leader. I've been selfish and have allowed my anger and my hate to cloud my judgement. I know that I was not good to you, and for that, I am s—"

"Alesh," she interrupted, "you were fine. It really isn't—"

"No, Katherine. No, I wasn't. I doubted myself, you see, and I allowed that doubt to make me angry. You deserved better." He glanced at those others, his friends, now moving toward the gate, thought, too, of Sonya. "You all did."

"It's okay, Alesh," she said. "We can talk about it later—"

"I don't know that there's going to be a later," he said, then he stepped forward taking her hands in his. "Listen, this isn't me being fearful or doubtful—but what we face now is no less than the most dangerous threat the world has ever come against, greater even than that which Olliman faced years ago, and I do not know that I will come back."

"We," she said, frowning. "You mean we."

He winced, meeting her eyes. "No, Katherine. I don't. You won't be coming."

"I'm not a child, Alesh. If you all are going, then I'm—"

"No," he interrupted, "no, you're right. You're not a child. But you're not a fighter either, Katherine. Besides, anyone with eyes can see that you're just about done in—I know what you did. I know that, without you, without your song, the city would have fallen. But you can barely stand. And I need you to do me a favor. In case...that is...I need you to look after Sonya for me. If things go wrong or..."

"Don't," she said softly, and he saw tears gathering in her eyes. "Don't say that."

He studied her then, trying to etch it all into his memory, the color of her eyes, the way her hair framed features that were kind and compassionate but strong, too. "I have to go now—we can't keep the Welians waiting."

"Alesh," she said, her voice breaking, "I...I mean, be safe. Okay?"

He smiled. "Of course." Then he turned, meaning to move toward the gate where the others waited but paused, realizing that those things which he had told himself he would tell her, if he did not tell her now, he might never be able to. So he took a slow breath, turning to look at her once more. "I love you, Katherine. Maybe you know that or not, I don't know. I know this isn't the best time or the best place but...well, I thought maybe, if things go badly, then there might not be another and...I need you to know that."

She smiled, unshed tears twinkling in her eyes, and then she was in his arms, both of them holding each other tight, a world of emotion shared in that embrace. "I love you too," she whispered.

Alesh felt a great warmth spreading through him, one that was, in many ways, far better than the power granted him by Amedan. It was a power, a magic which was the strict purview of mortals and them alone. A human magic. He smiled back.

"Come back to me," she said. "To us."

He nodded. "I'll do my best." Then he turned and moved to where the others waited.

"So what do we do?" Rion asked. "Are we going to try to sneak around the army to the Welians or..."

Alesh let his gaze travel along the small group of those gathered, men and women braver than any he had ever known or thought to know. "No, Rion. No the time for sneaking is done. The Light does not hide, for a light hidden loses its power." He met each of their gazes, and was once again humbled by what he saw there—not fear, but courage, not desperation but determination. "The night has been long, but even this night, of all nights, cannot last forever. Not so long as there is a single light left to stand against it. So let us go, soldiers of Valeria, defenders of the world. Let us go..." He paused, closing his eyes, feeling the power there, feeling each spark of each torch running along the walls and by the gate. He called to those flames, felt them answer, and strength and power suddenly suffused him so that he felt as if he could hardly contain them, then he opened his eyes to regard those soldiers who were staring at him with unmistakable awe as flames swirled and danced around him. "Let us go," he repeated, "and be the Light."

Chapter Thirty-Three

The lines of Kale's army had long since stopped being lines at all. Even Marta, whose only knowledge about warfare was what she had gathered over the last few weeks—mostly, that it was the worst thing in the world—could see that much. The forces who had recently retreated from the city were milling about in confused jumbles while the army's commanders tried—and largely failed—to bring some semblance of order to their chaotic ranks.

Meanwhile, those other soldiers, hundreds—thousands, even—who had been meant to make up the second wave of the attack were instead puking and shitting themselves, succumbing most effectively to Llanivere's herb. Marta reminded herself as she carried yet another bucket—one overrunning with a variety of bodily fluids which stank worse than anything she'd ever smelled—toward the edge of the army camp, never to get on the old woman's bad side.

She was focused on walking carefully—gods forbid she spill any of the foul waste on herself—when, suddenly, chaos erupted around her. Or perhaps it was more accurate to say that the chaos which had already existed grew *more* chaotic. The enemy soldiers began to shout and scream, some even hissing like cornered beasts. At first Marta had no idea what it was that was causing such an uproar. Then, she turned, following the soldiers' wild, panicked gestures and saw what it was that had driven such a panic into them.

A terrible bright light seemed to be flying directly at the army, one which originated from the city of Valeria. A light so bright, so powerful, that she was forced to shield her eyes. It was as if a star had crashed down to earth, or perhaps as if the sun itself had and was now rolling directly toward the enemy army.

At first, Marta could make out no details within that light, but as she watched, she thought she saw a figure she recognized at its head, and her breath caught in her throat. It was Alesh, the man blazing like some great beacon, his sword, blazing with the flames wreathing it, held aloft before him. And behind him were others, Darl and Rion among them, all of them charging directly toward the enemy camp. It was a beautiful, terrible, inspiring thing to behold.

But as amazing as it was, she noted that, upon closer inspection, there could be no more than around fifty men and women with Alesh all told, certainly less than a hundred. Gods, what was the man thinking? Such a small force would be met and swallowed whole by the enemy army with little effort. For while Kale's army had descended into chaos, even now the commanders, mostly through the use of brutal force, were forcing some order back into the ranks, getting the soldiers back into a line. They were all terrified, that much was clear, but it was also clear that they vastly outnumbered the force charging toward them.

At first, she could not imagine what Alesh could be thinking—had the man gone insane? But then it hit her. The Welians had come, and without the help of those defenders of Valeria, the Welians would be set upon by Kale and his forces the moment they struck land, though what Alesh thought he would accomplish with so small a force she couldn't imagine.

But then...it didn't have to be so small, did it? After all, there were several hundred slaves in the camp, women who'd had their rights—their very humanity—stripped from them by those of Kale's army and who were all too eager to take it back. She tossed away the bucket of foulness she'd been carrying then turned to start back toward the slave tents at a run.

She'd only made it a few steps when a large form stepped out of the chaos of the army to block her path. Marta stumbled, nearly falling, but the big man reached out a hand, catching her.

"Excuse me—" she began, trying to make her way past, but the big man did not let her go.

"You're her, aren't you?"

Marta paused, looking up at him. The man had a kind face, did not sneer or frown as Guardsman Blake had, but that meant nothing, she knew, for if the last weeks had taught her anything it was that evil came in many forms. "I'm no one," she said.

"Oh, I don't think that's true," the man said, smiling. "Everybody's someone, after all. What I mean, though, is that you're the slave girl, the one Fur came to see."

"Fur?" she asked, confused. "No, you must have me mistaken with someone else, forgive me, but my master—"

"Fermin, I mean," he amended. "You're her," he went on, nodding. "I'm sure of it."

She could have lied then. The gods knew she'd done it enough in her time, but she was tired of lying, tired of being scared, too, so she took a slow, deep breath, meeting his eyes. "My name's not girl. It's Marta. And yes—Fermin's my friend. So what happens now?" she asked, realizing that more soldiers had gathered behind the big man, several dozen at the least, and they were all watching her. "You going to kill me? Torture me, maybe?"

The man barked a laugh that was not menacing at all but was, in fact, somehow heartening. "Kill you? Gods no, girl. We've come to help." He reached out a hand that could have crushed her easily, if he'd wanted it to. "The name's Calden."

She took the hand—there wasn't really much else to do. "So...what's the plan, Calden?"

"You tell me," the big man said. "You're the boss."

Marta blinked, looking around at the soldiers all staring at her. It didn't make any sense, not any of it, but there was no time to worry over that, not now. It was a miracle, that much was sure, but she promised herself that she would thank the gods later, burn a goat or something, maybe, though what the gods did with all those burned goats she'd never been able to imagine. "Well...I need to get to the slave tents. There's some sla...that is, soldiers there, that will help us." She glanced over his shoulder at the chaos all around them, "though how we'll get through all that, I can't imagine."

The big man grunted, giving her a wink. "Don't worry about it, lass," he said, drawing the sword sheathed at his side. "You just have to ask nice, that's all. Now, you just tell us where to go—we'll get you there."

Chapter Thirty-Four

Alesh pivoted, his blade flashing out, and the fine steel, gifted him by Odrick and Larin, cut through his attacker's wrist as if it were nothing, separating his hand from the rest of his arm and the hand—along with the sword it held—flew away. The man screamed but not for long as Alesh's second strike took his head from his shoulders.

But there was another man to take his place, then another to replace that one when he'd cut him down, too, and on and on it went as the enemy forces continued to gather before them. It seemed, then, that the army was beginning to reorganize again, and a quick glance showed him that dozens, perhaps hundreds of soldiers had begun to surround him and the others, slowing their forward progress.

He spun, parrying a blade meant for one of the soldiers beside him then lashed out, impaling the attacker, but as fast as he moved, he was not fast enough to protect all those with him, and as the enemy soldiers continued to press in around them, he saw several of Valeria's defenders fall with more being swarmed and taken down with each passing moment.

He was slowly accepting the reality that he and those with him would make it no closer to the Welians, that they would be slaughtered here by the enemy soldiers that surrounded them, when something strange began to happen in the enemy lines. A *ripple* seemed to pass through them, and their shouts—ones of anger and bloodthirst moments before—turned to screams of pain and surprise. Those soldiers in front of Alesh and the others began to turn, ignoring those in front of them and spinning instead to look behind them, and Alesh stared, confused, as the enemy soldiers seemed to be fighting each other.

But not just each other. Women of varying ages had appeared in the enemy line as well. They wore dirty, linen shifts that looked as if they might have once been white, and wielded weapons ranging from broom handles to cast iron pots to rocks. They clearly had no training and no real weapons with which to exercise that training even if they had, yet the women fought with a ferocity and tenacity that overcame much of those shortcomings, attacking the enemy soldiers like wild beasts let loose of their cages, leaping on the enemy soldiers from behind, growling and hissing as they fought.

It was over in minutes. The ground was littered with the fallen, enemy soldiers and more than a few of those women in the linen shifts. Alesh and those with him were still surrounded. There appeared to be a couple of dozen men still dressed much as the other soldiers had been but there were also a few hundred of the women whose chests heaved and who gripped their makeshift weapons—most of them bloody—looking all too ready to use them once more.

A big man, one nearly as large as Odrick or Larin, stepped forward through the press, regarding Alesh and those with him. He glanced past Alesh at where Fermin stood, the older man's thin chest heaving, the club in his hand—where he'd gotten it Alesh had no idea—stained with blood. Then the big man winked. "Fur."

The manservant cleared his throat. "Calden."

Alesh turned back to the man, frowning. The soldier carried a sword and, unlike many of those Alesh and those with him had faced, held it like he knew how to use it. He, along with those with him, studied Alesh and his companions across the intervening space of a few feet. Several moments passed in silence, then, as Alesh—and no doubt everyone there—tried to reconcile his confused thoughts and understand what had happened.

"You are Chosen Alesh?" the man asked. "The one they call The Son of the Morning?"

"Yes," Alesh said. "I am he."

He didn't know what to expect, thought it likely that the man would attack him out of hand. Instead, the big man abruptly dropped to one knee, bowing his head and placing his sword on the ground at his side. The others followed his lead a moment later and, in seconds, Alesh and those with him were left surrounded by several hundred kneeling men and women. "I have done a lot of bad in my life, sir," the big man said. "All of us have. If you'll have me—if you'll have *us*—we'd like to do some good before the end."

Alesh shared a look with Rion who gave him a small, wide-eyed shrug, then he met Darl's gaze, and the Ferinan gave him a small smile, as if he had expected no less. Alesh cleared his throat. "We...of course, we would be happy to have you. But please, rise, all of you." They did, and Alesh stepped forward, offering the big man his hand. "My name is Alesh."

The big man took it, smiling. "As Fur said, the name's Calden."

He nodded. "So tell me, Calden, it's you that I have to thank for saving us?"

The man gave a hearty laugh at that, the sort of laugh that was infectious. "Oh, gods no, sir, not me. Her."

He turned then, and the soldiers and women spread out behind the big man separated, creating an avenue through which a small figure walked. Alesh took in a sharp breath, and he heard Rion and Darl do the same, for the person which walked toward them was no stranger, but one he—one *they*—knew well.

"Marta?" he managed in a surprised, breathless voice.

The young girl was smiling timidly as she walked toward him. "Gods, but it seems I can't leave you lot alone for anytime at all without you getting into some kind of—" She cut off, letting out an abrupt sound of surprise as Rion rushed forward, lifting her off the ground and pulling her into a tight embrace.

Several of the women in shifts started forward, clearly with violence on their mind, but Marta held up a hand, and Alesh was surprised to see them all freeze and back down like a pack of dogs at their master's command. Then Marta was laughing, hugging him back. "Okay, okay," she said, "I missed you too, now how about you let me down while I've still got some ribs unbroken?"

Rion smiled sheepishly, setting her down, and Alesh grinned, walking forward and pulling the girl into an embrace as well, though one a touch less likely to crack a rib. "I'm very glad you're okay, Marta," he said. "We were worried. Has it...has it been terrible for you?"

Marta grinned, sharing a meaningful glance with an older woman in a white shift who was near her before turning back to him. "Oh, you know, nothing to it. Just been sittin' with our feet propped up while men feed us grapes and rub our feet, that's all."

There was laughter from the gathered women at that, and Alesh, knowing Marta's penchant for understatement—and outright lying—thought that there was quite a bit more to it than that, but before he could ask any further questions, Marta turned and stared at Tarex. The little girl's amiable expression changed to one of fury, and her finger stabbed toward the man in a point. "*You,*" she growled.

The women—as well as the soldiers—around her reacted immediately, each taking a step forward as if by some silent command. "Where did you put Sonya?" she demanded. "I swear by all the gods of the Light and Darkness both, that if you hurt her in any way—"

"Wait, Marta, wait," Alesh said, stepping between Tarex and the girl, not to mention the slaves and soldiers nearest her who looked ready to charge the Ekirani. "Tarex is one of us."

Marta blinked at that, a confused expression on her face. "What?"

"He brought Sonya back to us," Alesh explained hurriedly, thinking he didn't have much time before one of those women or soldiers decided to take matters into their own hands. "He escaped from the camp and brought her to us—she's safe now, in Valeria. Or at least," he amended, "as safe as anyone can be. She's with the Tirinians."

"Lord and Lady Tirinian?" Marta asked.

"That's right."

She smiled sadly. "I miss them. I think I even miss the damned tutoring lessons." She gave her head a shake as if to clear it then glanced around, apparently noting for the first time the willingness of those others with her to attack the man, and she held up a hand to forestall them. "Well," she said. "I did hear something about him leaving with her but I thought...well, never mind what I thought." She turned back to the Ekirani. "Tarex, isn't it?"

The tattooed man knelt, bowing his head. "I am very sorry, Chosen, for the crimes which I committed against you and yours. If it is your will that you or those with you will seek your apology in the form of blood, then know that I will not resist."

Marta stared at the kneeling man in surprise then turned back to Alesh. He said nothing, for he had made his peace with Tarex already, and what forgiveness the man needed was not his to give. Finally, Marta turned back to the Ekirani, and he could see the anger he himself had felt flashing in her gaze, could see it in the way her hands knotted into fists at her sides over and over again. In the end, though, she let out a heavy sigh. "I think there's been enough blood, don't you?" At the words, the soldiers and women gathered visibly relaxed. "And likely," the girl went on, "there'll be more before its done. So stand up, alright? You're making me uncomfortable."

The Ekirani nodded. "As you wish," he said.

The man had only just stood again when a great roar came from nearby.

"*Enough!*" a voice thundered, and they all turned to see a giant approaching. And not just any giant, not this, but Paren, the God of Conflict, himself, and he looked furious. Yet for all the menace of the god, menace which radiated out from him in waves, the women and soldiers did not quail at his approach but looked ready to launch themselves at him.

Yet Alesh knew that fighting the God of Conflict was far different than fighting ill-equipped and ill-prepared soldiers, knew that the men and women, no matter their courage, stood no chance against the god. If they tried to fight him, they would only be cut down by the massive sword sheathed at the giant's back like wheat before the scythe.

"Rion, Tarex" he said, "make it to the Welians—help them, if you can. I will handle this."

He took a step forward, readying his sword, but a hand fell on his arm, and he turned to see Tarex beside him. "No, Son of the Morning," the Ekirani said softly. "You have your battle, it lies before you, and this is not it. Go, and bring aid to the Welians. I will buy you what time I am able."

Alesh glanced at the god standing there with a small smile on his face, his thick, muscled arms folded across his barrel chest, then back to the Ekirani. "You're sure?"

"I am sure," the man said. "My wife and my son, they wait for me, Son of the Morning. Long have they waited, and I think..." He paused, readying his weapon. "I think that soon, their waiting will come to an end."

"Wait a minute," Rion said in a harsh whisper, stepping forward, "we can't just *leave* him, I mean, it's the *God of Conflict.* He'll kill him!"

Alesh met Tarex's gaze again, and the Ekirani only gave him a small, knowing smile, nodding his head. He glanced at Marta then, and the girl met his eyes, waiting for what he would say. Finally, Alesh let out a heavy breath. "Come on, Rion," he said. "It's time to go—the Welians need us."

He turned back to Tarex the Ekirani, one final time. "Thank you, Tarex. For everything. It has been an honor."

The Ekirani smiled at that, and there was no fear in his gaze, no worry or doubt. There was only peace, peace greater than any he had ever seen on the Ekirani's face before. "The honor, Son of the Morning, has been mine."

Then, with a heavy heart, Alesh turned back to the others. Several hundred of them now that Marta had brought her own force, though from where she had gotten it he would have to discover later, when there was time. Not a great force, perhaps, to stand against the Darkness, but then even a single light could drive back the night. "Come on," he said. "It's time to go."

And then they were running, resuming their charge once more and driving toward the Welians, hoping to save those who had come to save them.

Chapter Thirty-Five

Tarex stood silently, his spear held at his side, one end resting on the ground, as he regarded the god before him. Some men in his situation would have been terrified by this avatar of war and battle which stood like some immovable mountain, but Tarex felt only peace. He had faced conflict and war for most of his life, after all, and he knew it well, knew all the shapes it might take.

"You are to be a sacrifice," the god observed, still smiling. "Know, then, Tarex, that it will make no difference in the end. Know that I will finish with you here, and then I will hunt down these friends of yours, will slaughter them and put an end to this misguided attempt."

"I know many things, God of War," Tarex said, "many things that you, yourself, seem to have forgotten. I know that for millennia you have whispered in the ears of warriors and kings, have spread your poison into the hearts and arms of men so that they might shed the blood of the innocent and call it valor, call it courage. Yet for all the pain, for all the agony and loss you have caused, you have always been above it, hidden from it like some historian, chronicling events but too scared to get your own hands bloody. You style yourself a warrior, but you have fought no war. Instead, you have watched, have urged others to fight, have allowed them to suffer in your stead. Now, though, you do not sit in safety. Now, you are here, in the world of men, a world of beauty and kindness yes, but one also of pain, a pain you do not understand, for you have never felt it. Now I will be your teacher."

"Enough talk," the god growled. "Are you ready to bleed, Tarex of the Ekirani?"

"Are you? Come, God of War," Tarex said, readying his weapon. "I will show you the Dance of the Ekirani."

Tarex had spent his life training in combat, had spent years mastering the art of the Dance, tutored by the best warriors in the world, those he had been privileged enough to call his people. He had been honed, over those years, into a fine instrument, one built for one purpose. And yet, for all his training, for all his skill, the god moved with an incredible speed, one no mortal could match, and the first swipe of his sword very nearly took Tarex's head from his shoulders.

He ducked, just in time, and felt the wind of the giant blade *swish* only inches over his head. And then they were in the midst of it, the god's blade moving with a speed far greater than any striking serpent, coming at him again and again in a metallic blur, and it was all Tarex could do to avoid the sweep of that deadly steel.

But he was not afraid, did not allow himself to feel fear, for he was in the midst of the Dance, and he would buy what time he could for those he would call his friends. He could only hope that it would be enough.

Chapter Thirty-Six

Argush crouched in the trees, flexing his taloned hands in anticipation, an anticipation he knew was shared by all the nightlings, his brothers. They were spread out in the forest around him, and though they blended in with the shadows so well that even he, with his god-blessed sight, had to focus to see them, he could hear them easily enough. Could hear their hisses and their growls as they gloried in the bloodshed to come. They were ready, waiting only on his command, the command of their king, one he would give the moment the bulk of the Welian force made landfall.

On the other side of the forest, spread out in a semi-circle so that the Welians, once they disembarked from their ships, would be surrounded, left with nowhere to go but to the company of the Keeper of the Dead, were the mortal troops.

They, too, were eager for the bloodshed to come, but to Argush, crouched among his true brothers, their two-legged forms, their defenseless skin lacking any scales to protect them, seemed pathetic, even perverse. He gave a snort, shaking his head and putting the mortals out of his mind.

Their commanders could deal with them. He was not a commander now, not a man to waste his hours poring over maps and reports. He had done that long enough, and it had brought nothing but grief and failure. No, it was time to let his bestial side free. It was hungry, that part of him, always hungry, but soon it would feast. For even now, the Welian ships approached the shore, so close that he could hear the sailors' calls as they shouted to each other.

In less than an hour, perhaps minutes, they would reach the shore, would leave the safety of their crafts and would find such devastation and bloodshed waiting for them that never again would they ever dare to meddle in his affairs. Not that they would have an opportunity to do so, for his—and the nightlings surrounding him—hunger would not be satisfied with the country of Entarna. He would not be content until the entire world—or what was left of it, at least—knelt at his feet.

The growls and hisses of those creatures around him suddenly rose in pitch, pulling him from thoughts of the bloodshed to come, and he turned to see a figure approaching. A man would have been unable to see the figure clearly, given that the only light was the pale illumination provided by the moon, but Argush was no normal man, was far more than that, and he could see the newcomer easily. A messenger, one who approached timidly, his entire body trembling.

Understandable, of course, for the nightlings were hungry, eager, and when they were in such a state, they were not so particular about whose flesh they devoured, just so long as they did. "C-Chosen?" the messenger asked, his voice quaking with terror.

The beast inside him felt a flash of annoyance at being forced to deal with another of the awkward mortals with their soft flesh and no claws or talons to defend themselves, nothing except the poor substitutes they were forced to craft in their forges. Still, he took a slow, deep breath, allowing some part of his mortal side to return, and he rose, moving to stand in front of the man. He did not wear the robe he often did, the one which covered the gifts Shira had given him, the changes her blessings had wrought on his flesh, and even in the poor light provided by the moon there was no way the man could miss the thick, black scales covering his body. The messenger let out a squeal, turning and perhaps meaning to flee, but Argush grabbed his jerkin, lifting him off the ground.

"*Speak,*" Argush growled.

"T-the captain," the man stammered, "he s-sent me to tell you. T-there's a force approaching."

Argush flexed his talons impatiently, fighting the urge to rip the man apart, to feast on his flesh for his foolishness. "*Yes, the Welians, I know. We wait here for them, fool, and—*"

"Forgive me, Chosen," the man interrupted in a breathless voice, "but not the Welians. This force approaches from Valeria, and will be on us any mo—"

The rest of the man's words were drowned out as sudden, dazzling light exploded in the darkness. The nightlings roared with anger and pain as the hated light burned their flesh. Argush also hissed with fury, but while he was still sensitive to light, he could not be destroyed by it as his brothers could, brothers which were currently scrambling behind trees, searching for the soothing comfort of what little shadows remained in the face of that hateful illumination.

His talons flexing with rage, Argush promised himself he would make whoever had dared light torches among his brothers suffer as he spun to look. His gaze traveled to the hillside, the source of the hateful brightness, and he froze, staring in disbelief.

The light did not come from several torches as he had expected. It came from a man, a man who was not, as he'd thought, a member of his army.

He stood there shining like some great beacon of power and strength, the sword in his hand swathed in flames that swirled and danced around the steel. Alesh. The so-called Son of the Morning, the man who had frustrated Argush's plans at every turn, the man who he wished to see dead more than anything in the world. And he did not stand alone. Others stood with him, a few hundred in all, men who, by their dress, were members of Argush's own army, and others, women in white shifts. After a moment, Argush realized who they were—the slaves from the slave tents.

He wanted to laugh at that, at this pathetic excuse for opposition which stood staring down at him and his forces. Only there was nothing funny about them, and they did not seem so pathetic, not at all. Perhaps it was only by a trick of the light, perhaps it was something else, but while the force should have seemed laughable, a small, token opposition that might be destroyed with a moment's effort, instead it sent a tremor of something—not fear, certainly, but concern, perhaps—roiling through Argush.

Such men and women, facing overwhelming odds as they did, should have been afraid, should have turned and ran as fast as their legs could carry them and never mind that it would never, *could* never be fast enough. But they did not appear afraid, those men and women. And they did not run. Instead, they stood confidently and seemed to brim with power in some way that he could not understand or define. Argush hissed, glancing back to see that the Welians were very close to the shore now, only moments away from making landfall.

He glanced between the two forces, uncertain, and was still trying to decide on his next course of action when a voice spoke. It did not scream or shout, that voice, yet it carried clearly, thundering and drowning out all the hisses and curses—and shouts of surprise—from his army's lines.

"*Kale Leandrian, servant of the Darkness,*" the voice, *his* voice said, "*I have come for you. We have come for you. This ends. Now.*"

Chapter Thirty-Seven

The giant sword whistled at him through the air, a metallic blur almost too fast to follow. Tarex was weary from the fight so far, one that, while brief, was easily the most desperate of his life. He knew that he could not evade the god's strike, not in time, so instead he was forced to bring the haft of his weapon up above his head to block the blow. It was a powerful blow, one that would have easily shattered any normal weapon, but the weapon he held was not normal, was one gifted him by the very same god with which he was now locked in combat, and it did not break. Yet even still, the strike, powered by the god's inhuman strength, was such that it made Tarex's arms go numb with its impact, and he was driven to his knees.

Tarex had no time to recover before the god swung again with hardly any hesitation at all. He rolled away desperately, narrowly avoiding the questing steel and just managed to gain his feet in time to leap away from another strike which would have cut him in half.

Tarex had been in many fights, many battles, had spent the greater part of his life in one or another, yet now he faced the greatest battle of his life. An impossible one, in fact. How could any man, after all, expect to stand against the God of Conflict himself?

He would die, could *only* die. He did not fear death, had sought for it many times for all the wrong reasons and now only felt privileged that he might sacrifice his life to do something good, to go some small way toward righting the many wrongs he had wrought upon the world. He could not win. He knew it, and the god knew it too, the god who, while Tarex stood panting for breath, his entire body weary from the brief bout, stood straight and proud, his breathing unlabored.

"Your end comes upon you, Tarex," the god growled.

"Our end comes upon us all, sooner or later, godling," Tarex responded. "All things with a beginning have also an end—men and animals alike. The world. Even gods."

"I, an end?" the god said, laughing with a sound like boulders cracking under some great pressure. "Do you not yet see, Tarex? *I am no mortal whose flesh will wither and rot. Your lives, all of your lives are no more than the blink of an eye to me, for I am a god.* I am eternal."

"Come then," Tarex said, straightening himself and taking a slow, deep breath to gather what strength remained to him. "Let us see if even that which is eternal can bleed."

He knew that he had little time left to him. Soon, in seconds, minutes at the most, he would have nothing left, no reserves on which to call, and the god would cut him down. Tarex did not fear death, no, but he feared failure. He gritted his teeth then, calling on all his strength and speed, pushed himself to limits greater than any he ever had before, and with a shout, he charged forward, and the god rushed to meet him.

The giant sword lashed out, moving with a speed Tarex could not hope to match, the same speed which had forced him to abandon any attempt at countering thus far and had forced him, instead, on the defensive. He could not match that speed, he realized, and another realization struck him in that instant, one that brought a small smile to his face. He could not match the god's speed, and so he did not try. Instead, he continued his forward charge, his own weapon flashing out.

He felt the steel slide into him, felt the truth of it and knew that the blow was a mortal one, yet he was not afraid, and he did not allow that wild shock of pain to cause him to hesitate. He continued with his own blow, and the god cried out in surprised pain as Tarex's blade cut a bloody furrow across his face.

Paren let out roar, stumbling away, his own weapon—still impaling Tarex—forgotten. The strength left Tarex's legs, and he fell to his knees with a sigh, held up by the giant sword protruding from him, the handle of which, propped as it was against the ground, was the only reason why he was able to stay upright.

The god brought a hand to his bloody cheek, an expression of shocked disbelief on his normally smug, arrogant features. "Y-you cut me," he said, stunned.

"So I did," Tarex breathed, feeling his blood flowing out, feeling his death coming. But he was not afraid, for it had been coming for a long time now. He had watched its approach for years, had courted it and now, finally, he had found it. "It seems, then," he went on, "that even the eternal can bleed."

"T-that's impossible," Paren said, "i-it can't be. Y-you are only a mortal. I'm a *god.*"

"Your greatest mistake, Paren, God of Conflict," Tarex breathed, "is thinking you understand the limits of men's potential, a potential even we ourselves rarely grasp."

The god stood there, disbelieving, then gave his head a shake. "It...it does not matter," he said in what was meant to be a confident tone but one that was belied by the tremor in it. "For you are finished, Tarex, and even now you d—" He cut off as his entire body seemed to *flicker* as if he were but a reflection in a lake which had just had a stone tossed into it. Another look came onto his face then, this one not of confusion or disbelief but of fear. "What?" he asked. "What's happening?"

"Do you not yet see, godling?" Tarex asked. "What is it..." He paused, coughing out blood. "What is it," he continued, "that gives life to the gods?"

Paren hissed. "I will not be lectured..." He hesitated as he flickered once more, and his features twisted with budding panic. "T-this makes no sense, it is only a tiny cut, barely noticeable and—"

Tarex smiled. "Your *will,* godling," he said, answering his own question. "It is that which keeps you alive, that keeps all your kind alive. And *your* will derives from your belief in war, and your belief—flawed and incorrect as it may be—that the impulses it causes in mortals, hate and rage and bloodthirst, might be controlled. And that *you* might be the one who can control them. You thought yourself a puppet master above it all, controlling it, enjoying the pain you caused, but always standing far enough away that none of the blood would be your own, so that that which spilled would not even stain the hem of your garments. But war is not so precise, godling. It is not an instrument for exactness. War is like a boulder pushed down a hill and once it begins its descent, not even a god who styles himself its master can control it. And when a man—or a god—lives for blood, Paren, then sooner or later, no matter how skilled or trained, the blood that is spilled will be his own."

"It matters not," the god growled angrily, touching his bloody cheek and then staring at the fingers that came away stained crimson. "It is a minor wound, of no consequence and..." He flickered again, a look of unmistakable pain coming across his face, stealing his words.

"But it *does* matter, godling," Tarex breathed, flashing the god a bloody smile. "For you thought yourself the master of war, but war has no master, and if it did it would not be some god but the mortals who so often bend their backs to its labor. You have come to think of yourself as invincible, untouchable, but no man—no god—is a true warrior, a true scholar of war, until he has felt the bite of its edge. The problem, Paren, is that you have allowed yourself to believe that you would never feel such a touch, that you were immune. You have, in fact, shaped your entire identity—your entire *will*—around that belief." He gave the godling a small smile. "A fact which any mortal, even down to small children only just able to speak, would have been able to tell you the truth of, had you only thought to ask. But you did not. You have been arrogant and vain, and now you pay the price of that arrogance—your own destruction."

"*Fool,*" the god hissed, anger and fear mingled in his gravelly voice. "You think that you have accomplished something? You have done *nothing*. You cannot defeat the anger in mortals' hearts. You cannot conquer *war*."

"No," Tarex said, blinking in an effort to keep his eyes open, to keep the darkness back, if only for a moment longer. "I cannot conquer war. But I can conquer you, Paren, once God of Conflict, now God of Nothing. You have chosen the Darkness, the shadows, and now the shadows will claim you."

The god's form had grown translucent, and he was flickering sporadically now, a reflection breaking again and again. His mouth worked, as if he might speak, but no words came and this time, if never again, war, it seemed, had no answer to give.

Tarex watched the apparition of the god's mouth open into a silent howl, watched him fade into nothingness, and he smiled again. The sword still pierced him, his blood still leaked out onto the ground, traveling down the thick steel in great rivulets, yet he felt no pain. And being a student of war, he knew well what that meant. Pain, after all, was for the living. He knew this, yet still he did not fear.

All around him, the men and women of the army scrambled, still confused and unsure, trying to bring some semblance of order to their lines, but that was his problem no longer, and he did not see them in any case. Nor did he see the darkness which many believed came upon all men in the end.

Instead, he saw a tent, one he remembered well from another life, when he had been a far different man.

He did not hear the soldiers' cries or shouts of outrage and fear, for he was in that place no longer. He stood in the tall grass outside the tent, could hear his wife's soft voice from inside as she spoke to their son, telling him a story before bed. A tear glided down his cheek. He had finally made it home. It had taken many years, hundreds of miles traveled, had taken death. Yet, he was home. A long, difficult journey, but one that had been well worth making. Tarex of the Ekirani, Broken no longer, smiled, and then he closed his eyes. And stepped inside the tent.

Chapter Thirty-Eight

The enemy forces were arrayed in a semi-circle, had been waiting on the Welians and so they were spread thin. Alesh knew, though, that given time, they would reform their lines to face his considerably smaller force, would surround them and swallow them whole. The only option, then, was to not give them that time. He turned to Rion and Darl, to Marta and Fermin and all the others standing beside him. "Ready?"

Rion grunted. "Race to see who dies first?"

Perhaps Alesh should have been afraid, but he was not. He had spent nearly his entire life being afraid, but he was afraid no longer. "We go for there," he said, pointing to indicate where Kale had risen from.

"Well, of course we do," Rion muttered.

Alesh nodded. "You all just keep them off me as best you can—I'll deal with Kale."

"I can't wait," Rion said, but he readied his knife.

Alesh turned to the others, a question in his gaze.

"We're with you, Chosen," Captain Nordin said.

"Very well," he said. "Let's finish this."

And then they were running, rushing toward their target like an arrow, one which, Alesh hoped, would find its heart, for he knew what was at stake as did those with him, and so they fought with a ferocity that the enemy soldiers, in their confusion, could not hope to match, and cut them down in droves.

Yet for all their confusion, the enemy army began to rouse itself to its own defense. The troops, the nightlings, too, turned away from the Welian ships and the anticipated slaughter and began to form up, mounting an increasingly effective defense which threatened to slow Alesh and the others' charge long before they ever reached their intended target.

More and more soldiers and nightlings threw themselves at him and his group, and Alesh, acting as the point of the spear, was forced to call on every ounce of strength and speed he possessed, forced to rely on lessons taught to him long ago by Chosen Olliman when his biggest worry had been being made fun of or being abandoned.

He and those with him, fought hard, fought as if the fate of the entire world, of everyone and every *thing* they loved hung in the balance—because it did. Yet for all his efforts, for all his skill, Alesh's blade could not be everywhere at once, and he shouted in anger and pain as a nightling's claw sliced across his arm. He ripped his sword free from where it had impaled another and his backswing sent the offending creature's head flying from its shoulders.

He meant to resume his charge then, but there were more troops in front of him, nightlings and men both, blocking his and the others' path, and they were forced to a standstill as they fought desperately against the attackers beginning to surround them. Alesh felt a shift in the battle, saw it, too, in the angry snarls of those men they faced, ones which had been wide-eyed with terror moments before. But they, like he, saw what was happening, saw their far greater numbers saw, too, that he and the others had lost whatever momentum they'd had.

The nightlings were hissing and growling in their eagerness, the men doing the same. In that moment, there seemed to be very little difference between the two, hardly any difference at all. The men and nightlings pressed in around them, and he and the others fought desperately to keep the inevitable at bay. The enemy troops were so eager to get at them, to finish it, that they forgot all about the Welian forces in their ships.

It was a mistake.

Arrows rained from the sky in their hundreds, not visible in the darkness and so seeming to appear as if by magic, sprouting from the bodies of the enemy forces further back who screamed and writhed and died beneath the deadly hail.

Alesh looked past those arrayed against them—an ever-thinning line as many fell to the Welian onslaught and others, panicked, fled into the darkness—and could see what appeared to be hundreds of archers on the Welians' ships. As the ships began to reach the shoreline, the archers knelt, wielding bows far bigger than any he had ever seen before, stringing them with arrows handed them by others before firing them into the sky, the missiles landing with deadly precision among man and beast alike.

It sowed confusion and fear in the ranks, taking some of the crushing pressure off them, and Alesh did not hesitate, driving toward where he had last seen Kale, now known as Argush, the man or at least what once had been a man, who had cast such a long shadow over the world. By rights—and despite the Welians assistance—they should have been cut down by the far greater numbers they faced, but they were not. For each of them fought better than they had ever fought before, found energy when they had thought they had none left. This was their last chance, the last chance for the light to drive back the darkness. If they failed here, there would be no other.

And so they charged into the army, cutting a bloody swath before them. They were not just men and women in that moment—they were lights, they were flames to drive back the darkness.

And drive it back they did.

Alesh did not know how long they fought. He was focused only on the rise and fall of his sword, of avoiding the blades and claws that sought his flesh. In time, though, the resistance before them began to falter, and those who did not fall before their attack fled before the merciless assault of these men and women who seemed invulnerable to their panicked minds.

A space opened up before them and there, standing less than a hundred feet away, was the man, the creature, responsible for so much of the recent suffering. Argush's chest heaved with fury, his taloned hands clenching tightly, and an inhuman growl issued from his throat as he stared at Alesh across the intervening space.

Alesh stared back, but he did not feel anger as he might have. Instead, with his gods-gifted sight, he saw into the truth of the creature before him, saw past those things he had done, saw past, also, what he had become, to the truth of him.

A nobleman who had been given all of life's benefits, so much so that he had come to believe he deserved them. But earning a thing and being given it freely were very different. A man grew from his struggles, from overcoming the obstacles life put before him—it had taken Alesh a long time to understand that, but he understood it now.

Kale, though, had been given no chance to struggle, no chance to win his own battles, for his parents and their wealth had fought those battles for him. And so he had not grown, but had remained that spoiled child who thought he deserved whatever he wanted simply from wanting it. And looking at him, Alesh did not feel anger—he felt pity.

An abrupt silence fell over the armies as the two forces—Alesh's own, diminished force, and Kale's hundreds of soldiers and the nightlings which remained—stood facing each other, their respective commanders in front of them. A silence which was shattered seconds later by the blast of a horn, and man and beast alike turned to the sound. Alesh saw then that the Welians had managed to disembark while Kale's army had been distracted by his and the others' charge and were now spreading out in formation. Thousands of fresh troops, all looking prepared to fight.

Kale roared in frustrated anger, turning back to Alesh. "*You!*" he shouted. "*You did this!*"

"No, Kale," Alesh said, and although he spoke softly, sadly, his words could be heard clearly. "Your ambition, your greed is what brought us here, to this place, to this darkness. But it is finished now—it's over."

Kale hesitated, as if unsure, a look of what might have been fear coming over his monstrous, scaled face. "I...I have beaten you before. Many times under that *fool* Olliman."

"Yes," Alesh said, "and were it just me here, you might beat me still." He glanced back at those remaining of his troops, those brave men and women who had risked everything to stand against the darkness, then turned back to Kale. "But it is not me you fight, Argush, Son of Darkness. It is the Light."

The man hesitated as if he might run, then the fear on his face was replaced with fury. "*Die!*" he roared. Then he charged.

Alesh's men started forward, but he held up a hand, stopping them. "Stay," he said. "Please. You have all brought us here, to this place, and what victory we have we have because of you. But this last part I must finish alone."

And then he was running, his blade at his side, and beast and mortal, servant of Light and servant of Darkness, watched in anticipation as their two leaders met.

Kale was fast, incredibly so, but Alesh had seen as much during their brief fight in the tunnels beneath the city, and he was ready for it. Perhaps he should have been exhausted after the battle at the gate, but he was not. Instead, his body, his muscles, seemed to thrum with practically limitless energy. Kale came at him, his talons flashing wildly, snarling and spitting in his rage, but Alesh evaded the strikes easily, gliding around each blow as it came.

It was a fight Alesh had anticipated, had yearned for since Kale had betrayed Olliman and usurped his power in Ilrika, one he had longed for since finding the dead body of the man who had taken him in and realizing that Kale was behind it. Now, though, he was surprised to find that he did not feel excitement or eagerness that the moment he had wished for had finally arrived. Instead, what he felt was disappointment. Regret. Most of all, he felt sadness, the sadness any person must feel when confronted with how low someone they once knew—enemy or friend—has fallen.

He sidestepped a lunge from Kale and pivoted, his foot flashing out and striking the man in the side, sending him sprawling. Kale hissed in anger, spinning quickly and making it to his feet—but not quick enough to avoid the tip of Alesh's blade before it came to rest at his throat. "Enough, Kale," Alesh said.

The man's monstrous, scaled chest heaved with impotent fury as he stared down the length of the blade at his throat. *"No,"* he hissed furiously, "this isn't how it's supposed to happen. Y-you have to die. She...she *promised.*"

"Who promised?" Alesh asked softly. "Shira?" He sighed, shaking his head. "She lies, Kale. It is all she does. Do you not yet know that?"

The man said nothing to that, only stared at him, studying him with a gaze that danced with rage, rage which, was the blade not at his throat, he would have no doubt tried to vent on Alesh's body.

But the blade was there, and so he only stood. Any other, looking at him, might have seen only a monster, but Alesh's gods-blessed sight could see past his grotesque exterior, past the rage and anger he wielded like a shield, to the frightened, scared man beneath. "Even now, it is not too late, Kale," he said softly. "You can end this—no man can travel so far into the darkness that he might not return to the light once more."

He saw some reason slowly come into the man's furious gaze. And in that moment, he felt hope...then the man gave his head a furious shake. "*No*," he growled. "*It is too late. End it. Kill me.*" And then, in a voice barely loud enough for Alesh to hear, but loud enough that he could make out the desperation in it. "*Please.*"

Alesh opened his mouth to answer, unsure, even in that moment, of what answer he might give, but then suddenly the ground shook with ear-splitting thunder, and he was forced to shield his eyes as a great, terrible bolt of lightning shot down from the sky. Men and beasts alike cried out in fear and pain, and when Alesh opened his eyes once more, he saw that Kale was no longer alone. Shira stood beside him.

There was no denying who it was, for he could feel the power of the goddess coming off her in waves and so, too, could he feel her fury. "*No*," she growled in a voice as terrible, as cold, as a winter storm. She raised her hands overhead and suddenly the air was split with another peal of thunder, and the sky began to churn with dark, malevolent storm clouds. "*You will die,*" she hissed, "*all of you will die and—*"

"Wife."

She cut off at the soft voice, soft but brimming with power, and suddenly the building storm faltered, the sky became clear once more, and Alesh followed the goddess's gaze to beside him where a figure in a white robe, one he recognized, stood. Amedan, the God of Fire and Light, looked much as he had when Alesh had first seen him what felt like a lifetime ago, when he had mistaken him for a priest gone mad during Ilrika's burning.

The god did not wear his power around him like a garment, the way Shira did. If the goddess was a raging storm, he was a still meadow bathed in sunlight, yet there was something greater to that quiet strength which felt no need to show itself.

Shira grinned madly. "Foolish, husband, to show yourself here, before me, for while your power might be greater than mine in normal times, you are weak now. It will be no difficult thing for me to—"

"I am sorry," Amedan said softly.

Shira hesitated, the expression of fury on her face changing to one of confusion. Then, finally, in a barely audible hiss. *"What?"*

"I said that I am sorry, dear one," the god said. "Our daughter is gone, our son, too, and I am sorry. I am sorry for their loss as I am sorry for the pain that I have caused you, for making you feel that you were second in my eyes and my heart. I am sorry...and I forgive you."

Shira's face twisted with what appeared to be a range of emotions, but she finally settled on anger. "How *dare* you?" she hissed. *"You* forgive *me?"* She laughed, but there was a mad sound to it. "You who have—"

"Yes," Amedan said. "I have wronged you, wife. I have wronged you greatly, for I allowed you to doubt the love I felt for you, the love I feel still, and for that, I am truly sorry. I am sorry, too," he continued, glancing past her as a figure stepped out from the lines of Kale's army, "that it took another to show me how much I had wounded you."

They all followed his gaze to watch the man moving forward to come to stand beside Amedan. The man's figure suddenly blurred, shifted, and when that shifting resolved it was no longer a soldier who stood there, but the God of Chance, a sad smile on his face. "Hello, Mother."

"You have taken a terrible wounding, wife," Amedan continued, "one caused by my own hand, though I knew it not, and for centuries that wound has been left to fester. I am sorry. And for that pain you have caused in your anger, in your grief, I forgive you, for it, all of it, is my fault."

Shira stared, stunned, at her son, then back to her husband. "Y-you...are sorry."

He said nothing, only watched her, his eyes bottomless pools of emotion, blue eyes deeper than the sea itself. Suddenly, Shira's body flickered, as if, for a split second, she was not there at all, and a look of panic came over her as she stared at her husband. "I...I don't understand."

Amedan sighed. "It is your hate, Shira, your will. You were great, once. Magnificent. You still are, in many ways, yet you allowed yourself to be consumed by your hate, your hatred for mankind yes, but mostly your hatred for me. It is the foundation on which you have built yourself for centuries and when a foundation falls..."

"Then that which sits upon it must fall also," she said, not angrily, not now, but in understanding.

Amedan gave a slow nod. "Yes, my dear one," he said, then he stepped forward and pulled the goddess—flickering by the second now—into a tight embrace. "It must fall."

She stood there, unmoving for several seconds, then, slowly, the hard lines of her face seemed to soften, and she reached up, hugging him back, laying her head on Amedan's shoulder. "I have missed you, husband."

"And I you," Amedan said. Then there was another flickering, and after it, the god was standing alone, holding nothing. Slowly, his arms fell to his sides, and his shoulders slumped in a very human expression of grief. He turned to Alesh and, as he did, the sun began to rise over the horizon, putting an end to the longest night of Alesh's life, the longest night, perhaps, of anyone's.

The nightlings that remained screamed and hissed for a moment, but then the light bloomed in earnest, chasing away the shadows, and the creatures vanished, turning to dust which blew away in a soft breeze as if they had never been. Kale himself looked about, confused, his face a mask of fear and anger. He opened his mouth to scream, then suddenly he vanished, and Alesh was left staring, stunned, at the place he had been.

"What shapes the shadows make," Amedan said softly, "vanish come the day."

As for those soldiers which had made up Kale's army, they were not soldiers, not any longer. The shadows were gone, the light come, and with it their thirst for blood which had served as a replacement for courage had faded, leaving them not monsters anymore but only confused, frightened men and women who fell to their knees and shielded their eyes, as if they were children seeking shelter beneath their blankets.

"Son of the Morning," Amedan said, meeting his gaze. "You have done well." He glanced behind Alesh at the others staring in wonder. "You all have."

Alesh saw some of the heartbreak in the god's gaze. "*We* all have," he said softly. Then he glanced around him at the men and women who were left, those who had made it through the long night just passed. Finally, he met the god's eyes again. "What will happen now?"

The god shook his head slowly. "That is not my decision to make. My daughter is gone, my son; my wife, too, is no more. No, Alesh, the age of the gods has passed. The age of men has come." He gave a smile to Alesh and the others, one that clearly cost him. "I wish you all luck."

He turned then and started away, but Alesh stepped forward, grabbing his arm. "Thank you," he said, then gave a small smile. "Priest."

Some of the pain and heartache left the god's face at that, and he smiled back. "It has been a pleasure," he said.

He started away again, but Alesh was not finished. "Where will you go? What will you do?"

The god turned back. "I will rest, I think. Who knows?" He paused. "Maybe I'll do some fishing."

"With any luck," Javen said, a sad smile on his face, "we might even catch something." He turned to Alesh and the others. "Well done, all of you. I must admit I did not see any chance of victory, but you managed it just the same."

Rion stepped forward, and Alesh saw him draw a coin, Javen's coin, from his pocket, offering it to the god almost meekly.

Javen laughed, shaking his head. "Keep it, Eriondrian Tirinian. Who knows?" He winked. "Perhaps there's some luck left."

Then the gods turned and, in another moment, were gone.

They were gone.

And the age of men had begun.

Epilogue

"Are you excited to be back?"

Alesh turned to Katherine where she sat in the wagon beside him and smiled. "I'm excited to see my friends again. You?"

She grinned. "The same."

Alesh clucked at the horses, giving the reins a light snap, and they started through the gate. No crowds waited to celebrate his coming, no soldiers listened for his orders, orders that might doom or save them, and for that he was glad.

There was only him and Katherine in the small wagon, and the men and women they passed in the streets gave them no more than a cursory glance before moving on, not recognizing him as Chosen Alesh, once ruler of Valeria, and she Chosen Katherine Elar, the woman whose song had inspired and fortified the troops on the wall during Valeria's final siege. As far as most knew, the two had given their lives in the defense of Valeria. And for that, too, he was glad.

They were not Chosen anymore, and what gifts, what magic the gods had given them had faded in the days following Shira's defeat, faded until it did not exist at all, but Alesh did not mind, and Katherine's song, to him, was still just as sweet, just as beautiful.

He took a slow, deep breath, gazing at the castle in the distance, the top of which he could see over the shops and houses around them. "Are you ready?"

She winked. "Lead the way, husband."

***

It had been over six months since the siege of Valeria and the end of what people were now calling The Nightfall Wars, yet Larin sat on Valeria's throne as if he were testing it out for the first time and, as it happened, finding it terribly uncomfortable.

Alesh glanced back as the guardsman who had escorted him and Katherine to the throne room closed the door behind him, then he grinned at Larin. "Maybe you could get a cushion."

The big man snorted, seeming all too happy to use the excuse of their arrival to rise from the throne and walk toward them. Alesh held out his hand, but the Chosen pulled him into a tight embrace, clapping him on the back before doing the same to Katherine. Then he took a step back, grinning widely at them. "Gods, but it's good to see you two. Tell me how are things?"

"Good," Alesh said, his grin slowly fading into a frown. "Well, mostly good. I saw the statue."

Larin roared with laughter, clapping him on the back again, apparently oblivious of the way Alesh was forced forward a step by the blow. "Thought you'd get a kick out of that. I went by yesterday mornin', told the Chief Sculptor they didn't get your nose anywhere near big enough."

Alesh scowled, and the big man shrugged. "Serves you right, makin' me king of Valeria, you bastard. What do I know about bein' king? I lived by myself in the desert, damn you. The biggest responsibility I had was keepin' the sand out of my boots, and now I've got a damned kingdom to run."

"And from what I hear," Alesh said, "you're doing pretty well. Anyway, if it's any consolation, the last leader of Valeria nearly lost a battle with the shadow and the one before that served it, so I'd say the bar is fairly low."

Larin grunted, glancing at Katherine. "You haven't strangled him to death yet, eh?"

She grinned. "Give it time."

Larin snorted, shaking his head. "Well. Best we go to the dining hall—gods, but I thought I was done with throne rooms and dining halls. Anyhow, the others'll be waiting."

Alesh and Katherine followed the big Chosen as he walked through the castle, and despite all his complaining, Alesh couldn't help but notice the way the man paused and spoke with each servant briefly, calling them by name and seeming as pleased as they did at the conversation.

In time, they reached the dining hall and one of the guards stationed outside started toward the door, meaning to open it, but Larin waved him away with a grunt. "I can open my own damn door, Dillon, or are you sayin' I'm too old and frail, that it?"

The young guard turned red, swallowing hard. "O-of course not, Highness."

Larin shook his head with a sigh, glancing at Alesh. "You see what you leave me to? Why, everyone's so damned serious." He turned then and swung the door open. Alesh could hear voices coming from inside, voices he recognized. The big man sighed again, giving Alesh a rueful look, then stepped inside.

Katherine glanced at Alesh, but he waved her through with a smile. "After you."

"For the rest of your life," she whispered, then she leaned forward and gave him a soft kiss before turning and walking through the door.

Alesh stood at the entrance, gazing into the dining hall as Marta and Sonya both leapt up from their chairs, leaving a consternated Fermin who—judging by his face—had been in the middle of some unappreciated lecture or another, and rushed to Katherine with shouts of joy.

Rion was there, too, only a step behind the girls in his eagerness to greet Katherine. Gone was the cynical nobleman who Alesh had first met. This man, instead, was unabashedly thrilled to see her as were his parents, and Odrick, the Royal Smith, who weren't far behind.

Alesh watched from the doorway, smiling. They were all here, all except for Darl who he and Katherine would go and see after they spent some time in Valeria. His friends, those he had come through so much with. At least, those who had walked the darkness with him and come out the other side. Not all of them had. There were those that had been lost along the way.

But those that remained, Katherine among them, were not the strangers they had been little over a year ago. Neither were they the friends they had become. Those that were left—those that were left behind, too—had become family.

So he stood there in the relative dim glow of the torches compared to that bright illumination put off by the lanterns placed regularly along the dining hall tables. He stood and watched his family laughing and hugging.

It had been a hard road, yes, but it had led here, to this, to men and women—and children—who would do anything for each other. A young orphan who had found a family, who had learned to trust, a nobleman who had learned to care, and a young girl who had, in truth, taught them all.

"Alesh!" It was Sonya's voice, the little girl, his sister running toward him, and then she was in his arms. He laughed, holding her.

"I've missed you."

"I missed you too, brother," she said, grinning widely.

"Hey, Alesh, get in here!" someone shouted.

Alesh grinned, waving at his his friends, his family.

And then, he stepped into the dining hall.

He stepped into the light.

THE END
of
THE NIGHTFALL WARS

We have reached the end of *The Age of Men*. It is my sincere hope that you enjoyed this book and this series. Now, if you're looking for something else to read and haven't yet, check out *A Sellsword's Compassion*, book one of the bestselling and complete Seven Virtues series!

If you've enjoyed *The Age of Men*, I would love it if you'd spare a second to leave an honest review. There are several cool things about being an author—wearing house shoes while I work comes to mind, but few things are better than hearing from readers.

If you'd like to reach out and chat, you can email me at JacobPeppersAuthor@gmail.com or visit my website. You can also give me a shout on Facebook or on Twitter. I'm looking forward to hearing from you!

Sign up for my new releases mailing list to hear about promotions, launches, and, for a limited time, get a FREE copy of *The Silent Blade,* the prequel book to the bestselling epic fantasy series, The Seven Virtues.

Go to JacobPeppersAuthor.com to claim your free book!

Note from the Author

And now, dear reader, we have reached the end of The Age of Men and, with it, the end of The Nightfall Wars. It is my sincere hope that you enjoyed the series, and I want to say thanks for taking this journey with me.

This journey is one that took longer than I intended when I set out on it, when *we* set out on it but then, is that not so often the case? And I would not change it for anything, for my wife and I had the privilege, in January, to welcome our new daughter, Norah Alaina Peppers, into the world.

And yes, I'm sure you've noticed that our daughter's initials are N.A.P. Probably it will make no difference considering that her brother, Gabriel, didn't really get down with the whole sleeping thing until he was two years old or so but still...it can't hurt, right?

Anyway, thank you again for coming on this journey with me and for all your support. It has been a blast to work on this series, and a privilege to hear from readers who have enjoyed it. For those of you who have been asking after the final book, well, I know it took longer than anticipated, but I can only hope that the wait was worth it.

We have traveled these books, this world, together, and while it has been one fraught with danger, one often sinking into despair, it is one which, in the end, has brought us to the light once more. And, call me an optimist, but I like to believe that, given time enough, given hope enough, such is always the case.

Now, I would like to take an opportunity to thank all of those without whom this book would have never seen the light (cue laugh track) of day.

Thank you, as always, to my wife, Andrea, who somehow manages to appear interested no matter how many times I run ideas by her. Thank you, also, to my family and friends, who have listened to me go on and on about this character or that one, never mind the fact that they aren't, by the strictest sense...or any sense, for that matter, "real." A special shout out to my son, Gabriel, who always helps jog my creative juices when I'm in a slump, usually by the expedient of throwing a toy ball...or train...or baseball bat, at my face. And, of course, a huge thank you to my daughter, Norah. Her reaction to the book was mostly crying, but I like to think those tears were shed over the difficulties our protagonists faced and not necessarily the quality of the book.

As always, thank you to those kind-souled beta readers who have braved the darkness with me and to the members of my launch team who were the first to follow us into it.

But above all else, thank you, dear reader. There are many books out there, many worlds, and I cannot express my thanks that you have taken the time to visit mine, to spend your time with Alesh and Katherine, with Rion and Darl, Marta and Sonya, and all the rest. It is because of you, after all, that this world, that these people, exist at all.

This journey is done but stick around, won't you? As is so often the case when a person finishes one journey, another is waiting around the corner. Often, sooner than you'd think.

Thank you and until next time,

Jacob Peppers

About the Author

Jacob Peppers lives in Georgia with his wife, his son, Gabriel, three dogs and, very soon, his newborn daughter. He is an avid reader and writer and when he's not exploring the worlds of others, he's creating his own. His short fiction has been published in various markets, and his short story, "The Lies of Autumn," was a finalist for the 2013 Eric Hoffer Award for Short Prose. He is also the author of the bestselling epic fantasy series, *The Seven Virtues*.

Made in the USA
Columbia, SC
06 June 2025

59037548R00180